HELLBOY
ODDEST JOBS

From the Library of

_____

HELLBOY

ODDEST JOBS

Edited by
Christopher Golden

Illustrated by
Mike Mignola

DARK HORSE BOOKS®

Mike Richardson ✠ *publisher*

Scott Allie ✠ *consulting editor*

Tina Alessi ✠ *designer*

Special thanks to Rachel Edidin, Annie Gullion, and Freddye Lins.

HELLBOY™: ODDEST JOBS

Published by Dark Horse Books
A division of Dark Horse Comics, Inc.
10956 SE Main St.
Milwaukie, OR 97222
www.darkhorse.com

July 2008
First edition
ISBN 978-1-59307-944-4

1 3 5 7 9 10 8 6 4 2

PRINTED IN THE UNITED STATES OF AMERICA

TABLE OF CONTENTS

INTRODUCTION

By Christopher Golden

I don't look much like a preacher. Once upon a time, though, spreading the good word wasn't so much about looking the part as about having passion. As a child, I worked to persuade my friends and family to come over to my religious beliefs and my way of worship—a church of monster movies, comic books, and ghost stories. I remember with amusement the year I turned twelve, when I turned out the lights at my birthday party, lit a candle, and read aloud from a horror novel.

Yeah, that went over just about how you'd expect. Oddly, the mockery didn't sting very much. I didn't really feel humiliated. Mostly, I was just baffled. I'd even say dumbfounded. How could they not all see what I see? How could my friends not love what I love, and understand how damn cool it all was?

Not much has changed. I live in a quiet Massachusetts suburb where people don't get why there's a concrete jack-o'-lantern on my front steps 365 days a year. Visitors come into my office and see my books and comics and DVDs, my statues of Hellboy and the Spectre and Daredevil, the movie posters and framed artwork, and they're the ones who are baffled. They don't get what's so amazing about the autographed pictures of Christopher Lee and Clint Eastwood and Darren McGavin (as Kolchak). They think, of course, that I'm weird.

The feeling is mutual.

My friend and frequent collaborator, Tom Sniegoski, and I have a shorthand reference to this phenomenon. With a certain disdain, we simply say, "They don't know what's *good*."

But that isn't enough for me. I'm a preacher, you see. If I had the time, I'd go door to door, ringing more bells than Jehovah's Witnesses, trying to spread the word. And the word would change every day.

"*You don't watch* The Shield? *It's the best show on television. You're missing out.*" "*Best Picture of 2007?* Gone Baby Gone, *and it wasn't even nominated. Unbelievable. Amy Ryan should've won best actress hands down.*"

"*You seriously have never read Joe Lansdale? You have to start right now. It's like legal crack without side effects.*"

"*Coolest place I've ever been? Croatia! You've gotta go!*"

Some people, I'm certain, find my preaching irritating. I honestly can't stop myself. When I've got a passion for something, I want to share it. I want it to make everyone as happy as it makes me.

Which is why everyone in the entire world should read *Hellboy*.

My association with Hellboy goes back at least a dozen years, maybe a little more, to an interview I did with Mike Mignola for a short-lived magazine called *Flux*. Since that time, I've been fortunate enough to indulge my love for the character and his world by writing three novels, editing a bundle of others, and cowriting (with Sniegoski) the first B.P.R.D. miniseries. All the while, I've tried to spread the word about how amazing and unique the series is, thanks to the extraordinary art and lunatic genius of its creator. Really, you see, Mignola is a preacher, too. He loves folklore and monsters and history and pulp adventure, and his way of making you love it, too, is by bringing you *Hellboy*, *B.P.R.D.*, *Lobster Johnson*, *Abe Sapien*, and a million other things he has planned.

But back to the little kid reading horror stories by candlelight at his birthday party.

I want everyone to love Hellboy as much as I do. Back in 1999, that love prompted me to put together *Odd Jobs*, an anthology of short stories featuring Hellboy and his world, written by authors I admired and who I thought would appreciate the series. I could share my love of Hellboy with them, and they could pass that on to their own readers as well. That first time up, we had Poppy Z. Brite, Brian Hodge, Max Allan Collins, Greg Rucka, even a cartoon by Gahan Wilson.

People who know what's *good*.

In 2004, *Odder Jobs* came along. We always knew we would do it when the timing was right. Then Frank Darabont sent Mignola a Hellboy story he'd written and we figured that meant it was time. In addition to Frank, we had another stellar lineup, including Charles de Lint, Sharyn McCrumb, Graham Joyce, and Tim Lebbon. Sniegoski stepped up for that one, as did *Hellboy*'s editor and good shepherd, Scott Allie. A story by Guillermo del Toro was the icing on the cake. As the director of the *Hellboy* movie, del Toro had officially become the world's best-known Hellboy preacher.

Now, here we are again, with more people who know what's good. Maybe you think *Oddest Jobs* was inevitable. You're probably right. But Mike and I weren't sure it would ever happen. Way back at the beginning, a decade ago, I asked Joe R. Lansdale to write a Hellboy story. He wanted to, but his schedule wouldn't allow it. We went back to him in 2003 for the second volume of this series, and again, it didn't work out. Then, a couple of years ago, Mike and I met up with Joe in New York and he asked if we were ever going to do another one. We threw down the gauntlet.

"When you write a Hellboy story, that's when we'll do *Oddest Jobs*."

Joe nodded. He'd wanted to all along, he said, but never could find the time. Now, though, he just had to put it on his schedule.

I waited, not sure he'd ever get around to it.

As you can see, he did. Boy, did he.

Instead of a short story, Joe wrote an absolutely insane novelette that's prime Joe Lansdale, and prime Hellboy as well. It felt like Christmas.

Once we had Joe's story in, it was time to go out and preach the word again, spread the love of Hellboy far and wide. Time to recruit.

One of the goals in choosing writers was variety, on several levels. The contributors to *Oddest Jobs* are, in some ways, an unlikely crew comprised of mystery writers, horror novelists, and fantasists, though many of them move fluidly amongst various genres. They hail from three continents, and myriad backgrounds. Some of them didn't know anything about Hellboy when I first approached them, and some were already passionate fans. Of course, they're all preachers now.

The other goal was to gather a list of contributors comprised of authors I routinely encourage others to read. Some of the names in here might be instantly familiar to you, and others may not be. Either way, they're people who know what's good. And now, so do you. Spread the word, my friends, about Hellboy and about these writers who share our passion.

Now turn the page, and read about the oddest of jobs . . .

—Christopher Golden
Bradford, Massachusetts
St. Patrick's Day, 2008

Jiving with Shadows and Dragons and Long, Black Trains

Joe R. Lansdale

Prologue in pulp

It was a long train and swift and dark as the inside of a dead man's gut. Its smoke stack chugged out dark wafts of choo-choo exhaust that climbed up high and momentarily bagged the full moon, stunk up the sky until the thin desert air smelled like something rotten and pissed on.

It ran not only between and around cacti and little rises of sand, it ran right smack dab through them, but didn't move them, didn't change them. Went through them as if the train were smoke, churning up clouds of dust.

Since its appearance, the moon had stayed the same, had not changed a bit; it was forever full and forever bright and it kept the same position in the sky. The train ran on invisible rails. The smoke from the stack broke up in patches, fluttered about like agitated birds of prey.

The desert town of Cold Shepherd lay cool and silent in the late of night. It was dark except for a few store lights. It was a little town and not very populated, most of the people middle-aged or old, a smattering of kids and infants, so after midnight there was very little activity. Everyone was tucked away in their beds by that time. Come early morning, many would drive into the city some twenty-five miles away to do their jobs or shopping. Old men would play dominoes down at the Community Hall, smoking and cussing and telling lies of youthful prowess. Old women would gather for a furious game of bridge and gossip; false teeth would clatter and the air would smell of too much perfume. There would be no school as it was the dead of summer, and the kids would be bored by midday, having played out video games and watched DVDs until they could quote the lines in all the movies. Mothers would be worn out with crying babies. Dogs and cats would lie about in any available shade.

So they slept, the next day looming, and then came the sound, from a distance and odd at first. No more noise than a rat straining to shit, and then there was a bit of clatter and rattle, like a drunk pot-and-pan salesman falling downstairs.

It was loud enough that lights went on and people came out of their houses, walked into the street for a look. In the distance they saw a perfectly round glow of gold the size of a thumb tip coming toward them beneath the higher glow of the harvest moon. The round glow kept coming on and on, faster and faster, becoming larger, and then they saw it was the light of a train, and then they could see the train, its cow catcher at the forefront, greasy smoke stack coughing up char-colored smoke; the stench was close now and worse than rotten and pissed on; it smelled like a butcher shop where the meat had hung too long.

As the machine heaved to a stop in the center of town, scattering people in pajamas and robes, it could clearly be seen that the train was right out of an old Western movie, something ripe for Jesse James to rob. There were boxcars, but they none of them appeared to be passenger cars—no windows. When it stopped there was the sound of the big hot engine cooling in the night air, the metal heaved and squealed like a soul caught up in barb wire, the box cars trembled as if cold, and the smoke stack coughed one last time and a huge puff of shadow swelled out and stuck in the stack for a moment, then broke loose with an uncorking sound, took to the sky and broke apart and made a batch of bats that flew up until the night absorbed them.

The people, stunned as if they had been whacked with a mallet, just stood there, staring, not even speaking, and then someone said, "Look at that," and pointed toward the sky. People looked, saw the smoke bats were coming back, and they were swelling in size until they were no longer bats but smoke dragons. They could see through the dragons in spots, hints of moonlight here and there. The dragons dropped down out of the sky. Their beating wings and twisting tails caused the dirt to spin on the street in tiny dust devils. The glass in window panes rattled like dry old bones.

People panicked. Old men and women hobbled on canes and walkers, and younger men and women broke and ran. Others scooped up their children, or encouraged them to run. They made for their homes.

No one made it. Not even the dogs and cats.

The smoke dragons were quick, and when they came down they scooped the people and animals up like hawks grabbing mice, scooped them up in their smoky talons which were solid as steel, and darted for the train.

The side door on the train flung open with a sound like a cough, and just before the shadow dragons carried the people inside, the victims got a whiff of the train's interior. It was enough to make the eyes water, the nose fill up, and the head go stone-cold drunk. It was a stench beyond the exterior butcher shop smell; it was a stench like all the dead things that ever were or ever would be, all the vomit, excrement, and foul odors of decaying man and animal, fruit and vegetable, composting in the heat of hell.

The shadow dragons darted into the train. The door slammed loudly shut, tight as a miser's wallet. The train cranked up with a chug, and another, another, and then it was moving again, down the street, right through a house without so much as breaking a board, leaving behind ectoplasmic cobwebs and drips of goo.

The train pumped on across the back end of the town, on out into the desert again, picked up speed. It began to look like an elongated shadow, and then there were only streaks of blackness, like some kind of poisonous infection running the length of a wound. The streaks joined with the natural shadows of the desert and were soon one with the night. There was only a hint of its stench left behind to mark its passing.

Bureau for Paranormal Research and Defense
New Mexico field office
Hallway security cam

It's not a good picture. It vibrates a little, goes scratchy (*got to get that fixed*, everyone thinks, but so far no one's fixed anything.)

Cam shows a tall man with a shaved head and a goose-step walk. He wears a black suit underneath a black leather raincoat, has on shiny black shoes, has the face of a man afraid to laugh. His eyes look like a couple of cigarette burns. With him is a woman, Kate Corrigan, folklore expert. She has to walk fast to keep up.

A large room

Hellboy, sitting in a chair, watches the security cam on the wall, says, "Now what?"

A light glows red above the door, and then the door opens, and Now What enters the room. The tall man and Kate. Kate, she looks okay today, like maybe she got some sleep, but she's all business, Hellboy can tell that. She's got that look, rested or not.

He takes hold of his tail and pulls it in an unconscious gesture, maybe hoping it will come off. Sawing off his horns worked out. The nubs looked pretty cool, like goggles. Maybe a nip of the tail and he'd look more presentable. Of course, there was his right arm, about the size of a cannon and not exactly the most dexterous of limbs. Had a lot of bad mojo about it, Right Hand of Doom and all that, formerly owned by someone else, real heavy, good to hit with, but not exactly the best hand for picking your nose. So, no matter what he did, unless he was willing to have a lot of amputation and one hell of a makeover and wear funny hats, he was always going to look like a big red guy with a tail.

When they come into the room, Hellboy doesn't leave his chair. He's too tired for that, too worn for that, too much late-night business with demons and ghosts, werewolves and nasties; even someone of demonic origin gets a little worn out, needs a break, thinks of Hawaiian shirts and smooth beaches and girls in bikinis, some kind of cool, alcoholic drink.

As the tall man and Kate approach, Hellboy says, "It's not good to see you. I'm taking a break. I don't want any. Gave at the office. Can I borrow five dollars? I have runny sores."

"Weak," Kate says, sauntering over.

"Yeah, well," Hellboy says, "I'm not feeling so good. My dog died. I have to wash my hair."

The tall guy just looks at Hellboy. Hellboy doesn't like those eyes. Human enough, but they're way too deep in the skull and too small and too close together, the pupils are like greasy B.B.s. Hellboy watches, wondering: Does this dude blink?

"This is Jim Jeff," Kate says. "He's a Reverend of sorts. He thinks it's the end of the world."

"Again?"

"Big time," Kate says.

"Ah, saw you blink," Hellboy says to the Reverend.

"What?" says the Reverend.

"Don't pay him any mind, Reverend," Kate says.

"Reverends have always got problems," Hellboy says. "I've come to the conclusion religion isn't any fun."

"Glad to meet you," says the Reverend, and he doesn't mean it, of course. Hellboy takes him for one of those self-righteous types, probably wondering what in the world he's doing associating with someone that has the stench of sulfur about him. That's all right, Hellboy thinks. I don't like you either.

"Salutations and all that stuff," Hellboy says. "What's up, Rev? Let's make it snappy. I got a manicure coming."

"Manicure?" says the Reverend.

"No, he doesn't," Kate says. "He thinks he's funny."

"I got a million of them," says Hellboy, "mostly Farmer's Daughter jokes, but they're good and I can really tell them, and boy are they nasty. I know some elephant jokes too. How many elephants can hide in a jelly bean jar? Buzz. Time's up. Twenty, if you paint their toenails the right color."

"Shadow train," the Reverend says, ignoring Hellboy. "It's been moving through the desert. It's touched a big spot of desert in Arizona. Now it's always night there and the moon is always full. It's something demonic, I'm sure of that," says the Reverend.

"Isn't it always?" Hellboy says. "And because it is, you need a big, red guy to help you out. Am I right?"

"I came here for help, and maybe I can help a little myself," the Reverend says. "Ms. Corrigan here has added a lot to what I know, and maybe I've given her something to work with. Did I mention the train doesn't run on tracks? That it comes out of the night and melts into the night?"

"Nope, you didn't mention that," says Hellboy.

"Well, that's the way it is."

"That's a curiosity item for sure," Hellboy says.

Reverend Jim Jeff nods. "And towns are disappearing."

"Towns?" Hellboy asks.

"The inhabitants to be exact," the Reverend says.

"Vacation?" Hellboy says.

"Everyone is missing, not just a few," the Reverend says, as if Hellboy's question is serious. "They couldn't all be on vacation. There aren't even any animals about. A bird won't fly over the place. And should I say again it's always night and the moon is always full?"

"Yeah, I got that part," Hellboy says. "Is there any way you can figure this out yourself? Maybe hire ten guys to do my job?"

"Not likely," the Reverend says. "You have . . . special abilities."

"You mean I'm a freak."

"I didn't say that."

"But you're thinking it. About those ten guys?"

The Reverend shakes his head.

"Just hopeful," Hellboy says. "Arizona is far."

Reverend Jeff says, "There are signs of interest, however. Handles, so to speak. Things we can grab onto. Ectoplasmic signs. The air is foul with decay, but there aren't any bodies. A family driving on the highway said they saw something from a distance, something rising up in front of the moon. Dragons. Not entirely solid creatures. The family was on their way toward Cold Shepherd, one of the towns where this happened. They were in daylight, and then they crossed into Cold Shepherd and it was night. They stopped and got out of their car and watched. They saw the dragons dive down into the town, then later they said they saw a ghost train. That's what they called it. And then it disappeared. Saw it go right by them and then it was gone. They said the air stunk so bad they got sick. They drove through the town. Not a soul. The motels were open, but no one was there. They told the sheriff in the next town about it, where it was still daylight, and of course he thought they were crazy. But the story got around. Some people went to Cold Shepherd. Dead of noon, and there was nothing but night. They found other towns that way as well. Three of them. And guess what?"

"No one was there either," Hellboy says.

"That is correct," says the Reverend. "And it's night there, too. And the moon is full. The towns are all in line with Cold Shepherd."

"We think they're linking up," says Kate. "Soon, it'll be a whole chain. Spreading across the country."

"Maybe it's done. Maybe four's enough," Hellboy says.

"Maybe," Kate says. "But we can't be certain."

"Why Arizona? Why these towns?" Hellboy asks.

Kate shakes her head. "All we know is we've brought the National Guard in to protect both ends of the towns that have been . . . evacuated, if that's the word. We don't really know what's happened there."

"Before I saddle up and ride, Rev," Hellboy says, "what's your place in this?"

"Outside investigator," Kate says. "Works for us. His own shop. But an outside contractor."

"I live near Cold Shepherd, at least most of the time. Phoenix. Normally, I deal with these things myself." The Reverend folds back the flaps of his long black coat. There are twin revolvers, butts turned forward, poking out of sleek, black holsters. "Sometimes I use these. They fire mojo bullets. You know, treated with spells and such."

"My gun is bigger," Hellboy says. "And I use really big bullets. They have all manner of stuff in them. And I have a lucky horseshoe on my belt. Crucifixes. All kinds of goodness. I think I got more mojo working."

The Reverend looks at Kate.

She just shakes her head.

"The Reverend," she says, "also writes for the psychic rags."

"How nice," Hellboy says.

"Everyone is busy," Kate says, "so we're sending you and him to check this out. It's the Reverend's area, so that's bound to be helpful."

Hellboy leans forward in his chair, latches an eye-lock on Kate, says, "The end of the world and everyone is busy?"

"There are all sorts of approaches to the end of the world," Kate says, "and some of them go on at the same time. You know that. You do your part, and we'll do ours. I've got some ideas on this, and I've put together a file. You'll be briefed en route. You should leave immediately . . . If that's all right with you, of course."

"Well," Hellboy says, "it is the end of the world and all."

How they traveled to Arizona
Taxi to the airport

A new hybrid, painted yellow, some checkerboard designs. Quick trip to the airport, light traffic. The driver talks about this and that and tries to engage them. He plays crappy disco music, circa 1970s. They arrive and Hellboy gives the driver a light tip. The driver complains he got them there really fast. Hellboy says, "You talk too much, and get a better brand of music, Chipmunks singing, anything, but dump that crap," and then Hellboy takes back the tip. The driver calls him something insulting and drives away.

Hellboy shoots him the finger.

Private jet to Phoenix

No security lines. On board there are no flight attendants. But there are peanuts and soft drinks and the seats are really big. Hellboy takes up two comfy seats and eats most of the peanuts and drinks a lot of the sodas and falls asleep.

The Reverend Jim Jeff sits in his seat with his seatbelt on, his hands folded in his lap, staring straight ahead. His little eyes hardly move at all. Except for the pilot and the copilot, no one else is on board.

It's a really quick flight because it's a really quick jet.

Rental car to Cold Shepherd, Arizona

Arranged for by the Bureau on arrival in Phoenix. Powder blue. Very nice. Handles well. The Reverend drives. Hellboy dozes. The miles melt.

Hellboy wakes up as they pass a hospital just outside of Phoenix. He wakes up in time to see that the sign out front says the place specializes in treating trauma and brain injury. Probably okay with gunshot wounds and splinters, too.

Hellboy's eyes are hardly open, and pretty soon, he closes them and is back asleep.

A little later on the Reverend nudges Hellboy. "Wake up. It's Kate."

Hellboy wakes up, smacks his lips. "I dreamed I was being attacked by squirrels. With machine guns," he says.

"Kate," the Reverend says again.

What they got is this little doohickey that they stick to the dash, and it opens up and there's a screen, and the Reverend has already done that, and what's on the screen is Kate. The image is very clear, much better than the hall cam back at the Bureau. She is leaning on her desk. She looks pretty sharp today.

Hellboy thinks, Man, her color is blue. That really makes her look good. I should tell her. Wear more blue. But he doesn't say anything. He just listens. Kate's voice comes through loud and clear.

"All right. We don't know all we need to know, but we never do. But of what we know, there's this. Pretty sure this is all a form of astral projection."

"Astral projection?" Hellboy says. "So, some train, it's sleeping, and projects itself into the desert—with dragons? Even for us, that's pretty weird."

"Astral projection isn't just a mind sending the form of its body somewhere else, solidifying that body. Sometimes, the mind sends surrogates."

"But a train that stinks and has dragons?" Hellboy says. "Maybe it's a Manitou. It is Native American country, by the way."

Before Kate can respond, the Reverend says, "It does sound peculiar, Kate. A Manitou from the metal of an old train might do something like this. I've never heard of such, but it could be possible. Astral projection, that seems far fetched."

Kate shakes her head. "No. Wrong M.O. Hear me out. A lot of folklore suggests that werewolves, certain kinds of werewolves, or vampires, were hidden desires that manifested themselves in the sleep of someone thinking about such things, and they became real. Bigfoot, the Yeti, Loch Ness Monster, same thing. Sometimes, instead of the eye sending a message to the brain, so that it then sees what it's looking at, there are times when the brain sends a message to the eye and sees things no one else sees. And then, there are those who, for whatever reason—perhaps a great ability to dream, stronger imaginations—they do the same, but what their brain sends to the eye, they not only see, but others see, and, for the most part, it's real. Fact is, the thoughts are sent to the invisible eye—the third eye—and the thoughts are then projected into the real word, where they exist as both dream and reality."

"So, what you're saying," Hellboy says, "is someone out there is dreaming of dragons and trains."

"That's right," Kate says. "Trains and dragons, and no telling what else. And they are not happy."

"Do you know for a fact it's a dream?" the Reverend Jim Jeff says, his manner as flat as a cardboard cutout and as cold as the bottom of an ice tray.

"No," says Kate, "but it has all the hallmarks. We've had minor cases like this before, but nothing that proved destructive. Often, the dreamer can't make the dreams concrete, but this is one of those who can. That's my take. The dreamer dreams and the dreamer is angry, and when he dreams bad things happen. But the projection of the dreams can only go so far, someplace he's familiar with, or an area he's familiar with."

"So he's not taking over the world?" Hellboy says.

"Yeah, we've rethought that," Kate says. "We think it's personal and local. Obviously, the dreams only last as long as he dreams. Thing is, though, the more the dreamer dreams, the stronger the dreamer's dreams become, and if he has unlimited access to dreaming, say he's in a deep, drug-induced sleep, the things he dreams become more and more real and more and more constant."

"Huh," Hellboy says. "If it's not one thing it's two. Hey, did you see that, Rev? A coyote. Uh, way back there now. Cute little fella. I think he was eating some kind of carcass."

"Pay attention," the Reverend says.

"Don't let him fool you," the image of Kate says. "He's paying attention. It's just his way. Am I right, Hellboy?"

"What was that?" Hellboy asks, straining, turning his head at an angle against the side window, looking up and out to see the aerial source of a vulture's shadow scooting across the ground.

A mind in shadow

Six months earlier
Down in the basement

Before the deep dreaming, Wilbur Cain lived in the basement. He came and went as he pleased, but the basement was his world, and it was the place he preferred to be. It was like a universe unto itself. It was cool and dark down there and the walls were lined with shelves filled with old pulp magazines in plastic sheaves, and there were stacks of bagged comics, and boxes of old science fiction and fantasy books, and there were cartoons of all manner on DVDs, and science fiction and fantasy and horror films, and there were the model trains and the tracks that were laid out on a table with a tunnel through which the trains could travel. There was mountainous terrain and there were bridges over lakes. There were little towns the train could chug through, and there were small plastic people who stood by the tracks to watch the train pass.

It was detailed.

Wilbur took his favorite position, the tall stool at the edge of the table where he could watch the trains when he ran them. There was a space on the huge table where he liked to sit and read his magazines, comics, or pulps. There was a strong light there, very concentrated on that area. Everything out from the glow of the light, his magazines and DVDs in racks, had the look of being hung in space. Sometimes, when he wasn't lying in bed looking out at the shapes of his magazines and his trains, he would sit on the stool and read. It was a big stool and well padded, because Wilbur was a big man, three hundred and fifty pounds, with ankles so deep in fat that when he stood the fat formed little rings around his ankles, like flesh bracelets, and the skin under his chin was almost like a bag, chock full of fat cells. His face was as if snakebit, big and swollen, the eyes near lost inside doughy flesh. His belly was a drum. When he moved, he moved slow, like a sloth with brain damage.

Wilbur worked his way to his stool and turned on the lamp, and in the glow of the light he began to read Henry Kuttner's "The Graveyard Rats" from an issue of *Weird Tales*. He had read it before, but it had been awhile, and he liked to reread certain stories from his collection from time to time, and this was one of his favorites. He read for a while, then lifted his massive head and looked at the walls and his magazines, and thought of everything that was there, just inside the pages, not far from his reach: Lovecraftian monsters, Robert Howard's barbarians, Bradbury's sweet, dark shadows. He thought of other stories, and then he fantasized about trains and dragons, shadows and blood.

Down here, in the dark, with only his lamp, the fact that he was overweight and unattractive was not important. He had his reading and films and cartoons, and he had his trains. He finished the Kuttner story and closed the aging magazine and carefully put it in its acid-free plastic bag. He looked out at the table and his train set, and he reached out and took the switches and set the train running. It was a favorite train of his, an old-style Western train. It even puffed little puffs of black smoke from its stack, courtesy of a device in the train that worked off machine oil.

He ran the train for a while and thought what a wonderful world his basement was, and then there was an interruption.

Mother.

Upstairs was mother, and she had come to the door of the basement, opened it, let in foreign light, and the light fell down the stairs, spread over his basement like some kind of laser beam seeking him out.

"Wilbur," his mother called. "Take me to the store."

"You don't need anything," he yelled back.

"I want some cigarettes and some sodas."

"Smoking isn't healthy," he said, turning on the stool, yelling up at the light and her bony shadow thrown up against the side of his basement wall.

"I know you want to play with your toys, but—"

"They're not toys!"

"Come on now, I need to go to the store. Who pays the bills around here? You or me?"

"What has that got to do with anything, mother?"

"It has to do with you not having a job and my check paying for everything, that's what it has to do with things." She had stepped onto the stairs now, and there wasn't just her shadow to see, there were her skinny legs in her ugly shoes, and the bottom of her old blue dress. "It has to do with that and the fact I can't drive a car, and I want to go to the store and you don't have a job and I'm the one who buys your toys. Now, Wilbur. Come up."

That was the end of it. She went upstairs, knowing he would comply. How could he not? He sat for a moment, though, and he thought about things, and none of the things he thought about were good. He didn't like to leave the basement, and more and more it was difficult to do. He didn't like to go out into the real world where people would stare at him and whisper things he often heard, like "How do you suppose he let himself get that fat?" and "My god, he's huge."

And his mother never let him forget that he couldn't hold a job, that he couldn't have a girlfriend . . . well, there had been Naomi. She had been a plain thing, and very small, but she liked him. He met her when he delivered newspapers for a while. He met her at the newspaper office where he picked up his papers and did his route through Cold Shepherd and four little towns beyond. They were not big and the route was really pretty easy and reasonably quick, and the money was enough to buy more pulp magazines and trains and old comics and old movies, but when he met Naomi, Wilbur found himself thinking of candlelit dinners, and trips to the movies, walks in the moonlight. He even lost a few pounds.

She was very shy and very quiet, and he couldn't even remember exactly how it happened, but soon they were something of an item, mostly going to her place for coffee and drinks, and he had even kissed her once, and she had given him a little black dragon on a chain; it wasn't much, and it was probably cheap, but he had told her how he liked stories of horror and fantasy, and was fond of dragons, and maybe she thought this was some connection. Didn't matter. He loved it. He wore it on a chain around his neck. For the first time in his life he thought that perhaps love was a real thing, not just something said.

But his mother wouldn't stand for it. She found out he had a girlfriend and the griping never ceased. She said women were the wreck of men, and until Naomi he thought this was probably true, his mother being the only example of a woman that he really knew. She had been enough for his dad, who in this very basement had tied a rope around a ladder and, standing on a chair, had kicked it out from under him, having left a note pinned to his shirt that read: "Try and nag me now, bitch."

But he had given Naomi and the paper route up. He kept the dragon on the chain, forever hanging around his neck, under his clothes. As he had gained weight, the chain had grown tighter, but it was still there, and from time to time he took it off and looked at it, and thought: I didn't give this up and I shouldn't have given up Naomi, either.

Doing what his mother wanted had become so much of a habit he hadn't had the will to fight back. He thought about that a lot these days, his lack of will, and he thought a lot about Naomi. He wondered if she still worked at the newspaper; he wished he had a job of his own, money of his own. He had gained a hundred pounds since then. Now, it was all he could do to go up the stairs, and soon, that might not be possible; he was gradually committing suicide by food.

Wilbur climbed off his stool and started up the stairs. It was laborious, but he worked the steps carefully, listening to them creak with the strain of his weight. He went up and into the light of the world above, into his mother's bright little home with its perfect furniture all covered in plastic, on into the spotless living room that smelled like a doctor's waiting room, a place where no one came, not even her. She lived in the kitchen, smoking cigarettes and drinking coffee, watching soap operas on a little television that nestled on the counter close to the sink. She just sat there in her chair with a cigarette hanging out her mouth, an ashtray in her lap, a cup of coffee on the table beside her, or a soda, as she called all soft drinks. She would sit there and eat most of the day, not gaining one pound, and she would go to bed before the sun was down, and he had to sit by her bedside as she tried to sleep, her head propped up high, her eyes closed, talking incessantly about nothing. She asked for coffee and he brought it. She asked for a soda and he brought it. She asked for him to hand her a cigarette and light it and he did. She asked for him to read to her from the newspaper and he did. She asked him to read from books about romance and he did. Sometimes he wanted to take one of his copies of *Weird Tales* and read that to her in its place.

That would be neat, he thought. Maybe she would die of fright, because she couldn't stand much of anything. Bugs made her scream. Bad news on the TV she couldn't stand and wouldn't watch. She liked a world that was controlled. And so did he. That's why he had his basement. It scared him to think that maybe, at least in some ways, he and she were much alike.

He thought about all this as he came up the stairs. He could feel the sweat on the back of his neck, and his heart was beating fast, his knees ached from carrying his weight.

When he came into the kitchen, his mother was standing there, her purse tucked under her arm like some kind of growth.

"You took long enough," she said. "Get the keys."

Wilbur got the keys and they went outside. The world out there was more and more foreign to him. He didn't like it. It couldn't be controlled.

They got in the car, which was a big old thing, and dated. The only driving that was done was from the house to the store and back, and to the car dealer for its checkup, so the car was almost brand new and ran as well as the day it had come off the showroom floor.

Wilbur turned the key and the car purred. "Now don't drive fast, Wilbur, and obey the laws, and be sure your seatbelt is tight," his mother said.

"Yes, Mother," Wilbur said, and he eased the car out of the garage.

They drove by the newspaper office, and as they did, Wilbur craned his neck to look and see if he could see Naomi's car, and he did. He saw it, and somehow the sight of it made his insides flutter.

His mother said, "You're thinking about that girl, aren't you, Wilbur?"

"Leave me alone, Mother," Wilbur said, and gave the car a little gas.

"She was no good."

"You didn't even know her."

"I knew her type."

"You didn't know her, so you didn't know her type."

"I know she was a tramp and she would have ruined your life."

Wilbur took his eyes off the road, looked at his mother. "Ruined my life? What life? You ruined my life, like you ruined Dad's life. He killed himself over you."

"Put your eyes on the road, Wilbur."

Wilbur looked at the road. A car whizzed by close.

"You're not being careful . . . And your father, he was weak. That's why he died. He couldn't stand life because he was a coward. Watch the road, Wilbur."

Wilbur looked ahead and saw the Cold Shepherd courthouse. The road went left and right when you got to the courthouse. The steps of the courthouse were dead center of his path. He had to turn right to go to the store.

"Mother," Wilbur said. "You make cowards of us all."

And with that Wilbur hit the gas.

"Wilbur," his mother said, "you're driving too fast."

"Yes. Yes, I am."

"You won't make the turn."

"No. No. I won't."

More gas. The car leaped like some kind of great fish. It hit the steps of the courthouse, and surprised Wilbur by climbing them, running right up them. As the car completed the steps and made the concrete landing above, a tire blew. His mother screamed.

"Crom!" Wilbur said, mimicking one of his pulp heroes, Conan.

The door of the courthouse jumped up in front of them. Wilbur drove the car into it and everything went black. When he opened his eyes, he saw his mother, smashed up against the cracked windshield like a bug, having been snapped right out of her belt (didn't fasten it right, he thought, all that nagging, and she didn't fasten her belt right, oh, boy, that serves her), and then blood ran into his eyes and his head felt as if it was coming apart and the pain was so intense in his skull that the world went dark again, dark like his basement, and he was glad of that, and dove right in just as the car exploded and the flames licked throughout its interior and wiped the flesh off the corpse of his mother, and wiped him as well, nearly down to the bone.

Three or four times he came out of the basement into the light of the world, and between the flutters of his eyes, he saw it was a world he didn't like, full of men and women in white coats in a bright, white room. He could see that he was wired up like a spaceman and he was being asked questions, none of which made sense, and then he closed his eyes again, and he could feel himself walking downstairs, into the dark, but walking much more swiftly than usual. He felt good and lean and strong.

He heard something just before he reached the bottom of the stairs.

"Can you hear me? My name is Doctor Stone. Can you hear me?"

He understood that, but somehow, it still didn't mean anything to him.

Wilbur looked up from his position at the bottom of the stairs, and all he could see was the doctor's shadow against the wall. He willed the door at the top of the stairs closed, and it closed, snapping away the doctor's shadow and all the light there was in the world.

Snap back to the present
Excerpted from Hellboy's report
Delivered late, as usual

Ten miles outside of Cold Shepherd was the National Guard. They saw me and waved us through. No faking a big red guy.

When we arrived at the border of Cold Shepherd, at first it looked as if there was a great wall of dark rain in our path. The not-so-cheery Reverend Jim Jeff pulled over and we got out of the car and stood near the sign that read *Cold Shepherd, Pop. 2,895.*

I studied the darkness in my usual astute manner, and it is my belief that I cut quite a figure standing there in the sun, the average left hand in my trenchcoat pocket, looking at darkness where light should have been, thrashing my tail out from under my coat, looking like Satan's aviator with my sawed-off horns.

The darkness was maybe three feet away from me. It looked less like a wall of rain close up. It was more like a gossamer curtain stained in ink. We walked past the sign, into the darkness, and I stuck out my hand. The big one that I like to call, in my more poetic moments, *The Big One.* I think this matches my *Big Gun* and my *Big Bullets.* Other large accoutrements are not discussed in mixed company, or in the company of dour reverends, or in reports to the Bureau, but if you would like to ask in private, I can explain.

Anyway, nothing happened to my big paw, so I pulled it back and poked the other one out there. The darkness had texture. I put this fact into the great computer that is my brain, let that evaluate, came up with my response.

"Huh."

The moon hung high in the sky, bright as pirate's gold, but it looked like a big plate up there, not the moon we knew, the one made of cheese. Sorry, couldn't help myself. Back to the moon we don't know. It was shiny and smooth as a baby's ass and it made me want to sing Moon River. I had the force of will not to, but I did hum a few bars of Blue Moon.

Reverend Jim Jeff, ever stylish in all black with an expression as warm as stone in shade, walked up to me, said, "Look over there."

I looked where the Reverend was pointing. The horizon. The darkness was starting to melt away, from the ground up, melting in streaks. Daylight was poking through. "The illusion is coming apart," the Reverend said.

"It's more than illusion," I said. "It's true matter. If it's like Kate said," (not that I doubt you), "maybe whoever is projecting this universe is coming awake, and it's all going away."

"Someday," the Reverend said, "I suppose the god I believe in will do the same. Come awake, and we will all go away."

And I'm thinking, maybe that's not all a bad thing. I have those kinds of days, you understand, and I'm also thinking if God is dreaming, is our world a sweet dream to him or a nightmare? Some place in between? I know this is a report, but I think we all profit when I wax philosophical, don't you?

But back to our story, which is something I've always wanted to say.

Not having a witticism at hand, I said to Reverend Jim Jeff, "Then let's drive on through," and we did.

We coasted down the highway, into the dying darkness and the melting moon, and by the time we came to the back end of Cold Shepherd, all the shadows had been torn away and flung out of sight and the moon was less than a thin circle through which the sun shone.

The Reverend cranked up the air conditioner and we drove on through the connecting towns, little clutches of civilizations that had gathered near a thin trickle of water that the residents called a river—or so stated a sign that named said body of flowing water something most likely Native American in origin, and something I couldn't pronounce. I can't even spell it, which is why it does not appear here. So, look it up.

I could give you some neato geographical descriptions of the countryside, but I don't want to, so all I'll say is that when we came to those towns in line with Cold Shepherd, they were all losing their darkness and their moons. And when we reached the far end of the farthest of the three towns, there was no more darkness, just light. The towns were empty. Not a thing moved, not even a bird flew overhead. I wondered if there were even insects on the ground. I was tempted to have the Reverend pull over so I could stop and look for ants. But not tempted enough.

We drove on and I realized something important. I was hungry.

When we came to the next town, Sand Rock, it was so different. There were cars moving about and people walking here and there, and when I let the window down I could hear the noise of the cars and people and I could smell exhaust and the normal smells you would expect, food cooking, a whiff of sweat, and pops of women's perfume. This town was alive.

We stopped at a Mom and Pop place and ordered something to eat, and of course, I was someone who drew the eye. I signed some autographs. The waitress came over and she had a camera, had Reverend Jim Jeff take her picture with me. She was cute. I prolonged that one as long as I could.

Anyway, we sat and ate, and Reverend Jim Jeff said, "Considering your origin, you don't have to be on our side."

"One way of looking at it," I said, "but I never really give it any thought. I do what's right because it's right and I don't need another reason."

"That's good. I like that. But right is sort of in the eye of the beholder, isn't it?"

"Well, a lot of people say they are doing right and believe it, but to me, if it involves helping out innocent folks against nefarious supernatural badness, then right is as obvious and clear as the nose on your face. Which, by the way, is not any kind of comment on your nose."

"I was raised by wolves," the Reverend said.

"And your manners are so respectable."

"No. Really. Werewolves. My parents had the curse. They couldn't help it. They knew right from wrong, but it's a disease. Not some kind of astral werewolf like Kate was talking about. I don't doubt her word on that, but we weren't astral. We were werewolves."

"Not a lot of twelve-step programs for that, are there?"

"No. But they raised me and taught me and showed me how to live in a proper way. They didn't kill humans. They raised sheep. It wasn't like the old stories, the full moon and all that."

"Different kinds of werewolves, just like there are different kinds of dogs," I said.

The Reverend nodded. "They could become a werewolf any time of the month, whatever the phase of the moon. It had to be night, and that was it. They locked themselves up in cages on those nights. With a sheep in each cage."

"I suppose the sheep didn't get much sleep."

"In the morning, an automatic timer let them free, unlocked their cages when the curse was worn off."

"How did they come by the curse?"

"Not a bite, but they were cursed. It's a long story. Let me put it this way: our background is Romanian. They came from there. They had the evil eye thrown on them."

"That can be nasty."

"Most of that stuff, it's just talk, bluff, but the woman who put it on them was not kidding. They don't even know why she did it. It made their lives miserable, of course."

"Didn't do the sheep any good, either."

"No, guess it didn't. When I was growing up I was taught to manage the cages. The automatic locks, once they opened too soon and my father went on a kind of . . . well, rampage. He was shot, and not by a silver bullet. As a werewolf he was strong, but still he could be killed."

"Silver is something for the super-werewolves. Those are bad dudes. My Big Bullets would kill one, I might add. Silver in them, holy water, shavings from crucifixes, not to mention good old gunpowder. Did your father die?"

"Not from that. Old age. Anyway, he discovered . . . I don't know how to put this delicately . . . he ate his neighbor's wife."

"Ouch. That's bad for neighbors."

"No one knew of their affliction other than them and me."

"Is them and me correct English?"

The Reverend didn't crack a smile. He said, "I'm not sure."

"Anyway, I became their keeper. And then I discovered something as I grew older. I too had the curse. It had been passed on by the Evil Eye to their children, or their child in this case. I was the only child they had. So we all spent the nights in our respective cages, and we went back to the timers. Never had any trouble with that again, by the way, and our neighbor never figured out who killed and ate his wife. A pack of wild dogs was suspected, and for a while, every stray or dog that had gotten loose of their pen or their home ended up shot."

"Werewolfery is tough on the animal community," I said.

"You don't take anything serious, do you?"

"Problem is, I take everything serious. Come on, Reverend. Look at me. Do you think I'm living large? I got a life going, and a lot of it's good, but this body is, as they say, a blessing and a curse. I don't laugh a little, I don't see life with a little humor, well, I might as well take my Big Gun and put it to my red head and shoot myself with one of my Big Bullets. And I wouldn't want to do that, because it would surely leave one hell of a mess. But don't think I don't hear you. I do. You've had a strange life. So have I. So, baby, here we sit eating a meal and bonding."

I stuck out my fist. The Reverend just looked at it. "Come on," I said. "Show me some knuckles." He made a fist and touched mine with a light tap. He looked as awkward doing that as a cow trying to put on house slippers.

"So, how's the werewolfery?" I asked.

"I learned to keep it under control by force of will, and then, one day, it just went away. I don't have it anymore. I can't even turn into a werewolf if I try."

"Sometimes curses are like that. They wear thin. Want to know my guess? The woman who put the curse on your parents, one that got passed on to you, she died, and the curse ended."

"That's what I surmise. Anyway, because of the curse, I vowed to fight evil. And here I am."

"Good plan," I said.

"All right, then," the Reverend said. "So, what's the plan, or do we have one?"

"I like to just show up and handle it as it goes, which, of course, doesn't exactly sound like the height of intellectual reasoning. But, hey, it works for me. Way I see it, this town is next. If it is some form of astral connection, it appears the human projector loves trains and shadows and dragons and there's some connection with his life and these towns. Maybe he's all done. Maybe he'll never even know he did it. But if he's not through, if whatever his connection is keeps running along this route, he gets to this town, people will die. We are in the business of not wanting that to happen?"

"We are," he said.

The cute waitress came over with coffee. She said, "Can you move that tail around?"

I showed her I could. I reached out and took hold of her wrist with a twist of my tail. "How's that?"

"It gives me certain thoughts," she said.

"Sometimes thoughts can become reality," I said. "Believe me, I know."

She smiled and poured the coffee and went away. I watched her go away.

The Reverend said, "So, we wait here for . . . the train?"

"Nope. What we do is we go back to the town in front of this one, go to its outskirts, and see if the dark starts coming, and along with it, a train, and some shadow dragons. I got this idea he always starts in the same place, and just moves forward, and then dreaming the nightmare wears him out, he has to regroup. Then he starts again, moving faster as he comes to each town all over again, seeing no one's there, moving on."

"What if you're wrong?"

"This town gets empty," I said. "What I figure is somewhere, for some reason, someone with enough bile in their bones to burn through the fabric of reality, or rather enough bile to create a reality of their own, is traveling through this line of towns, letting out their anger. My guess is it's a guy. Gals can love trains, but I figure this is a guy. He's got this stuff inside him and he wants to let it out, and it's all connected to some kind of route. Maybe he was a salesman. Maybe he feels the company done him wrong. In his mind, someone did. That means he manifests all his anger into his thoughts, and here he comes."

"As a train?"

"The train, the dragons, and most likely a ton of things we haven't even seen yet."

"But why would he take it out on the townspeople? Surely they haven't all done something to him?"

"He's been someone powerless, and in his dreams he has power, but because of a number of quirks in his makeup, in his experience, the intensity of his anger, his thoughts have become solid. And like some murderers, he kills near someplace he is familiar with. Perhaps in real life he would never do these things, but in his dreams . . . well, it's different."

"Just someone going to sleep at night and they are able to do this? That is some kind of power."

"They may not be doing this when they sleep. Not a normal sleep anyway. It may have to do with some kind of suspended state. It's not about sleeping. It's about dreaming. And for him, his dreams are about jiving with shadows and dragons and long, black trains."

"Like being under medication?" the Reverend said, sipping his coffee. "Something drug induced?"

"Something like that," I said.

"So, this probably isn't an end-of-the-world situation?"

"Probably not. Disappointed?"

"Evil is evil."

"Now you're talking."

"You know, Hellboy, you're a lot smarter than you look."

"And you really do have a big nose," I said.

Down in the coma, the king of his domain

Sometimes he felt himself float up, and when he did he would glimpse the whiteness, the light, and he knew he had come too far, and he would feel pain, and he didn't like it there.

Sometimes he knew he was in a hospital, and that he hurt, and that there was morphine pumping through him, and there were moments when it was stronger and moments when it was weaker, and in those weak moments he almost surfaced. That was when he could feel himself bobbing below the light like a fish in a dark pond, looking up at movement just above his metaphorical waters.

But it was cool dark when he swam down into the darkness, and he felt that he had considerable abilities there. He lived in a very nice boxcar with all his magazines and toy trains, and the dragon necklace was magical. All he had to do was think about the necklace and the dragon would jump out of the little shape around his neck and it would grow and move about his dark boxcar with its black walls and black curtains and a light that was no light at all, but an ability to see in the blackness without brightening it. Sometimes the dragon divided. Sometimes it was smoke. It could leak out from under the boxcar doors, and it could fade through the boxcar walls and make its way toward the engine where no engineer resided. It could go into the big hot box of coals that Wilbur continued to imagine in the furnace, and the dragon could become smoke, go right up the stack and out into the night. The dragon was his eyes. What it saw, he saw. What the light of the train saw, he saw. And the very walls of the train were shadows of rats and bats, and what they saw he saw.

He had powers down there in the depths of the coma, and down there in those depths he stewed and felt mad and thought of Naomi and his horrible witch of a mother who he had seen licked clean of flesh by a wave of explosive flame; a big old orange and yellow tongue that with but a flick changed the nature of all it touched; it had robbed him of skin, he knew that upon surfacing a few times, going up there into the light. But he wasn't going back. Never again. He was staying down here in the cool dark where he could do magic.

He thought of his old paper route, and when he did, he thought of Naomi, and then he remembered she had been in Cold Shepherd, and that he had gone and got her and that she was down here with him. They were part of the very fabric of the darkness he lived inside of, and when he thought that way he could see Cold Shepherd, and it was an empty place because his train had come to town, and he could see the other empty towns beyond it, one, two, three. He had done it. He had made it happen. But he was in the hospital. How did that work? Where exactly was he? Was it all in his head? Was Cold Shepherd still thriving? Was he no more powerful than before?

He must have been moved to Phoenix, to a bigger city, a burn unit. Yeah, that was it. Had to be it. He was operating inside the coma while his body lay scalded and peeled and fat and destroyed in the light of a Phoenix hospital.

Down here in the dark his blood was morphine, his soul was shadow, and he began to move through Cold Shepherd in his big black train, and when the train moved the darkness gathered around it and his mind hung a big old bright yellow moon in the sky. It was the way the moon looked when he first went out with Naomi, and they had sat in the park in Cold Shepherd, not really saying much, but liking each other's company.

And now, she was down here with him. He turned his head, and there she was, lying in the bed, her skin dark in the shadow and her hair gone black as a raven's wing, her lips full and thick and black with dried blood. He sat up in bed and the black sheet fell away from them, and he saw that he was not fat at all, but slim, and muscular, and Naomi, whom he loved, had grown beautiful, if forever draped in the colors of night, the darkness of narrow corners and deep wells and empty pockets. He felt hungry, and he called to the dragon. And the door at the far end of the boxcar flew open, and there was no more light in the car beyond than in the one where they rode along, gently rocking. Behind the dragon in the dark were the people of Cold Shepherd, and the other little towns, and they hung by their feet on ebony hooks poked through their ankles. They had been split open by the dragon and cooked by the dark flame that came from inside its gut and spewed from its long, knotty snout like a flame thrower.

The dragon stood in the doorway and looked at them. Wilbur nodded. The dragon turned, whipping his long dark tail along the floor. With his sharp talons and sharp teeth, he tore loose the already burned flesh of a large woman, and dragged the flesh along the floor, and into the lair (and Wilbur so dearly loved to think of it as his lair), where he dropped it on the bed between Wilbur and Naomi. Wilbur patted the dragon, said, "Have your fill." The dragon nodded happily and moved quickly into the other car, found a corpse of his liking, tore the testicles from it with his fangs, and ate them as an appetizer. And then the dragon really turned hungry and began to rip savagely at the corpse, and he moved so violently that all the other corpses on their hooks swung back and forth, stirring the shadows and causing them to spin.

Wilbur closed the door with his mind, leaving the dragon to his meal. He and Naomi ate like lions.

When they were satiated, Naomi said, "You brought me here."

"That's right," Wilbur said. "What do you think?"

"I love it. I feel different. But what about your mother?"

"We need not worry about her anymore. Would you like me to read aloud from an issue of *Weird Tales*?"

"Oh, yes. That would be grand. Please do, Wilbur."

"Very well," he said, and he flowed over the floor as softly as a windblown ball of cotton. He reached up into his rows of magazines in nice plastic bags and took down an issue, and read to her. He began by reading the title. "'The Graveyard Rats.'"

And so Wilbur's train moved through the towns he had already devastated and turned them dark again and hung the moon again in each. He came to the border of Sand Rock, and the daylight there began to fade. What the train saw he saw. And what it was looking at was Hellboy, and a lean guy in a trench coat with fists full of pistols.

Further excerpts from the journal of Hellboy
(Actually signed as Honorary Human—Gee, thanks)

So it showed up, the train. And it was a big ole dark baby coughing out some really nasty-smelling smoke. It wasn't running on tracks. Right over the highway, and there we stood in the middle of aforementioned highway, watching, me and Reverend Jim Jeff, our nice blue rental off to the side.

The night came with the train. It was like some kind of window dresser from the heart of Halloween showed up, started tossing black confetti, 'cause pretty soon the day sky was night and the real moon waded up and went away. Up there, pinned to the sky, was a perfectly round moon as big as a platter and shiny as a freshly waxed plastic melon.

The train came on fast, and I can't tell you exactly what got into me, but I said, "Reverend, step aside or you'll be run over."

And he stepped aside, and me, I stepped forward and swung the Big Right Hand with all my might. Hit that train so hard it rattled the minerals right beneath it. Hit it so hard the big cow catcher on the front of the train came loose and tumbled over the ground and turned to smoke, and then the engine started to slide, and it caught me broadside as it turned. It knocked me about a hundred feet through the air, causing my tail to whip around and clip me one on the lip, and then I was rolling, and through glimpses I saw the train's boxcars jackknife and overturn and one of the boxcars exploded, and bodies, burned and cut up and chewed up, came sliding out of them and into the dirt. The rest of the boxcars went twisting off to the side and remained upright.

I got to my feet, gathered my thoughts, which were mostly *ouch*, and looked at the train more carefully. The engine had broken loose from the boxcars. The engine turned quickly, as if on a swivel; it moved as easily as a cartoon train. And then it blew a burp of black smoke out of its stack, and screamed its whistle, and came for me.

I had kind of lost track of the Reverend, but now I heard those big guns of his bark, cling-clang, and ping-ding on the side of the train. He might as well have been spitting jelly beans at it; whatever mojo was in his bullets wasn't enough to stop the train.

I glanced at the Reverend, saw him walking and firing, looking so strange in that long black overcoat flowing in the wind, sunglasses covering his eyes, bright orange bursts jumping out of the barrels of his guns.

Pushing back my overcoat, and trying to be stylish about it, I pulled out my really Big Gun and shot a really Big Bullet at the train as it pumped and thundered toward me.

Now, let me tell you. I'm not a squeamish kind of guy, and I've been known to take some serious blows, and just moments before I had actually hit a train with my fist, knocking it and the boxcars spinning, but this whole business, that train not running on tracks and all that horrid meat, the bodies of those humans sliding along the ground, had given me a bit of acid reflux. When my Big Bullet from my Big Gun hit the train engine, the bullet was sucked into it like a cashew dropped into chocolate pudding. The train just sort of slurped it in, and the great light at the front of the engine glowed brighter, and something moved behind the light.

When it hit me, that's when I lost my meal, which was not nearly so good coming up as it had been going down. The waitress flashed before my eyes, and I thought, damn it, I had that one sewed up, and now I'm going to be dead. The impact of the engine was worse this time, like it had gathered its forces, and as I spewed my meal, I clung to the front of it and it pushed me across the street and off the street, across an abandoned lot, and through a little ice-cream shop (I got a whiff of vanilla gone sour; glimpsed a flying waffle cone), and it slammed me into the side of a general store and knocked one of my teeth loose.

So there I was, pinned between engine and store wall, and I could feel the wall giving way behind me, and I tried to move, but was stuck there too tight, and I looked up, and what did I see, but the Reverend, climbing up the side of the engine. He had removed his trench coat and had it wrapped around his hands, which, considering steam was coming off the engine in a hiss of black smoke, was not a bad bit of thinking.

He was climbing on it as it pushed forward, trying to kill our hero (that would be me, if you're wondering), and it heaved steam off its surface in big, hot waves. The heat didn't bother me. Heat I can do. I'm not crazy about cold, but heat, that's my element, baby.

Anyway, I was pinned at a high point on the engine, and I could see the Reverend scrambling up there, using that trench coat, and he got up close to the stack, and out came his bag of tricks, which was mostly a large bottle of something that I figured was Holy Water, and with a deft flick of the wrist, he tossed it inside the stack.

Nothing happened.

At least not at first.

And then there was a sound from inside the engine like a hungry stomach rumbling, and then another sound, like someone demure passing a fart in attempted secrecy, and then the engine exploded in a blur of shadows and steam. It was such an explosion that it knocked down the wall my back was pressed against. It sent me ass over hooves through the general store and through the far wall and into a boutique store and rolled me right over the ladies' section. When I stood up from all that, I was wearing women's panties on my head, and my arm, the Big One, was draped with a nice pink teddy.

I charged through the ruins, the teddy and the panties flying free, crunched over the glass and the charred lumber. I found particles of the engine. They appeared to be flesh and bone, bleeding blood the color of rerun thirty-weight oil. Its ribs were sticking up here and there and the front of the engine, the great light, had burst open, and there was a big eye on tendons inside, and it was dangling out in the dirt, squirming. It was about the size of a grapefruit, but less appetizing.

I stomped it and it squirted like a water balloon. It was kind of nauseating, not to mention creepy, but you know how fun it is to stomp things that squirt.

I looked around for the Reverend, didn't see him.

I heard a creak, and I looked. It was one of the boxcars. The door came open. And something came out of it, so quick at first I couldn't recognize what it was, but between breaths it moved again, and this time I saw it real good, because it was right up in my face, and it definitely needed a breath mint. It was a dragon, a kind of wavery dragon, all black with wet black eyes that somehow seemed blacker than the rest of it. It breathed black flames.

I wrinkled my nose. The breath stank, but as you know, the fire didn't bother me. I felt like I was in a comfortable sauna. I punched the dragon and my hand went right through it. It wasn't like the train. It wasn't solid.

Except when it hit me with a swipe of one of its talons. When it did that I can attest to the Amen Corner (testify, brother), that the dragon was as solid as a wall of politician lies. It knocked me winding. Swatted me so hard that I hit the ground with enough impact to crack the highway and send up twirls of dust that filled my nose and pissed me off.

I pushed up, and there came the dragon, beating its great wings and skimming low over the earth. I thought about my Big Gun with the Big Bullets, and realized when the engine had hit me, it had been knocked out of my grasp. I tried to duck, but the dragon hit me. It wasn't any worse than being clipped by a 747. I went flying and twisting along the ground (hey, got a glimpse of the Reverend, lying over in the dirt, taking a nap while I'm doing the hard work). I had no sooner stopped than I felt myself being lifted. The dragon had me, was flying up toward the moon.

We went up and up and I tried to twist free, then I decided maybe that wasn't what I wanted. And then a very odd thing happened. The dragon bumped into the moon. The moon shook and rattled like a dinner platter, and I realized that this fake moon was not so high up and neither was the sky, and neither were we.

I twisted and got hold of my personal bag of tricks, and jerked out a lucky horseshoe (blessed by a holy man whose horse had died), and managed to bend a little so that I was in front of the dragon's face, tight in its talons. The dragon gave me another fire bath, but that was nothing. I cocked back my arm (not the Big One) and threw the horseshoe into the mouth of the black-fire-breathing dragon. The horseshoe melted a little, but it went in, and the dragon gulped, and then it did a thing with its throat, like it was about to bleat like a sheep, but no sound came out. No fire came out. There was a small sound that I can't think of any neat simile or metaphor to describe, and then the dragon let me go.

It was actually higher up than I thought. I hit the ground pretty darn hard. I made an impact that left a small crater. I crawled out of the crater and looked up. The dragon was twisting and turning all over the sky. You know how you blow up a balloon and you pinch off the bottom of it with your thumb and your forefinger, and then you let go, and the air starts coming out of the balloon, shooting it up and all over? It was like that.

The dragon collided with the moon. The moon shook, swung down a little, then came loose of its fixings, clattered to the ground. I looked where it had been. There was a little hook up there, like the sort of thing you'd hang a picture on. Whoever had created this universe within the real one was doing it in a very methodical and cheap manner. Anyway, about that dragon. He spewed this way and that, finally hit the ground and broke apart in a burst of shadows.

Without the moon up there it was really dark, but I see well in the dark. I started walking back toward the overturned boxcars, and the couple that were still upright. One of which had been the source for the dragon.

I stopped and thought things over. Maybe I didn't want to do that just yet. I went back to the wreckage of the building and looked around and found my Big Gun with the Big Bullets, went back to the boxcars.

"Come out, come out, wherever you are," I said, "because you don't want me to come in there after you."

Pulp

Inside the train, Wilbur, an ebony body with shiny ridgelike muscles, a skull like a huge, bumpy turnip, arose from his bed. When he did, the black satin sheet fell away, and he saw his darling, Naomi, exposed. Naked and beautiful as a Frazetta heroine, dark as sin, shiny as fresh-licked licorice. He was everything here he wasn't back there, in the world. He was strong and virile as Tarzan and Conan, crafty as Elak of Atlantis. He was all the heroes of his memory and his imagination. But he was a lot more pissed off.

He tried to will his train back together, but he couldn't. Someone out there was messing with his thoughts by messing with his train, and they had to be stopped.

He could sense his dragon was dead. The one he had once worn around his neck. It was dead. But there were others, and he called out to them, and they came out of the shadows in a clutch of beating wings and spurts of dark flame and hisses of chocolate-colored steam.

"Take him," said he who was master of all he surveyed.

Further excerpts from Hellboy's report

I'm creeping up, you see, quiet as a mouse in sneakers, some of those gel cushions on the shoe soles, that's how quiet I am, and the side door of the boxcar flies open, and out comes a whole batch of shadow dragons. They aren't as big as the guy I dealt with before, and their eyes are red, like burning coals, as we like to say when referencing hell. They're smaller boogers than the one I dealt with before. They are whipping about like huge dragonflies. They do not look happy, and they do not hesitate to take in the sights, speculate on the nature of the universe. They come right at me, moving like jets.

I have my Big Gun with the Big Bullets pointed, but before I can fire, a shot comes from off to my right. I glance, and there's the Reverend Jim Jeff, walking toward the dragons with his head turned slightly to the side like a curious dog, walking like he has one foot in a ditch, the other on a stump, and he's firing fast, with his big gun, which is not really all that big, and he's not hitting every shot, because I think inside his head he's still spinning from that explosion, probably can't hear a thing, got a humming in his head like a seashell pressed to the ear. Didn't bother me a bit, that explosion, except it made some holes in my nifty trench coat, but I been around regular people (I am, after all, an honorary human) enough to know how it could affect him. He also looks a little scalded; one side of his face is as bright as a baboon's ass and a bit of it is peeling off like old wallpaper. The other side of his face has grown hair and teeth that stick out of one corner of his lips; the werewolf has jumped out of him after a long time being dormant, or at least a little of it has. That funny walk, he's probably got one wolf leg, and a long tail crammed up under his pants. That can't be comfortable.

He has a gun in either hand and they are barking like a cage full of dogs. Dragons are taking a dive; stuff in his bullets is enough for these guys. I get off some shots, drop two, and then one has me. I can't get a good shot at him. We wrestle all over the ground, me dropping the Big Gun again, him holding onto my trench coat with one talon, trying to scratch my eyes out with the other, succeeding primarily in making my face look like a tic-tac-toe board.

I roll up on top of him, try to get him in some kind of hold, but a stepover toehold doesn't work so good on a dragon. Finally, I grab him by the snout, the top one, in such a way I'm pinching his nose holes together, and then I raise the Big Right Hand and I hit him so hard he spurts into a splatter of shadows, hit him so hard the blow smacks through him and knocks a hole in the ground big enough to fill up and make a nice wading pool.

I get up and rush toward the boxcar, forgetting my Big Gun with the Big Bullets, lying back there somewhere on the ground. I go at the boxcar, whacking at dragons with my Big Right Hand. One of the Reverend's bullets clips me on the shoulder, sends a spray of blood upward, causing it to make an umbrella of red drops.

"Hey," I yell back at him. "Watch it."

"Sorry," the Reverend says, and then he falls down. Doesn't melt, just goes down straight and flat as a dropped two-by-four, shakes a little when he hits. Nose forward, right in the dirt. His wolf tail rips up out of his pants and waves in the wind, then droops.

No time to consider his condition further.

I rush inside the open boxcar door.

Inside the air was cool and it was dark and there was a stench so strong it could wear an overcoat and boots and take a walk. I moved through the boxcar. There were bodies hanging on hooks. There was blood on the walls. My feet were tromping through entrails. There was a black shadow flowing between the corpses and moving about me, and it was ectoplasmic, sticky as a wad of Kleenex beside a teenage boy's bed.

I went on through and came to a door that was closed, pulsing like it was breathing. I could see all this clearly, thanks to those nifty see-in-the-dark eyes of mine. It goes with my ability to see long distances. I'm a walking, talking, night-vision, telescopic kind of guy. (I know you know this, but I like to remind you of my skills because it makes me feel good and . . . well, that's mostly it. It makes me feel good.)

The door was dark, but it had veins and arteries and they were pumping with the rhythm of a heartbeat. I kicked out at it, and that really hurt my foot. I did then what I should have done all along. I hit it with my right hand and it came apart and fled away in a flow of black rats and flapping bats.

The next room stank only a little less than the first, and the walls were the same, breathing, lined with veins and arteries. As I looked, the veins and arteries became less obvious and I could see rats and bats crawling all over the wall, or rather, they were the wall. The place smelled of not only dead bodies, but of rodent shit.

I went along the floor and the floor swayed. It too was made of bats and rats, and they nipped at my hooves, not causing me any damage (I have pretty tough hooves, as you know), and I came to a black (of course) curtain, and pushed it aside with my very fine and dexterous left hand. In there, on the bed, which was as black as all night, was a man, big and muscular and nude, his head propped against black pillows. His forehead pulsed like a knotted water hose, and beside him on the bed was a woman's corpse, split down the middle, the innards gone, the face gnawed on. She appeared to have on some kind of see-through negligee, stretched over her rotting meat, the blood from her wounds sticking to it like a bandage.

I thought, wow, now that is different—and, as you know, I've seen a few things.

He got out of the bed as if he might be merely thinking of putting on his pants and checking his mail. He was tall, taller than me, and he came for me at a run.

I ran at him, hard as I could. When we collided in the middle of the dark room, we made a noise like—pardon this—but it was a noise like two trains running together. We hit so hard we were both knocked backward.

I wobbled to an upright position. He climbed to his feet.

"I am a living hell," he said. "I am fire and brimstone and shadow and hate. I'm the whole package. I am all the pulp horror that can be in a world."

"No argument," I said.

And then he came for me again.

Hellboy comic panel
Splash page
Pulp cover style

Dynamic. We're talking so beautifully pulp it makes trees in the forest tremble for fear of more like it. You got this big, big, now we're talking *big*, obsidian guy coming at Hellboy with his fist drawn back. The right one. And it's a big fist. Almost looks as if the clenched fingers are an anvil. The body is like a black ice sculpture. Perfect. The head however, not so nice. Big and bulbous as if something inside is about to explode at any moment. Rising out of one ear, pushing to get free, is a bat. It's snarling, showing some real ugly bat teeth.

Hellboy, he looks impressive as well. He and Wilbur (a.k.a. the Obsidian Giant) are about the same size, and Hellboy, he has a look on his face that looks very far away from pleasant, and his Big Right Hand (a.k.a. the Right Hand of

Doom) is drawn back so far it looks like this punch (lacking economy of motion all the way) is being drawn all the way from hell, and when it hits it will knock its target all the way to the heavens.

And for those paying close attention to detail, in this splash panel we can see on the bed the horrible slab of meat that is Naomi. It is boiling with maggots. Her hair is coming off on the bed in patches.

Another note: The walls are literally made of wing-flapping bats and squirming rats that look half the size of an armadillo.

Darkness swells around the feet of Hellboy and the Obsidian Giant, like a splashing pool of sewage. This is drawn and inked and painted so carefully, so perfectly, we can almost hear the wind from their fists.

Freeze on this panel. Hold this panel. Now—

—*Let it go.*

Further excerpts from Hellboy's report

We came together like two bulls of the woods, and it was a collision that made my back teeth tremble, and that was just our chests meeting, and then there were the fists.

Now, let me tell you, when I reflect on this, it comes across as kind of cool. But at that precise moment in time, cool was not what I was thinking.

The big obsidian fist came at me so fast it was a blink within the blink of an eye. It hit me as hard as the train engine had hit me. And here's the part that I can look back on as kind of cool, or at least unusual: I hit him at the same time.

Next thing I remember I'm slammed against a wall and rats are squirming all over me, and I'm grabbing them and slinging them against the floor and they are exploding like bottles of ink.

I look across the way, and there is my foe, this Obsidian Giant. My blow has knocked him back on his bed, right on top of that hunk of meat that was once a woman. He's rising up slowly, shaking his head, and as he does, the walls of the train strip in spots and I can see light through them. Then the light goes black and the strips seal, and he's up, and I'm thinking, man, this sucks. He took a pretty good shot from the ol' Right Hand of Doom, and he's still got his head on.

He's up.

I'm up.

We come together again, and it's Fist City, dear hearts. Slinging knuckles like blackjacks. He gets in some good blows, but this time I'm slipping them a little, and I'm not winding up so much, jabbing out with my Left Hand of Not So Much

Consequence, saving the Big Boy (I just started calling it that, and it worries me a bit, naming parts of the anatomy) for the Big Moment.

The jabs are working. When I jab him, shadows fly out of his face. I go for a right, but the Big Boy misses, because the guy is as slippery as a greased eel. He pops me one hard enough to make numbered sheep jump across my vision. But then I've got him. I come low and grab all the way down to his ankles, butt him with my head, and back he goes on the bed. I drop a knee into his groin, and then I give him the Big Boy.

It's a perfect shot. He doesn't roll with it. It's more solid than the first shot, and that would have knocked over an SUV. This one, it's right in the middle of his face and when I hit him, it's like my fist is diving down in dark waters, and the waters splash up and go high and come down on me and splatter against my face and chest, and even over my back. I'm thinking about my nifty trench coat, that it's no longer nifty, and then the light rips in through the blackness. The bats break free and show more light as they climb to the sky. The rats scuttle and squeak. Then there is a tornado effect of spinning bats and rats and shadow, and I'm caught up in it, pulled up into it like a leaf, and away I go, doing the Pecos Bill thing, riding the tornado, and the next thing I know I'm flung out of the storm and I'm crashing into a building, which does neither building nor me any good. And then, there is much light.

I look. Tornado gone, baby. Gone.

The sky is blue and the sun is bright, and I feel like I've been run through a blender then hammered out with a mallet. I lay there, trying to breathe again. And then I'm feeling woozy, and I roll over, thinking something is coming up from my insides, but I only cough out a piece of a bat hung in the back of my throat. Yuk.

Lying where the boxcar was—for now there is no boxcar—are hunks of meat, body portions, pieces of the missing townspeople. My figure is there will be no Cactus Festival this year.

One body lies separate from the others. The body that had lain in his bed. I stagger over for a look see. Withered. Split apart. Did he not realize she was dead, that he had done it with his dragons and bats and rats and trains?

I figure not.

And who was *he*?

No answer. I know him only as I have labeled him: *The Obsidian Giant.*

I had to look around for the Reverend Jim Jeff. No idea where he was. I finally found him where the explosion of the boxcar and the whirl of the tornado had thrown him. He'd been knocked through a plate-glass window, knocked so hard his clothes were almost cut off of him and he looked a little like a butcher's hamburger special. But he was breathing. The wolfiness had gone away.

Don't move an injured person they say, but they were not there with me and they couldn't see how bad he needed a doctor. I thought about a few tricks in my bag, but none of them would do for this. I put him in the rental, which, though upright, had been flipped a few times, and though still blue, did not look so fine anymore: roof bent in, headlights shattered, the doors all stuck from the car having rolled.

I put the Reverend down and just jerked the door off the driver's side. I slid him across the seat, to the passenger's side, cranked back the seat, strapped him in. I got behind the wheel. The key was still in the ignition. I drove furiously.

I was doing at least one hundred and twenty. The car started to rock. I whipped through that line of little towns until I came to Cold Shepherd. Just like all the other towns it was now a place of blue sky and sunlight and no people.

As I passed the *Leaving Cold Shepherd* sign I saw the National Guard. The soldiers raised their rifles either in warning or greeting; probably the latter. No one shot at me.

I arrived at the Phoenix Hospital, and there were all manner of things you were supposed to do to park, but they bored me. I ran through a striped bar and made a guy in the little house that gave out parking permits jump (caught that out of the corner of my eye), and then I banged the car up some steps so hard and fast I tore out a chunk of its bottom.

I parked on the grass in front of the sign that said *Stay Off The Grass*, and got Reverend Jim Jeff out of there and ran with him in my arms to the hospital. At the desk I was told to wait, and I told them I wasn't waiting, and if they didn't get a doctor down quick, I would tear the place up. They all knew who I was. Everyone does. Tabloids. News.

Anyway, everyone's staring because I'm not exactly your everyday view, and my tail is twitching nervously.

They get a stretcher down there, and then we're in the elevator, going up, and then we're on the floor, and as we wheel Reverend Jim Jeff out, I let the orderlies take him, glide him along toward surgery, 'cause that's what he needs (ribs are broken and poking out of him like porcupine quills), and I say, "You might want to worry if he starts growing hair."

Then I hear this awful scream, and go rushing along the corridor, 'cause that's what I do, help people, even when I might rather be somewhere else. I rush into the room where the scream is coming from, and what do I see on the big (formerly white-sheeted) bed in the room: a nude body, burned all over, minus genitals (flames got them), toes fused together, fingers fused together, and the face . . . Well, there isn't any face (and this is the source of the no-longer-white sheets), because he's got a hole right through the middle of where his face is, and that hole is just about the size of the Right Hand of Doom, the Big Boy, and it is from that hole that blood has leaped, all the way to the ceiling and all over the walls, coloring the sheets apple-ripe red, but a lot less appetizing.

The nurse who has come in to check the temp is screaming, and then she sees me, and maybe she's not hip to the tabloids and the TV appearances, or maybe it's just too much to take: the discovery of a face that has exploded and a big red demon with a Big Right Hand and sawed-off horns and a twitchy tail in her path, but she really screams now, and then . . . well, you really know the rest.

I have his name now. Wilbur Cain. A guy who must have had some real bile inside him. And as Kate suggested, he had to have astral-projected all the things he loved into something sour and mean. Something about the woman he had in the bed with him. Something about his mother, because he had tried to commit suicide, maybe more hoping it would kill her than him, and he managed that.

Can't figure the whole story. It's a confusion, a big ole baffle.

Whatever.

May his soul fly free.

Reverend Jim Jeff. He's got the best care they can give him. I've checked on him and he's conscious now, and he even took hold of the Right Hand of Doom, one finger anyway, and he said, "We make a pretty good team."

"Well, you're the one gets the nurses," I said. "Me, the doctor looked over my cuts and poured alcohol on them."

"Nurse I got is named Bob and he always has a growth of beard and his breath smells like chewing tobacco . . . Hellboy, thanks, my friend."

"You're welcome. I had to drive back this direction anyway."

Okay. That's the report, all emailed out. I can fill in the rest of it later. Oh yeah. I'm not coming back for a while.

Send.

Bora Bora
A unique wedding chapel

Hellboy sat in a very comfortable lawn chair on top of a big glass floor with the ocean underneath. It was a place designed for weddings. Couple came in, had their wedding on the glass floor, looked down, they could see fish swimming. Groovy, baby.

Hellboy bent over and watched the fish for a while.

He sat up and leaned back and looked out beyond the glass and beyond the open walls. He could see the blue sea and the blue sky, and the way they met, it was almost as if there were no heaven and earth, but only a big bright ball of blue.

It was nice.

A cool wind blew.

A man in a white coat, with hair slicked down with so much grease you could have run your finger through it and used the tip of it to oil a squeaky door, came over with a tray with a tall drink on it that was as blue as the sky and the sea, a wedge of orange draped the edge of the glass, and there was a big straw in it that had a hinge that let the straw bend. It was a really long straw.

Hellboy took the drink and gave the waiter a tip.

The waiter paused. "It's mostly just the couples come here."

"Aren't I big enough for a couple?"

The waiter smiled. "Sure. You're plenty big."

"Good."

"Can I ask you a favor?" the waiter said.

"As long as I don't have to get out of this chair."

"How'd you get all those scratches?"

"Cat."

"Cat?"

"Yep."

"Oh. Can I, like, have your autograph on a napkin?"

"Got a pen?"

The waiter dug a pen from his coat pocket, gave it to Hellboy, put the napkin on the tray and held it. Hellboy signed. He did it with a flourish.

"Thank you, sir. Are you comfortable?"

"I am. And, may I make a request? When you see this glass go empty, bring another, and every time you do, I'm going to double your tip."

"Yes, sir," said the waiter, and went away.

Hellboy sat, not moving, slowly closing his eyes, sipping his drink lazily through the straw.

STRAIGHT, NO CHASER
MARK CHADBOURN

Brodie's is the kind of club you rarely come across these days. You know it the moment you step through those art-deco swing doors and breathe deeply: it's in the air, soaked deep into the grain of the bare-wood floorboards, and the scratched tables and the long, oak bar, like seventy years of spilled bourbon; it's in the very fabric of that long, low-ceilinged space. Brodie's is a club where music matters, where the syncopation celebrates the off-step skip and jump of life itself.

You'd never guess it by checking out the finger-snapping, nodding, knowledgeable clientele. They're all dead. But even the dead deserve a nightlife.

For a jazz joint of such high regard, it's a little off the beaten track. On the last leg of his journey, Hellboy stood with his back to St Paul's Cathedral, facing the River Thames as Big Ben chimed midnight, and then raced east to Spitalfields. In the shadow of Nicholas Hawksmoor's mysterious Christ Church, a street visible only for five minutes led into the depths of the quarter where the dead like to hang out. Clubs and pubs and bars sprawled along a labyrinth of narrow streets and alleys, lit by neon and flickering torches. And there, overlooking a small, cobbled courtyard, was Brodie's.

Hellboy had barely stepped through the door when an elderly man shambled up, grinning broadly. That was partly because most of his mouth was missing, but there was a definite sparkle in his glassy eyes. He wore a sharp if moldy suit in a 1930s style, and a hat pushed back on his head, a beetle nestling on the brim.

"Not much life in here," Hellboy said.

"You know we've heard that one before?" The man chuckled throatily, did a few sprightly steps, then shook Hellboy's hand. "Been expecting you, my man. The name's Eubie Parkhouse. You want a drink?"

"No time. I'm on a deadline. I need the shoes by dawn or a pretty girl gets her wedding day ruined big time."

"That's a dangerous path you've chosen. Those shoes are powerful mojo. They've been lost for a long time, and some mighty important people round these parts don't want them to be found."

"I've come prepared."

On stage, a tall, thin man tapped the microphone. He had pomaded hair and half his face charred to the bone, but he had the pearly smile of someone who thought they were in heaven. The stage lights came on the instant the band behind him launched into a version of "Mercy, Mercy, Mercy." Eubie snapped his fingers and did another little dance and spin.

Hellboy's attention was drawn to a member of the band. "Hey, isn't that—?"

"Sure is. You know who has all the best tunes. We got some of the finest jazz- and bluesmen ever to grace a stage playing round here on a nightly basis."

Eubie carefully searched the shadowy corners of the club and then whispered, "I help you, I'm putting this club . . . everything . . . on the line."

"I know that," Hellboy replied. "But I was told you were the only one who could help, and that if I told you why you'd probably do it."

"The music was my life, and it's my death too. Without it . . ." Stifling a desperate edge in his voice, he examined his dead hands, the desiccated skin, flesh hanging loosely from the bone. "Let's just say, this whole deal ain't exactly a fat night at Radio City. I think I know what you're going to say, but come on—let's go somewhere quiet."

Eubie led the way through the smoky atmosphere. "You found this old place easy enough?"

"Depends what you call easy. It took me five days, three countries, and a whole mess of breakages to get the next scheduled appearance of the entrance to the Night Quarter."

"Yeah? Where was it this time?"

"London."

Eubie nodded thoughtfully. "Always did fancy seeing the world. As it was, never got much out of my backyard."

They went up a flight of rickety stairs to a cluttered office. Old black-and-white photos of famous and forgotten musicians lined three of the walls. On the fourth was an enormous protective sigil, etched in blood.

Hellboy inspected it. "Human?"

"We didn't take every last drop," Eubie said sheepishly. "What are you gonna do about it? We're zombies. Besides, gotta look after my club."

"And yourself. You're supposed to know everything there is to know. That's got to be a threat to those *mighty important people,* too."

Eubie poured himself a shot and slumped into his chair. "I've been around a long time, in this place and the world. Can't help but pick up information if you keep your ears and eyes open."

He pointed to the most faded photo, a band posing with their instruments, faces serious but hats pushed back in the same jaunty angle that Eubie still wore his.

"Yeah, that's me," he said. "I played horn with Kid Ory's Original Creole Jazz Band for a while. That would be back in '21, when they were on their way. The first black jazz band to make a recording." He shrugged. "Dropped out before they made their place in history—story of my life. After that, I played with a lot of bands, some jazz, some blues, traveling up and down the Delta, hopping trains, thumbing a ride. Different night, different town, same beautiful sounds from my magic horn." He eyed the instrument, which gleamed in a glass case on a shelf.

"Yow!" Hellboy snatched his hand back from the case as a flash of power crackled out from the horn.

"Yeah, ain't that the thing," Eubie said. "In our lives, we all carry round somethin' special, somethin' we hold in our hearts. And at the moment of our passing, those things soak up a deal of power. The stranger the passing, the bigger the power."

"That's what happened to the shoes?"

"Yeah, 'cept the shoes got a double dose. You see, you're thinking shoes, right? They're, like, nothing, like a newspaper you leave on a park bench, or a comb, or a toothpick. Use 'em up and throw 'em away. But back in those days, shoes meant something, for my brothers and sisters. A lot of us didn't have shoes, and if you did, you were on the way somewhere! You earned those shoes, and you showed them off, and you'd walk right up to hell's door in them!"

The clock on the wall struck a quarter to one. "Time's running out. Are you going to help me?"

Eubie weighed Hellboy's words, then asked, "Tell me about this girl and her wedding."

"Her name's Clarice Masterson. She's one of the immortals."

"Yeah, I heard of those dudes. The immortals and the dead, we got a lot in common. Time on our hands, for one."

"You hit the nail on the head. Clarice got herself wrapped up in an arranged marriage, with one of your guys—Malecula?"

Eubie rolled his eyes. "Oh, yeah. *The Favored One.*"

"It's a symbolic thing. Bring the two families together, peace in our time. No more trouble between the immortals and the dead, like the one I got caught up in over in Capetown in '59. But if it doesn't happen there's going to be a big war, and hell to pay for the rest of us caught in the crossfire."

" 'Cept it's also a risk, right? The rules say 'no immortal and no dead shall ever wed.' It's an alchemy thing, or like pouring gasoline on a blaze. But the shoes . . . the power in 'em, anyway . . . will stop the whole fire raining from the heavens and judgment from on high thing?"

Hellboy nodded. "The ceremony starts at dawn. And I want cake."

Eubie sighed. "Big stakes. I can see why you've got yourself so worked up."

"That's not all. If the shoes don't arrive on time, they're going to press on with the wedding anyway. And if that happens, Clarice dies."

"That's crazy. She's an immortal."

"When the rules are broken, everything changes. She dies, just like everyone else." Downstairs the band kicked into a song that Hellboy recognized. " 'I Got My Mojo Working.' That's our cue. Let's go."

Hellboy followed Eubie out of Brodie's and into the maze of streets until they found a blues and soul club called Green Onions, all skinny ties and porkpie hats on the men, and tight, colorful dresses on the women. The dead danced exuberantly, but always in silence, and never blinking, their staring eyes alive with the colors of the flashing lights.

"You know we were followed from your club?" Hellboy said.

Eubie sucked on what remained of his lower lip. "Not left that place in fifty years or more. People tend to notice when routines like that get broken."

Hellboy realized how vulnerable Eubie now was away from his sigils, and that made his motivations even harder to understand. Why risk so much, so quickly? There was no point asking; the dead kept their secrets close to them, and any hidden agenda would be buried deep.

"Any idea who it is?" Hellboy pressed.

"Somebody we don't want to meet too quick, so let's keep moving." As Bob and Earl sang "Harlem Shuffle" over the sound system, Eubie pushed through the dancing bodies until they came to an extremely overweight woman sitting at her own table not far from the stage. Her hair hung in greasy dreads and the skulls of various small animals lay amid a mass of beads, amulets, and other charms around her neck. As Hellboy neared he could see her eyes were all white and her face was strangely implacable.

She shrieked when Eubie stood before her, though her lips didn't move and she showed as little animation as a regular corpse.

Eubie greeted her with a slight bow of his head. "Mama Secordia."

"Lord! You're out! Here!" Her lips and face remained still. The voice appeared to be coming from the fat jowls that hung around her throat. "You got a death wish, boy? You had enough of not-living?" A deep chuckle rolled out from some secret part of her.

"I'm looking for the shoes, Mama."

Silence for a moment, then: "After all these years? And with all that it's going to bring down on your head?"

"We don't need to talk about that. Just point me in the direction of Willie Davis."

"Not so fast, Master Parkhouse. You got it?"

Eubie weighed his response, then said, "Yeah, I got it."

"Show me." When Eubie didn't move, Mama Secordia pressed, "You think I'm just going to set you in the direction of one of the most powerful things we got round these parts 'cause you say so? You show me, Eubie Parkhouse, or you're heading back to your club and all your big risk has been for nothin'."

"You know what Willie's got is no good on its own, Mama."

"Never you mind that. Show me."

Reluctantly, Eubie pulled a leather thong from inside his pristine white shirt. Hanging from it was a small piece of flat, carved bone.

"Woooo," Mama Secordia whistled. "Robert Johnson's plectrum."

"Carved from the skull of a man who tried to kill him." Eubie quickly tucked away the artifact.

"Half the key—you do have it." She released—from somewhere—a tremulous sigh of awe. "With that and Willie's piece you can get Johnson's shoes. After all these years."

"They're Robert Johnson's shoes?" Hellboy exclaimed.

"Who's this you brought before me, Eubie? Who's this?" Mama Secordia shrieked, seemingly shocked that Eubie was not alone.

"Name's Hellboy, Mama. You might have heard of him. Had some dealings with our kind."

"I don't like it, Eubie. I don't like it at all."

Hellboy was shocked to hear another voice emanate from Mama Secordia. "Hush. Don't rile him," it hissed.

"Hey! What's going on?" Hellboy asked.

"Let me tell you about Robert Johnson," Mama Secordia said to Hellboy in a now-oily voice. "When he was a boy he dreamed of being the greatest bluesman there ever was or would be. Dreams like that don't just happen. You make 'em happen through force of will . . . and a little help here and there. And so he asked around, and begged and pleaded and cajoled, and eventually he was told to take his ol' guitar down to the crossroads near Dockery's plantation. And the Devil came to him there—yes sir, ol' Scratch hisself—and Johnson was trembling mightily but he kept his nerve. And the Devil took his guitar and tuned it so he could play anything he wanted. All he had to pay was his soul."

"I told you those shoes got a double dose," Eubie said. "One blast then, when Old Nick did his work, and another when Mr. Johnson passed over on August 16 in '38. They're fueled with the heavenly, God-given magic of the music he was born with, and the Hellfire super-charge that took him into eternity. Why, with those shoes I reckon you could do anything."

"So why didn't you get hold of them before?" Hellboy asked.

"I got no use for them. There's only one thing I want, and the shoes ain't no use there." He turned back to Mama Secordia. "Come on now, Mama. Where's Willie been all these years?"

"Someplace safe."

"We had us an agreement, Mama."

"Let me see the half-key again."

"Back off." Hellboy could see something was wrong with Mama Secordia: ripples ran through the fat encasing her body, though no body movement appeared to be generating them.

"Give it to me!"

Mama Secordia tore open from chin to crotch, pivoting wide like the jaws of a venus flytrap. In the sticky interior, five small figures squirmed before suddenly launching themselves at Eubie. He went over backward under the force of the attack.

"Gahhh! Zombie babies!" Hellboy exclaimed.

Snapping and snarling, the babies swarmed over Eubie, trying to get at the plectrum. One by one, Hellboy grasped them by the backs of their necks and tore them free. With a flick of the wrist, he hurled them across the room where they bounced off walls and dancers before renewing their attack with an even greater frenzy. This time they went for Hellboy, tearing all over his body like cats. When he went for one, it was already somewhere else, sinking needle-sharp milk teeth into Hellboy's flesh. And when he did grab hold of a baby, it was back as quickly as he could throw it away.

"Get off!" Hellboy hated the way their baby skins felt, not soft, but dry as a bundle of sticks.

"They won't let up!" Eubie called. "Mama Secordia's brood always gets what it wants!"

"We'll see about that."

Hellboy caught the ankle of the biggest of the babies, the one he was sure had been the spokesbaby for the Secordia clan. He hauled it over and slapped it on the bar, snatching a bottle of bourbon from the bemused barman and dousing the baby in it. Cursing as the other babies tore at his arms and back with their teeth and talons, Hellboy marched to one of the blazing wall torches and dangled the biggest baby next to it.

It shrieked and cried, "Stop! Have mercy!"

"Yeah, that's what I thought. You'd go up like a kindling. Now tell him what you know."

The baby protested wildly, but the other four had dropped off Hellboy and scurried under the table where they clung on to the still-splayed-open Mama Secordia's ankles.

"Last chance," Hellboy said as he moved the biggest baby closer to the flame.

"Wait, wait! I'll tell all! Willie Davis is in the basement of the Blue Note."

"For fifty years?" Eubie said contemptuously.

"We walled him up to keep him safe!"

"Yeah, safe for you to come back to when you'd found the other half-key."

Eubie plucked his hat from the floor and replaced it on the back of his head. "I thought you were smarter. No good's going to come from getting ahold of those shoes."

"Okay, I'm pretending you didn't say that." Hellboy threw the baby into the slimy insides of Mama Secordia. The other four scurried inside and the carcass closed up around them.

"You're a fool to do this now, Eubie Parkhouse," she said. "You're gonna lose everything you fought for."

"Ain't that the story of the blues?" Eubie adjusted his tie and took a lurching step toward the door as the speakers blared out "I'm Gonna Tear Your Playhouse Down."

The Blue Note was darker than the other two clubs, with an unpleasant air of threat hanging oppressively in the cramped space. It was standing room only, men and women in dark suits pressed tightly together, swaying gently to the rhythm of the music. Their faces were turned toward the floor, and they kneaded their hands incessantly. Hellboy could feel the palpable waves of despair coming off the lone musician on the stage at the far end of the room. He sat on a stool, head bowed intently, his fingers flying across the fretboard, his voice a low growl of misery.

"The Blue Note's a real thing," Eubie noted. "Played right, it can tear your heart out. Literally."

"Ever thought about listening to something uplifting? Like the Funeral March?"

"This is our music, Hellboy. It speaks to us about the truth, that life's a long road of pain, and it don't get any better once you've passed on."

"Okay, I can see how most of your kind would think that. But you look like you've got a pretty good deal. Nice club, drinks, music round the clock."

"The trick is making the best of the hand fate's dealt you." Eubie paused to watch the bluesman on stage deftly move into another heartbreaking song.

"How'd you end up . . . you know . . . dead?"

"Stupidity. A smart mouth. Wanting something so bad you'll do anything to get it. The usual. I met Johnson in May '31, just after he got married. The word was out all over Mississippi about this guitarist who could make heaven and earth move. And the stories . . . he wasn't human . . . some kind of thing sent out to tempt poor souls off the path of righteousness . . . guitar playin' that could turn even a preacher bad. And the other story, the one that really got me goin'—that he'd sold his soul to Old Nick to get his heart's desire."

"It always amazes me how people keep falling for that."

"People are people, that's the long and the short of it. The Devil always wins, 'cause people want things so bad they can taste it. They're always trying to fill that hole they carry around inside them—money an' fame an' power an' sex an' drugs. They always look like they just might do it, but after you've been filling that hole for a good lifetime you start to realize you'll never get to the top, an' then it's too late. Only one thing fills it, only one. And that's the hardest thing to find."

"So you realized how Johnson bought his skill and thought you'd do the same?"

Eubie began to push his way through the wall of swaying bodies filling the hall. "I'm not proud of what I did. I was a weak man. I thought my need overrode anything, even a man's life. I knew in my heart, I guess, but you make an . . . accommodation with yourself."

"Who did you kill?"

"Johnson. Not by my own hand—even I couldn't have done that. But I had to make sure he was at a certain place at a certain time, so the Devil could collect his due. It was 1938, August, and as hot as hell. A crossroads out in the country, not far from Greenwood, Mississippi. I guess even the Devil likes his poetry and his balance. Johnson was poisoned by some other sucker who thought the Devil would do him a good deal. Robert Johnson, RIP. Only twenty-seven. He lost what I wanted—eternal life. Never getting any older."

Hellboy winced at the pain in Eubie's voice.

"Yeah, I never did get any older. I just rotted away. My body turned like my black, stinking soul. There's that poetry again." He laughed bitterly. "A zombie. I shoulda read the small print."

Hellboy came to a halt in the middle of the audience. The bluesman had changed to a new song, low, rumbling, dangerous.

"That wasn't the only part of my punishment . . ." Eubie realized Hellboy was no longer following him. "What's wrong, big guy?"

"Why'd everyone stop dancing?" Hellboy slowly turned to survey the motionless crowd. The music tugged sensations of unease from deep within him.

"That song," Eubie said. "Nobody's allowed to play it round here. 'Hellhound on My Trail.' Robert Johnson's song."

Every pair of dead eyes in the room was fixed on Hellboy and Eubie.

"Uh-oh," Hellboy said. "This can't be good."

There was a hanging moment filled with the full intensity of those desolate gazes, and then the dead moved as one, hands reaching, grasping, tearing. Broken, dirty nails raked Hellboy's head and back. Eubie went down under the weight of bodies.

"Son of a—! Hang on!" Lashing out, Hellboy drove a path to Eubie. A wave of dead flesh washed hard against him, however much he smashed the bodies back. Ducking beneath the surface, he scooped Eubie up in his arms. The club owner was as light as a bundle of sticks. There's nothing in him, Hellboy thought. A pretend-man. A memory, that was all.

The dead attacked in complete silence. In the background, the bluesman played with mounting intensity.

"It's elevator music for me from now on." With the blows raining off his back, Hellboy bowed his head and shoulders to shield Eubie and forced a route through the crowd. Bursting out near the stage, he allowed himself one glance at the performer. The bluesman gave a small, mean-spirited smile.

Hellboy tore open a door beside the stage and locked it behind him. It bowed with the relentless pressure, but held, though the tearing of nails on wood set Hellboy on edge.

Eubie released himself from Hellboy's grip and dusted himself down. "I shoulda seen that coming. We're getting closer to the real business. People are going to start getting agitated."

"When you say *people* you don't really mean that, do you?"

A flight of rickety wooden stairs led down through damp, salt-encrusted brick into a dank, mud-floored basement filled with broken furniture, boxes of bottles, rotting drapes, and unused lights and microphones.

"Before all that started, somebody came in through the door after us. I think it was whoever followed us from your club." Hellboy examined a cardboard box of old 78 rpm records. "You going to tell me who that is?"

"Me. Or something that looks just like me."

"Yeah? Some kind of doppelgänger?"

"My own personal Hellhound. The part I like to keep locked away, but couldn't on that night I led Johnson to his death. I told you there was another part to my punishment. It's not enough I get to spend eternity slowly rotting away—my shade gets to hunt me down, slicing off a part of me every time he catches me." Eubie held up his left hand; two fingers were missing. "Whittling me down a bit at a time. But still alive, you know? Always alive, however much he removes. Yeah, and I used to be such a good-looking fella." He gave another throaty chuckle, but the bitterness in it made it too painful to bear.

"So that's why you hid away in your club all that time, hiding behind your sigils."

"One of the reasons." Eubie wouldn't meet Hellboy's gaze.

"And after fifty years in hiding, you decide to come out and help me today because I asked nicely? Come on, Eubie. You want those shoes for yourself."

"I could've got them at any time. You're doin' me a disservice." Eubie shuffled into the depths of the basement, calling out Willie's name. Once the echoes had faded, they heard a faint muffled sound.

"Willie was involved in Johnson's murder too?"

"Yeah, we both earned our dues."

"What did he want from the Devil?"

"A plate of beans and some franks."

"What?"

"He was hungry. Hadn't eaten for days. I asked for more, for my eternal soul, but at least he got a full belly. That shows which of us is the biggest sucker."

The muffled sound came from an oily patch on the plaster of one wall. A dark spot was prominent about six feet off the floor. "What's this?" Hellboy touched it gently with his index finger. "Hmm. Soft."

"The tip of his nose." Eubie inspected it closely. "They didn't wall him up. They built him into the wall and plastered over him."

"Fifty years as fixtures and fittings. That's got to be boring. Here. Let me." Hellboy swung his hefty fist at the wall, shattering the plaster and the brick beneath it. A dusty, wide-eyed Willie pitched forward onto the boards.

"Probably take a while to get those legs working," Hellboy mused.

A mewling sound emanated from the prone Willie. Eubie examined him and discovered his tongue was missing. "Guess they cut it out so he wouldn't call for help." Eubie fished inside Willie's shirt and removed a straight razor on a thong. "Johnson carried it for defense," Eubie said. "You needed to look after yourself on those lonely country roads, late at night."

"Okay, you got what you need to find the shoes?" Hellboy asked.

Figures," Eubie said.

They stood at a crossroads of alleyways. A brass plaque set into the cobbles was in the shape of a large black dog. There was no inscription.

"This looks like the place." Hellboy checked all four alleys. They were dark, but empty. "Now what?"

As Eubie gradually brought the plectrum and the razor together, they began to glow with an inner light, growing stronger as the two artifacts neared each other. With shaking hands, Eubie touched them and a bolt of force shot down, blowing the brass plaque into the air. Beneath it were a pair of spit-shined black leather shoes, the soles worn thin.

"I'm watching you, Eubie," Hellboy said.

"I tol' you, big guy. I'm as straight as the night is long."

Before Hellboy could pick up the shoes, a deep rumbling began far beneath their feet. It grew louder until the cobbles erupted, throwing both of them back into one of the alleys. When the smoke had cleared, a squat figure with a blazing body was standing in the middle of a ragged, blasted pit. Twin horns curled out of a soot-blackened head in which two yellow eyes burned.

"Ukobach!" Hellboy said. "Keeper of the Devil's boilers. What the hell are you doing here?"

"You cannot take the shoes." Ukobach's voice sounded like the clanging of hammers on iron pipes.

"We'll see about that." Hellboy launched himself at Ukobach. Before he made contact, he was hit by a column of liquid fire that rammed him into a wall. Cursing, he renewed his attack. Every time he neared, Ukobach blasted him again, driving him back, superheating the air so it boomed and screamed. A change in strategy was the only way to go. Hellboy hammered the nearest wall so hard it collapsed on top of Ukobach. By the time the demon had clawed his blazing form out from under the pile, Hellboy was standing over him, gently dangling the shoes by the laces.

"Ulp," Ukobach muttered. In a flash of brimstone-reeking smoke, he disappeared.

"I don't know what he was thinking," Hellboy sighed.

Dawn lit the sky silver and scarlet. The clubs were closed, the clientele shambling their way back to their resting places. The sound of a lone horn rose up, filled with jazzy life. A procession wound its way toward Hellboy and Eubie as they perched on a wall in the main square.

"You hanging around for the party?" Hellboy asked.

"I'm hangin' around to see her." Eubie shifted uneasily.

"Who? Clarice? Yeah, she's a real beauty."

"I know."

"You've seen her before?"

Eubie let out a long, low sigh. "I told you—the Devil always wins 'cause people want things so bad they can taste it, and I wanted her. We met when I was playing New Orleans with Kid Ory's Original Creole Jazz Band. I looked up from my solo, and there she was, at the back of the hall, watchin' me like I was a god or something. She was the prettiest, classiest girl I'd ever seen. She's got this *quality*, right? Everybody sees it. You know you're in the presence of somethin' special. And she was lookin' at me. I knew right then and there my heart was taken."

He beat a rhythm on the wall, lost to his memories. The procession moved into the square, Clarice in her ivory wedding dress at the head of the line. Hellboy thought she probably was the most beautiful woman he had ever seen, and the saddest. Her eyes met Eubie's for a long moment.

"That's why she told me to look you up to find the shoes," Hellboy said. "She knew you'd help."

"I quit Kid Ory to be with her, right when they were hittin' the big time. I didn't mind. I'd have done anything for her. For a while, I had everything a man could ever want in this world. We were in heaven."

"What happened?"

"I found a gray hair, and another, and a wrinkle. I got old. And she stayed as young as the day we met."

"That's the thing about immortals."

"I just got obsessed. How could an angel like her hang around with an old, wrinkled guy like me? How would she feel when I was drooling into a cup? I didn't want her to hate me. I didn't want her pity. I just wanted her love."

"She ever say anything to you about it?"

Eubie shook his head. "She loved me. I always thought I was a smart guy. But I wasn't. I should've made the most of the time we had together."

The procession came to a halt. Clarice adjusted her dress and tried not to look at her soon-to-be husband, a grotesquely fat zombie with one eye and a missing rib cage.

Hellboy nodded thoughtfully. "You've given up everything you earned to save her. That's a heck of a sacrifice."

"It's too late for me now. My time of doing anything worthwhile is long gone. But she'll always have that ahead of her, even stuck with that dumbass Malecula as a partner. That's how she is—always filled with hope." He stood up and cracked the bones of his fingers with finality. "I'd do anything for her."

He looked for a long time toward one of the shadowy alleyways leading off the square. Eventually a figure emerged. It was Eubie, but this Eubie's face was filled with a fierce hatred, greed, and murder.

"No point running anymore," Eubie said.

"Hang on." Hellboy went over to the wedding party, and as he handed the shoes to Clarice he whispered briefly in her ear. She raised the shoes above her head, and as the sun came over the rooftops and hit the other Eubie, he faded into nothing. Clarice's smile was brighter than the dawn, and for a moment Eubie was back in New Orleans, listening to the dying notes of his solo and thinking everything would be all right forever.

Hellboy came back over. "She wants a word with you before the ceremony starts."

"An old dead guy like me?"

"Yeah, there's no accounting for taste."

Second Honeymoon
John Skipp & Cody Goodfellow

Sea of Crete
April 22, 1999
9:47 a.m.

I t was a beautiful day for the end of mankind, sun high and crisp in the cheerful blue sky. The wind was warm. Brisk. Salty with life. The possibility of lovin'.

And the certainty of death.

Watching the light dance across the lazy waves from the wide-open door of the descending cargo plane, you'd almost think that Gunter Herzog was right. That Nature had a hand in this insanity, and had put on her brightest, sunniest face to see them off.

Hellboy wasn't buyin' it for a second.

"You know what I hate?" he said, shrugging on the rocket pack. "This stupid thing."

"They did a lot of work on them," said Roger the Homunculus, already strapped into his. "I think we will fly just fine."

"Uh-huh."

They were scanning the skyline for Herzog and his eco-terrorist cronies: a batch of Earth-Firsters so determined to *save the world from humanity* that they were willing to do the single stupidest thing imaginable.

Unleash the father and mother of all monsters, set them up on a date, and let nature take its course.

This is what the crew knew going in, based on Kate's ongoing brief from HQ:

Eight hours ago, a seismic research camp on Mount Etna was raided by a crack paramilitary team. Everyone at the camp was killed. The volcano erupted, grounding carabinieri and Italian-army aircraft. Then it got weird.

The terrorists lifted off under cover of smoke and flying lava bombs with a sixty-ton core sample, towed in an enormous carbon-steel sling by four cargo-lifting choppers, with two Soviet-surplus gunships walking point. Interpol flagged down the B.P.R.D. when the choppers and cargo cleared the coast, and vanished into a hole in the sky.

Then came the prerecorded message from Gunter Herzog, a pasty, bespectacled East German sorcerer who'd been held in Spandau for most of the Cold War. He was a most scary little man: frail in form, but rabid with conviction, and burning with awful power.

"We are Silent Summer," he declared from the smoking ruins of the Etna camp. "We are the vengeful arm of Gaia, whom you have all but murdered in her sleep. On this very special Earth Day, we have pledged our lives to give teeth and claws to our Mother, so that she might save herself.

"Now the terrible Hundred-Headed One awakens, to be reunited with his magnificent bride. And all who serve the Machine shall perish. May Gaia forgive you.

"We assure you: all virtuous people, who bow to Mother Earth, have nothing to fear. Nature loves her children, and is kind and just.

"But the old days, the old ways, are come again. We are Silent Summer . . . and you will know us by our triumph!"

End of ultra-stupid broadcast.

Beginning of red alert.

Fifty miles from the nearest land, the B.P.R.D. cargo plane circled above the waves. They had no mystical cloaking spell or ingenious device to hide them from view. Their only element of surprise was that they were out here, too.

Silent Summer believed there was something enormous and terrible waiting deep beneath the surface. It had been waiting for untold thousands of years. Waiting for a moment just like this.

Abe was down there, checking it out. Evidently, the doomsaying lunatics were right again.

Hellboy spotted the massive shadows on the water a mile out to the west, in the moment before the choppers blinked in and out of view as Herzog's invisibility spell wore out at last.

"Holy cow," said Omar the pilot, banking them into a brutal U-turn. "That guy's gotta be *pooped.*"

Four miles away, but closing fast, the huge Sikorsky cargo choppers swooped low, so their enormous payload skimmed the suddenly choppy whitecaps of the sea the ancient Greeks called the Icarian, after the last fool who tried to fly across it.

Hellboy told Roger, "You wait here with Omar and Liz. I'll call you if I need ya."

"Are you sure . . . ?"

"*Gah!*" Hellboy answered, as he stepped out through the cargo door and plummeted into space.

Roger was right. The new jet pack kicked right in at the first push of the button. Yanked from freefall by jet propulsion, Hellboy righted himself, then rocketed straight at the gunships.

"Nice," he said.

The closer he jetted, the clearer the immense gray object in the sling became: a colossal severed tongue of metamorphic stone—wide at the base, tapered at the tip—roughly the size of a subway car.

"Typhon was buried alive beneath Mount Etna while preparing to throw it at the gods of Olympus," Kate lectured. "At a guess, that's only a segment of one of his tentacles."

Hellboy growled, "It damn well *better be* a tentacle."

He was close enough now to see the terrified faces gaping at him through the windows of the lead chopper: fey, vegan Euro-hippies, way the hell out of their depth. He almost felt sorry for their dumb asses. But it was definitely time to grow up.

As if on poop-your-pants cue, *great red clouds and globs of blood and meat* began to flume out from all four load-bearing choppers, misting the air and plopping down onto the monstrous slab.

Which, almost instantly, began to shudder with life.

Typhon had awakened.

"Oh, crap," Hellboy said.

On board the Sikorskys, all was jittering chaos and Teutonic gloom. Between the woodchippers consuming the dozens of wine-bloated goats on slaughterhouse hooks, and the sudden appearance of a rocket-powered monster, Silent Summer's starry-eyed fling with radical eco-shamanism was over. Luckily, the day's festivities were about to take on a life of their own, and would need no human hand to guide them.

From the lead gunship, Gunter Herzog gloated over Hellboy's confusion. The B.P.R.D.'s pet devil seemed to stall in midair, watching the bloody rain of rebirth, unsure of which way to go.

Perfect.

"*Set him free!*" Herzog screamed into the radio mic.

All at once, the bolts holding the sling exploded. The tethers, untethering. The Hundred-Headed One, falling.

The helicopters, darting away like frightened mosquitoes—from the splash of sixty tons of petrified titan hitting the sea.

And the stone-fisted monster followed it, heading straight for the churning depths into which Typhon had disappeared.

"Behold!" Herzog crowed, fingering a remote detonator. "Typhon calls, and I open the door!"

Abe looked up when the colossal stone hit the water, like the door to heaven slamming shut. Churning, bloody foam cast a purple sunset pall over the depths, but he could hear the sound of the abominable thing growing as he stroked down into the azure void, so swiftly that his skull ached with the uncanny pressure and . . . heat?

Abe swam for the blunt, broad peak of a seamount that reared up off the sea floor like the stump of a blasted volcano. The jumbled stones of the mountaintop were softened by cobwebs of pale, slimy algae, but they had the unmistakable uniformity of chiseled blocks and columns.

Abe recognized the pillars as Minoan, but the scale was absurd. To build such an oversized temple on a tiny island would break even the maddest emperor.

But Abe doubted that this place was made for, or by, men.

And perhaps it wasn't sent to the bottom of the sea. Perhaps it was built *down here . . .*

As Abe paddled closer, the warmth abruptly became a most unpleasant heat. A solitary boulder loomed up out of a clearing among the ruins, embedded in the buckled flagstone floor, like the eroded remains of a colossal idol.

Or, Abe thought darkly, *the plug in a bathtub.*

Beneath the silt and slime, the cyclopean boulder was inscribed everywhere with spirals, circles—serpents. And it was not merely wedged into the hole, Abe noted with a twinge of admiration.

The boulder was the head of a gigantic Archimedes' screw, with threads winding down its shaft to lock it into the hole for all time.

This isn't a temple, Abe realized. *It's a tomb.*

Or a prison?

Abe swam closer. The unnatural heat was coming from the sealed pit. Even if Silent Summer revived it, the fragment of Typhon would never get through this. Not without help.

That's when he noticed the blinking green lights underneath the head of the titanic screw. And the strobing red timers.

Oh, no . . .

Abe keyed his throat mic. Every static-blasted channel dragged barbed wire through his brain.

"Hellboy? Liz? Anyone?"

Hellboy hit the red waves skull first, letting the jet pack's ballistic momentum propel him deep, then deeper still, until Typhon rose up to intercept him, block him, plow him back toward the surface. Hellboy came in swinging his right fist like a wrecking ball, in a slow but unstoppable arc of stone on stone.

Given time and room to work, Hellboy could reduce the Great Pyramid to paperweights. But the water dragged on his fist, and the thrashing behemoth shrugged off his love taps like he wasn't even there.

Then Typhon picked up speed, and Hellboy clung like a remora on a shark's back to the pitted living stone as the monster tentacle reared up into the dazzling daylight.

Still coughing seawater, Hellboy was suddenly fifty feet up in the air again, riding the Earthshaker into the middle of the outraged swarm of Silent Summer helicopters. And Typhon was not only angry, but growing.

That was when Herzog pushed the button, and the bombs went off below.

First there was the punishing sound, deafening underwater. Then the shockwave knocked Abe senseless.

The head blew off the giant screw, spinning away like an aborted rocket launch. The next thing he knew, the explosion collapsed into a vortex, drawing the sea down into the opened pit.

It was a strange feeling, to be swimming for his life one moment, only to find himself falling the next. He wrenched one arm out of its socket, fighting the current, but was sucked helplessly down, like a spider down a drain.

Plunging through pitch blackness, he could only flail in the tumbling seawater and rising steam. That he'd fallen long enough to *realize* he was falling gave him serious cause to worry.

But nothing could prepare him for the return of light.

The scalding steam became a writhing fire that flayed the scales from his flesh. The distant walls of the cavern glowed with livid green phosphorescence, arching away on all sides, to form a spherical grotto bigger than the Astrodome.

His Geiger counter keened on his belt. The chamber was evidently lined with uranium, or some even more radioactive metal. With the water that had seeped inside it over millennia, it had become a natural nuclear reactor.

The water was like molten lead. Abe's gills curled up, eye membranes clouded over. Shrieking like a lobster in the pot, kicking for the surface, Abe tried to call Hellboy. *Don't try to save me,* was what he would have said. *Nothing could survive down here—*

Then something gargantuan stirred below, and rose up out of the boiling blackness.

Even as Abe struggled against the sucking undertow, the leviathan slurped him back. It stretched out forelimbs like bridges, tipped with fossilized talons long enough to flay whales. A leering mountain of jellied, colorless flesh—pickled almost to translucency over a gigantic pagoda of bone—parted the waves.

Trapped by the lighthouse lamps of its eyes, Abe could only marvel at the yawning hangar of its mouth, as it swallowed him.

Abe threw out his arms, but he couldn't even touch the sides.

As he tumbled down the gullet of Typhon's wife.

At first, wrestling with Typhon had seemed like a perfect vacation. With no mouth, the stubborn chunk of a titan couldn't try to eat him or bore him to death with grandiose monologues, and its seeming indifference to pain left him free to unload on the bastard without holding back.

Like any vacation, however, it got old fast.

Typhon's stone armor had split in a thousand gasping mouthlike gills, to suck up the goat chowder that coated its surface.

This was good, because Hellboy was able to grab a gaping slat and peel it back like an envelope, exposing a soft interior that was less like stone than meat.

Not so good, because Typhon was gulping down goat so fast—growing so immense and alive—that Hellboy was becoming less of a threat by the second.

It wasn't like riding a subway anymore. It was more like a runaway firehose, a bucking bronco the size of a nuclear sub.

Hellboy ripped a thirsty flap into a foxhole, felt the whole titanic mass twitch as if stung. At least it knew he was here . . . He pulled a concussion grenade off his belt, armed it, stuffed it into the hole, and jumped back.

This time, he could feel it scream. A big step in the right direction.

A huge cloud of bubbles broke the churning surface all around them. The sea began to *bend*, spiraling powerfully counterclockwise and down. Spinning Typhon like a Tilt-A-Whirl.

"Oh, man . . ." Hellboy groaned.

And then they were both dragged beneath the surface, once again.

Up until now, Omar, Liz, and Roger had been reduced to stunned spectator status. But as Typhon and Hellboy disappeared into the yawning whirlpool, the Silent Summer choppers turned on them with guns blazing, and the dogfight was on.

Liz hit the deck as bullets stitched down the hull of the cargo plane. "Hang on to something!" Omar shouted, executing a textbook vomit-comet barrel roll.

Liz enjoyed a moment of true weightlessness, spoiled only by the imminent mutiny of her breakfast. Roger clung to the wall, oblivious as a bullet glanced off his temple.

Almost too soon, Omar deftly returned the deck beneath their feet. "I'm bringin' us around! Get ready!"

Liz scrambled to the open aft door and dangled out into the wind. She saw the lead attack chopper pacing them like a shark. It must have been dry on ammo, because the guns were swiveling without spitting tracers; but a silver-haired man splashed with blood hung out the gunner's door, waving his fist and roaring air-curdling curses at them. It could only be Herzog.

"You brought this on yourself," she muttered. "This was all your stupid idea . . ."

She drew in a breath, let out a wordless curse of her own. This curse was made of fire, and bent the winds with an ear-splitting snap as it was unleashed.

The last she saw of Herzog, he was screaming through a faceful of burning glass.

Then the gunship was engulfed: a huge blazing dragonfly full of dying people, tumbling end over end into the sea.

No time to dwell. Plenty for that, later. The second gunship dropped onto their tail and began to fire.

So did she.

Then, and only then—as the bullets melted in midair, followed by the guns and the people who fired them—did Liz remember her friends.

"*Hellboy!*" she bellowed into her headset. "*Abe! Are you all right . . . ?*"

She jumped when Roger touched her arm. "Hellboy went down with it," he said, staring down into the bloody sea. "Abe doesn't answer. I should help them."

Liz stepped in front of him, tried to make pushing him away into a hug. The first time they met, Roger almost killed her. Even among the sideshow ranks of the B.P.R.D., the manmade man took some getting used to. "Roger, you're . . . here to observe, to learn what to do."

"But they will be hurt . . ."

Liz tightened her lips in an expression even the homunculus could tell was not a smile. "Then you'll learn what not to do . . ."

Back in the whirlpool, Typhon turned itself skinny-end first to ride the maelstrom like a gigantic kayak. Not so far below, the glowing mouth of the vortex was a hungry hole in the ocean floor.

Hellboy hung on like a barnacle, tried to rally his thoughts. Fighting was useless. But something had to be done.

The rocket pack clonked him hard on the back of the head.

"Ouch!" he gurgled.

And cracked a devilish grin.

Hot damn, he thought, *this stupid thing might wind up useful, after all.*

Working as fast as he dared, he armed the rest of the concussion grenades and strapped his utility belt to his rocket. He shrugged the pack off, punched the thrusters, and sent the rocket whipping down the throat of the vortex, just ahead of the unstoppable tentacle of Typhon.

The eager tip of the titan slipped into the mouth of the pit. And with a concussive slam of whirling currents and awful stillness, the whirlpool sputtered and died.

Hellboy kicked off the wriggling behemoth and tried to swim for the surface, but the shearing currents from the trapped giant spun him helplessly horns over heels in orbit around itself.

Shame he was trapped at the bottom of the sea, because the monster's predicament was worthy of a good belly laugh.

The pit was a big one, but not quite big enough. About a third of Typhon's ever-expanding mass could fit, but try as it might—thrashing like a salmon on the make—it could not squeeze into the hole.

Clearly, they'd fed it too much goat.

Finally, the rocket pack draped in grenades went off in the pit. Trapped between the walls and Typhon's thrusting bulk, the explosion was enough to collapse the pit and shear off a good third of the rogue tentacle's length, leaving it wedged in the ocean floor.

Thrashing in agony, rage, and frustration, Typhon went out of its mind. It had suffered through eons, waiting for this day, only to be blocked by a chunk of itself.

It slammed against the barrier, trying to beat its way through. When that didn't work, it whipped up a whirlpool of its own, like a drunken wife-beating worm screaming "*Stelllllla!*" at the top of its lungless lungs.

That didn't work, either.

Meanwhile, Hellboy battled the rip current and stroked desperately for the surface. Wondering how his friends were faring.

In particular, Abe . . .

Plummeting down the smokestack of Echidna's throat, Abe decided he'd had quite enough of being swallowed. He drew his knife and stabbed the wall.

The blade sank into soft, overripe tissue like the waterlogged lining of a coffin, barely slowing his descent until it snagged on something like bone.

He climbed into the door he'd made and slithered into a stagnant capillary swamp, clogged with the corroded shields and armor of forgotten heroes.

Turning upstream, Abe chased gruesome blind cavefish out of the glare of his flashlight, possessed by a maddening but unshakable calm. His seared gills greedily pulled oxygen out of the plasma flooding her ancient organs, syrupy tides stirred by the sluggish rhythm of Echidna's endless dreaming.

Lost in the empty avenues and alleys of an unfamiliar city in the dark of night, anonymous, unrecognized, Abe Sapien could always count on a kind of peace.

And Echidna was nothing, if not a city unto herself.

She had dense fortresses of muscle, cathedrals of bone, and silos of rancid fat and curdled milk; endless sewers, reservoirs, and canals, guttering furnaces, deserted avenues, and silent factories; the drowned harbors of her lungs, the skyscraping flesh-foundries of her womb, where the great work of the city was executed, and all of it animated by the volcanic throb of her heart.

When he strayed too near to the skin, Abe could look out through milky porthole lesions in Echidna's parboiled hide, and see her terrible shape.

She was not a city, and if she was not a goddess, she was much more than a monster. A First Daughter of the Living Earth. She bore no resemblance to her mate, Typhon, mostly depicted as a winged giant with tentacles for legs, and sometimes a hundred heads. But none of her abominable brood resembled her, or each other, either.

The bride of Typhon mingled features of eel and anglerfish with the torso of a human hag whose lower half terminated in a serpentine tail longer than an aircraft carrier.

But Abe's fleeting glimpse of her eyes as she swallowed him told him how very wise this creature—this woman—was. She radiated hunger and hate as she ate him, but there had also been hope. *The cruelest of Pandora's curses . . .*

Abe only noticed the faint, echoing voices when he realized that he was following them.

Abe swam into a cavernous chapel filled with membranous towers like the façades of sagging tenements. If he had searched unconsciously for this place to plant his bombs, or to satisfy some grim curiosity, now it had been satisfied. Here was where the end of the world would begin.

The voices sang a curious, incomprehensible song. Bitterly old, yet innocent; grimly keen on death and destruction, yet so tenderly naive, that Abe wondered to hear it in such a haunted, hopeless place.

He approached the ovaries with extreme caution. If anything inside Echidna was guarded, it would be these.

Her eggs.

Like any female creature, Echidna had carried the same eggs all her life, and they had aged within her. Now, they sang in a vulgar mother root of Greek that some golden-age eavesdropper might have cribbed from the speech of the Olympians. But their tone was like that of children everywhere.

"Are you our father's seed?" cried one ovum in a shell. "Have you come to make us?"

"I will be a dragon," cried another, "with a hundred heads, like Typhon . . ."

"Choose me! My shadow will drown the sun . . . !"

"When I am hatched, I will devour you all . . . !"

"I want to be a dog, and play all day . . . !"

"Be still!" Abe hissed, but his plea spread the alarm to the other ovary towers. Soon, the whole hatchery trembled with the demands of unborn monsters.

Abe kicked away for the duct from which he'd emerged, but the sphincter door puckered shut. Trapped. Perhaps, if he sang them a lullaby . . .

"I am old, and not so terrible as I once was," said the walls of the womb. "And now, I must have forgotten how to chew my food . . ."

Hellboy broke the surface with a throaty, deafening, "Damn it!" If the bubbles that preceded him could speak as they burst, he'd owe a fortune to the office swear jar.

He beat some sense back into his pressure-wracked ears, but he'd given himself a wicked case of the bends, going to the bottom and back so fast. Cramps wrung him out like a dishrag.

At least it was still a beautiful day . . .

Suddenly, in the full view of that cloudless blue sky, Hellboy found himself surfing a wave in a cold, dark shadow.

Coming up, and up, and *bam!* Like getting hit by a subway train.

Typhon reacted like any jilted lover when it hit the surface. Its crude overtures had been foiled, and all it wanted now was to lash out hard.

The severed tentacle stump whipped up savagely, lofting Hellboy a hundred feet in the air. He hung on, helplessly along for the ride once again, watching the overeager Silent Summer choppers get closer by the second. Armed only with more goats, but bristling with cameras for the waking-of documentary.

One darted within reach, and the mammoth tentacle cracked at it like a bullwhip.

Hellboy knew that this was gonna hurt.

As usual, he was correct.

He slammed tail first through a laminated glass windshield, too fast to get more than a glimpse of the screaming pilots before the chopper's engine exploded, and the rotor blades shivered to shrapnel all around him.

Still, he hung on, squeezing until Typhon seemed to scream out loud, as if a real, live mouth had opened somewhere on its monstrous form.

Then he looked down, and wondered, *Why am I always right about the bad stuff?*

The blunt stump of the tentacle had awakened to a new purpose. Now it yawned in a rude mockery of a mouth, dripping stalactite fangs and even something like a tongue, reaching up to meet him as the tentacle dangled him over it.

The flesh in his grip went all runny, bulging into a hemispheric bubble. Hellboy scrambled like he'd had a rug pulled out from under him.

The bubble trembled, and blinked.

It was an eyelid, newly formed.

Which left him staring into an eye nearly as large as himself.

The blank, black eye stared back, clearly unimpressed. When Hellboy punched it, it popped like a water balloon.

At last, he had a way in, with no teeth.

The walls of Echidna shook. The plasma around and inside Abe trembled with her voice.

There was no point in looking around, but he did, anyway. Every duct, every pore, every cell, spoke. She was all around him.

And she knew exactly where he was.

"I did not come to be eaten," Abe replied, in passable Homeric Greek.

"Miserable meal that you are . . . perhaps a rival suitor?" Echidna's seismic rumble quivered with coy curiosity.

How sad, hoping for flattery from the contents of one's own innards. But she had absolute power over him. If he threatened her with the explosives, she might call his bluff. Perhaps she yearned for the peace of death.

Perhaps she only wanted what any woman, locked away from the world and her mate, would want.

"My lady," he began, fumbling for the proper sincerity, "your beauty and fertility are eternal . . ."

"*Yessss . . .*"

" . . . But the world has moved on. It is not what it was."

"I hear them outside, battling for my favor. Your tiny champion will fall before my terrible one."

"Typhon . . . is—"

"How I hated him," she sighed. "But he was made for me, and our young ones were so fierce. You would do well to go to my stomach and be eaten, before he finds you here—"

"He's not coming," Abe said, and braced himself. "He is dead."

The hatchery spasmed. The eggs redoubled their whispering.

"*None shall stand before him!*" Echidna raved. "He scattered the pretty ones of Olympus, and routed the house of Man. Our children feast on manflesh, from Thebes to the gates of Hades!"

"They are no more, lady." Perhaps setting off the bombs would be a mercy. He would die outside, but he could not bear to breathe the sour plasma of her panic. "The gods let them live only to challenge men to prove their heroism."

"Heroes! Pretty monsters who kill children for sport! How our Mother hates them! I would bear a thousand young and choke the Styx with their bones! You . . ." Now terribly lucid, her voice seemed to come from right behind him. "Which Olympian's pretty bastard are you, hero?"

"I am not that kind of hero," Abe Sapien replied, "and I am not pretty."

As Echidna raved, Abe stretched out one webbed hand, gentler than a breath, to touch the membrane of the nearest ovary tower. The hatchery still buzzed with their chatter and childish hymns, but the eggs crumbled at his touch, like orbs of ash.

"I am sorry, my lady," Abe said, "but there is no place for monsters, anymore. The earth has begun to take her own revenge on mankind."

"My Typhon will come! He will save me—"

"Only a small piece of him lives, Echidna. It fights to get to you, but it is not the one you loved—" How sad, he thought, and how wondrous. Was it only a ghostly instinct that drove Typhon's severed limb to come to her, or was every bit of that ancient abomination so infused with the same doomed love that Romeo felt for Juliet, that a moth felt for the flame? Was that all there was to love?

"A hundred heads and nothing like a brain," Echidna grumbled, "but if he is gone, then I am better off dead." Her self-pity was like a toxin released into her bloodstream. "Kill me, little hero . . . Ugly as you are, they would sing such songs of the slayer of Echidna, that women would still love you . . ."

"You should sleep," Abe replied, "and wait for a better husband. Maybe Briareus the Hundred-Handed . . ."

"Silence!" The hatchery walls crumbled; clouds of black blood spurting from ulcers and tears in tired flesh. "Would you kill me with lies alone?" Eggs exploded in puffs of dust, whispers of unborn ghosts. "Kill me if you can, or I'll rip myself open to get at you!"

The brick of plastique in his hands did not feel like a hero's sword. "No one will sing your praises, if none lives to tell the tale."

She paused in shaking herself to pieces. The sly, serpentine monster coiled close about him again, starved for one more kind word. "What will you tell them?"

He smiled. "I will tell them you were magnificent . . . and terrible."

In a lifetime of foolish choices, few seemed crazier or scarier than strapping a tank of explosive gas to her back. But she had no other choice.

If I get out of this alive, Liz thought, *I'll never rag HB about these things again.*

The new rocket pack was indeed a cinch to fly, if not so easy to land. And Typhon was working to make it even harder. No longer thrashing like a severed lizard's tail, the colossal limb had changed its tactics by sprouting a mouth, and breaking out in a rash of malevolent eyes. Hellboy waded waist deep into one of them, but the rest observed Liz with incendiary contempt as Typhon's obscene bulk tried to swat her out of the sky.

"*I'm goin' in!*" Hellboy yelled, then plunged headfirst into the socket, as if tunneling his way to China by hand.

The second he disappeared under Typhon's skin, Liz hurled howling sheets of fire into those all-seeing eyes. The leviathan howled with rage, but all she could do from here was singe it.

She would have to get closer, land right on it and do that which most terrified and exhilarated her: let loose completely on the thick-skinned bastard.

Typhon plucked another cargo chopper out of the air and threw it at her. Liz narrowly dodged the whirling rotors and launched herself at the thickest span of the monster, just above its newly formed mouth.

She touched down and damped her thrusters, but the explosion from the crashing cargo chopper swept her off the slick surface.

Impervious to fire, but flying metal was another matter entirely. Ass over teakettle, Liz tumbled into the waves splashing against Typhon's flanks.

Stupid!

She was totally helpless, soaked to the skin, and not even a good swimmer. The rocket tugged her downward, so she ditched it at once, and good riddance.

Fighting to keep her head above water, she saw only the rampant arch of the monster rearing up above her to block out the sun, but she could get no closer to it.

What the hell was she trying to do, anyway? Typhon breathed fire, and slept in a volcano.

But Kate had recited Hesiod and Homer all the way across the Atlantic, until Liz wanted to put her cigs out in her ears. To defeat Typhon, Zeus had to master the lightning: "the bolt that never sleeps, thunder with breath of flame."

A forest fire of fury sparked and sputtered inside her, but she couldn't even snap her fingers and make a satisfying noise, let alone a thunderbolt.

She did not see Roger until he'd caught her outstretched arms and ripped her out of the water like a slingshot. "I've got you," he called out. "Where do you want to go?"

Kicking, screaming, Liz flew up out of the water and motioned for Roger to drop her back onto Typhon.

A measure of her misplaced fear of Roger lit up like kindling inside her, and it was not rage that dried her and singed even Roger's clay hands as he set her down, but love.

A corona erupted around her and blazed hot enough to make a firebreathing monster scream. Terrible in her solar beauty, Liz Sherman knelt to lay her hands on the titan's hide, and let it all out.

Like a thousand years of drought, her unbound fire seared the flesh beneath her feet, in faults and fissures, and returning it to charred stone so violently that boulders broke free and lofted like meteors to burst in the steaming sea.

She walked down Typhon's paralyzed length and stuffed a supernova down its throat. She felt the white-hot plasma race up the shaft of the tentacle to blow out its host of ogling eyes like the windows of a demolished skyscraper.

Hellboy punched his way out of a blazing socket near the penthouse, then somersaulted down the heaving length of the monster to join her. "*Yowch!*" he yelled. "Way to go, Liz!"

"It's not slowing down!" she shouted over the roar of her own flame. Typhon's hide was a bed of coals, but the monster's frenzied gyrations were, if anything, only more desperate. From a mating dance to a death dance.

"I couldn't find anything like a heart or a brain in it. That thing's an idiot."
Hellboy pounded the glowing red stone like an anvil, bellowing, "*You lost, damn it!
Cut it out, already!*"

The surface of the sea about fifty yards out bulged and broke as the gas from an
underwater explosion broke free of the waves. Hellboy pinched his nose. Roger flew
through the noxious fog and almost crashed, but Liz's fire gushed out over the water,
turning green with the methane-rich upwelling.

It was the unmistakable miasma of a belch, suppressed and festering for millennia.
And out of the thick of it, smeared with something fouler than ambergris, came
someone who waved to them.

"A be!" Hellboy's joyous roar cut through the earsplitting spasms of the defiantly
undying monster.

Despite Hellboy's warnings, Abe swam toward Typhon's gasping mouth, almost
pulled headfirst over its teeth in a swallow of seawater that leaked out its sundered
sides in plumes of steam.

Abe caught himself on its lower lip and shouted something down the titan's
gullet. Hellboy could not understand it, but he thought he recognized the scholarly
cadence of Abe's ancient Greek.

And just like that, Typhon finally gave up the ghost.

With a shudder and a sigh that was softer and more unsettling than the cacophony
of destruction he and Liz had wrought, the heaving monstrosity subsided into its
natural petrified state, as whatever mad energy the deluge of blood and wine and
magic had awakened in it simply and suddenly went away.

Typhon's stone carcass sank like the *Titanic,* and would have sucked them down
after it, had Roger not snatched each of them clear of the undertow and dropped
them beside the emergency raft Omar had left behind, before he ran out of fuel.

Looking at the bobbing hulks of helicopters in the smoking black-red water, Liz
lit a cigarette from her watertight pack and smirked, "Best Earth Day ever."

"Be careful," Abe warned. "I'm a bit soiled, and more than a little radioactive."

"Nuts to that," Hellboy replied. Still holding his nose, he pulled Abe into the raft
and said, "I'm sorry if I made that harder than it had to be. You give a monster an
inch, and they think they're a ruler. What happened to you down there, anyway?"

"I was trapped." Like one dimly awakened from a dream, Abe searched for the
right words. "I had . . . help getting out."

"Did you cast some kind of spell on Typhon?" Roger asked.

"I didn't cast a spell." Abe smiled, but the warmth of it never reached his icy blue
eyes. "I broke one."

"I'm sorry?" Roger, as always, keenly trying to understand.

"I told him that she just didn't love him anymore."

"Awww," Liz said. "That's kind of sad . . ."

"Mm-hmm," said Hellboy, and left it at that.

Together, they bobbed on the current for a while, while Omar circled and lowered the ladder. Each sifting their own measure of sunshine and melancholy, in the light and shadow of still-abiding Mother Nature.

Taking her course, once again.

Someday it might end. But not today. Magnificent and terrible, life went on. The waves still waved. The sun still shone.

All in all, a very beautiful day.

Tomorrow, there might even be another.

End

I told her there was no more room in the world for monsters," Abe said.

Liz just looked from the begrimed amphibian to the homunculus to the wryly smiling devil with whom she shared the raft.

"Yes, there is," she said.

DANNY BOY
KEN BRUEN

The robbery happened so fast, it was like jig time

    I was behind the counter, doing my usual mundane boring job when the two guys came roaring in, screaming obscenities and waving sawn-offs though one looked like a pump

They scared the be-jaysus out of everyone which was the whole point

And they had three bags of serious cash packed and ready to roll in, I'd guess, four minutes, we were lying on the floor

Normally, sleepy midwestern towns, we have an old security guard whose toughest task is to stay awake

But recently, a young kid named Jason, due to ship out to Iraq, had been doing the job

He had long black hair, shades, and a whole attitude of gung-ho

He was itching for aggro

He got it

They'd taken his weapon but this was a kid of the movies, carried an ankle piece, he's shown it to me often enough

I didn't like him and he thought I was a nerd

He'd go

"So Danny Boy, ever feel like having a brew or doing some guy stuff?"

The robbers were at the door, the three stashed bags in their arms when Jason got on one knee, no shout of

"Freeze motherfuckers."

Nope

He just started blasting away

The first guy managed to make it out the door, the second guy, did a little dance of dance and I registered the bag of cash fly across the floor and lodge in an alcove, hidden in plain sight almost and the thought came to me

"Dare I?"

Jason had taken off after the other guy and I was on me feet, screaming

"Everybody out, move move."

They did

I had about sixty seconds

I grabbed the bag, vaulted the counter, put it in my locker and then ran out of there like all the other sheep

Cop cars were wailing in from everywhere and the second guy got blasted to hell from about six different directions and miraculously, kept driving and got away

We were all of course interviewed and offered counseling and the manager confirmed the guy had gotten away with three full bags of serious bills

I nearly wet meself

Jason was on a jagged rush and didn't seem to notice the third bag had never left the building

My whole body was shaking

Jason, being congratulated by all, finally got a moment to speak to me, said

"Shitting yourself there buddy . . . right?"

The prick

I said

"That was an amazing display."

He'd been basking in praise from all and said

"No biggie, it's what men do."

I bit down on my smile, he might have the glory but me, I had the loot

You'll have gathered I'm not American, I'm working on the accent but it ain't coming in so good, it's hard to shed a Mick mindset, ask any Brit, they'll endorse that Bill Clinton is a saint in Ireland, never no mind his little peccadilloes, he's good-looking, that's enough for us, reminds us of John F. Kennedy and God bless him, he'd initiated a number of schemes whereby we exchanged personnel, especially in the financial sector.

So the Irish banks sent a batch of us stateside and a bevy of Americans came to Ireland.

In my branch in Dublin, everyone wanted

New York

Boston

San Francisco

Washington

Who wouldn't

But the powers that be felt it was important we also gain experience of small-town

America to apply to our minor branches in the less-sophisticated parts of rural Ireland.

Every bastard was praying to God's Mother that they get the plum gigs

My prayers were obviously ignored, I got the sticks and this nowhereville and did I hate it

Take a wild fucking guess

But now, a chance to get free, not only of this shithole but of banking and all that plain

Joe bollocks, I felt the rush of the freedom beckoning

I was exhilarated, so excited, that I stopped by Joe's, had two boilermakers and Joe said

"On the house after all the ruckus you had today."

Meaning

"Tell us the story for the fourteenth time."

I did

Got out of there, a little unsteady, I wasn't used to drinking in the afternoon or indeed any other time, I was to pun . . . *steady*

I had rented a small house, it was one up, one down as the Brits say

I let myself in, contemplating a warm bath and early night and nearly dropped dead of fright

Sitting in my armchair was a massive red figure, with what looked like horns on his head and a curiously disfigured right hand, as if someone had attached a distorted hammer on it

Boilermakers!

Already in the DTs

I shook my head to dispel the vision, opened my eyes and it was still there but smiling now and it spoke, rich baritone masculine voice

"Danny, hope I didn't give you too much of a scare but believe me, if I'd have approached you on the street, you wouldn't like the attention.

"I'm Hellboy."

I decided that events of the day had temporarily unhinged me and if I just humored it, he'd simply fade away

He shook his huge head, said

"My instinct tells me there is going to be serious crap coming down the pike."

I went to the fridge, got some iced tea and asked

"Get you something?"

He laughed, if a cackle blended with a gutted larynx can be called that

"I'm good . . . Well, not always, but that's another dimension."

I sat, a hell of a headache building, a real stormtrooper and he said

"That's mild compared to the headache you have coming."

I said

"Go fuck yourself."

He made a sound that might have been a snarl, said

"It's to prevent you from doing exactly that to yourself that I'm here."

I had a pretty good idea of where this was going, well, then, I thought I did, if I really had

known,

I'd have fled, right then and there

He said

"All around you the black forces are swirling, you've given them a tiny window, don't make it a portal."

I said

"I have no idea what you're talking about."

He leaned over, a languid move, all stealth and dark grace, said

"That money already cost one life, the bank is built on the site of an Indian burial ground and the story goes, a shaman blessed it to keep the evil spirits away . . . On condition that nothing bad occurred there, even something like stealing money, and the shaman emphasized that if blood was shed on that hallowed ground, then forces would be released that would bring chaos in their wake."

"You're saying it's cursed."

"Bank robber's already suffering thanks to that shaman but we've got it covered . . . We can probably prevent it getting out of control, and save your life, if you don't steal the money."

Alas, I choose that moment to look down and saw . . . I fucking kid thee not . . . *cloven hooves!*

And shuddered, he said

"Shudder now, pay later."

Staring more closely at that deformed right hand, for all the world like a slab of granite that some very bad sculptor had tried to insert fingers into and oh fuck, the things on his head were horns, but as if they'd been sawn down, he stood and then he did a little turn, right there in the middle of my room, and I saw a tail, beneath the red mac he was wearing

He sat back down, the chair creaking under his weight

He asked

"You never heard of me?"

I gave him my banker's smile, all malice and bad intent, said

"Barney the dinosaur is about our speed here."

He seemed genuinely surprised, said

"Guess you don't read *Life* or *People* magazines."

"Welcome to Hicksville and dare one ask as to what exactly you hope to accomplish?"

He sighed, sounded more like a bellow, he must have been over seven foot and that massive frame rattled, he said

"I work for the Bureau for Paranormal Research and Defense, lately it's been quiet so we've been experimenting with pre-recognizance, see if we can avert an event before it happens, your actions are likely to set off some serious murder and mayhem."

What can you say save

"Good luck with that."

He reached in his mac, extracted the largest gun I've ever seen, flung it on the table, asked

"See if you can lift that."

I tried

Couldn't

He picked it up like it was a feather, put it in a massive holster, said

"The security guard, he's the key to chaos and you and he are linked, this is your opportunity to prevent disaster."

I said

"Great story, now if you'll excuse me."

He stood up, his huge presence looming over me, used his other hand to touch those growths on his head, said

"It's not too late, I'll be hanging round, see if I might talk some sense into you, my car is parked out back."

He had a car?

I watched him stride out, get into a red '59 ragtop Cadillac, it had huge fins, and I bet it was hell on gas but I doubt if he'd have fit in anything smaller

He rolled down the window, shouted

"Cheerio."

Did he have a Brit accent?

I did what any normal person would do who's just had a chat with Hellboy, I had another drink, okay, drinks but who's counting eh?

As I finally got into bed, I began to plan what I'd do with the money, if it meant having the odd red devil-ed hallucination, cheap at the price

Amazing the lies that booze will tell you

I didn't touch the money for another four days, the excitement was finally easing down and people were beginning to talk of other stuff, like the Red Sox and Britney Spears, you know, bank stuff.

Jason had a new swagger in his strut, he'd been unbearable before, now he was Dirty Harry in a cheap security uniform. Was it my imagination or was he watching me a lot? I kept my head down and did what I do best

Blend

If I was a color, I'd be beige

On the outside, what lay beneath, ah . . .

Whole different animal

Seething, uncoiling, longing, resentful and oh, so much smarter than any of those dickheads who'd dismissed me as a geek

Beware of geeks bearing stolen cash

Come lunch time, I did the same thing I'd done for years, put on my tan raincoat, and headed for Joe's Diner

There is no Joe

There is certainly a Sandy

Oh sweet Jesus

A wet dream in a waitress outfit, she ran that diner like clockwork and always, over her top lip, a tiny line of perspiration, I was fascinated by that, dreamt of licking it off, and her body

Lush

One of her eyes had a slight defect and did that put me off

Duh

It only accentuated her whole radiance, for three years I'd been trying to work up the courage to ask her out, she called me Mr. D . . . I'd asked

"Call me Danny."

Licking her tongue along her top gorgeous white teeth, she'd said

"I only call guys I'm banging by their first names."

Yeah, a mouth on her

Like a fishwife

Made me love her all the more

One of the tellers, Joan, fifty, bitter, single, and ugly as fuck, said to me one time

"That Sandy, she ain't nothing but trailer trash."

Part of the attraction

During that four days, when I got back to my home, I'd smell . . . cordite? . . . a heavy acrid stench . . . like brimstone and would chide myself

"Get real buddy."

The third day, the remains of a meal left in a mess on my kitchen table and I laughed, shouted

"You might at least wash up yah red bastard."

If he heard, he didn't answer

The day I finally took the money, the omens were not good, first my boss had told me to

"Snap to it."

When I looked at him, he said

"You're daydreaming all the time, and don't tell me it's the robbery, look at Jason, more alert than ever so *get over it.*"

And yes, did shout that last bit

I saw the smile of sheer malice on Jason's face

Lunch time, Sandy served everyone else before me and then Jason sauntered in just as I was about to finally get my order and she literally rushed to hand him a menu and oh fuck

"Jason."

Any reservations about taking the money evaporated in a cloud of hatred

I'd brought my gym bag to work, not that I ever worked out, not that we even had a gym . . . and come closing, it was a tight fit but I got the money sack in there, put my bag on my shoulder and near fell under the weight

My body was covered in sweat and just as I'd cleared the front door, a voice asked

"What's in the bag dude?"

Jason

Hand on his holstered gun, his hip stuck out like a hooker

I said

"All the rubbish that has accumulated over too long."

He moved toward me, said

"Lemme give you a hand there."

And I said too quickly

"*No,* I mean, thanks and all but I can manage."

He watched me for a moment, said

"Pretty damn jumpy there fellah, hope you're not robbing us, you know how I deal with scum like that."

Then he took a long intense size up of me, said

"I thought you Micks were like, party animals, loved to get down but you Danny, you're like some uptight Mormon."

I had no reply to that and started to move toward the street

He . . . I swear to God . . . he made a gun of his right hand and as I walked away,

he dropped the hammer

I got home, my clothes drenched in sweat, and made a large bourbon rocks,

I'd been buying more of the stuff in the last few days, it kind of sneaks up on you

I drank off a lethal bourbon, emptied the bag onto the kitchen floor and muttered

"Sweet fuck."

As a cashier, I could almost tell how much was there in the hundred-dollar bands, and oh bliss, so many of them

I sat down and began to count

One to count cadence

Took my time and I punctuated the count with frequent trips to the bourbon bottle, my heart was pounding and the plans, getting out of this shithole, moving to Mexico, and best of all, bringing Sandy with me. She'd come, not for me but for the money. I was under no illusion about my appeal but I'd watched her eyes whenever a guy flashed a roll. I was money-dazzled, and bourbon-saturated, I never heard the porch door and nearly jumped out of my skin when a voice said

"Oh Danny Boy."

Jason

With a smirk as wide as the Grand Canyon

He had his new Ruger in his right hand, not pointing, just dangling casually by his right leg

He lifted the bourbon bottle, asked

"Mind if I join the party."

Took a large swig, then wiping his lips, said

"Everyone knows you've been depressed since the robbery, all that macho gunplay too much for your delicate sensibility and it's already known you're hitting the sauce so how surprising is it you shot yourself?"

He produced another gun, a .22, said

"Mickey Mouse gun for a Mickey Mouse guy."

A booming voice said

"You don't want to do that kid."

There was Hellboy, his gun pointed at Jason

Jason asked

"The fuck are you, Halloween isn't for another three months."

Hellboy said

"Drop the guns."

He did

As if pleading, dropped to one knee and I knew, the ankle weapon, and before I could shout, he had it out and Hellboy fired, blew off his gun hand

Hellboy looked at me, said over the screaming

"Oh Danny boy, them pipes are calling."

Sure enough, the sound of sirens could be heard
I pleaded
"Get me out of this."
And he smiled, almost a tender one if such a grotesque face could achieve that,
said
"Now wouldn't that be a hell of a thing."

STRANGE FISHING IN THE WESTERN HIGHLANDS
GARTH NIX

It is forty years and more since I first went fishing with Hellboy. I was a young man then, with a fresh-minted medical degree from St. Andrews and what I thought was a wholly rational view of the world. Bachelor of Medicine and Bachelor of Surgery I was, with Mb ChB after my name, and a head stuffed full of scientific knowledge and a bare modicum of practical surgery from the hospital in Dundee.

The last few years of my medical studies had been extraordinarily busy, and in that time I'd seen very little of my father, my sole living relative. He hadn't made it any easier, choosing when he retired to live not in our comfortable former family home in Edinburgh, instead moving to the house he had inherited from his uncle, a remote place on the shore of Loch Torridon in the Western Highlands. It was four miles from where the road terminated, had no telephone, only occasional electricity from a diesel generator, and for the most part, could only be easily reached by boat from Lower Diabaig or Shieldaig, across the loch.

So, having unexpectedly been given four days off duty from the hospital due to what I supposed was a rostering error but may have in fact been a direction from on high that I was working too hard, I decided to visit my father. I sent a telegram to advise him, but as it was February, and the winter storms busy on the west coast, I thought it unlikely it would reach him before I did. Though I had no doubts about his filial affection, we did not enjoy the closest of father-son relationships. So I took the precaution of purchasing a ham, a dozen bottles of his favorite burgundy, and a few other odds and ends to offer as gifts, all of which went into a hamper that I could only just jam into the very slim boot of my senior colleague Dr. Teague's Austin-Healey 3000, which he had reluctantly lent me for my journey.

The road trip was uneventful, save that I drove toward bad weather rather than away from it, and regretted borrowing a convertible rather than something more sensible from one of my other friends, as while the car looked very fine and was quite fast, it also leaked and the heater was either too hot or completely ineffective.

I arrived at Lower Diabaig around four o'clock and parked near the pier, which marked the terminus of the road. It was already quite dark, and the latest in a steady series of heavy showers was coming down, with the promise of more to follow. There were two fishing boats tied up at the pier, so I walked up to see if anyone was aboard who might take me to my father's. If not, I would have to knock on some doors to see who might be at home in the village, as there was no pub or hotel where I might otherwise find a fisherman.

I thought I was in luck as I saw someone aboard the first vessel, as I even knew the man slightly. His name was Toller, though I didn't know if this was his Christian or surname. He had taken me to my father's on several previous occasions, so I was rather surprised when he answered my cheerful greeting with a grunt and immediately returned his attention to coiling a rope that he had, in fact, just perfectly coiled, only to unroll it at my approach.

"I'm sorry to interrupt, Mister Toller," I called. "I was hoping you might be able to take me over to Owtwauch House."

Toller turned away from me, ignoring me completely, as I stood stupidly in the rain looking at his broad, oilskin-clad back. I was surprised, for Toller had never shown me any animosity before. True, he was a Highland Scot, and I a Lowlander born and bred, and an anglified one at that, but I'd never felt that this was a problem before, though I'd heard of such prejudices.

I was momentarily tempted to step aboard his boat and give him a piece of my mind, but fortunately was prevented from doing so by a hail from the other fishing boat. A fisherman I hadn't met before waved at me, so I left Toller and walked along the pier.

"Old Toller's having a Presbyterian sulk today," said the man, who was not much older than myself, though considerably more weathered. His accent was unusual. He spoke excellent English, and sounded Scottish most of the time, but he placed a different emphasis on the syllables of some words. "Did ye say you wanted to go over to the Owtwauch?"

"Aye," I answered. "It's my father's house, Colonel MacAndrew. I'm his son, Malcolm."

"Pleased to meet you, then," said the fisherman. "I'm Erik Haakon. I'll take you over."

"That's very kind," I said, leaning down to shake hands as he reached up from the deck. "I'll just nip back and get my things. You don't think the weather's too tough to cross, then?"

Erik looked startled, following this by a glance at the sky.

"Ach, no! There's plenty of rain, but the wind's dying already. Full moon tonight, and all."

I'd forgotten it was a full moon. If it cleared, it would be a beautiful night. The view from my father's house was particularly spectacular on a moonlit night, with its panoramic vista of the loch and the western sea toward Skye. I supposed that was why it had been called Owtwauch House, "Owtwauch" being Gaelic for something like a sentry post. My father was very keen on the Gaelic and spoke it fluently, and it had been drummed into me as a small boy, but like any rarely used language it had faded from my mind. Mostly to be replaced by medical Latin, of which I had been required to memorize far more than was really sensible in the modern age.

Erik and I chatted a little as we chugged away across the Loch. He was Norwegian, but had married a local girl, and was older than I thought, in his mid-thirties at least. We discussed the parlous state of the fisheries, and the recent purchase by the National Trust of most of the land around Loch Torridon from one of the old estates. In fact, my father's property was one of the few remaining pockets of freehold not to go to the National Trust. It had been held by our family for a very long time, apparently all the way back to Somerled, King of the Isles, and perhaps before.

We were bumping up against the rough wooden jetty that served as a landing stage for Owtwauch House before I noticed, through the curtain of rain, that there was a helicopter sitting on the front lawn, a broad expanse which ran down almost to the stony beach, ending in a retaining wall that was as green with tidal weed as the grass of the lawn. There were also many more lights than usual burning in the house, far more than the one generator could support.

"Remember me to your father," said Erik, and he made a curious gesture, a fist hammering the air, as I gaped at the helicopter. "I'd best make for home."

Absently, my mind awhirl, I tried to pay him for the short voyage, but he would have none of it, instead helping me get my hamper onto the jetty, and helping me out as well as I continued to try and press a five-pound note into his hand.

I had hardly taken four steps when I saw two men emerge out of the rain-hazed lights and block the end of the jetty. They were dressed in the typical style of country gentlemen, as I was myself, in Harris tweed, corduroy, and Wellingtons, and it would not have been too out of place if they had shotguns under their arms. But it was definitely out of place for them to be carrying Sten submachine guns, relics of the past war, instantly recognizable to me not only from hundreds of comic books of commando adventures, but also from many visits to the various bases where my father had served the latter part of his thirty-five years under the colors.

Fortunately, I half-recognized one of the two men, and perhaps even more fortunately he knew me.

"Malcolm MacAndrew! What are you doing here?"

"I've come to see my father," I stammered. "What's going on?"

"You'd better come inside," replied the man. He was a major, or had been when I had last met him, though I'd forgotten his name. He was one of my father's former subordinates from his last posting before retirement, when he commanded the King's Own Scottish Borderers.

Cradling the Sten in the crook of his left elbow, he shook hands with me. I almost dropped the hamper in the process, and felt a clumsy fool in the presence of these soldiers.

"Colonel Strahan," said the man, reminding me. "Call me Neil. This is Bob Mumfort."

The other man nodded, but it couldn't be described as an overly friendly gesture. Reluctant acceptance at best.

Strahan led us across the lawn, past the helicopter. It wasn't a type I recognized, and the only marking on its dark gray hull was a small acronym in darker gray on the door.

"B.P.R.D.? What's that?"

"Your father will explain," said Strahan. We continued past the helicopter, further into the light. There were portable floodlights like those used in filmmaking rigged up around the house, encircling it with harsh white illumination, and I could hear the deep thrum of several diesel generators out the back.

The front door was open, but guarded by two more men, this time with Lee-Enfield rifles, who looked familiar and were almost certainly some of my father's former military colleagues.

There were a lot more men inside the house, dozens of them in the reception rooms, all armed to the teeth, with rifles, submachine guns, and even a couple of Bren light machine guns. They stopped talking as I was led through to the kitchen.

My father was there, tall and authoritarian-looking as ever, though I had never before seen him as he was now, with his face painted in strange whorls of a blue so dark it was almost black and a wreath of holly in his silver hair. He was also wearing a long white robe with the hood pushed back.

He was waving a green stick, a branch recently torn from a tree, over a pile of .303 ball ammunition boxes on the kitchen table, tapping the boxes as he chanted something in what was not exactly Gaelic. There was also a pile of what looked like gilded pruning hooks under the table, thirty or forty of them, and every third tap he bent down to wave the stick over them as well.

I started to go in, but Strahan held me back and emphasized his grip on my arm with an urgent whisper.

"Wait! Not until he puts the rod down."

I opened my mouth, but shut it again before anyone needed to tell me. I suppose I was in mild shock, the kind of dissonance you experience when you see your extremely proper, military father wearing a white robe while he performed something that could only be described as a rite or spell of some kind.

Then I really did go into shock, as I took in the figure at the far end of the room. A man, or a manlike humanoid, whose skin was as red as a boiled lobster, and his head a strange confabulation of angular lines, with two circular growths sprouting from his forehead like opaque goggles of that same red flesh. He wore a khaki trenchcoat, and I was further staggered when I saw a tail twist out behind the coat, a tail that could only be described as demonic.

I must have gasped, for Strahan pulled me back, and the strange red creature looked at me. He put down his pewter mug and waved, shocking me still further, as his right hand was a massive, oversized fist that apart from being the same color as his flesh, would have been more in keeping on a mighty statue of some medieval hero.

My father finished his chant, and laid the wand upon the ammunition boxes. The branch withered as he did so, and crumbled into a light ash, which he bent down to blow off with three carefully controlled breaths. Then he turned to see who had almost interrupted him, controlled anger on his painted face, which eased as he saw me staring, the hamper clutched to my chest almost like a shield.

"Malcolm! What are you doing here?"

"I . . . I got some days off," I stammered. "Spur of the moment—"

I was looking past him at the creature. I couldn't think of him as a man, for he looked to be so far beyond the physical norm. In fact I didn't know what to think, and a good part of my previously extremely secure worldview was crumbling.

My father saw me looking, and clearly understood.

"Let me introduce you to a colleague," he said. "Hellboy, may I present my son, Doctor Malcolm MacAndrew. A medical doctor, not one of those philosophers."

"Hi," growled the apparition. He sounded human enough, with the hint of an American accent. "How ya doing, doc?"

"Fine, thank you," I said automatically. Then I dropped the hamper. I heard the wine bottles break, but it didn't really register.

"But I don't understand what is going on," I added, and suddenly felt ten years old again, and not at all a well-qualified professional with a grasp of every situation, which was how I liked to perceive myself. "Why is your face painted? And why are you wearing a . . . a robe?"

"It's not the right time to tell you," said my father slowly.

"Got to tell the kid sometime, Mac," said the red apparition, this Hellboy. "Must be a shock to see your father wearing a dress."

"It's not a dress, it's a druidical robe," said my father. "As you very well know, Hellboy. But I wasn't initiated into the mysteries until I was thirty-three, that is the proper age—"

"What mysteries?" I interjected. "Just tell me what is going on, please!"

"We might need a doctor to come along," said Hellboy.

"We have a doctor," replied my father.

"Doc Hendricks is a bit old to be wandering across the bottom of the loch," said Hellboy. He looked at me and winked. "What say you come along, Doc?"

"The bottom of the loch?"

"Oh very well, I suppose I don't have much choice," grumbled my father. "You B.P.R.D. types just don't respect tradition sometimes. Strahan, issue the blessed ammunition and the sickles to the men. You come upstairs with me, Malcolm, and I'll fill you in. Hellboy . . . I don't suppose there's any point giving you any orders, is there?"

"Nope," said Hellboy. He finished whatever he was drinking from the silver flagon and took a cigarette from an inside pocket of his trench coat and lit it up. "I might take a walk along the water's edge, see if anything pops up."

"Nothing will happen till the moon is high," said my father.

"The Russians might not know that," replied Hellboy. He bit down on his cigarette and talked through a clenched jaw, while he busied himself checking the most oversized handgun I'd ever seen, at least outside the picture of a medieval hand-cannon that had adorned the cover of one of my childhood books.

"The Russians?"

I felt like I'd inadvertently taken some delirium-inducing drug. My father was apparently a druid in charge of some paramilitary organization in league with an American semihuman . . . I felt a strong urge to get out my medical bag and take my own temperature, except that I knew it would not indicate a fever. I had stumbled into a hidden world, but I knew it was a real one, as real as the discovery of my father's secret relationship with my cousin Susan, after my mother died. That had been a shock too, but to some degree it had prepared me for this, the realization that my father had a number of layers to his life, many of them hidden to me.

I followed him upstairs to his study, which was as orderly as ever, his books of military and natural history arrayed in alphabetical order by author behind the glass doors of the bookshelves, his desk devoid of paper, several pens lined up on the green baize top in order of size.

We sat in his studded leather armchairs, and he looked at me with an expression I knew well, that of a gentleman of a certain age uncertain how to impart to his son the facts of life. He took a breath to start, stopped, let it out, took another breath and started off, all while not really looking me in the eye.

"We come from a long line of what many people call druids, Malcolm. Uncle Andrew, your great-uncle, was in fact the Arch-Druid of Britain until his death and in due course I will probably succeed him. At present I hold the post of Sentinel of the West and the Isles, and it is in that capacity that I have gathered the lesser druids and deodars here and sought the help of the B.P.R.D.—"

"Deodars? B.P.R.D.?"

"Deodars are sworn laymen in our service. The Bureau for Paranormal Research and Defense is an organization that has a lot of experience in dealing with the kind of situation we're facing. Particularly Hellboy, who is their chief operative—"

"What situation? And what is Hellboy anyway?"

"Hellboy is a fine young man," replied my father stiffly. "Just think of him as having a different background. Like a Gurkha or a chap from Africa. I met him in Malaya during the Emergency, got a lot of respect for the fellow."

"He's not a Gurkha," I protested weakly. "He's got a tail, and he's red—"

"Hellboy is an absolutely essential ally in the fight we face tonight," interrupted my father grimly. "I expect you to show him the respect you would accord one of my brother officers."

"I don't understand, but of course I will behave properly toward him," I said. "What exactly is the situation? What fight?"

My father walked to the window and drew back the curtain. Beyond the floodlights, the surface of the loch glimmered silver, catching the light of the full moon which had begun to climb up, half its disc now visible.

"This house has been here a very long time," he said. "It is not called the Owt-wauch for nothing, for it is indeed a sentry post, from where we druids have watched over the sacred circle of Maponos since time immemorial."

He gestured out toward the water.

"When the moon is full, there is a silver road to the stone circle that now lies at the bottom of the loch. A silver road that we guard against those who would attempt to use the circle for evil ends. Hellboy has brought us word that just such evildoers will seek to enter the circle tonight, and we must prevent them."

"Russian evildoers?"

"Their nationality is not their primary identification. They serve a Russian master, and have bent the power of the Soviets to their own ends. Now, there is little time, and I must prepare you. We cannot do the full initiation of course, but Maponos will need to know you as one of his own."

"I've heard that name before," I said. "I vaguely remember . . . when I was a child . . ."

"Aye, I'd forgotten you'd met a presence of the god," said my father, as matter-of-fact as if he were talking about the village grocer. "That will help. You were eight or nine at the time, it would have been 1946, when we were last all here."

"I thought he was a fisherman," I said. I had forgotten the name, but I remembered the occasion very well. There was a stream that ran into the loch not far away, and I had been paddling in it. A man had come out of the water, and given me a very large and splendid sea trout, which I'd taken back to my mother, who had not been as thrilled as I was to receive it.

"Well, he might remember you anyway, but we shall paint your face to make sure, and you can wear one of my spare robes."

I acquiesced to this without protest. It didn't even feel particularly strange to have my father smear the curiously sweet-smelling dye upon my cheeks. He'd painted my face before, when I was a child. Perhaps those occasions had been more significant than I thought.

The robe was slightly more troublesome, since it was extremely reminiscent of a large, loose dress. But if my battle-veteran father could wear one, I supposed I could too, and when we went downstairs I was not that surprised to see several others also wearing the white robes, though most of the younger men were not. I supposed they were the deodars.

Hellboy was back inside too. A man wearing a similar trench coat was talking to him, reading from a clipboard. Hellboy nodded as the man spoke. When he'd finished, he stood up and raised that strange clublike fist. Everyone fell silent and looked at him.

"Okay guys, the sonar buoy says there's a sub in the loch. Gotta be the Russians. Mac, what's the deal with the silver road?"

My father looked out the window.

"The road is forming. They will be able to enter it, from the mouth of the loch, as will you. We had best deploy."

"Yeah, we'd best," said Hellboy. "Remember, you hold 'em off from the circle, while I come at them from behind."

"They will not reach the keystone," said my father grimly. "Not alive, at any rate."

"That's what I'm worried about," growled Hellboy. "I don't want any of them reaching the keystone dead, either."

"None of the unworthy will gain a boon from Maponos," added my father. "Dead or alive."

"They'd better not or we'll all be into some serious regretting time. Those old gods ought to be more choosy who they dish the goods out to. I'll see you later. Good luck, guys."

Pausing only to throw his cigarette butt into the fireplace, Hellboy left. He moved very swiftly, I noted, weaving through the men with deft, precise movements that belied his bulky chest and that massive fist. I thought then that he would be a very interesting subject to examine more closely, before I even knew about his immense strength and durability.

We all left the house soon after Hellboy. I carried my doctor's bag, and one of the gilded pruning hooks. I had declined the offer of a Browning Hi-Power pistol, having a somewhat romantic notion of being true to my Hippocratic oath. I wished I had taken it soon enough.

The moon had not quite completely risen, but its light was bright enough to cast shadows. By virtue of the surrounding mountains or some meteorological phenomenon it did shine most brightly on the surface of the loch, lighting a silver trail that extended from the sheltered waters far out to sea.

"The silver road is present," pronounced my father, and he added something in Gaelic that I didn't catch, but was repeated by the men around me.

We marched down to the water's edge. I had no idea what was to happen next, but given the earlier events of the night, I was not overly surprised when we just kept going into what should have been water, but was not. My father gestured, and the men spread out into a skirmish line and I followed them into the strange, silver-lit atmosphere that was neither air nor water.

After a few yards I noted that though I could see a membrane above my head that was where the water level should be, and the ground beneath my feet was by turns both weeded and stony, there were no fish sharing this temporary environment we had entered. The water had not been made breathable to us; it had been transformed entirely, and that transformation had also removed the usual inhabitants of the loch's waters.

We continued down the slope of the loch floor for several minutes, in watchful silence. I found it both frightening and wonderful, that I should be walking deeper and deeper into the heart of the sea. But even this strange experience could not hide the underlying fear I felt, that soon I would be under fire, that I would be taking part in a battle and my father would see that I had not chosen a medical career because of some deep calling to the profession, but because it represented a respectable way for me not to become a soldier like him. It had even allowed me to avoid National Service, and I had fully expected that my occupation would keep me safe even in the event of another world war.

It was not being wounded that I feared. I had treated all kinds of wounds, and could easily imagine myself being shot, or peppered with shell fragments, or burned. I was afraid of being put in a position where I might show my fear, where my natural instinct to run would take over.

I knew that my father would soon know I was a coward. But I had no choice. I was under his eye, and deeply programmed from my earliest years, I knew no other course but to obey.

Half a mile from the shore, at the deepest part of the loch, I saw the ring of standing stones. We were easily six hundred feet below the notional surface, but the same soft moonlight continued to illuminate everything. My father gestured again, and his troops quickened their pace, as he circled his hand and indicated that we should form a defensive ring, mimicking the posture of the stones themselves.

"The enemy has to take the longer way, coming from the western end of the silver road," said my father quietly as the two of us continued on, and entered the ring of stones. "We may take a quicker path, as befits the children of Maponos."

"Where is Hellboy?" I asked. I could see no sign of our fire-skinned friend.

"He too, must take a longer path. He is not a child of Maponos. Now, we must pay our respects, before the hurly-burly starts."

There was a single stone in the middle of the circle. It was no higher than the others, and in fact all the stones of the ring were quite modest sarsens, little taller than myself, and of a not particularly inspiring gray-green color.

Even so, I knew that central stone was different. If I looked at it from the corner of my eye, it was not a stone I saw, but a hunched figure, with the hint of a grin too wide for a human face, and clasped hands that were not hands, but taloned claws.

I fell back as we drew closer. My father stopped and looked at me.

"There's nothing to be afraid of. Maponos knows his own. Those others, who come, they will seek to bend him to their will. He would never turn against us of his own accord."

I felt six years old again, listening to my father explaining why I should not be afraid of a cow in a field, because it was not a bull. Only when we did cross the field, there was a bull there that we hadn't seen and it had frightened me so much I dreamed of it for years afterward. He'd thought it was funny at the time, and of course, was not the parent who responded to a small boy's nightmares.

"We need merely grant him a small taste of our blood," continued my father. He lifted his pruning hook and sliced the end of his finger, and wiped the blood upon the stone.

Out of the corner of my eye, I saw a tongue curl and lick it off, and then there was no blood.

"Hold your finger up."

I shook my head.

"I *am* a surgeon," I answered. "I can cut my own finger when necessary."

I did it too, clumsily enough that if I'd been doing a prac I would never have passed my finals. Without looking, I wiped my finger on the front of the stone, and suppressed a shudder as I felt a warm, soft touch upon my flesh.

My father recited something in Gaelic and stepped back. I stepped back too, very readily.

The stone was the same, but there was no blood, and I saw that grin again.

"Right, that's done. I wonder where these Reds are?"

He sounded confident, as perhaps he had every right to be, with some forty heavily armed men in position, their ammunition blessed by ancient ceremony, and the god Maponos along for the ride.

Then we saw the first of the approaching enemy. I don't know what my father expected, but I had a hazy idea that some sort of Soviet marine force would be attacking, that apart from our strange location, it would be a relatively conventional battle.

But the figures who came toward us did not walk across the loch floor as we had, but descended from above, floating down as if they still moved through sea, not the silver atmosphere we experienced.

They were not Soviet marines either, but the rotten, skeletal remnants of long-dead men, clad in waterlogged rags that had once been the working uniforms of Hitler's Kriegsmarine.

They were dead U-Boat crews from the last war and they were coming for us.

"Aerial targets! Open fire!" shouted my father, and before even the word "open" was out of his mouth, the sharp crack of rifles and the chatter of the Stens and the deeper beat of the Brens exploded all around us. I knelt down and opened my bag, but continued to look up at the enemy. They looked like target dummies, or puppets on long, loose strings being lowered to a stage, jumping and dancing as they were struck by bullets, bits of uniform and bone and faint fragments of decayed flesh spraying out above them.

"They have some protection," muttered my father, who was watching them intently. "The bullets are charged with the power of Maponos. They should be falling apart."

But the dead sailors kept coming, inexorably drifting toward us. The first of them touched down some twenty yards distant, and for a moment I thought it would just settle in place, a sodden, long-drowned relict, its flesh long stripped away. But it jerked upright, as if those puppet strings were suddenly under command, and advanced upon the nearest of our defenders. He emptied the magazine from his Sten into its head, but even though its skull was blown to pieces, the headless thing kept coming, skeletal hands grasping as he chopped at it with his gilded pruning hook. He took one arm off, but it got a grip on the blade, and pulled it from his grasp and before he could retreat, another revenant fell upon his head and thrust its long fingers through his eyes and into his brain.

"We must call the god himself," said my father quickly. He looked down at me. "We will need a sacrifice."

I gaped up at him, as he loomed over me, his sickle in hand. Long-dead German submariners sank like falling flowers behind and above him, far too many for us to fight off, even if they had been susceptible to our weapons.

"Dad—"

"Not you, Malcolm!" exclaimed my father testily. He pulled me to my feet and forced the sickle into my hand. "Do you really know me no better than that? Now cut my throat and let the blood fall upon the stone!"

Those taloned hands were cupped now, ready to catch my father's blood and drink it up.

"Hurry!"

I raised the sickle. My father quickly gripped it and tried to bring it down across his throat. But I was faster, and held it back. I had seen something, beyond the outer stones. A red shape, moving fast, accompanied by a sound like a miniature sonic boom, or a mallet struck against a giant kettledrum—or the sound of an arcane fist smashing undead skulls.

Hellboy came charging through the undead sailors, smiting them as he advanced. Where his fist hit, the enemy simply blew apart, the fragments being carried away on unseen tides.

I dragged the sickle back, and the grin on the stone became a scowl, and the clawed hands twisted together in annoyance.

"Hellboy!" I exclaimed.

"What?" asked my father. He craned his head around to look, and stopped trying to drag the sickle down. I let my own grip ease, and the sickle suddenly moved of its own accord, falling across my father's throat.

At almost the same moment, two of the undead sailors threw a net of steel mesh and heavy lead weights over Hellboy's head, and down he went.

I threw the sickle away and held my father as he slowly fell. The cut to his neck was deep, but I saw in a moment that it had missed the major blood vessels. I pressed my hand against the wound, and lowered him down, as I groped about for my bag.

I so badly wanted to run, but while my father no longer held me back, I was holding him. His right hand scrabbled at his neck, painting his fingers with blood, and then he splayed that same hand against the stone.

I felt a voice speak to me, a voice that felt as if it was coming from deep inside my own heart, the words rushing to my head with the pulse of my blood.

"There," said Maponos angrily. "Our foe! Strike him down!"

I looked, and saw that amid the melee of our few remaining men and the undead sailors, there was one who I knew was different. He looked like a ragged skeleton, but he hung back from the affray, and when he walked, he did not bounce and glide as if he moved through some other more buoyant medium.

Hellboy had torn the steel net apart and was using it to snag enemies and drag them into smashing range, but there were just too many of them. From the look of things he'd definitely beat them, but it would be too late for me, and way too late for my father. I needed to investigate and suture the wound, and there was no time to lose.

"Hellboy!" I shouted, pointing with my free hand. "Maponos says shoot that one in the back!"

"You got it!" replied Hellboy. His hand-cannon boomed out, and this time I saw the bloom of real red blood. The man fell, and so did the U-boat crews, all at once, before the echo of Hellboy's shot even came back from the sides of the loch.

"Mine," said the voice inside me.

"Drag that one Hellboy shot over here!" I shouted, not looking to see who heard. I was busy, plying my trade, my hands bloody in a different way.

I had just finished stitching up my father's wound when Hellboy himself dumped the still-bleeding corpse at the foot of the keystone. I saw the talons reach, but also saw nothing, the stone completely still. But the body was gone, and I heard a self-satisfied chuckle that slowly faded.

"Thanks," I said to Hellboy, as I stood up and looked around for other wounded. My father raised a finger at me from where he lay, by way of a salute.

"No trouble, kid," said Hellboy. But it was a distracted answer and I saw that he was looking at the sole small remnant of the man that Maponos had consumed. A metal badge that the man had worn on his tunic, a swastika variation that incorporated some kind of serpent.

Hellboy suddenly stomped on the badge, mashing it beyond recognition. One of our men called to me, and I picked up my bag. At the same time, my father croaked, his voice barely understandable.

"Moonset . . . early . . . feel it. Get . . . moving!"

We moved. I stabilized the few wounded who had managed to survive, but we had to leave our dead. There were only ten of us left, eleven counting Hellboy. He carried my father, and Maponos made no trouble about all of us taking the short way back.

We went fishing the next day, just Hellboy and I. Hellboy had a purpose-made strap to lash a rod to his fist, so he could wind the reel with his left hand. A friend of his called Abe had made it for him, or so he said. He caught a dozen salmon to my three sea trout, the fish teeming on his side of the boat, which was certainly unnatural, but by that point I did not find it particularly strange. We didn't talk, but I believe he enjoyed the shared solitude.

He must have done, for we have been fishing a dozen times or more since then, not always when there is also business to be done for the B.P.R.D., though always at the loch.

Hellboy is quite a regular visitor here, and has become known to some of the locals as a lucky fisherman, which stands him in even better stead than being known as the friend of the only doctor for miles, or even for those who know that I am more than a country doctor, but also the Sentinel of the West and the Isles, and favored son of the sunken god Maponos.

Who, I think, should work *much* harder to help me catch more fish than Hellboy.

SALAMANDER BLUES
BRIAN KEENE

I s it too late to get a stack of pancakes?"

I thought my order would snap the waitress out of her trance, but she continued staring at me, slack jawed and wide eyed. My red skin and filed-down horn stumps tend to have that effect on people. Smiling, I waited, patiently. When she finally spoke, her southern accent was strong.

"You're that guy?"

"That's what they tell me. About those pancakes . . ."

"Oh, sorry. Yes, you can absolutely have pancakes. We serve breakfast around the clock. Coffee or juice?"

That's when some damned fool started pounding on the window.

"Go home, Ralph," Bethany shouted. "You been drinking again?"

Ralph's babbling was incomprehensible through the plate glass, but I don't think his panicked expression had anything to do with alcohol. He pointed an arthritic finger up the street, at something we couldn't see. His face turned alabaster. It didn't take a lip reader to understand what he shouted at us next.

They're coming! Run!

He hightailed it up the street, away from whatever it was that spooked him. I got that familiar bad feeling, but I slid off the stool and headed for the door anyway.

Bethany grabbed my arm. "You don't really think anything is out there, do you?"

"Get back in the kitchen and stay there."

"What if it's nothing?"

"Then I'll be back for those pancakes."

The chime above the door dinged once as I walked out into the dark street. The shadows were long and deep.

One of them moved.

I got my stone right hand up just in time to block the spiked club aimed at my noggin, and busted my attacker in the chops with my left. His face felt slimy. Rubbery. He toppled to the sidewalk, sprawling on his back. The light from the diner window gave me a good look at his smooth, black skin and the red stripe that started just above his eyes and ran back down the center of his head. He blinked bulbous, black eyes and gasped for breath. It was a wet, phlegmy sound. A long tongue flicked across his angular snout as his eyes focused on me. Snarling, he bared a wide row of narrow, pointy teeth, and got back on his feet.

He said something that sounded a lot like "Bubba wok gleep snack!" but probably wasn't.

"Whatever you say, pal."

The salamander man circled like a boxer, sizing me up for the next strike. His club looked like stone, or maybe coral, with a row of shark teeth embedded in the tip. He wore a cuirass of tortoiseshell fragments strung together with kelp. The shards rattled when he moved. He darted in again, swinging.

I caught the club in my hand and squeezed. It crumbled easily, and while he watched the blue and pink powder tumble to the ground, I kicked him hard between the legs. He dropped, bleating a miserable croak as he curled into a ball. Yep, he was definitely a *he*. I thumped him on the head with what remained of the club handle and his lights went out.

A distant scream caught my attention. I ran to the end of the block and found two more of the salamanders dragging a woman out of her house by her hair. Another carried an unconscious man over his shoulder, and there were three more salamanders roaming nearby. All their eyes turned toward me.

"Ah, crap."

They rushed me as I drew my gun. Unable to get the gun up, I introduced the face of the first opponent to my fist. The second dodged and knocked my gun from my hand with his coral staff. He followed that with a thrust to my gut. Something slammed me in the back of my head. My knees buckled and then they were on me. I may be tough, but a whack on the head is a whack on the head. I saw stars between the salamanders. Blows rained down on me from all around. A row of shark teeth slashed the back of my jacket. One of them kicked my gun and it skittered along the gutter.

I took their hits and gave back in kind. I felt teeth shatter and ribs break. A back kick to one of their knees produced a satisfying crack. The first two didn't go down easy, but they went down hard. The one with the ruined knee limped away.

"Where you going, Limpy?"

The remaining three backed off, surrounding me. They started shouting gibberish. I got the feeling they were interrogating me as they circled.

"No comprendo, amigos."

One of them leaped on my back. I snagged his wrist and yanked him down. He hit the pavement with a satisfying sound and rolled around screaming. A thrust kick across the chin put him out. I straddled him while his brothers charged. One got a good whack on my shoulder, but once I got a hold of their collars and smashed them together a few times, the fight went out of them.

Limpy was gone by then. I found my gun and brushed the grit off. The town came alive with more screams. Someone fired a shotgun. There was no second shot. Ugly croaks punctuated the violence.

"Let's see what you guys are up to."

The Atlantic shore was only a half mile away. It seemed like a good place to get started.

An SUV squealed around the corner. I held up a hand, shielding my eyes from the headlights. The driver slammed on the brakes and the SUV screeched to a halt. I could just make out the terrified driver at the wheel as he caught sight of me and screamed. Then he shifted to reverse and drove away. It wouldn't have done any good to tell him I was the good guy. That's the downside to being in the middle of a monster attack and looking like I do.

With a little luck, nobody would take a shot at me as I walked down the street. With even more luck, I'd still get those pancakes when this was over.

A few blocks later, I heard more salamander gibberish. Hugging a wall, I peered around the corner and saw another group of them surrounding a handful of frightened townspeople in the street. One of the salamanders held onto a young boy's arms. The boy, maybe eight years old, cried. A woman I assumed was his mother was being held back by two men. A third man was pleading with the creatures. One of the salamanders kept pointing at the boy and the surrounding houses.

I stepped around the corner. "Hey, fish face! Let the boy go."

Several heads, human and salamander alike, turned in my direction. Half of the monsters fanned out, brandishing their primitive weapons. I held my gun loose at my side. They released the boy and he tumbled into his mother's arms. Their leader barked something at me. His tone was quizzical. Again with the interrogation?

I paused, resting my thumb on the hammer of my pistol. I was confused. Sure, I could take out a few of them before they got to me, but was that the right thing to do? I felt they sought answers more than blood.

The salamanders shuffled closer. My thumb itched to pull back the hammer, but I refrained. Abe and Liz were always better at the thinkin' and talkin' part of the job. Me? I just pound on Big Bad Things. Against my instincts, I returned my pistol to its holster.

"This would be a lot easier if you were just a bunch of slavering piranha men." Two of them unfurled a large kelp net.

"You know what? Good idea. Take me to your leader."

I let them close the distance. When they threw their net, I put up a token resistance and earned a few whacks. Like their comrades, they couldn't do any real harm to me, but that didn't stop me from handing a few bruises back. Then I let them snare me, and let them pull me along. They snarled and pushed, but at least they stopped hitting me.

The salamanders herded the captives ahead of me. We walked to the edge of town, then onto the beach and along the surf for a couple hundred yards. The new moon left the beach cloaked in darkness, but something glowed in the distance—a blob of phosphorescence that dissolved into several blobs, and then into a cluster of glowing orbs.

I got a sinking feeling in the pit of my stomach when I saw the army of salamander men standing around them. There had to be fifty at least, and more burbled in the darkness and splashed in the tide. Human women and children sobbed all around us. Most of the men cried along with them.

We came to a halt. I saw three men laid out in a row on the sand. Two were still breathing. The third wasn't. Probably because the side of his head had been bashed in.

A pinched croak sounded from the group, and the salamanders fell silent. Our handlers moved us to one side. The crowd parted as one of the creatures approached. He was taller than the others, and his shell armor was streaked with a bright yellow and red pattern. The largest pearl I'd ever seen dangled from a cord around his neck.

"You must be the fearless leader," I said.

He warbled back at me.

"Listen, pal, you best get your butt back into the ocean and take your goons with you. The National Guard's going to roll in here any time now, and I don't think either of us wants to deal with that."

A murmur ran through the human captives. The leader looked past me at something in the distance. I glanced over my shoulder in time to see the town's lights flicker and die. The salamander man said something else. I swear it sounded smug.

"Not bad," I said. "I guess if I were smarter than the average newt, first thing I'd do, too, is cut off communication when I brought my invasion ashore."

Burble-burble-something-something. This was getting nowhere fast. Time for a show. I tore a big hole in the kelp net, and then ripped another section to pieces just because I could. After all, it was just seaweed. My guards jumped back, but Fearless Leader held fast.

"We done playing around, now? Can we talk like big boys?"

Crrooak. He thrust a slate shingle in my face. There was a pictogram on it, something that looked like a circle with a blob in it. He pointed to it, emphatically, and made a few gestures.

Charades. I hate charades. One wrong gesture and we'd officially have an Inter-Species Incident on our hands.

"You are looking for this?" I pointed at him, at my eyes, and then at the shingle. "What is it?"

He put his hands together, as if cradling something.

"I'll be damned. It's an egg, isn't it?"

He blinked at me.

"I will find this, if you give me all of them." I pointed at myself, my eyes, the egg, then at him, my cupped palm, and the prisoners.

He responded with some pointing of his own. The town, the egg, himself, the people, and me.

"I think we understand each other." I nodded.

Fearless Leader waved off his goon squad. I started to turn but he grabbed my arm. This time he did more pointing at me, the egg, and himself. Then he held out a flat hand and slowly raised his other fist from below it to above it. He finished with a stabbing motion at his chest and pointed at the people.

It took me a second to process.

"Find the egg by dawn or the villagers die. Right. Guess I better get started."

It sounded easy enough at the time. As I walked back to town, I felt confident I'd find it in some jerk's living room or kitchen. Then I'd bring it back to the salamanders and they'd be on their way.

Then I'd get some pancakes.

Best-laid plans . . .

Little did I know how big a haystack this particular needle was hiding in. An hour into the job I'd barely cleared a block. I searched garages, refrigerators, closets, and under beds. I checked sheds, cellars, attics, and even a doghouse. All without luck. It didn't help matters that I didn't have a very good idea of what I was looking for. Maybe I should have asked if it was bigger than a breadbox.

Around three, I thought about getting help, but the salamanders had sequestered most of the townsfolk, so I couldn't just recruit people.

By four, the salamanders had set up a perimeter around the town. They commandeered a sheriff's patrol car and pushed it just north of town, blocking the road. I guess living at the bottom of the ocean, they didn't know how to drive.

There was no sign of the deputy. The National Guard wasn't coming. Neither was the army or the FBI or Black Lodge or any of the other alphabet-soup agencies.

At five, I wondered if negotiation was the wrong tactic after all. Maybe I should have just fallen back on instinct and kicked their asses. I probably could have saved some of the people, right? Had to be better than skulking around in the dark on this scavenger hunt.

At five-thirty, I considered just sucking it up and calling the Bureau. I could be long gone by the time anyone showed up. Of course, the townspeople would be long gone, too.

I had about forty-five minutes to sunrise. I reloaded my pistol and wondered if maybe taking out Fearless Leader would get the rest of them to bail.

Then I heard shouting.

"This can't be. None of this should be here. None of it!"

A male voice. Young, by the sound. I followed it.

"You fish-eating sons of bitches! Get back here and finish the job. You hear me?"

I found him stumbling down the center of Main Street, yelling at the rooftops. He aimed a large flashlight at the homes and buildings. In its backlight, I saw that he had long, black hair and a dark complexion. He might have been twenty-five. He wore a denim jacket and jeans, and his cowboy boots clattered on the asphalt.

My hooves were louder.

"Something wrong?"

He turned his flashlight on me.

"Sweet Lucifer," he gasped, crossing himself with his free hand.

"Afraid you've got the wrong guy," I said.

"You've come to punish me."

"That all depends." I held my hands up, trying not to frighten him any worse than he already was. "You're an Indian, aren't you? Or, wait, how does that go these days . . . an 'Indigenous Person,' yeah?"

He nodded briskly. "N-native American."

I studied him. "Croatoan descent?"

Another nod.

I could almost hear Liz's voice: *Now you're thinking, HB.*

Roanoke Island couldn't have been more than ten or fifteen miles down the coast. If I hadn't been too busy tearing through people's bedrooms, I would have put it together sooner.

Stop me if you've heard this one. Back in the sixteenth century, Sir Walter Raleigh attempts to establish a colony on Roanoke Island, just off the coast of North Carolina. John White, the guy in charge of the colony, sails back to England for supplies and gets delayed by the war with Spain. When he finally returns, the settlement is deserted. All of the colonists have vanished. The only thing he finds is the word *Croatoan* carved into a tree—the name of an Indian tribe on another island. Roanoke becomes known as the Lost Colony, and the fate of those missing colonists remains unknown.

The frightened man spoke. "May I go?"

I glanced upward. The sky was turning gray and orange. Time to get a move on. "Where's the egg?" I asked.

"They don't have it yet?"

Roaring, I rushed him. He screamed and tried to run, but I slammed him up against the wall.

"The boiler room," he blurted. "At the grade school!"

"Show me. Fast."

"N-no."

I slammed my stone fist through the wall beside his head.

"Um, okay." He blinked brick dust from his eye.

I shoved him down the street, keeping a grip on his collar so he couldn't rabbit. "What's your name?"

"W-will Talon."

"How'd you know about the egg?"

"My ancestors have always known. Once a generation, the mermen lay their eggs in the shallow coastal waters to be nourished by the warmer water and the sun. My grandfather knew many tales about them."

"So you stole one? Framed the townspeople like the Croatoan did back in 1590?"

"No! That is not true. *I* stole one, yes. But not my *people*. The white settlers found the eggs and tried to farm them, destroying many in the process. The Croatoan tried to warn them, to stop them, but they wouldn't listen. When the mermen returned, they were enraged, and they destroyed the settlement. As usual, the white man sealed his fate with his own greed and ignorance."

"Is that what this is about—teaching the white man a lesson?"

"My father was a crab fisherman. A good one. But when he fell on hard times, the government took his boat. He couldn't find work. My mother took sick, and we couldn't care for her. Shortly after she died, my father hung himself."

I nodded, encouraging him to continue.

"That was five years ago. Ever since then I've been watching the shallows, waiting for the mermen to return. When they did, I stole an egg. I thought they would come looking for their young and destroy this town."

I could hardly wait to spring the surprise on him.

"You condemned a town full of innocents to death because your father committed suicide? That sounds more like petty revenge to me."

"No, it's punishment. Nobody should have to go through what my father went through! Did my mother deserve to die because we couldn't pay for her surgeries? Because we didn't have the same health insurance as white people?"

"Things are tough all over, kid."

"Five hundred years ago, my people could fend for themselves. Villages thrived on the land. Then the white man came with his concept of property, with his banks and his money. He stole the land and parceled it out, made it so nobody could live there without his say so. It's those concepts that destroyed my people. This town is an example of the punishment due."

"Who are you really trying to convince, me or you?"

"You couldn't understand. You have red skin but you are not one of us."

"I understand plenty. You're like any other man, thinking only about himself. You got a beef with the government? Vote."

He laughed. "Vote?"

"Sure. Write a letter or organize a protest. But don't kill two thousand innocent people."

"Nobody listens to a letter."

"Nobody listens to a murderer, either."

We arrived at the school. Will led me to a smashed classroom window. He climbed in first, and I promised to shoot him if he tried to run. We made our way down the hall to another door. He'd jimmied it open with a crowbar. A narrow set of stairs led us down into a large, hot, and humid room dominated by a water tank. He led me between the boiler and the damp concrete wall to a narrow nook with a sump pump and drain in the floor.

"It's down there." Will sat his flashlight down next to the opening and stood back.

I crouched down and pulled the cover off the drain. The egg, an opaque, gelatinous mass about twice the size of a basketball, was at the bottom. I scooped it up with my left hand.

"This is gross." Slime oozed between my fingers. I felt the shape of the merchild inside through the outer film of the egg.

Behind me, metal scraped on concrete. I turned to see Will swinging a length of pipe at me. He struck me hard on the shoulder blades, then again across the center of my back. The egg slipped from my grasp. Growling, I kicked his legs out from under him. He hit the boiler before hitting the floor.

I picked up the egg and made sure it was still intact. The fetus squirmed inside. I stood to kick Will again, but he scurried around the boiler, whimpering. I shifted the egg to my right hand and picked up the flashlight with my left. I went around the boiler.

"Get up."

Groaning, Will reached up and gently explored the huge knot forming near the top of his forehead. He stood slowly, and then made his way toward the door. I kept the flashlight aimed ahead of him as we navigated the halls.

When we reached the schoolyard, I noticed that the gray on the horizon was shifting to blue. The sun would clear the horizon soon.

"The beach," I told Will. "Hurry up."

The walk didn't take long. Will stopped short when he saw the two groups up ahead. I dropped the flashlight in the sand and shoved him along.

He struggled. "You lied to me!"

"No, you assumed. Keep moving." I dragged him by the arm.

"Wait! Stop it! What are you doing?"

"We're about to make a trade."

Protesting, he dragged his feet. A group of salamanders scurried toward us. Fearless Leader appeared, and I pointed to Will.

"See this guy? Get a whiff of him. Remember that scent. Anybody screws with you again, you leave the other folks in town alone and just hunt down this guy."

Fearless Leader stepped up to Will, inhaled, checked him up and down, then turned to me and nodded.

I handed him the egg. He croaked his thanks.

"But what if it isn't me?" Will squeaked. "What if someone else bothers them?"

"Guess you better make sure that doesn't happen."

He took two steps back, then cut and ran. I let him go. They could find him now, anytime they wanted.

The sun crept over the horizon, glittering off the waves, and I was anxious for another game of charades. I looked at Fearless Leader. "Set the people free, take the egg, and go home." I punctuated this by pointing to the people and the town, the egg, Fearless Leader.

He ran his hand lovingly across the surface of the egg, chattered at his people, then made a circular motion in the air and turned toward the ocean.

Silently, the salamanders waded into the waves. The townspeople whispered, quickly escalating to cries of joy and relief.

The humans fled for their homes. A few made awkward attempts at thanking me, but most of them just ran away. Soon as power was restored, the authorities would be notified. Eventually, the Bureau would get a call. It was time for me to go.

I walked south along the shore. The water lapped at my feet. Overhead, seabirds wheeled and squawked. I glanced out at the ocean as the sun broke across it, and wondered what else might be lurking in the depths. What kinds of things did the mermen deal with on their own turf? Something vicious, judging from the coral clubs and turtleshell armor. Maybe they had to fight things much bigger and scarier than human monsters who stole their young.

There are some things I'd rather not know.

I wandered along the beach, wishing for some pancakes.

THE THURSDAY MEN

TAD WILLIAMS

"You know anyone famous named *Monday?*" Liz asked.

"You mean like Rick Monday? Used to play for the Dodgers back in the '70s?" That was from Ted the technician. I never cared much about baseball myself.

"Okay," said Liz. "So that's one for Monday. And there's Tuesday Weld, the actress."

"I thought of another one—'Ruby Tuesday,' that Rolling Stones song," said Ted, and began to hum it—or at least he hummed what he thought, in his tuneless way, it sounded like. He's a decent-enough kid and a pretty good tech, but if the B.P.R.D. ever fires him he's not going to be making a living on the pro-karaoke circuit.

"I thought we were going to play cards," I said. "What is all this crap?"

"I've just been thinking about the days of the week and people who have them as names," Liz said. "Wednesday from *The Addams Family*. Robinson Crusoe's Man Friday."

"No!" shouted Ted. "Has to be Joe Friday! From *Dragnet.*"

"You weren't even alive when that was on," I growled.

Liz went on as if we weren't talking. "And there's Baron Saturday—he's one of the voodoo gods, I guess you'd call them. You know about them, right, HB?"

I have had more than a few strange adventures in the New Orleans area over the years. "Yeah. But that doesn't mean I want to talk about it. What's your point?"

"And Billy Sunday was a famous evangelist or something—my grandmother used to talk about him." She frowned. "But I still can't come up with a Thursday. I don't think there are any."

"Ooh, I thought of one," said Ted. "There's a pretty famous spy book called *The Man Who Was Thursday*."

"Yeah, but it was just his code name," I pointed out.

Ted looked at me in surprise. "You read G.K. Chesterton?"

"Why, you think I only read comic books?" When you're seven feet tall, literally ugly as sin, and red as a fire truck from head to foot, people always doubt your intellectual credentials. "But I'll give you a real one, if you promise to shut up and play some damn cards. Grayson Thursday. In fact, there were a whole bunch of Thursdays, when you get down to it."

"It doesn't count if nobody's ever heard of them," Liz said, pouting. She makes those grumpy-kid faces, you almost forget she could napalm a city block if the urge took her.

"But it does sound familiar," said Ted. "Why is that?"

"Maybe you read the file," I said, knowing he probably had. The kid studied up on me when he came here like a Yankees fan memorizing all the stats of his favorite player. When it came to my Bureau career, he could tell you the equivalent of my average with runners in scoring position for every year.

Hey, I said I didn't care much about baseball, I didn't say I didn't know anything about it.

I looked at the two of them. They were waiting expectantly. "Crap," I said. "We're not going to play cards, are we?"

"Come on, tell about this Thursday guy," Liz said. "If I know who he is, then maybe it'll count for my list."

"Wait, was that back in the '80s? The guy with the magical grandfather clock?" Ted said. "I think I remember . . ."

"Shut it," I suggested. "And keep it shut. I'm the one telling the story."

It was the first time I'd been on the California coast above San Francisco. It's interesting how quick you can go from a place packed with people and lights and car horns and things like that to the middle of nowhere. Once you get about an hour or so north of the Golden Gate Bridge most of it's like that—the kind of place where you realize you've been listening to the seagulls and the ocean all day and not much else. Or at least that's how it was when I went to Monk's Point back in early March of 1984. Maybe it's different now.

Albie Bayless met me off the B.P.R.D. plane at Sonoma County Airport. Bayless was a former reporter with the *San Francisco Examiner* who'd retired to his hometown a few years back and taken over the local shopper, the *Monk's Point Beacon*. He'd had some past contact with the B.P.R.D. and me—you remember that Zodiac guy, the murderer everyone says was never caught? No, nobody knows the B.P.R.D. had anything to do with that—I didn't file an official report on that one. Probably never will. Anyway, when Bayless stumbled onto the weird death of Rufino Gentle and what happened after, he called my bosses at the Bureau and suggested they send me out to have a look-see.

Bayless was wearing shorts and had grown a beard. He looked a good bit older and saggier than the last time I'd seen him, but I was there to work with him, not marry him. "Still got that bad sunburn, I see," he said as I came down the ladder. Funny guy. I squeezed into the passenger seat of his car and he filled me in on details along the way. The town was called Monk's Point because there used to be a Russian monastery out on the rocky headland overlooking a dent in the coastline called Caldo Bay. The population of monks had dwindled until the last of them went back to Russia. Later the monastery was turned into a lighthouse when the Caldo Bay fishing industry hit its stride. Those glory days passed too, and the lighthouse was decommissioned in the 1960s. The property on the point now belonged to some out-of-town rich guy who hardly anybody ever saw. But the place itself had a bad reputation going back even before the Russians arrived. The local Indians had been a tribe called Zegrado—which, Bayless informed me cheerfully, was a corruption of the Spanish word for *cursed*.

As I discovered, *cursed* and *dying* were two words that seemed to come up often in almost any conversation about Monk's Point. The reasons became clear when we drove through the center of town, a handful of weathered plank buildings beside a tiny harbor at the mouth of Caldo Bay. Half a dozen shops, a coffee joint, and a bar made up the business district, along with a few other stores that looked like they'd been boarded up for a while. I doubt there were a thousand people in total living in the place. Things had gone downhill since the cannery closed. The town's young people were leaving as soon as they were old enough, and except for Albie Bayless, no one was moving back in.

"Everybody always says the place is dying," Bayless told me as we waited for a dog to cross the main street in front of our car. "But they still get upset when someone actually dies—at least when there's no good explanation for it. That's what happened here last week. A kid named Gentle—Rufino Tamayo Gentle, how's *that* for a name?—was out here with some friends. I guess Gentle and his buddies were troublemakers by small-town standards, but nothing too bad—a couple of busts for pot and loitering, some suspicion of breaking into tourists' cars. Anyway, on a bet, young Gentle climbed over the fence and went up to the famous haunted house. His friends waited for him. He never came back, never showed up for school. One of the kids mentioned it to a teacher. Result was, a local cop came by, cut off the bolt and walked up to the house. He found young Gentle standing on the front path, head slumped like he'd fallen asleep standing up. Body was stone cold—he'd been dead for hours."

"Standing up?"

"That's what the cop swears. He's not the type to make things up, either."

"You said one of the kid's friends told a teacher. What about Gentle's parents? Didn't they notice he didn't come back?"

Bayless smirked. "You'll have to meet the kid's dad. *There's* a piece of work."

"Okay," I said, "*dead standing up* is definitely an interesting trick, but it isn't why you called us, is it?"

"Nope. That would be Rufino's *escape*. But first I'm gonna take you to my place, get you some dinner."

Just a half mile or so past not-so-bustling midtown, Bayless pulled up to a gate across a private road. It was surrounded by weeds and sawgrass and looked like it didn't get opened much. Beyond it a long, curving driveway led away toward the top of the hill. The house itself, the ex-monastery, was mostly hidden from view behind the headland but the lighthouse loomed in clear view, pale as a mushroom. The windows at the top went all the way around, yet the impression was of someone looking away from you, staring out over the sea—someone you didn't want to disturb, and not just out of courtesy.

"I don't like it," I said.

"You're not alone," said Bayless. "Nobody likes it. Nobody ever has. The local Indians hated the place. The monks only stayed about thirty years, then they all went back to Russia, saying the place was unholy, and nobody's actually lived in it since. Even the guy who owns it now hardly ever shows up."

Albie Bayless had a mobile home on the outskirts of town—not a trailer, but one of those things that look pretty much like a house with tin sides. He kept it up nice and he wasn't too bad a cook, either. As I listened to him I spooned up my bowl of chili. He made his with raisins and wild mushrooms, which actually worked out pretty good.

"The reason the dad didn't report his son missing is that he's a drunk," Albie said. "Bobby Gentle. Supposedly an artist, but hasn't sold anything that I know of. One of those bohemian types who moved here in the '60s. Kid's mother left about five or six years back. Sad."

"But that's not why you called us."

"I'm coming to it. So they found the kid dead, like I told you. No question about it. No pulse, body cold. Took him to the local medical examiner over in Craneville and here's the good part. The body got up off the examination table, sort of accidentally slugged the examiner—it was thrashing around a lot, I think—and escaped."

"So he wasn't actually dead."

Albie fixed me with a significant look. "Think again, Kemo Sabe. This was after the autopsy."

That didn't sound good at all. "After?"

"Yeah. Chest cracked and sewn up again. Skull sawed open. Veins full of embalming fluid."

"Jesus. That's nasty."

"Imagine how the guy felt who'd just done the sewing."

"And you're sure the coroner's not in on some body-selling scam?"

"Kind of a stupidly vivid story to tell if you don't want to attract attention, don't you think?"

I had to concede that one. "Okay, so the kid goes to Monk's Point lighthouse on a dare, dies standing up, then walks off the autopsy table and runs away. Weird. Anything else?"

"Oh, yeah. You see, I was already doing research as soon as I heard about the boy being found dead. I didn't know him, but I thought it might make an interesting wire-service piece—you know, *Old Ghost Story Haunts Modern Murder . . .*"

"*Old Ghost Story?*"

"Like I said, everybody's scared of this place . . . and it turns out there's good reason. A lot of weird stuff's happened there and in the area just around it, going back as far as I can research, everything from noise complaints to murders, old ghost stories, local kid's rhymes and other odd stuff, even some UFO sightings. It kind of goes in cycles, some years almost nothing, other years things happening a few times a month. It began to remind me of some of the places you told me about back in San Francisco, when we were working on, y'know . . ."

"I know," I growled. I could hear the frogs outside kicking up their evening fuss, and, dimly, the sound of seabirds. "I think I want to see this place close up."

I stood in front of the gate. The lighthouse was nothing much more than a big dark line blocking the stars like paint. "You were going to tell me something about the guy who owns the place."

Bayless pulled his jacket a bit tighter. It was cold for the time of year. "Grayson Thursday. It's been in his family for a long time. He's hard to get hold of, but he's supposed to see us the day after tomorrow."

"Good enough," I said. "See you in the morning—I'm going to have a look around."

"Are you sure you want to do that?" He looked upset, but I didn't know whether it was because he was scared for me or he'd been looking forward to the company. "What if you're not back in the morning?"

"Tell the children that Daddy died a hero." I grabbed the top bar and vaulted over the gate. "See ya, Albie."

The local real estate market wasn't losing anything by having the Monk's Point property in the hands of one family. It was kind of butt ugly, to tell the truth. As I came around the headland and I could see the buildings properly, my first thought was, *So what?* There really wasn't much to it—the lighthouse, plain and white as vanilla, and a big, three-story barnlike structure with a few outbuildings pushed up against it like they were all huddled together against the hilltop wind. Still, my feelings from earlier hadn't changed: something about the place, as subtle as a trick of light or angle of land, made it easy not to like it. In the dark it had a thin, rotten sheen like fungus.

I stopped on the pathway in front of the barnlike building's front door, figuring this must be where the kid had ended up. I looked around carefully but couldn't see anything that was going to stop someone's heart. The front door was locked but the pockets of my coat were full of remedies for a problem like that. A few moments later I was inside, swinging a flashlight around.

If this Thursday guy and his family had hung on to the house for a while, it looked like it was mainly to keep their old junk. The inside was like some weird flea market with the stuffed heads of deer and other wild animals on the wall and dozens of other examples of the taxidermist's art in glass cases or stands all over the huge front room, even a stuffed, snarling Kodiak bear looming almost ten feet high on its hind legs. The shelves were piled with books and curios, an old pipe organ stood against one wall, and a grandfather clock the size of a phone booth stood against another. Some of the junk actually looked kind of interesting and I strolled around picking things up at random—a model sailing ship, a conch shell the size of a tuba, some giant South American beetles that had been preserved and posed and dressed like a mariachi band. Three quarters of an hour or so passed as I wandered in and out of the various rooms, some of which seemed to have been dormitory rooms for the monastery, all of which seemed to have the same kitschy decorator as downstairs, as though the place had been planned as a museum but never opened. I even walked up the winding stairs of the lighthouse itself, which was as bare as the rest of the place was cluttered. It didn't look like the beacon had been lit in recorded memory—the wires had been torn out, the big lamp removed. I took the long walk back down.

I looked at my watch. A little after eleven. I sat on an overstuffed chair that didn't cramp my tail too badly, switched off my flashlight, and settled in to wait.

I may have dozed off. The first thing I noticed was a glow in the high windows, a sickly, pale gleam, slowly pulsing. It took me a moment to realize what it was—above my head the lighthouse had smoldered into a sort of weird half-life. I started across the room but before I got to the foot of the stairs I heard a rustling sound, as though a flock of birds was nesting in the high rafters. I stopped. The noises were getting louder, not just rustles but creaks, crackles, pops, and snaps, as if the room was a bowl full of cereal and someone had just poured the milk.

I swung my flashlight around. A stuffed seagull on a stand meant to look like a dock piling was stretching its wings, glaring at me. The deer head on the wall behind it was straining to get loose, gnashing its teeth, rattling and bumping its wooden plaque against the wall. Something moved beside me and I snatched my hand back. It was a replica of a Spanish galleon, the sails inflating and deflating like an agitated blowfish.

"Oh, this is just *crap!*" I said.

Outside the windows the green light was still dim but the pulses were becoming more rapid and the whole room was growing more wrong by the moment—the air had gone icy cold and smelled harsh and strange, full of scents I had no name for. I took a few steps back and something broke on the other side of the room with a splintering crash, then a huge shape came thumping and stumbling out of the shadows. It was the stuffed bear, walking like a stiff-legged drunk, swinging its clawed arms as it went.

"You've gotta be kidding me," I said, but the thing wasn't answering. It wasn't even alive, just moving. One of its glass eyes had popped out, leaving behind a hole full of dangling straw. I stared at this for half a second too long and the thing caught me on the side of the head with one of those swinging paws. It might have been stuffed but it felt like it was poured full of wet cement. It knocked me halfway across the room and I'm no feather. Something other than the latest improvements in taxidermy was definitely going on, but I didn't really have time to think about it too much, since the giant bear was on top of me and trying to rip my head off my neck. It felt like it weighed about twice as much as a real bear, and trying to throw it off was already making me tired. I dragged out my pistol and shoved it up against the furry belly.

"No picnic basket for *you*, Yogi!" I shouted and emptied the gun into it. *Bam! Bam! Bam! Bam!* No soap. The thing just kept bashing me. Trying to shoot a stuffed bear—stupid, stupid, stupid.

Eventually, I rammed the thing through the wall and got its head stuck deep enough that I could finally pull myself loose. No sooner had I got rid of the bear than a tiger rug wrapped itself around my ankles and started trying to gnaw off my hooves. The whole place was nuts—the paintings on the wall with their eyeballs bulging, trying to talk, the stuffed animals jerking around like they'd been electrified. I'd had enough of this crap. I kicked the rug up into the rafters where it hung, gnashing its teeth and swiping at me with its claws, then I made a run for the front door. I couldn't help but notice as I ran past that the grandfather clock was lit up from within like a jukebox, glowing and, well, sort of *throbbing*. And the air around it was murky with strange, colored shadows which were streaming into the clock like salmon swimming upstream to spawn. Every one that went past me burned icy cold and made my skin tingle. It didn't take much to know that this was the center of the haunting or whatever it was. It was pulling on me, too, a strong, steady suction like a whirlpool in dark, cold water. I had to struggle against it to reach the door.

I was happy enough to get outside, at first.

The sickly glow from the top of the lighthouse was barely strong enough to light the long grass waving on the hilltop, but it was enough to illuminate the thin shape standing at the bottom of the path, swaying a little, head hanging down as though in some kind of hypnotic trance. Whoever it was, they didn't have a prayer against that stuff behind me.

"Hey!" I shouted. "Get out of here!" I hurried down the path. If I had to, I'd just throw whoever it was over my shoulder and carry him . . .

The first weird thing I noticed was that the Y-shaped pattern on the guy's chest wasn't a design on a shirt. I realized that because of the second weird thing—he was naked. The design on his chest was made of stitches. Big ones. In fact, it wasn't a guy in any normal sense at all—it was Rufino Gentle's body, fresh off the autopsy table, standing just about where it must have been found in the first place.

I've seen a lot of creepy stuff in my time, but that doesn't mean you get *used* to it, you know.

I grabbed at his hair as I got close and lifted his head so I could look into his eyes. No resistance at all. Nothing in his eyes, either. Dead—I'm telling you, dead. Not like you say it about someone who doesn't care any more, I mean dead as in *not alive*. There was nothing like a soul or a sensibility in that corpse, but it was still standing there, swaying a little in the wind, long dark hair flipping around, a livid new autopsy scar incision stretching up past his navel and forking to both collarbones. When the wind caught his hair again I couldn't help noticing that the top of his skull was gone, too, his brain sitting right there like a soft-boiled egg in a cup. He was clutching the rest of his skull in his dead hand like it was an ashtray he'd made at summer camp.

I'd had a rough night. I don't think anyone will blame me for not bringing Rufino Gentle's body back with me—he looked pretty comfortable standing there, anyway. I hurried down to the fence and Albie Bayless, waiting in his car.

"Did you see the lights?" Albie asked me, wide eyed.

"We'll talk about it," I said. "But first I need to drink about nine beers. Do you have nine beers at your place, maybe ten? Because if not I really, really hope there's somewhere open in this godforsaken little town where we can get some."

"The Gentle kid's body, just . . . standing there?" Albie asked again as we got into the car the next morning. This was about the twentieth time. "You really saw it?"

I don't think Albie had slept very well. I wondered if maybe I'd told him too much.

"Trust me—I've seen worse things in my day. I have to admit, though, you've developed a few new wrinkles here."

Grayson Thursday was waiting for us in his office, a little storefront place just off the town's main street that looked like it might have been the site of one of those telemarketing boiler rooms. There was a computer—the 1980s kind, so it looked like the mating of a Hammond organ and a typewriter—and a single telephone and that was about it. A notepad sat on top of his desk. Not a file cabinet in sight. Thursday himself was a kindly looking gentleman of about sixty, although his face was a little odd in a way I couldn't entirely put my finger on at first. Like he'd been in an accident and had gone through some cosmetic surgery afterward that didn't quite iron out all the bumps. His voice was a little odd, too, as though he'd been born deaf but had learned to talk anyway. But what really worried me was that he didn't seem to think there was anything unusual about me at all—didn't even look twice when we were introduced. *That* I'm not used to, and it gave me a bad feeling.

"I'm sorry to have kept you waiting for this meeting, Mr. Bayless, Mr. Boy," he said. "I don't get into town very often."

"Oh, yeah? Where do you live?" I asked him.

"Quite a long way away." He smiled as if he was thinking of something else entirely and adjusted the sleeves of his expensive sweater. "Now, what can I do for you gentlemen?"

"My associate and I want to ask you a few things about the Monk's Point property," Albie told him.

"Is this about the Gentle boy?" He shook his head. "Terrible thing—tragic."

Oddly enough, he really sounded like he felt bad about it. It didn't make me any more comfortable with him, though.

Thursday proceeded to answer a bunch of questions about the house—how long his family had owned it (seventy years or so), what they used it for (storing an old family collection of treasures and knickknacks), and why they didn't sell it to a hotel company (sentiment and the historical value of the property). All very expected, but I was watching Thursday more than listening to the answers. Something about him just didn't quite seem right. He seemed . . . distant. Not like he was on drugs, or senile, just weirdly slow and detached.

"I hope that's been some help to you," he said and stood up, indicating that our time was over. "What happened to the boy was very sad, but as I told the police already, it's nothing to do with me. Now I'm afraid I have some important errands to run. Please leave a message with my answering service if there's anything else I can do for you. I won't be back in town until next week."

As we went out into the parking lot, I asked Albie, "Did he say he wasn't going to be back until next week?"

"Yeah, why?"

"And didn't you tell me he made you wait a week for this meeting?"

"I guess."

"And it just happens today's Thursday. And his last name's Thursday."

"I'm not following you."

"Never mind. Can you look some stuff up for me this afternoon? I'll give you a list. And before you start, drop me off at Bobby Gentle's house."

"The dead boy's father? Why?"

"His name was on a notepad on Thursday's desk."

Albie shrugged. "You're the boss. Try not to scare anyone to death."

"There's been enough of that already," I said.

After the Bayless-mobile rolled away, I walked up the long, overgrown driveway toward Gentle's place, but stopped and stepped into the trees before I reached the house. I stood there for only a short time before Grayson Thursday rolled up the driveway past me in his spanking-new Mercedes. I waited a couple of minutes, then followed, but the yard around the ramshackle house was covered with dry grass that hadn't been mowed in months, not to mention all kinds of other trash, and it was hard to get close without making a noise. Thursday didn't stay very long, anyway. I had to duck back into the trees again as he came out, got into his beautiful car and bumped off down the driveway.

When he was gone I knocked on the peeling paint of the front door.

"Jesus Christ!" said Bobby Gentle when he saw me, and jumped back into his shabby living room, then darted out of sight. That was the kind of reaction I was used to. I felt better already.

"Don't bother getting out a gun," I called after him. "I don't mean you any harm, but I am armed and I'm probably a better shot than you are. I just want to talk." I looked around the living room. The place was a mess, cigarette butts and beer bottles everywhere, along with greasy fast-food wrappers, months' worth. A couple of not-very-good seascapes hung on the nicotine-stained walls. If they were Gentle's, I knew why he wasn't selling much.

He came out of the back room slowly, his hands open wide. He hadn't been able to find the gun, anyway.

"Swear you ain't gonna hurt me?"

"I promise. Sit down."

He squinted. "I saw you in the papers, didn't I?"

"Could be."

Gentle Sr. truly was a piece of work, no doubt about it. He stank of booze and it wasn't even noon yet, so I figured he must be sweating it out of every pore. He was as pale as his son, but without the excuse of having had all the blood pumped out of him. I kind of doubted he'd been outside more than a couple of times in the last six months. His hair was long in the back, thin on the top, and stringy and greasy all over. He wasn't killing himself keeping up with his shaving, either. Still, the last week couldn't have been easy on anyone. "Sorry about your son," I said. "Rufino, that was his name, right?"

"Yeah. His mama named him after some famous spic painter. Before she took off and left me. But I got the boy back off her. Went to court for it." For a moment his angry little red eyes lost what focus they'd had. "Bitch wasn't taking my boy to live in some commune full of tofu-eatin' losers."

Tempting as it was, I didn't really want to spend the whole day with this charmer. "I'll cut to the chase, Mr. Gentle. You've just had a visit from Grayson Thursday. I suspect it had something to do with your son's death. Would you mind telling me what he saw you about?"

He looked at me in surprise and confusion, then his pale skin turned almost as red as mine. Before I could react he bolted out of the living room and down the hall. He pulled a door shut behind him and locked it. I was patting my pockets for a lockpick when I looked again at the state of the rest of the place, then I just broke off the knob.

The bathroom was empty except for a stack of *Hustler* magazines beside the toilet and an ancient no-pest strip dangling from the light bulb. The window was open, the screen kicked out.

I caught him in the woods a hundred yards away. He was pretty fast for a rummy, but for some reason he was carrying a suitcase, and I can get this bulk of mine moving pretty quick when I want to.

"No!" he screamed when he saw me, and threw the suitcase end over end into the deep undergrowth. "You can't have it! I never got anything else for him! All that boy ever did was cost me! You can't take it away!"

I picked him up by one arm and let him sway in the wind a little bit until he stopped yelling and started whimpering. "What are you talking about?" I asked him. "Why did you run away? What did you just throw?"

He stared at me, or did his best to focus in my direction, anyway. "You don't want to take it away from me? You're not going to steal it?" He grimaced. "Damn! I shoulda kept my big mouth shut!"

"I'm sure that's not the first time you've said those words—and I'll bet it won't be the last." I put my face really close to his, doing my best not to breathe in. "Now, if you don't want me to swing you around in a circle until this arm of yours comes off, you'd better tell me what you're babbling about."

"The money Mr. Thursday gave me. It was 'cause my boy died! He said so! There's no crime in me having it!"

I shook my head. "He gave you money? How much?"

Now his eyes got shifty. "I don't know. A couple of thousand . . ."

I lifted him higher. I heard something pop in his shoulder and he shrieked. "Don't lie to me, Gentle."

"A hundred thousand! He said it was a hundred thousand!"

I set him down. A hundred thousand? That was crazy. "Go get it."

He came back with the suitcase cradled in his arms. I swear he was getting tearful at the thought I was going to take it off him. I couldn't help wondering if he'd ever expressed that much care and concern for his son. "Open it," I told him. He did. If it wasn't a hundred thousand dollars, you could have fooled me. Stacks of new bills, side by side. I made a face and turned around, heading back toward the road. This whole thing was pissing me off.

"So . . . I can keep it?" he called.

"Far as I'm concerned. But you'd better keep your mouth shut about it or someone less polite than me will come out here and take it away from you."

Last I saw of him he was scurrying back toward his falling-down house, suitcase once more gripped tight against his chest.

It was well into the afternoon by the time I had hiked back to Albie's mobile home. He met me at the front door.

"Guess what I found out," he said. "Oh, and do you want some chili? I was just going to heat some up."

"Later," I said. "And you can tell me what you found out while you're driving me back into town. We're going to talk with that lying son of a bitch Thursday before he takes off again."

"Why's he a liar?" Albie asked as he maneuvered his car out onto the main road.

"You remember him saying the murder was nothing to do with him, right? Well, he was just over at Bobby Gentle's place and gave the guy a hundred thousand dollars. Does that sound like nothing-to-do-with-me money? Or like some kind of payoff instead?"

Albie whistled. "I never knew my little town was so exciting."

I scowled. "In my business, there's a thin line between *exciting* and *multiple fatalities*. I hope we stay on one side of it."

Nobody was in at the office so I sent Albie to the coffee shop to buy me a couple of burgers and we sat in the car and ate while we kept a watch on the place. "What did you find out?" I asked him.

He handed me a stack of green printout pages about the width of my thumb. My bigger thumb. "I pulled every story I could on weird stuff happening near that house, going back to the monastery days. There are lots of Indian legends, but they didn't have what we're looking for, of course . . ."

"And?"

"And guess what I found. Almost every single murder, UFO sighting, public panic, you name it, for the last hundred and forty years, happened on . . ."

"Thursday," I said.

"Well, no."

I was stunned—my theory had just been shot to hell. "I don't get it . . ."

"But you were half right. Look—a few did happen on Thursday, or at least that's when they were reported. And a few seemed to have happened on Tuesdays. But almost every other freaky thing—dozens of them—happened on a *Wednesday*, between midnight and midnight. Which, if you remember, was also when the Gentle kid must have died."

So it wasn't back to square one, after all. I felt mighty relieved. But it probably meant I was going to be spending at least another week on this one, so I was a bit disappointed, too. "Wednesday, huh?"

"Thursday."

Now I was losing my temper. "But you just said . . . !"

"No, I mean that's Thursday—over there." He pointed to where a silky black Mercedes was just pulling into the reserved parking space in front of the office. "He's back."

We waited until our guy had gone in before following. I didn't want to spook him. I'd chased enough weirdos for one day.

The inner office door was locked, but I leaned on it and it popped open. Grayson Thursday didn't look as surprised as he should have, but I don't think it's because he was expecting us. He just wasn't very good at showing human emotions.

"Okay," I growled. "Sit down. You aren't going anywhere until we have some answers."

He did manage *puzzled* pretty well. "Didn't we finish our conversation earlier?"

"Can that crap. Tell us the truth about Monk's Point." I flopped the stack of printouts down on his desk. "Tell us why stuff's been happening there for a hundred years, and probably more. And why it always seems to happen on the same damn day of the week."

His mouth worked for a moment. He really didn't look right and it was starting to bug me. If you're going to wear a disguise, at least *try* to be convincing. I yanked out my gun and stuck it in his face. "I'm losing my temper here. You're a lousy fake, you know? Your watch is upside down, your shoes are on the wrong feet, and your pupils don't contract when the light changes. Now talk to us or I'll blow your head into little bits. That may not bother you personally, but I'm betting that at the least it'll be an inconvenience." I was also betting on the fact that he wouldn't know and couldn't guess that I'm not the kind of guy to shoot except in self-defense. Sometimes when you're huge and red and scary looking like me, a bluff is your best move.

He waved his hands frantically. "No! Don't! We have no right!"

Now he'd confused me again. "No right to what?"

"We have no right to damage this body." He patted himself gingerly, as if it was a rented tux and he was afraid he might wrinkle it. "It is only borrowed. Its owner is in a comatose state, but he may recover someday. Please do not ignite your weapon."

I turned to Albie Bayless, who looked pretty confused. I felt sorry for him. Even I'm not completely used to this stuff, even though I do it for a living. "Sit down, Albie," I said. "I think we're finally going to get some answers."

As you've guessed," Grayson Thursday said, "my people are not natives of your earth. Or, to be more exact, we are native only to a small part of your world— the portion that happens on the day you call Thursday."

"I'm lost already," said Albie cheerfully. "Or I've finally gone crazy."

"Our dimension intersects with yours, but at an angle, so to speak—our lives only touch yours once every seven of your days. We have explored your dimension, but we have no physical existence here and normally cannot interact with the inhabitants, so our visits had only ever been for the furtherance of science . . . until things went wrong. You are so far from us, so different, that other than these few scientific expeditions we might as well be in different universes."

"Thursday's child has far to go," I said.

"What's that?" Thursday asked.

"A nursery rhyme. Bayless, you must know it. Monday's child is fair of face, Tuesday's child is full of grace, Wednesday's child is full of woe, Thursday's child has far to go . . . And so Grayson's people are Thursday's children, I guess."

Grayson Thursday nodded. "Very appropriate—disturbingly so. Because it is not us but Wednesday's children who are the problem. They are indeed *full of woe*, and it is our fault. We bred them too well. We gave them enough life to be aware of their own condition, their own . . . shortcomings."

"Okay, now you lost me," I said. "Try again."

"We are an old race." He shook his head. "We were tired of striving, of struggling. We wanted rest. So we created a race of servants for ourselves. Not like us—we made them primitive, without emotions . . . or so we thought. Creatures that would not object to servitude."

"To slavery, you mean." I scowled. "Let me guess. They didn't feel the same way about it as you expected them to."

"After many thousands of years, yes, they did become restless." It was hard to tell, but the stiff face looked a little ashamed. "There was an . . . uprising. We realized that we had created a permanent problem. Our servants were more numerous than us. We could not destroy them—we are not that kind of race."

"In other words, you could make and keep slaves but you couldn't kill them."

"You mock the complexity of our problem," Thursday said sadly. "But it is more or less true. So our greatest thinkers devised a way to solve the problem. We found a parallel dimension, one that had no outlet back into our world. We transported our unruly servants there and left them to make their own lives. We even apologized, but they were too savage, too discontented to feel anything but hatred toward us."

"Imagine that." I sat up and tucked my gun back in its holster. "Let me guess. The place you dumped your slaves leaks into our dimension. Right here at Monk's Point."

He sighed. It was the closest to human he'd seemed so far. "Yes. We did not know that at the time, of course, or we would have sent them somewhere else. Apparently all our parallel dimensions intersect your timeline here in this dimension. Thus, the Wednesday Men, as you might term them, imprisoned one dimension over from us, full of woe—and anger. And once a week, if conditions are right, their prison touches on this world."

"So why are *you* here? And what are you doing about Monk's Point?"

Thursday grimaced. "We have done the best we could to keep them there. We have filled the place with attractive host bodies—you see, like my people and I, they have no physical forms of their own here, and must find things to occupy. Thus, we have filled the house with once-living shells and other objects to attract them—the things you supposed to be museum pieces, the preserved animals and such. And the house is warded with various other defenses designed to hold our former servants inside. The combination of these two is generally effective, but not perfect, I'm sad to say. Sometimes the flow from what you would call the Wednesday dimension is very strong and they spill out even past these restraints. That is when . . . unfortunate things happen."

"Yeah. And your job is to show up here once a week after the damage has been done, when your Thursday dimension opens into ours, and pay off the victims or their families. To keep them quiet, or just to ease your own consciences?"

"Please." He actually looked pained. "We encourage silence, of course, but I am here only to repair, in a small measure, the harm we have done." He shook his head. "We did not mean this to happen, but we no longer have the power to move our former servants to another place. They have grown too strong, too canny—we could never trick them again as we did the first time."

"Well, isn't this just sweet," I said, and looked at Albie, who was busy scribbling notes. "Why are you bothering, Bayless? You'll never be able to print this story."

He looked shocked, his face suddenly old and helpless. "What do you mean?"

"Well, leaving out the fact that you'd get put in a nuthouse, let's not forget that you called in the B.P.R.D., and this is now government jurisdiction. But we've got a bigger problem, anyway." I turned back to Grayson Thursday. "Do you want to make up for what you've done? End this problem once and for all?"

"Of course, but it cannot be done . . ."

"Hey, buddy, in our dimension, we never say *cannot*. For one thing, we use contractions." I stood up. "I'll tell you what you need to do." I grabbed Albie's pen and handed it to him. "You'd better write this down, because I'm guessing your dimension goes back out of phase with us at midnight, so we won't be seeing each other for a week. If you get this wrong, we're all in big, *big* trouble."

"Like what?" Albie Bayless asked.

I would have liked to reassure him, but I wasn't in a reassuring mood. "Like end-of-the-world trouble."

It was Tuesday morning when they flew me back into Sonoma County Airport. Albie was waiting for me. He was definitely looking old and tired, like maybe he was wishing he'd taken this being-retired thing more seriously. Getting a glimpse of what squirms under the rock of everyday reality can do that for you. I definitely wasn't going to let him get any closer to the lighthouse than I had to.

"How was your trip?" he asked.

"Connecticut, what's there to say?" I told him. "The guys at the Bureau say hi. A bunch of them still remember you from '69."

"That's nice," he said. "And how was New Orleans?"

"Even freakier than usual. I did get to spend a nice night on the town." I have some good friends in New Orleans, and there are a few places I can go and eat red beans and listen to music where nobody bats an eye at me. I like that.

"And your . . . shopping?"

"Good, I think—I hope. We'll see. There's no recipe book for this stuff—we kind of make it up as we go along."

It was a pleasant-enough trip west to the coast and Caldo Bay—you could smell and see spring on the way—but I wasn't really looking forward to visiting Monk's Point. As he drove, Albie filled me in on what had been happening, not that there was much news. The only excitement in town was that Bobby Gentle was spending what he called *his insurance money* like it was water, and there was a permanent twenty-four-hour party going on out at his house, with all the local rummies and freeloaders prominently represented.

"I can't help thinking about that poor kid—or at least his body," I said. "The Wednesday Men must have squeezed his soul right out of it, then kept the body running until they got bored or lost control over it. You never saw anything so empty and so lost."

Albie shuddered. "Come on, don't."

When we arrived chez Bayless, I opened my two suitcases and started spreading stuff out on the table. Albie watched me with wide eyes as I counted and sorted. "What is all that?"

"Fighting gear," I said as I shoved things into a knapsack. "And some other tricks. It's how we're going to take it to the Wednesday boys, basically."

"How's that going to work?"

"You mean, how do I *hope* it's going to work? I'd rather tell you after I live through it—if I manage. It'll be less embarrassing that way." I wasn't feeling all that confident, to be honest. "You got a beer?"

The afternoon ticked away in small talk and me packing and repacking my knapsack and coat pockets about a hundred times. At one point I was making Albie so nervous I got up and took a walk along the headlands above the ocean. The lighthouse at Monk's Point stuck up like a warning finger. I turned my back on it and concentrated on the dark-green water and the white chop kicked up by the rising wind. Seagulls banked and keened. It was like standing at the edge of the universe. Which, if I thought about what was going to open up in a few hours just half a mile away, was pretty much the case.

So much for putting my mind at ease.

After dark had come down good and solid, I let Albie drive me up to the bottom of the hill at the edge of the Monk's Point property. "You go home now," I said. "Don't get any stupid ideas about coming to help me, no matter what happens—you'll wind up doing the 'Thriller' dance alongside the Gentle kid. Come back at dawn Thursday."

"That's more than twenty-four hours from now!"

"I'm aware. If I'm not waiting for you then, go home and call the Bureau."

Albie shook my hand and tried to smile. "Second time, damn it," he said.

"Second time what?"

"First Zodiac, then this," he said. "Second time I've been sitting on the story of the century and both times you wouldn't let me write it."

"Oh, you can write it," I told him as I got out and headed for the fence. "Feel free. You just can't show it to anyone."

Inside the house I picked a spot just a few yards away from the grandfather clock, which was almost ten feet tall and as ornate as a baroque chapel. Once I'd got my equipment set up, I hunkered down to wait. About ten minutes to midnight, with the wind blowing hard outside and the breakers crashing below, I turned on the special lights. They didn't make the place any brighter, of course—they weren't that kind of lights. But when I put on the blue quartz goggles the boys at the Bureau had whipped up for me, all of a sudden I could see all kinds of things I couldn't before, including how the air seethed and glowed around the big clock, and how the thing itself didn't look much like a clock anymore, but like something a lot less ordinary and a lot more complex.

"We put it there to keep the fabric of the wound in space-time from getting any larger," Thursday had told me. "We can't close the hole back up, but the clock construct will keep it from getting any worse."

Based on what he could tell me, I'd had the Bureau's tech boys and girls get to work, and so, with my special lights and special goggles, I was actually able to see what was happening as midnight came and the Wednesday dimension opened into our own.

It wasn't pretty.

The clock began to strike midnight. On the twelfth toll, the space around the clock—there's no other way to put it—split open. What came pouring out was light like a bad bruise and wisps of something smoky yet as liquid as dripping glue that nevertheless had the shape of living creatures, with limbs and a depressing bump where a head should be. Their eyes were empty black holes, but they were holes that melted and ran like the yolks of soft-boiled eggs. Flapping, ragged mouths gaped beneath them, and I was grateful I couldn't hear the noise they made, because I could feel it vibrating in my bones and even that was sickening. Some of them floated off to occupy the stuffed animals, but the rest headed straight toward me, figuring maybe they'd force me out of my body like they'd forced the Gentle kid out of his. Just thinking about it made me really angry.

I turned on the "brass knuckles," as the technicians had named them, which looked like a couple of glass-and-wire watchbands, one of them big enough to stretch over the Hand of Doom. For a moment I felt the vibration they made, then my hands just . . . *weren't* anymore. I couldn't feel them at all. I hoped that meant that the Wednesday Men would. I stepped toward the clock.

"You're not going anywhere, Sloppy Face," I told the nearest of them as he came at me. I took a swing. There wasn't much in the way of a satisfying impact, but a kind of snap and sizzle like an electrical shock. The thing flailed backward, its nasty mouth all hooty and shocked. I grinned. "Didn't like that, huh? Well, come and see what we're serving on Wednesdays around here from now on!"

I waded into them. It was the donnybrook of all donnybrooks and it went on for hours. It was like flying all the way to Asia with in-flight entertainment by the Spanish Inquisition. I could only touch them with my hands, but they could climb into the bodies around me and hit, scratch, and bite. But the gloves put me partially on their plane, I guess. Sometimes they grabbed me and it burned, burned bad.

It went on and on. First they'd push me back, swarm over me until I thought I was done, but I'd keep slugging until they started to cry. Then for a little while they'd retreat and huddle in the glowing depths of the clock, just inside the gap into their dimension, and look out at me like eels hiding in the rocks, whispering to each other in a deep, soundless rumble I could feel in my teeth. That would give me a few minutes to rest before they broke out and tried me again. Like I said, hours went by, and I had only one thought: Keep 'em here till Wednesday's almost over. Don't let 'em past.

I had a few other weapons from the tech boys, but I knew ultimately I wouldn't be able to push them all back by myself. I just had to hang in and keep them in the vicinity of the clock until the rest of the plan kicked in. When I absolutely couldn't make it another moment without rest, I chucked one of my precious supply of vibration-augmented grenades at them, which disrupted them and probably hurt them like hell, too—in any case, each grenade sent them flapping and slurping back into the breach for a bit. Then they'd get back their courage and come at me again.

It was pretty much like the Spartans at Thermopylae. I had to stop them and keep them here. As long as they were busy trying to kill me, either in the bodiless form that I could only see because of the goggles, or occupying the various stuffed-animal corpses, we had a chance. If they got beyond the perimeter, we were in trouble.

And, yeah, they used everything—stag and boar heads jumping off the walls, gouging and biting, stuffed ferrets breaking loose from their pedestals to run snapping up my trouser legs. Even the giant Kodiak bear made a reappearance about six in the morning, at a moment when I was feeling particularly exhausted. Still, after about half an hour rolling around with it I managed to break off its arms, then let out all its stuffing with a Gurkha knife.

Things got a little quieter as the sun rose Wednesday morning—the W. Men didn't seem to like the light very much—but I couldn't afford to turn my back on them and I certainly didn't dare sleep. I popped a few amphetamine tablets I'd brought with me and did my best to pay attention. I walked around the place beating the random crap out of anything alive that shouldn't have been, trying to keep all activity confined to the area around the clock. I did have time to down a sandwich in the middle of the day, which was nice. I'd brought a sack lunch, including two packages of Twinkies. It's the little things that make fighting for the survival of our dimension worthwhile.

Damn, I was tired, though. Things began to ramp up again as the sun set on Wednesday night—the things might not have understood who I was or what I was doing, but they were clearly getting frustrated as hell. As soon as the dark came they were all over me again in earnest. I can't really tell you what happened for the next several hours. I just fought to stay alive, using my vibration-enhanced hands and weapons on the things themselves, using the clubs and knives I'd brought with me to beat the unholy bejabbers out of any of the stuffed corpses that they hid them-selves in the way hermit crabs used seashells.

The last hour before midnight was the worst. I think they'd begun to get an inkling that I meant to do more than deprive them of their fun for a single week, and if I thought they'd fought hard before, I hadn't seen anything. I wished for about the hundredth time I'd brought more help from the Bureau, but I hadn't wanted to risk anyone else. I still had no idea what was going to happen at the end—for all I knew, we'd wind up with a scorched hole a mile wide where the town had been, or something even worse, like a smoking rip in the space-time continuum.

At the end, they finally got me. I was boneless as a flatworm, exhausted, battered, sucking air but not catching my breath, and to be honest, I couldn't even remember why I was fighting. A bunch of them charged and pulled me down, then they swarmed over me like giant moaning jellyfish. That was it, I knew. All over. I was too tired to care.

Then, from what seemed like a hundred miles away, I heard the grandfather clock begin to chime, a surprisingly deep, slow sound, and suddenly the light around me changed color, from purple-blue to a bright reddish-orange. The things on top of me slithered off, buzzing in surprise, as a host of new shapes burst from the clock. These didn't look a thing like human beings, but they didn't look like the Wednesday Men either, and I knew that Grayson Thursday had kept his word and brought his friends. The cavalry had come.

"Pull them back in!" I shouted, although the Thursday folk probably couldn't understand me or perhaps even hear me. Nevertheless, they knew what to do. The orange, glowing shapes grabbed my attackers and all the other Wednesday Men and began to drag them back toward the shimmering lights of the big clock. Not that the moaning jellyfish-things went without a fight—people were dying here, that was clear, even if they didn't look like people.

It seemed to go on for an hour, but it must have happened during the twelve times the clock struck. At the end, the last of the glowering Wednesday shapes had been pulled back into the breach, and one of the Thursday Men looked back at me with his face that wasn't a face.

"Thanks, buddy!" I shouted. "Now I suggest you all duck!" I pulled out the egg grenade. I'd saved it for last, saved it carefully. Not only was it set to the same vibrational field as the Wednesday Men, and that of their entire dimension, but I'd had one of my friends down in New Orleans prepare it for me, so the grenade itself was taped to a black hen's egg full of serious hoodoo powder. See, hoodoo magic is crossroads magic, and if a place where one world runs into another isn't a crossroad, I don't know what is. I'd gone to see the folks who knew how to deal with such things. *Gris gris gumbo ya ya,* baby.

One of the Wednesday Men had got away and was oozing back toward the breach and our world, mouth wide in an unheard roar of frustration. "Hey, Soupy,"

I shouted. "Regards from Baron Saturday!" I pulled the pin and threw the hoodoo-egg grenade.

I'd never seen half the colors that explosion made and I hope I never see them again—they hurt my eyes something fierce and made my brain all itchy. Not only did the blast seem to close the breach, it blew the clock itself to fragments and started big pieces of roof beam falling down as well. It was all I could do to crawl out into the post-midnight darkness before the walls themselves started to collapse. The last thing I saw before I passed out was the lighthouse tower shiver and then crumble, falling down into the ocean in big white chunks.

Albie Bayless found me in the morning. He stared at the ruins like a kid who's not only seen Santa Claus but been given a supersonic ride to the North Pole strapped onto the runners of the fat man's sleigh.

"What happened?"

"I held the pass," I told him. "It's closed now."

"For good?"

I groaned as I sat up. "I'm not sure. That's why I've got one more thing to do." I limped over to the spot at the edge of the property where I'd left my last little surprise. I ached all over, and judging by the worried expression on Albie Bayless's face, I must have looked pretty bad, too. It hurt even to lift the lead box, which was about the size of a tool chest. Normally I could have picked it up with a finger and thumb.

"What's that?"

"Something we're going to leave behind." I led him back to the wreckage of the Monk's Point house and picked a blackened patch of open ground. I dug a hole and put the lead box in it. I tried not to read the stuff scratched on it. My friend in New Orleans had said it would work and that's all I needed to know. She's a smart lady.

"But what *is* it?" Albie asked, as I kicked dirt over it.

"That box contains the mortal remains of a man named Albert Dupage," I said. "Killed half a dozen men because he claimed they were cheating him at cards. Killed his family too, wife and kids, but that was another time. Killed a sheriff and a deputy, and the local circuit preacher as well. Meanest, craziest man in all of St. Bernard Parish, everyone says. When a posse finally tracked him in the swamp and shot him down like a mad dog, he was buried at the crossroads just to keep his evil spirit from finding its way back home." I smiled. Even that hurt. "I figure we'll leave him here to guard *this* crossroad, just in case those Wednesday boys get an idea about coming back. They'll have to get through Albert, and I don't think it'll be easy."

There was one more part of the Monk's Point story. As I was recuperating the next afternoon in the sunshine of the front yard at Albie Bayless's place—Albie himself was in the house, putting raisins or some other damn thing in his chili—I heard a rustling in the bushes and looked up. The figure standing there wasn't naked any more. It was wearing somebody's pink bathrobe stolen off a wash line, but the new garment was a little too small to conceal the Y-shaped autopsy scar. This time, though, he was looking right at me, and there was an intelligence to his face that hadn't been there last time.

"Rufino?" I asked. "That you?" I asked calmly, but I was a little worried in case it was one of the Wednesday Men who'd got out before the breach was shut.

"Roof," he said. "That's what everyone calls me." The boy shook his head slowly. "Used to call me. 'Cause I'm dead now."

"So I heard." I beckoned him over. "Sit down. How are you feeling?"

"Not too bad. I don't like the sun much, though, so I think I'll stay here in the shade. It makes my skin feel bad—makes it smell, too. Kinda like bad bologna. You know what that smells like?"

"Yeah, 'fraid so. What brings you here?"

He shrugged. He was still a teenager, just a dead one. "I don't know. You saved me, kind of. I mean, I got out of that place when you blew up the door. Found my way back into my body, I guess."

"Ah. So they were sort of—holding you prisoner?"

"I guess. It's all kind of confusing. One minute I was looking at the old haunted lighthouse, the next minute I get, I don't know, sucked out of my body, and I'm in some kind of dark, windy place listening to these weird noises. It was like going to a really, really slow Day on the Green concert. On bad acid, even. Then a bunch of *really* weird stuff happened, and there was you, and an explosion, and I got out . . . and I was back in here again." He frowned and shook his lank hair out of his face. "But look what those doctors did to my body! I don't even have blood any more."

"Yeah, that can't be fun."

"Thing is, you're leaving, right?" He looked at me with the most hope I've ever seen on a dead person's face. "I want to go with you. I already hated this place when I was alive. Can you imagine how messed up it's going to be for me now I'm dead?"

I thought about it for a moment. "You know, I think the folks at the Bureau would be willing to give you a place to stay, Rufin . . . Roof." I nodded. "Just hang around for a little while, then Bayless can drive both of us. I've got a private Bureau plane waiting for me." I smiled. "It's not like you've got a lot of stuff to pack."

"No," he said seriously. "But there is one thing I gotta do first. Can you come along?"

"Where?"

"I need to say goodbye to my dad."

You haven't heard a houseful of drunken rummies scream until you've heard what happened when Roof showed up at his dad's house in mid-party, bloodless, scalpless, and very obviously dead. The few who could keep their legs (and bladders, and sphincters) under control long enough to run outside all ran into me, which probably didn't help their state of mind, either. Albie told me later that about half Bobby Gentle's friends sprinted straight to town after this life-changing experience and threw themselves on the mercy of Jesus, care of the nearby Monk's Point Presbyterian Church.

"I told him he ought to get his act together," Roof said as he rejoined me. I could see his dad lying slumped in the doorway of the house where he'd fainted, a beer still clutched in his fist. "I don't think he'll listen, though."

"Don't underestimate your powers of persuasion," I said as we walked away. I could hear some of the guests still shrieking inside. "You may have a future on the religious circuit, kid."

I took him back to Albie's place and found him some duct tape so he could stick the top of his head back on until we could fix him properly back at the Bureau.

Wow," said Ted. He looked a little pale himself. "I mean . . . Jeez. That's pretty . . . So what happened to the kid?"

"He stayed with us for a couple of years. Worked a few missions for the B.P.R.D., but his heart wasn't in it. So to speak." I smiled as I thought of Roof. He had been a slacker before the word existed—he just happened to be a dead one. The last thing he wanted to do was spend his afterlife working an office job. "Last I heard, he was in Yakutata, Alaska, surfing year round. He likes it 'cause it's real cold there, and nobody ever asks why he always wears a wetsuit."

"And the Thursday Men?" asked Liz.

"Haven't heard from them—or their woeful buddies. But I can't help worrying about it sometimes."

"Why's that?" Liz smiled at me. She thinks I think too much. She's probably right.

"Well, if those two dimensions just happened to run smack into ours, what about the others? What about the rest of the days of the week? Why haven't we heard anything yet from the Monday Men or the Tuesday Men?" I leaned forward. "They're probably *already here* and we don't even know it. In fact, you could be one of them, Ted. It would explain your singing voice." I slapped my hand on the table. "Now, who's playing cards?"

PRODUCE
AMBER BENSON

Bertha knelt by the shelf that held up the packages of cottony white toilet paper and listened to the slow clop-clop sound, like horses made. She peered under the shelf, but didn't see any horses. Instead, she noticed a snaky, scarlet-red thing that drew her eye just as surely as if it were a screaming fire engine racing down the road.

She knew this because just such a thing had happened that very morning while she'd been strapped inside her car seat watching the world rush by the car window. There had been three men in yellow hanging from the back end of the truck, their fluorescent-striped arms tied to their sides by equipment and the onrushing air. She didn't know why, but the experience had tickled her fancy more than anything she could remember. She'd laughed out loud and pointed with a sticky finger (she'd just eaten a marshmallow) at the fire truck as it disappeared around the corner and out of sight.

It had been an eventful morning.

Now, here she was, the cold floor biting into her knees, staring at something that might very well turn out to be even more interesting than the fire truck. She got down on her elbows, the cold floor biting them, too, and reached her hand into the small space between the floor and the grocery-store shelving unit. It fit with a little bit of room left over. Having gotten her whole hand into the space easily enough, she pushed the rest of her arm—right up to her shoulder—inside, as well. She stretched out her fingers, extending them as far as they would go. Angrily, she realized that her reach wasn't going to be long enough: she was still much too far away from her prey even with the lip of the shelf pressing painfully into her shoulder blade and her fingers stiff as fish sticks.

She made a weird sound that she had never made before low in her throat—it reminded her of the sound Henry, her kitty cat, made when she tried to touch his fur, and opened and closed her hand in frustration. It seemed that no matter what she did fate was gonna keep her from reaching her goal and it made her mad!

Bertha peeked under the shelf again. The red snaky thing was all the way in the next aisle. No way her arm was gonna reach that far. Sometimes she could be so silly.

Suddenly, fate put another crimp in her plan.

She watched in horror as the rubbery red thing began to move away from her, sliding down the next aisle. If she didn't do something now, it was gonna be gone forever!

She kept her cheek pressed against the floor, her eyes locked on the disappearing red thing, its slinky redness like a silent Pied Piper beckoning her to follow. She began to crawl along her own aisle, the polished floor like ice, hoping she was fast enough to keep pace with the swishing red thing.

At the end of the aisle she came to an abrupt halt, daunted by the vastness of the space that loomed above her. The grocery store hadn't seemed very scary when she was safe back in the aisle, or even when she had originally come into the building with Esmeralda, but now that it had opened up in such a strange manner—the shelving replaced by gleaming basins of silver into which piles of brightly colored fruits and vegetables had been piled—the whole thing frightened her terribly.

Too scared to move forward, she sat back on her haunches, her little legs splayed out in front of her. She put her fingers in her mouth and chewed, hoping the sweet repetition of sucking would calm her down.

It did.

When she felt a little better, she got back onto her hands and knees, and took a tentative crawl forward. That's when she caught sight of the red thing again, but now it was further away than before. It was hiding behind one of the big tables that held up the basins of fruit, just peeking out enough to make her drool with anticipation. She moved forward, ignoring the feet and other obstacles she encountered in her path.

She decided that when she finally caught the thing, she was gonna put it in her mouth and chew it until it fell apart like her teething ring had.

Then the red thing moved again, sliding behind the fruit table and disappearing, making Bertha want to cry with frustration. Instead, she just kept crawling toward the place where she'd last seen her prey. She slid along the glossy floor, her knees and hands beginning to hurt, but when she reached the fruit table and turned the corner, the red thing wasn't there.

She flopped down and pressed her body into the cold floor tiles, her eyes shut tightly in rage and frustration. She began to cry. The tears coursed down her face, pooling on the dirty floor.

Her wails grew in pitch and fervor until they began to draw a crowd, gawkers that just stood there like dollies instead of helping her out, instead of finding the glorious red thing and bringing it to her to chew on!

Suddenly, she felt something strong and warm curl around her, sliding her across the floor. Then a huge hand picked her up, like *she* was a dolly. She opened one eye and looked up at her savior. The face that greeted her was strange and wonderful. She reached out a plump finger and poked it into one of the man's red cheeks. The man raised an eyebrow, an inscrutable look on his face, making Bertha giggle.

"Whatcha got there, HB?"

It was a woman's voice. Lower than Esmeralda's, but just as soft and melodious. Bertha tilted her head so that she could see the owner of the voice. The woman was thin and beautiful with twinkling eyes and cherry-colored lips. Bertha instantly liked the look of the dark-haired lady . . . but she liked the man with the thick red face more, so she turned her attention back to him. He was wearing a long dark coat and had two stubs on his head like round, thick pancakes. They looked like they were broken, and she wondered if they hurt. She reached out to touch them, but he gently lowered her out of reach.

"I don't know, Liz, but it's in the produce aisle so it must be edible."

There was a shout from across the room, and Bertha heard the hysterical lilt of Esmeralda's broken English getting louder as the old woman rushed toward them. Bertha watched, fascinated, as Esmeralda reached them, her eyes filled with a terror that Bertha realized could only be directed at the big, red man. She stared as Esmeralda made the sign of the cross before holding out shaking arms to take her. The red man gave up his prize easily, and Bertha found her body instantly folded into the old woman's expansive bosom, her face pressed against Esmeralda's collarbone.

Feeling warm and protected now, but still curious about the red man and his friend, she clambered into a sitting position in Esmeralda's arms so she could get a final look at them as she was taken back to where she knew the stroller she'd escaped from was parked.

That's when she saw it, the red thing that had so eluded her in her quest. It was the red man's tail! She reached out her hand, wanting desperately to escape her nanny's arms and go back for the big red chew toy! She began to cry hysterically, but she knew it would be to no avail.

It was too late. She had completely missed her chance.

Hellboy and Liz watched the sobbing little girl and her keeper as they disappeared down the cold-beverage aisle. It was a long time before the toddler's cries finally died away.

"And *that* is exactly why I hate grocery stores," Hellboy said, as he watched Liz pick up an apple and put it in her basket.

Liz only smiled thoughtfully to herself and moved on down the produce aisle.

REPOSSESSION
BARBARA HAMBLY

Aswan
1962

The south of Egypt was a weird place to be in the summer of 1962, especially if you happened to have horns and a tail. Workers were tearing up the red-gold hills above the First Cataract for the Aswan Dam; archaeologists were tramping around figuring out which temples they were going to cut to pieces and save, and which they'd leave to the rising waters of Lake Nasser. Spirits who used to be gods were coming to the surface, who'd sunk away into the parched wadis a thousand years ago; nasty little dust-devil afreets that had spent the last three millennia sliding in and out of mummies' brains in the rock-cut tombs now whispered in the date groves along the river, looking for something to bite. The air stank with psychic debris, supernatural slime stirred up from the bottom of Time.

At the Bureau for Paranormal Research and Defense, we *knew* every demon-hunter on the planet had to be out there with their little magic jars.

They flew me into Aswan with a Professor Harik from the American University of Beirut. His Arabic was better than mine at the time and he was supposed to act as my contact with Yusef ibn-Karim, Our Man in Aswan. The night I met Raisha bint-Tahayet, Harik was back at the hotel, feebly sipping warm Seven-Up in between trips to the john. One of the best things about having my particular consti-tution is that I can eat anything anywhere in the world without spending the rest of the night looking at the plumbing fixtures.

But the dumb bastard had insisted on having Scotch on the rocks at the airport instead of a beer—which doesn't need ice in it, or in his case, frozen amoeba soup pumped up from the river.

But maybe it was just something he needed to learn, along with, *let's not* ever *do that again.*

Whatever. That night in 1962, I was out on a red-rock promontory across the Nile from Elephantine Island at sunset, waiting for Yusef ibn-Karim alone.

The B.P.R.D. had budgeted a permanent agent in Aswan in 1959, when the surveyors were still making their plans. But good boony ops are hard to recruit. Who the hell wants to live in deep cover for three years in one-room workers' housing in a company town where the big news is the weekly shipment of cigarettes from Cairo? This was before the internet, or even TV, in most of Egypt. Hell, in that neighborhood it was before indoor toilets. Ibn-Karim wasn't bad, just inexpe-rienced. And though the Professor knew in the marrow of his bones that somebody *had* to be out there collecting thaumaturgical hairballs, we hadn't heard a thing.

Until last week.

So here I was, smoking in the fast-falling African twilight and listening to the demons whisper in the rocks. Across the river I could see the faint glow in the sky above Aswan, though the dark mass of the island blocked out most of the town itself. Behind me, where bone-dry hills merged with the biggest desert in the world, the sky faded, cinnamon to indigo to star-splattered black.

Feet crunched on the path. Tobacco, frankincense, and ras el hanout. I stubbed out my smoke.

"Who is there?" Whoever it was, she spoke fair English. "I am here from ibn-Karim."

"Where is he?" I didn't move. In the shadows, I can look pretty much like a rock if I need to.

"He is dead." She turned her face in my direction, and I could see she saw my eyes. In darkness they're kind of hard to miss. I saw her step back, and her breath hissed, flattening the black cotton of her veil against her lips. *"Al-walad al-Jahannum—"* My Arabic was for crap, but I knew damn well what *that* meant. Then instead of running screaming back to the river, like most people who come on me unawares in the dark, she stepped toward me again and said, "Ibn-Ghaalib killed him, the thief who steals demons. The thief who stole the demon out of my own flesh, Azuzar, that has dwelt in me for thirty years."

The moon, just clearing temple ruins on the crest of the island, showed me the glitter of her tears.

Her name was Raisha bint-Tahayet. She was a Berber out of western Sudan—the veil was for the benefit of her Egyptian neighbors, and she took it off once she was clear there weren't any Muslim men around. She was forty-two and looked nearly sixty, which is what living on the fringe of a desert does to people with no money (among other things, I found out later). She'd been possessed by a zar spirit since the age of thirteen.

"One cannot be the *kodia* of the zar dance, unless one is possessed oneself," she told me, as we passed through the date groves that fringed the river here. In her dark *hijab* and *abaya* she moved like a shadow, silent. A small motorboat was tied up on the bank: ibn-Karim's, whose friend she'd been. It's not a popular opinion, but I was damn glad just about then that the government had told every crocodile hunter in Africa to come to Aswan and help themselves. "One lives with the zar. Azuzar gave me strength. Here in this country, many women have need of a zar's strength to survive."

I could believe it. I hadn't been in southern Egypt long, but it sure wasn't New York.

"What'd your husband think?"

Raisha bint-Tahayet smiled. She was missing a couple of side teeth. With its elegant bone structure, her face was still beautiful. "My husband was an exceptional man," she said. "My sons—" Dark eyes, hollow from sleepless grief, ducked away from mine. "The zar dance is forbidden by our faith. I think it was my sons who helped ibn-Ghaalib lay hold of me ten nights ago and take the zar away 'for the good of my soul.' Allah knows what is good for a woman's soul—"

We got into the boat, cast off. My weight sank it to the gunwales.

"—but the loss of Azuzar has all but destroyed my heart. Yusef said this man he was to meet sought ibn-Ghaalib because of what he does; because he traps demons, and makes them his slaves. Is this true?"

"Something like that."

"Are you this man's slave, then?"

"Nope." The word came out maybe a little too fast and a little too hard, and I turned away from her gaze and lit another cigarette. After a minute, I looked back at her and asked, "The zar your slave?"

She shook her head.

"You his?"

No. "You don't understand," she said.

Something about her eyes told me I probably didn't want to.

But I'm curious. Always have been. It would have been safer for me to wait out in the alleyway of the old town where she took me, and to grab ibn-Ghaalib when he came out of the joint they'd rented for the dance. But I wanted to see.

Professor Bruttenholm, I knew, would want to know what the zar ceremony was like from my perspective.

So instead of going back to Raisha's room in the Old Town and drinking coffee for a couple hours—the Egyptian kind you have to chew for awhile before it quits chewing back—I had her smuggle me in through the back door of the old house where the zar dance was being held.

A couple of women were in the front room when we got there, setting up an altar on one of those brass tray tables in the center of the room. Raisha waited till they'd gone out to bring in whatever else they needed, then led me to what could have started life as a changing room or an office; anyhow, it had a wooden door with a grille on it, and a hook on the inside. We shut ourselves in just as the Decorations Committee came back with an armload of white tablecloths and bowls of munchies to put on the altar. Somebody set out a jar for contributions.

"Many women are possessed by the zar," murmured Raisha. "Like me, they draw their strength from these spirits—if their husbands are harsh, or their families misuse them. This girl tonight, Naseeba, is wed to an older man, a shoemaker, who treats her like a servant and whose sons show her no respect. So the zar in her rose up, and made her do things she would not have done in her right senses, like smashing the things in his shop, and striking the oldest boy with his own walking stick when he slapped her. It was clear that Naseeba was possessed, so the women of the neighborhood called on the women who dance the zar, to calm the angry spirit, and permit peace to return to the house. The shoemaker," she added, and glanced at me sidelong in the spots of naked electric-bulb glare that came in through the grille, "is paying for the food and the hall.

"I was to have led in this dance," she went on after a minute, while I thought this over in the light of the Psych 101 text I'd read at the Bureau. "I have been *kodia* of the zar dance here for ten years, and my teacher a *kodia* in her turn. With so many women coming in with the workers for the dam, our numbers have grown large here. A year ago a man —ibn-Ghaalib—came to join us, a thing not unheard of, though men on the whole do not approve of the zar. He was kind, and had gentle manners. A great many of the women liked him. I never did. In the dance, the zar—*my* zar, Azuzar—would warn me to keep away from him. When I watched him lead a dance some months ago, it seemed to me that instead of simply drawing the possessing spirit out of its subject to the surface, to calm it, he drew it out entirely, captured it in a vessel made of horn and glass that he had put on the altar. There," she said softly, and moved closer to the grille. "There he is."

Yep. It was him. I'd seen his pictures at the Bureau.

The name the Bureau knew him under was Muzafar al-Tair, but he'd had a couple of others; they were all the same guy, anyway. Ectomorph, dark eyes, major schnozz, long dark hair past his shoulders, which changed the way he looked. Since the last shot we'd had of him he'd sprouted one of those foofy little Prince Albert beards, too. There were flecks of silver in it, and a few in his hair, but they didn't fool me. There's a look people get, when they're using occult assistance to keep young. He'd graduated from Oxford in 1910.

It was ibn-Ghaalib, all right.

He came in with the musicians—they were guys, also—and had a boy to carry a big metal trunk for him. Out of this he took his own contributions to the altar—frankincense, bones, a root wrapped in string—then locked it back up again. It reminded me of the voodoo I'd seen, especially once everybody arrived and the music started. Ibn-Ghaalib killed a goat, out in the yard—Mr. Shoemaker's special contribution to the proceedings, and in my opinion they should have stuck the bastard for a camel—and during the dancing, which went on all that night and through the next day and the next night as well, women were coming and going from the kitchen, cooking it. In ceremonies like this—and the same goes for voodoo—there's a big streak of church picnic: everybody brought food.

And everybody danced.

There must have been nearly a hundred people showed up. Most of them were women, neighbors, and friends. You could tell which ones were possessed. As the night deepened and they moved around the altar, whirling in smaller circles, heads lolling, long hair hanging free, you'd see their faces change, sometimes their whole bodies, as other entities than good Muslim wives came up out of their hindbrains and took over. They'd swagger and shout—you see this in voodoo as well—and run to the altar, sometimes drinking from the bottles of rum and Jim Beam standing open there, sometimes chugging from the bowls of the goat's blood, splattering their white clothing with red. A lot of them smoked—demons love tobacco—and the more aggressive of them would grab up swords off the altar and make mock attacks on the male musicians, or the boy who'd carried in ibn-Ghaalib's box, or Mr. Shoemaker, who sat in a corner looking plenty grim. And I've got to admit, a lot of the ladies who did all of the above weren't possessed in the least.

Only glad to have the excuse to act as if they were.

Like I said, you could tell. Or I could, anyway. The music always changed when a zar rose to the surface: goatskin drum, tambourine, a big bronze chime whose note went straight through my skull, and an aluminum washtub. Intricate rhythms, different for each zar, and as the night got later I could feel the mingled energy of frustration and hate and friendship and fear and joy build and focus in that room, like hot sunlight when a kid tortures a slug with a magnifying glass. I could feel the rhythms pulling at me in a way I'd never experienced before—or not within conscious memory, anyway. A way that made my flesh crawl.

The first flash hit me when Naseeba—that good little wife whose zar needed calming down—fell on her knees in front of ibn-Ghaalib, raising her hands palm to palm like a Christian and shouting, of all things, the Hail Mary in Latin. Ibn-Ghaalib reached out to her—they were both swaying in wild circles—and I saw signs written on his palms in green henna, not the usual *baraka* you see all over North Africa, but Lemurian occult marks for the summoning and protection from demons, straight out of Abdul Alhazred's *Necronomicon*. It was hard to hear much, between the music and the shouting in the rest of the room, but I almost didn't need to.

I felt the spells he was calling out. Felt them in my bones.

And for one instant I saw myself—this seven-foot-tall, massive, red-skinned guy in a trench coat—pressed up against the door of that tiny room, the skinny little Berber woman at my side. It didn't last more than a second, then I was back looking through the grille again, gasping, heart pounding—*What the—?*

Swaying together, ibn-Ghaalib brushed Naseeba's face with his spell-written fingers, then rocked his body back, withdrawing slowly, and I could see the zar coming out of her, long strings of glowing ectoplasm trailing from his hands.

Smoke from the kitchen mixed with the overwhelming reek of burning frankincense, and the room was like a stove. Dizziness swamped me, though heat never affects me much, not even Africa in midsummer. The music was deafening but over it I could hear, clear as the hellish chime of that bronze gong striking, ibn-Ghaalib's voice, shouting in the language of the Great Old Ones. *I have to get out of here,* I thought. *I have to . . .*

There was a jolt like I'd been picked up and whacked like a rag doll against a wall, and I was standing on the other side of the little room again, looking at myself: ugly, crimson, not of human flesh. Raisha was gripping my arm, calling my name: "Al-Jahannum—*al-Jahannum*—!" but her voice seemed to come from a long distance away. I felt like I was falling but my body against the door didn't move. The yellow hue in its eyes had dimmed and I knew the heart had stopped. I knew what was going to happen next and memories—those nightmare memories from before my birth on this world—flooded my brain. Helplessness. Panic. Agony.

Raisha pulled a small knife from her belt and drove it with all her strength into my arm.

That tiny sharpness gave me a focus, like a spot of light. I flung my mind on it, gripped at it. Oxygen flooded my lungs and my heart raced like a blender, before I crashed unconscious to the floor.

I think the only reason ibn-Ghaalib didn't take me captive then was because he only had one bottle out on the altar, among all the almonds and dried apricots and smoking pots of frankincense, and that one was for Naseeba's zar. In my dream I was moving through the crowd in the front room, with the women spinning all around me, circling the altar as they spun, their *hijabs* cast aside and sweat splattering from the ends of their long hair. He was moving among them, the zar inside him now, captive, screaming and thrashing to get out. I saw him shed it out of him, weakened and tangled up in the weirds of power like a moth in a web, saw it go into the jar on the altar, that miniature dimensional enclave bounded by silver, pig tusk, and meteor iron. He looked around as he spun. *Who is that?* he shouted, over the clangor of the music. *Who is that?*

He knew I was there, all right.

There were other jars and bottles in his trunk.

As I sank deeper into dreams I could see them—Roman glass, fossil ivory, amber that had been gently carved in vats of human blood. About half of them contained other demons, not all of them zar and not all of them even from Egypt. He'd been collecting for a while.

Why?

They called to me, curses or pleas. One of them had a face that was scarily like Raisha's, only green like a moldering corpse's; and Raisha's long silver-gray hair.

I drifted down past them, into deeper dreams.

At the B.P.R.D., a lot of my education involved stuff that's generally referred to as "things mankind was not meant to know." That's because over the centuries, a hefty percentage of those who *could* figure it out used that knowledge to make trouble for everybody around them. And a lot of it had involved the summoning—and control—of supernatural or ab-natural entities whose psychic energy was greater than what humans could normally utilize without their brains imploding.

Like demons.

Since most of these unhuman entities don't give a rat's ass about human beings except as hors d'oeuvres, when they get out of control—and they often do—the result usually involves somebody having to scrape body parts off the ceiling. That's the tame end of the *What-could-go-wrong?* spectrum.

Having been summoned into this world by the Nazis myself for exactly that reason, I learned a lot about how necromancers use these entities once they get hold of them. Sometimes they end up as slaves and sometimes just as energy sources, cells in an ectoplasmic battery. Sometimes, if the entities are too powerful, they'll be enlisted as allies, but the results of that are never pretty. The B.P.R.D. had already had to clean up a couple of those. I dunno why people never learn, but they don't.

Anyway, for that reason I'd put in a lot of my spare time since the Egyptian government had announced work on the Aswan Dam reading up on folks who were known to be, or suspected of being, interested in collecting demons in bottles.

A lot of these are the usual shlubs who figure their lives will work better if they have a little astral help in getting rich or getting laid, and don't look further than that. Some of them are out to further a Cause—politics or whatever flavor of religion they think will save people in spite of themselves, which pretty much amounts to the same thing.

Ibn-Ghaalib was one of the very dangerous kind because he worked far under the radar and was hard to catch, like a cockroach. He collected enslaved supernatural power sources to sell.

There was no telling where this stuff would go, or to whom.

All that was in my mind as I floated back to the surface of consciousness. It was dim and blast-furnace hot, and smelled like harissa and coffee. By the sounds in the street outside it was full day. I was starving.

In a room close by a door opened and Professor Scotch-and-Dysentery Harik asked softly, "Any change?"

"Not so far." The other voice was Carmichael's, the pilot who'd flown us in from London. I opened my eyes, turned my head on the pillow of a narrow bed. "What'd you find out?" Carmichael went on.

"Yusef ibn-Karim was found slashed to death in the alleyway behind his rooms the day after he contacted the Bureau," reported Harik. "I saw the pictures; it was clearly the work of a demon." The door between the bed-sit where I lay with my feet sticking out over the end of the bed, and the closet-sized kitchen where Carmichael sat, stood open. There were awnings and cheap straw blinds over the kitchen windows but the room was still bright enough to make me squint and hot enough to give an elephant a stroke. The pilot knocked a couple of Camels out of his pack and held one out to Harik, just closing the street door behind him.

"Gimme one of those," I said.

"You okay, Hellboy?" They brought in the kitchen's solitary chair—it seemed to be the only one in the whole apartment—and Harik asked, "Does the light disturb you?"

"No, I'm fine." I sat up, looked around.

"Bint-Tahayet sought me at the hotel when she could not restore you to consciousness." Harik straddled the chair. He looked like he'd lost about ten pounds—which a guy that thin already couldn't afford—and sweat stood out on the long fjords of skin that went back into his graying hairline. "We brought you here, to her room in the Old City. She is out now, making enquiries as to where ibn-Ghaalib might have gone—"

"He's at the dance." I felt gingerly at my bandaged arm where she'd stabbed me. "The zar ceremony—"

"—ended this morning," said Harik. "It took her almost twenty-four hours to find me."

I said, "Crap." No wonder I was hungry.

"She on the level?" Carmichael went back into the kitchen and brought me a wad of flatbread, covered with cooked goat and hummus, takeaway from the ceremony, I guess—never let anybody tell you even the pilots from the B.P.R.D. aren't psychic. "Yeah, it sounds like poor Yusef got his from a demon, but that doesn't mean it wasn't her that sicced one on him."

I shook my head, the dreams coming back to me. "No, ibn-Ghaalib's a demon-hunter, all right. I saw Azuzar, shut up in an amber bottle—"

I winced, a stab of pain going through my head again. Azuzar. The other bottles and jars. Some were old—some were *damn* old. Demon hunters pass these traps along to each other, or steal them from each other and from unsuspecting museums. They have their own whispered network where they're bought and sold. Most of the traps are pretty poozley—they'll hold a poltergeist or a little water-pook, and most of the zar I'd seen at the dance weren't much stronger than that—but there'd been two or three in the collection that could have disabled low-level gods.

One of them—the strongest—I remembered had been empty, set aside in a separate compartment, packed in iron filings and salt.

"He's after something big." I opened my eyes again, looked from Carmichael to Harik. "He came here to fuel up. To trap the little stuff so he can use them when he goes after King Kong."

"He has not been seen since the ceremony," said Harik, as I proceeded to make short work of the flatbread. "When bint-Tahayet found us, it still took time to bring you here—"

"He see you at the dance?" Carmichael handed me a beer. It was warm, but I wasn't bitching.

I nodded, and winced. I'd hit that floor pretty hard. "Who would he be after, Professor?" I looked over at Harik. "What demons—what . . . *entities*—would a man like that go after, if he had the power of about a dozen captive demons to back him up?"

Harik thought about that. He didn't look happy. I wasn't thrilled myself. There's scary crap out there that Necromancers over the millennia have called across into this world and used—or tried to use—to get things their way.

Before he could answer feet clunked on the wooden steps outside the door, and a second later Raisha came into the kitchen, then through into the room where the three of us were. "Allah be praised, the all-merciful, the all-compassionate." She pulled off her veil—I guess she'd established that Harik was a Catholic and didn't care whether she was veiled or not—and sat beside Carmichael on the edge of the bed, making it pretty crowded. "I feared ibn-Ghaalib had taken you, al-Jahannum, as he took Azuzar—"

"I think we are all of us fortunate he did not," said Harik softly. "Egypt is a land full of spirits, even in times of quiet. Had your self, your soul, been drawn out of your body—" He turned to look earnestly at me, "—I think there would be real danger that another demon—an earth-spirit, not a hell-spirit—might have possessed it."

Oh, swell. "You mean *I'd* have been possessed?"

"More like . . ." He paused, thinking. "More like *sublet.* The problem is that none of us understands—I have discussed this with Trevor and I think he has spoken of it to you also—none of us understands the precise relationship of the demon spirit to its flesh. We know it is different from that of mortals; we do not know *how* different. Or what elements—what secrets, what dangers—may be hidden within you."

In the silence that followed the tinny blare of a Cairo radio station from the apartment next door sounded very loud. I knew there'd been a school of thought, while I was being raised in secret in New Mexico, that I should simply have been destroyed while humankind had the chance to do it. I'd heard also that some in the Bureau thought I should have been kept permanently under wraps and studied, instead of being brought up like a more or less normal person. It was only now that I began to realize what a risk the Professor had taken, insisting that I was a human being and should be treated like one. Which party, I found myself wondering, would Professor Harik have been in?

At the moment, there seemed to be only one thing I could say about the whole subject.

"Got another cigarette?" I turned to Raisha. "What'd you find out?"

She pressed one hand swiftly to her mouth, shut her eyes, trying to steady herself. "He was gone from the ceremony by the time I returned there," she whispered. Under decades of sunburn her face looked ashen, sick with anxiety and grief. "No one could say where. I checked at the airport and they knew nothing. But later one of the men there who loads planes for the smugglers—not the official flights, you understand—said that they'd left this morning, that ibn-Ghaalib had his box with him—"

A shiver went through her, and the gaze she turned on me was haunted. "What will they do with him? What do they want with him?"

"What happens to him," I said slowly, "depends on where ibn-Ghaalib was going."

She shook her head, fighting to keep calm against the unthinkable fear that she'd never find him again. Had she been that shook up, when her husband died? *You do not understand,* she'd said . . .

Silently Carmichael got her a Coke from the kitchen, and lit a cigarette for her.

"There is a man named Fuad," she said after a minute, "who flies cargoes in and out of Cairo. Sometimes cigarettes, sometimes *kif,* or women for the workmen's brothels. Or he will take pilgrims to Mecca—anywhere that anyone will pay for the fuel." She swallowed hard, fingers trembling on her cigarette. "These are not official cargo companies, you understand. They pay the men in the tower, and no papers are filed."

Carmichael said, "Shit."

I said, "What kind of plane?"

Raisha looked blank, the way most people do when you ask that question.

"This Fuad ain't the only cargo runner working the airstrip," I said. With Russian money funding an army of manual laborers, I knew Aswan had to be chin deep in smuggled goods. "I saw a lot of old C-40s and gooney birds left over from the War out there when we came in; bigger craft as well. If we know what kind of plane our boy rented, we might get some idea how far he thinks he'll need to go."

We'd come down from London to Aswan in an old C-46 that a grateful government had bestowed on the B.P.R.D., stopping off to refuel in Rome. From Professor Harik's rental Chevy at the edge of the unofficial end of the airstrip, Raisha and I watched while Harik and Carmichael went in and put the fear of God into the boys in the tower.

"Ibn-Ghaalib beat feet out of here the minute the zar ceremony was done," I told her. "So he knows we're on his tail. If he knew to kill Yusef, he may even know who we are. He's been around long enough. So he'll stay away from commercial flights." I gestured at the small planes scattered on the flat pale sand that stretched beyond the regular commercial runway under the brutal glare of the noon sun. "Now, if our pal Fuad flies a C-40, like half the smugglers in Africa, that could be bad news, because he could just be headed for Cairo, to pick up a flight anyplace in the world. A C-40 would also put him in Syria, in Mecca, along the trade routes through the north of Arabia, in Greece, or at the site of ancient Carthage. Any of those places had enough sophisticated occult knowledge in the past to be hiding some truly nasty bogeymen."

Carmichael and Harik emerged from the door at the base of the tower and walked toward us, Carmichael keeping an eye behind him on the airstrip staff. They looked like they'd sell a load of Mecca pilgrims to be chopped up for dog food if the price was right.

"A gooney bird—a DC-3—would expand ibn-Ghaalib's range to sixteen hundred miles before they have to refuel," I went on. "That's the Empty Quarter of Arabia, Baghdad, the mountains of Azerbaijan where there's supposed to be some *really* weird stuff walled up under old monasteries, and the sources of the Nile. Anything bigger is going to cost more, and means one of their hops is longer than sixteen hundred. And that," I said, as Carmichael opened the driver's side door, "means only one place, from here."

"Fuad flies a C-46," Carmichael said.

"All right." I glanced at Harik; he nodded agreement. He knew. "That means he's headed for Timbuktu."

We refueled in Cairo, and again in Tripoli with the sun sinking red over the mountains to the west. The ground crew said another old C-46 had refueled around noon. The descriptions fit ibn-Ghaalib, Fuad, and Fuad's two-man crew. To be on the safe side we kept west and fueled again in Casablanca, because there was no airport then in Timbuktu and we'd have to go from there to Lagos—if we survived.

Harik and I both knew what was supposed to be in Timbuktu.

We took off and headed southeast across the desert, a thousand miles of nothing in the dark.

For four hundred years, Timbuktu was one of the greatest trading cities in the world, the last port on a deadly ocean of sand. Even after the Portuguese cut into the trade in slaves and gold in the sixteenth century, the universities there were famous throughout Islam, both for their studies of the Holy Qur'an and for their production—and preservation—of manuscripts. "We know that a line of adepts of occult knowledge lived and taught there," Professor Harik said softly to Raisha, as those black miles unspooled down below us and Carmichael's flight crew—a young Brit named Thomas and a jarhead Carmichael had borrowed from an air base in Germany—passed around thermos coffee in paper cups. And if you think there was any way we could have left Raisha on the ground in Aswan, think again.

"I will not leave him," she'd said. The look in her eyes was scary. And to me, "You owe me your life."

Well, she was right. I had the uncomfortable feeling that if it hadn't been for her knowing what ibn-Ghaalib could do with demons, I'd have been in that other plane, not this one, cursing and screaming in one of those damn alabaster jars. And God only knew what would be occupying my flesh. Harik knew he—and the Bureau—owed her, too.

Now she sat on one of the carpet-covered wall benches that were the only furnishings in the dark cabin, listening to Harik while I tried to pull together in my mind everything I'd picked up from the Professor, over the years, about what it was ibn-Ghaalib had to be seeking in that pink mud city on the banks of the Niger.

"Manuscripts were preserved among the ancient families of the city," Harik went on, "vast libraries dating back to the days long before the Prophet. Manuscripts collected from Arabia, Persia, Moorish Spain, and India, and brought to the city on the caravans that brought in slaves and ivory and salt. During colonial days wealthy Europeans plundered some of these libraries, carrying them off wholesale to Paris or Berlin. Seeing this, the scholars of Timbuktu hid many of those that remained—thousands of volumes—in caves along the dry rock watercourses in the desert, or buried them in the sand."

Raisha asked, "And that is what he seeks, this ibn-Ghaalib?" Her brows pulled together under the dark edge of the *hijab* that covered her hair. She knew there had to be more. "Why does he need to capture spirits, only in order to discover a book?"

Harik glanced at her, then at me, asking how much of this an outsider would understand.

An outsider who's been possessed by a demon for thirty years? Beats me.

"We think so," he said. "There was . . . a great Arab scholar, a master of occult lore." Which I guess is one way of describing Abdul Alhazred, author of the *Necronomicon*. "We know that he studied in Timbuktu. It was there that he wrote portions of . . . of a work of frightening scholarship, a work that can be used to summon forth terrible beings from the abysses beyond Space and Time as we understand them. And a tradition exists, that he not only taught students of his own in Timbuktu, but that he left his notes, his early drafts of that dreadful manuscript, with these students: notes on sources that are lost now to the outside world."

"Legends say," I took up the story, "that Abdul Alhazred—that was his name—had a slave. He probably did; Timbuktu was the big center for the slave trade. This slave had come from the tribal south with his wife, but the woman had been mistreated on the way and died. Legend says the slave kept the spirit of his wife in a bottle, and every time a new caravan of slaves came in, he'd go down to the markets with the bottle, and the spirit inside would eat the spirits of women slaves when they died in the slave compounds."

Raisha said softly, "A zar. Many of the zar had life as humans, or take on the humanity of those they possessed before."

"Sounds like it," I agreed. I remembered the woman at the dance, swaying with empty eyes as she shouted the Hail Mary in Latin. "The story goes that after Abdul left town, our pal the slave went on living in Abdul's palace outside Timbuktu, and became a scholar in his own right. Years later he got religion, bricked up the palace, the bottle, and it sounds like his boss's old notes, and became a hermit in the desert."

"And this spirit," Raisha whispered, "this wife—this woman who died in hatred and in hatred lives on in the form of a zar—it is she who guards this evil book. I see." She closed her eyes. She looked dead tired; God knows how much sleep she'd gotten in the past two days, if any. "As the zar give women strength—as Azuzar gave me the strength to survive—now this ibn-Ghaalib thinks to use their strength to defeat her. Dog," she breathed. "Pig and dog."

Her eyes opened, burning up into mine. "She will devour him," she said. "This woman who died in anger, this Guardian Zar. She will destroy him, and eat the spirits he brings with him, as she ate the others long ago."

I didn't think it was wise at that point to say that was what we were all hoping would happen. If ibn-Ghaalib had power over demons—the power I'd felt at the zar ceremony—I sure didn't want to lay money on *us* being able to get near him before he laid hands on whatever notes Alhazred had left. He had six hours' lead on us, and personally, I was coming to realize that getting killed outright would probably be the least of my worries.

It wasn't a pleasant thought.

We sighted Timbuktu at first light. Sand swept and crumbling, it stood on a slight rise above the river surrounded by the baked-out remains of what used to be marshes, the Sahara moving in on all sides. In 1962, there wasn't a modern building in the place, just pink mud-brick, weird triangular mosque towers with log ends sticking out of them, elaborate old gates and dome-shaped ovens like beehives in every street. Farther out in the desert, fumaroles smoked where the peat of vanished marshlands burned under the ground, and little lumps of rubble marked where old villages or forts had stood, protecting the caravan route.

"It could be any of those, couldn't it?" asked Professor Harik, kneeling on the bench beside me—carefully, because Raisha had fallen asleep there—and looking down out the window. "The slave's old palace, where he hid Alhazred's notes?"

I shook my head. "Bureau's checked 'em out already." And don't think *that* had been easy, while the Algerian War was going on. I'd seen photographs, and the map, in the Professor's office, a couple months back. Like I said, the whole subject of Africa had been talked about a lot at the Bureau, between the breakup of the French dependencies and the start of surveying on the dam.

"Can we simply guard their plane, then?" For a fussy little stick who thought alcohol would kill germs in a glass of Scotch, Professor Harik had a nice, logical mind. I like that. It makes things lots easier.

"Too late," I said. "If ibn-Ghaalib gets hold of those manuscripts, he'll probably be able to command the Guardian Zar as well. Then we're all screwed."

"Ah."

Beside us, Raisha breathed, "*Azuzar,*" and opened her eyes.

There was something about them—blank, smoky, still tangled in dreams—that made me lean down and whisper to her, "Did he speak to you?" and she murmured, "Yes."

Her eyes slipped closed again and as gently as I could, I laid my hand on her forehead. "Can you speak to him now? Ask him where he is?"

If she hadn't been that tired I'm not sure it would have worked, or if she hadn't been used to putting herself in trances for the zar dance. "Overhead." The word passed her lips like a dying breath. "We crossed overhead, and he saw us. A chamber—rocks—stairs going down. Water was there once and now there is only dust."

"Tell Carmichael to swing this thing around and take us straight back over our tracks," I said softly. "Not you," I added, as Harik would have gone, and flicked with my stone hand to Thomas, who ducked fast through the cockpit door. "You watch for landmarks—"

"There is nothing." A thin, steady wind was blowing across the desert below, driving little crescents of dust before it. Enough to take out whatever tracks there might have been. "I have been watching."

"Don't look for a building; it's too old," I said. "Look for ground that'd take a building; bedrock where you could dig an underground cistern."

On the other side of the plane, the jarhead called out softly, "Something down there." I hadn't thought he'd been listening. A minute later it came into view with the turning of the plane: a big thicket of dried-out camelthorn that didn't move right in the wind. Raisha whispered again, "Azuzar," and at the same time the sun came up, marking every irregularity of the ground with huge violet shadows, showing up what looked like a long island above an arm of the far-off river, that had sunk away centuries ago into the sand. Timbuktu lay about ten miles to the south, an easy ride if you were rich and had horses—or could rent a jeep in the town. On the sunny side of that slight rise of ground there were what looked like rock formations, and a couple more withered trees. There'd been water there longer than the rest of the area.

I said, "Tell Carmichael to put this thing down."

I went in first because I'm big, I'm scary, and I was betting ibn-Ghaalib hadn't told Fuad the cigarette smuggler that the people after him included a seven-foot-tall red guy. The mud flat where Carmichael put the plane down was on the sun side of the island and the two guards ibn-Ghaalib had left on the entrance to the old palace's cistern started shooting while we were still taxiing, long before we were in range. Amateurs. Back at the start of this expedition we hadn't expected trouble, so we didn't have professional muscle, but the jarhead was a fair sharpshooter and we did have rifles, as well as a box of grenades.

I took off my trench coat so they could get a good look at me, hooves, tail, and all, then ran toward them, dodging and weaving enough—I hoped—not to take a bullet that probably wouldn't kill me but that could be a real pain in the ass.

It worked. Even from the plane I heard one of them scream, "*Yallah!*" and saw him break cover from the rock formation and throw aside his rifle, and head over the rise to where I was pretty sure they had a jeep hidden under the camelthorn. The other guy had an AK-47 and fired two bursts at me, which showed him up to the jarhead, who fired back with aim a lot better than his or mine. Then he ran, too. I'd gone flat at the first semiauto burst and stayed flat until Carmichael zigzagged up to me, though there wasn't any shooting after that. Then we went up to check out the area to be sure.

"Why're they still here?" whispered Carmichael. "They had six hours' lead on us—"

"—and probably a wall to dig through," I said. "We may still be in time." Whatever was down there guarding those notes, I'd much rather deal with ibn-Ghaalib before he got it riled up than after.

We'd barely reached the rocks when a scream came from the other side of the rise, a scream of purest, hellish agony, and a man's voice shouted frantically, "Hassan! Hassan!" And the next second, the stink of burning flesh.

I went to look, though I'd guessed ibn-Ghaalib had booby-trapped the jeep with a geas of some kind, and I was right. Hassan lay in the sand near the jeep, dead—most of the flesh was melted off his arms and his right leg. The other man, kneeling beside him, emptied a handgun in my general direction and then threw it at me and took off running straight across the desert.

Midsummer in the Sahara, you can die in less than ten miles, and he wasn't even headed in the right direction for town. My guess was, he wouldn't be back.

As I crossed back to the rocks where Carmichael waited, I felt, deep beneath the ground, a shudder, not like the jar and roll of an earthquake but a kind of sustained quivering, like a horse twitching its skin. I didn't know what that meant, but none of my guesses sounded good. I broke into a run.

Professor Harik and Raisha had joined the group by the rocks. Carmichael said, "What the hell is that?" and Harik, "There's no way in."

"There has to be, they were guarding here—" Carmichael began, and behind him I could see, behind fragments of half-buried masonry, the dark mouth of an ancient shaft.

Demons can see certain things that people can't. And so can I. I'd seen the runes ibn-Ghaalib had put on the jeep, and I could sure as hell see the marks he'd drawn on the old threshold, the broken wall, that slipped the human consciousness past them. It's an old trick and it doesn't work if your attention is drawn to whatever they're trying to hide, as I drew it by stepping into the shaft entrance; they all looked startled as hell. "How about this?" I said, and took the gun from my holster. Around us, the stone of the low hill shivered again, sending down a shower of pebbles and vibrating a cloud of dust from the walls. Harik coughed, backed out a step, then returned, taking a flashlight from his pocket; Carmichael muttered, "Damn straight." Raisha only stood, listening to something only she could hear.

"He's down there," she whispered. "He's calling—calling for help. Can you hear them?"

I couldn't, but what the hell. Down we went.

One member of ibn-Ghaalib's hired flight crew was still unaccounted for, and from the runes on the jeep I knew ibn-Ghaalib himself had a pretty high degree of supernatural power, so I wasn't really surprised at what happened next. Didn't make it easier to cope with, but I wasn't surprised. Because of the shaking of the hill the air was thick with dust, cutting the flashlight's beam to a few feet, and the soft, subsonic rumble of the earth hid every sound but one. Below us somewhere in the darkness I could hear a man's voice—ibn-Ghaalib's—chanting or singing, not in Arabic but in something else, some language unheard on the earth for millennia, words that existed only in those forbidden texts the Bureau tried to trace and keep under lock and key. And under that, woven around it like silver wire around a core of burning iron, a kind of wailing vibration that twisted the heart inside my body and made me want to turn and run.

Damn, I thought, knowing it for what it was. *Damn*—

A gunshot cracked, somewhere below us. Carmichael gasped and I heard his Walther-PK clatter on the broken stone steps underfoot, smelled his blood as I shot back. Whoever was down there was shooting up into the narrow shaft, like firing at fish in a barrel. I felt a bullet tear my shoulder as I barreled down the stairs, blazing away—*Hell*, he *had to be in a direct line with* us—

And I walked smack into it. A line—a field—of spells that necromancers form, to trap and hold the demons they summon. Energy went through my head, through my body, paralyzing me and turning me cold. Bluish light showed me the dry cistern chamber at the bottom of the stairs, the ring of bottles and jars set up in their own protective ring at one side of the long stone room, blurred by the haze of dust. The jars themselves glowed and above each one burned a heatless, terrible little flame. In front of me ibn-Ghaalib swung around from the hole he'd opened in the rear wall, a hole cut through ancient masonry, opening into blackness. His pick, and Fuad's, lay on the floor beside him, and before him the jar I'd seen in his trunk, the ancient one he'd packed by itself, a skull with its eyes sealed with silver.

He faced me with a face like nothing human, eyes glowing with demon light. Damn.

I tried to bring up my gun to shoot and my fingers loosened, my knees turned to water.

The bastard smiled. He opened his mouth and light came out of it, and he spoke words in the tongue of the Great Old Ones, and the trembling of the hill seemed to pass into my own flesh, loosening it around the bones.

For not quite twenty years, I'd lived on the earth. Now I felt my spirit—my soul—tearing loose, being drawn out of me the way ibn-Ghaalib had drawn the zar out of that girl Naseeba at the dance, the way he'd drawn the spirit Azuzar out of Raisha's body. From an ammo pouch on his belt—he was still wearing the white *galibeya* he'd had on at the zar ceremony—he brought another one of those jars he'd had in his trunk, a little one made of alabaster, and I hated it, hated it like the mouth of Hell because that's exactly what it was. He stretched out his hand toward me, palms marked with the ancient Lemurian signs of mastery, and there was no way I could stop him . . .

Because of what I am.

Cold pale skeleton light flared in the black hole in the wall behind him. He swung around to face it, dropping the alabaster jar as he flung up his hands. The jar shattered and it was like an iron noose around my throat being let out one quarter of an inch: I couldn't move, but breath trickled through my lips. Not that that would do me any good, with the thing that was squeezing, soft and horrible, through the hole in the wall, soundless mouths working, eyes the eyes of a woman who's been raped to death—and has dwelled in that last moment ever since.

Get me out of here. Whatever was going to happen next, it was *not* going to be good news for me.

Ibn-Ghaalib swayed, turned, moving as he'd moved in the zar dance. In the flame glow of the circle of jars I could see the thing that faced him; sometimes a woman—or two women or three women—sometimes like a great, glowing snake. I don't know what Fuad saw—Fuad crouched with a gun in his hand at the other side of the dry cistern chamber—but he was paralyzed by it, either too hypnotized to notice me moving or maybe too scared to break his boss's concentration by so much as drawing breath.

Made sense to me.

I managed to shift one elbow, move one hoof—it was like trying to crawl out from under a mountain. I pushed myself toward the steps again, toward the line of chill-burning signs that delineated the demon field.

I couldn't cross it.

Hands reached out of the dark, grabbed my wrist. Dragged me. It was like having the meat combed off my bones. I think I blacked out. Next thing I knew I was lying curled in the small stone space at the bottom of the stairs, Harik and Raisha crouched above me, the stone of floor and walls quivering like a Chihuahua on cold linoleum and the sound of ibn-Ghaalib's trapped demons wailing going through my brain like splinters of glass. Light and shadow flickered from the cistern, flashes of fire, the crack of lightning and the ozone stink of demonic power.

Raisha took my hand. Bony little claws, and warm. Despite the hammering African heat, my flesh was cold as the dead.

She whispered, "Possess me."

"*What?*"

She brought my hand up, pressed it to the side of her face. "You are a demon. If I am shot, you can carry me through, to do what I must do. And my human flesh will protect you from the runes."

"No." The alabaster jar had broken, but I knew there were others, including the one he'd prepared for Big Mama. And that strange coldness still flooded me, the shuddering sense that any minute soul and body were going to peel apart . . .

Death? *Could* I die? I'd always thought so, but now I wasn't so sure.

And what would happen to me then?

"You must." She leaned over me, forced me to look into her eyes. "If the Guardian Zar destroys ibn-Ghaalib we will all of us be killed. Azuzar and all the others will be taken into her forever, to who knows what end, now that she has been freed? And if ibn-Ghaalib destroys her . . ."

Metal scraped on the stairway above. Carmichael whispered, "You ever shot one of these things, honey?" By the smell of the blood he'd lost a lot of it, but he was hanging on.

She said again, "You must."

Maybe I could have let her die—though I doubt it. But not all three of them. And either way, I was toast.

I closed my eyes. Felt her bend down, her mouth pressing mine.

My breath went into her. My spirit, into the place where Azuzar had dwelled for so many years.

It was . . .

. . . It was nothing I ever, *ever* want to do again.

Pain. Hate. Human memories of a life enslaved and oppressed. Thermonuclear rage ignited in me and I staggered to my feet, swaying like a drunken thing, barely even conscious of the great crimson carcass lying on the stone at my feet. Barely conscious of Harik staring up at me—at us—with naked horror and shock. I scooped up Carmichael's pistol and charged across the line of demon signs and yes, her human flesh protected me, though I felt as if I'd run through barbed wire, and yes, Fuad shot her and I/we didn't care. I broke his neck before he got off a second shot, before I even turned to see what was happening in the center of the cistern. Ibn-Ghaalib swung to face me—us—with his eyes red with hellfire and that demon smile on his mouth, his hands gripping the pale half-visible limbs of the Guardian Zar. It—she—writhed, snapping at him with her snake mouth as he drew her toward the silver-sealed skull. I strode toward them, knowing he would devour her in the next moment and have the strength of both, undefeatable. He'd devour us both before we were out of the room. I shot at him as I strode—almost point-blank range—and saw the bullets tear through his flesh, and he began to laugh; light poured out of the holes instead of blood. I stretched out my hand—Raisha's long, delicate fingers—and felt her scream inside, wrench at me, make me stumble. I reeled against her dragging strength, pulling me aside, away, across the square stone room. I yelled at her, *You crazy bitch—!* as she flipped Carmichael's gun around in her hand, and the next second she flung herself down on her knees in the circle of demon jars, gun butt raised like a hammer.

Ibn-Ghaalib shrieked something, let go of the Guardian and threw himself at us like a tsunami of fire as Raisha brought the gun butt down on the first of the jars.

I convulsed, gasped, and nearly broke the back of my skull on the stone steps beside which I lay. Harik grabbed my flailing hand—my own hand, my more or less human left hand—and shouted, "Hellboy!" at me, in the same second a blast of searing, oily heat pounded over us from the cistern. I don't know who screamed louder in there, Raisha or ibn-Ghaalib. The sound was nothing human, anyway. With the dust and the fire and the whirlwind of demon energies as all the entities ibn-Ghaalib had absorbed into his body ripped out of him again as the jars were smashed, it was pretty hard to tell what was going on.

When I got to my feet a few minutes later—feeling strange in my own body again and shaking like a leaf—and shined the flashlight into the cistern chamber, the result was not pretty.

Raisha lay in the middle of the room, covered with—well, let's just call it mess. Ibn-Ghaalib wasn't the first person I'd seen torn apart from the inside by demons, but he sure was the most comprehensive.

I don't think Professor Harik saw the Guardian whipping and flickering around the chamber through the slow-settling dust, but she wasn't pretty, either. I held him back as he started to go in. There was someone else in there, too. A shining shape, like a man in a white *galibeya*, knelt beside Raisha's head. "You owe her a debt," he said, and the Guardian bared her fangs at him—several mouthfuls of them. "In the name of the woman that once you were," he said.

She didn't look a whole lot like a woman these days, that's for sure, but she withdrew, coiling herself just outside the hole in the wall that led to the inner chamber. I thought I saw an iron chest in there, with a simple gourd bottle sitting on top of it, but I wasn't going to get any closer. All the things that a woman can have done to her—all the things I'd learned, from those few minutes within Raisha's brain and Raisha's memory—looked out at me, unanswerably, from those unspeakable eyes. Azuzar turned for a moment toward me, dark eyes in a face green as a corpse's, and beckoned with a long-fingered green hand. As I stepped across the dead line of demon runes, he turned Raisha over gently, bent down, and kissed her mouth, pouring into her like a breath-drawn mist.

I kept a wary eye on the Guardian Zar as I picked Raisha up—careful not to even *think* about getting near that iron box and I don't care *whose* notes were in it—and said, "All right with you if we lock up when we leave?"

She bared her teeth again. There was ibn-Ghaalib's blood on them, and little chunks of other stuff. She didn't look like she'd mind.

While Thomas was talking Harik through flight prep and the jarhead bandaged Carmichael and Raisha, I took a couple of grenades from a box at the back of the plane and tossed 'em down the shaft to the old cistern. When we took off, I could see the subsidence in the ground where the stairway had fallen in. So far as I know, nobody's ever been back there.

On the bench in the back of the plane, Raisha rested easily, her breath gentle, her face the face of a woman wrapped in the sweetest of dreams. I went to the other side of the cabin and lit a cigarette. Looked out the window at the red towers of Timbuktu shrinking behind us in the hot noon light. I knew everything that was in Raisha bint-Tahayet's heart; everything that was in her mind, in her dreams, in her past. Her sweetest hopes and her vilest hatreds: love poisoned, betrayal endured smiling for years. Everything that had happened to her in her life, had happened to me.

And I knew she knew that about me.

I knew—and I was right—that I'd be dreaming her dreams for years, waking in the morning feeling stained and shaken and hating myself and her, for what we both knew. You should never know someone *that* intimately. I knew—and I was right—that I'd have a bad night, when years down the road she finally came to die. She was a strong, wise, likable woman who'd had a hard life and had gotten through it gracefully, and under other circumstances I'd probably have liked her.

But I knew I didn't ever want to look on her face again.

And God help her, I knew she wouldn't ever want to look on mine.

In Cupboards and Bookshelves
Gary A. Braunbeck

We should be thankful we cannot see the horrors and degradations lying
around our childhood, in cupboards and bookshelves, everywhere.
—Graham Greene
The Power and the Glory

During those times when Hellboy found his thoughts wandering down
paths he knew from experience were best avoided, Trevor Bruttenholm
would take him aside and say precisely the right thing to soothe the
disquiet and discomfort that were Hellboy's constant companions. Neither
Bruttenholm nor Hellboy ever used the word *loneliness* when they spoke of such
things, although, sometimes, Hellboy would acknowledge a certain *aloneness* at the
core of his existence, and Bruttenholm would smile and laugh and say something
like, "Well, it *does* have that impenetrable Kierkegaard ring to it that I so often in
my thoughts associate with you."

"Are you laughing at me, sir?"

"No, dear boy, I am laughing *near* you. You ought to try joining in sometime."

"Only if there will be pancakes later."

"Dear boy, there will *always* be pancakes."

But Trevor Bruttenholm—the closest thing Hellboy had known to a father—was no longer here, yet that *aloneness* remained, a constant aide-mémoire that he wasn't merely the last of his kind, he was *alone* of his kind, with no heritage, no real sense of purpose or meaning, and no promise of ever finding the answers to and behind his existence. Sometimes Hellboy felt as if he were one breath away from being cast afloat into the darker corners of the universe, unbound, unfocused, but never un-*made* (something that would be a mercy, especially at times like this). Sure, he had friends, good friends like Abe, like Kate Corrigan, like Liz and a small handful of others at the Bureau for Paranormal Research and Defense, but they hadn't come along this time, so if he were feeling a bit, well . . . *anxious*, he had no one to blame but himself.

"How many children do you have here?" asked Hellboy, craning his neck to try and take in the enormity of this place. The walls of the cave—or whatever the hell it was—soared upward at either end like the sides of a ravine. Looking up, it seemed to Hellboy they could never meet in the darkness overhead.

He stood at the crossroad of several different paths, all strewn with random stones and loose piles of scree. Illuminated by the light from the dozens, possibly hundreds, of torches, he saw that these paths became narrow and steep, the rocks growing fewer but larger, stacked one on top of the other. In the distance he could make out something that looked like a chaotic staircase of massive, wedge-shaped boulders. This was evidently the anteroom of some vast, silent, ancient chamber.

Ahead, he could see a bluish radiance, haloing some kind of rock formation. On a small plateau, under an overhang of white calcite that curved gracefully upward like a snowdrift hollowed by the wind, stood a cluster of meticulously carved stones, each roughly the size and shape of a woman, arms outstretched, holding something whose shape he could not quite discern. Their bodies were complete but all of them lacked faces.

Hellboy turned slowly around, looking upward, and felt his breath catch in his throat.

"Holy crap," he whispered.

Crisscrossing above his head like strands of a web was an intricate network of handmade bridges, some constructed from disparate sections of metal, others made from rope and planks of wood. Below these bridges was a catwalk, also made from wood, that seemed to encircle the entire chamber. Lighted torches and battery-operated lanterns hung from the surrounding walls, and every ten or fifteen feet there would be a rope ladder, some leading down, some leading up.

And everywhere above there were hollowed spaces that looked like small tombs, each of them lit from within and tenanted by children. Hellboy could hear music coming from some of the chambers, laughter from others. Other chambers were cut off by means of curtains that had been nailed into place somehow. The more he stared, awestruck, the more apparent the ingenuity that had gone into constructing this place. The curtains were not nailed into position as he'd first thought; expandable shower curtain rods had been used in each doorway, so that if the tenant desired privacy, they had only to slide their particular curtain closed. Some used quilts, others blankets.

"How . . . how many of you are there?" he asked again.

"I quit counting almost fifty years ago," replied a voice near Hellboy's side. "These catacombs go on for miles, and where one series of chambers ends, there are passageways to others just like this. There's an underground spring not too far from here—the cleanest water you've ever tasted. I'd offer to give you a tour but you don't look to me like you're up for much sightseeing at the moment. In fact, you kind of look like a sick walrus trying to climb over a rock, so I'd have a seat if I were you."

A moment later, the children erupted from their rooms with squeals of laughter and anticipation, scurrying down the ladders, running across the catwalk, dashing over the bridges. Hellboy thought for a moment that this cavern perhaps opened somewhere near the top because he was again seeing stars—some so far away they were mere pinpoints of light—but as he watched, he became aware that these distant stars too were moving, circling around other catwalks, traversing higher bridges, descending other ladders, or being lowered in their wheelchairs on wood-and-steel elevator platforms that were operated through a massive and ingeniously constructed system of chains, pulleys, winches, and counterweights, all coming toward him, not stars at all but yet more torches and lanterns being carried by children whose rooms were hundreds of feet above those he had first seen.

It was incredible. He'd thought there might be only a few dozen children living here, maybe a hundred, but now saw that their numbers were legion; there had to be at least two thousand children, maybe even more. He tried again to pull all the shadow-children into his vision but was overwhelmed with dizziness and vertigo. There were just too many of them.

"Are you all right?" asked another voice, this one a child's.

Hellboy nodded, then took a deep breath, and then shook his head. "I am feeling a bit dizzy, now that you mention it."

The children continued to descend from above until the chamber was packed; never before had Hellboy seen so many in one place. He tried to regain his balance before the dizziness got the better of him but managed only to drop onto his ass, his tail getting entangled with his oilskin coat and sending a sharp lance of pain up through his back. He looked around at the sea of surrounding faces and realized he couldn't see where the crowd ended.

"I'll be passing out now, if that's all right."

"I'm surprised you remained conscious for this long," someone said.

"I'll expect pancakes later . . ."

"Beg pardon?"

" . . . was told . . . there would always be pancakes . . ."

And, as he'd always suspected would one day happen, Hellboy was cast afloat into a dark corner of the universe.

He'd known something was up before he'd even entered Tom Manning's office. The director of the B.P.R.D. had this *air* about him any time his authority was overridden by someone, or something, higher up. Manning had been named director while Trevor Bruttenholm was still alive—the professor had wanted to use his time for research and field work—but Hellboy knew that many in the B.P.R.D. viewed him as a simple bureaucrat, a poor replacement for the accomplished Bruttenholm. In the wake of the professor's death, Tom Manning, Hellboy suspected, needed no one to remind him that he was the consolation prize. For a while, Hellboy himself had felt this way, but as Manning proved time and again just how well qualified he was for the directorship, what had first been an outright resentment on Hellboy's part became a gruff form of respect and, sometimes, even admiration.

Still, sometimes it was easy to see that Manning, for all of his stiff-backed demeanor and even steely manner, felt as if he were sometimes reduced to the role of errand boy—especially when it came to honoring requests made by Trevor Bruttenholm prior to his death. Who would dare argue with Hellboy's dead father, after all?

So when Hellboy saw the way in which Manning did not so much walk to his office as plow through the hallway, eyes not making contact with anyone along the way, he knew something wasn't right. That suspicion doubled when he received the call not one minute later to come to the director's office immediately. If any doubts were still lingering, they vanished as soon as Hellboy closed Manning's office door and saw the look on the director's face; Tom Manning looked humiliated beyond words; helpless, ineffectual, inept.

"Hellboy," said Manning, gesturing for him to take a seat.

"Sir," replied Hellboy, hoping that the tone of his voice was as neutral as he tried making it sound.

Manning met Hellboy's gaze for only a moment before returning it to the telegram on his desk. Reading it over once more, he pushed it across the desk, then sat back and rubbed his eyes. "That arrived less than an hour ago."

Hellboy nodded, then picked up the telegram:

HB
I hope this doesn't get you into trouble. I need your help. Please get here as soon as you can. Urgent.
The Reverend

"I promised Professor Bruttenholm a lot of things before his death," said Manning. "Not the least of which was that I'd respect certain matters the two of you wished to be kept private. Your friend the Reverend was near the very top of that privacy list. I never pressed Trevor and I've never pressed you about who or what he is. I know he's helped the Bureau on several occasions and has never asked for anything in return. Hell, even in the telegram, he doesn't demand your help, he *asks* for it. That tells me the man's got integrity and knows how to show respect."

"That he does, sir."

Manning tried to smile, didn't quite make it. Hellboy felt kind of bad for the guy.

"One of the other things I promised Trevor," said Manning, "was that anytime the Reverend requested your help or that of the Bureau, it would be given immediately and without question. Care to guess which part of this I'm having trouble with right now?"

Hellboy placed the telegram back on the desk. "Sorry, Tom, but I promised the professor that I'd keep the Reverend a private matter, as well."

Manning stared at him for a few moments, and Hellboy could sense the director trying to search for just the right words, or some small gesture that would say, *I know I'm not Professor Bruttenholm, but I could be your friend, I'm just no damn good at making the first move. A little help, maybe?*

"He's never used the word *urgent* before," said Hellboy. "Trust me . . . Tom, this is a guy who doesn't scare easy. He's not in the habit of overreacting. If the Reverend says it's urgent, then it's probably something that would make most people here crap their pants just to think about it, let alone deal with it."

Manning nodded. "So you have no reason to doubt that it's serious, whatever it is he needs you for?"

"I don't doubt it at all."

"You trust him that much?"

"Yeah, Tom, I do. So would you. I, um . . . I could introduce you sometime." The change in Manning's expression was subtle, but it was all Hellboy needed to know that he'd put the director at ease on several unasked questions.

"I would appreciate that," said Manning. "So . . . what do you need from the Bureau?"

"Just a ride to Ohio. I can make do with the chopper."

Manning tried to smile, actually made it this time. "Is there no end to the sacrifices you make?"

"*Is* kind of inspiring, isn't it?"

Ninety minutes later, just before one a.m., the B.P.R.D. chopper lifted off from a field one mile east of the Heath airport. Hellboy stood in the field, waited until the chopper was high enough, and then waved at the pilot. He never understood why he liked doing that *so much*, but he did, and what did it hurt? So he waved again, and then turned toward the direction of Cedar Hill and took off running.

He liked his infrequent visits to Cedar Hill because they allowed him the time and distance to really *run*, flat out, for miles at a time, across empty fields, through abandoned buildings, across construction sites, through countless alleyways . . . he often wondered if the people living in Cedar Hill knew what an amazing, confounding *maze* their city was. And if they thought it was bad on the *surface* . . .

He ran until he reached downtown, just off the square, and ducked into the alley beside Riley's Bakery. Was it just him, or could you still smell the pastries from this morning? Have to pop in sometime and ask. Maybe his celebrity would be good for a free box of glazed, or a bagful of crullers.

He reached the end of the alley and took the five short cement steps that led down and to the right. The door was locked, but that was to be expected. The Reverend had long ago provided Hellboy with the key to this door—not that it was exactly state-of-the-art security; a strong-enough breeze would probably snap the padlock one day, but Hellboy used the key out of courtesy to the Reverend. It wasn't everyone who knew that this old door at the bottom of those five ill-kept steps opened into a series of underground maintenance tunnels that spread out underneath a full sixty percent of the city.

Hellboy went down the short flight of steps on the inside until he came to another, unlocked, door. Opening that door, he reached in and around to the side, turning on the emergency lights that were strung through every foot of the tunnels.

There was a golf cart waiting for him, a note on its windshield: *Never say I don't let my friends travel in style. R.*

Laughing, Hellboy climbed into the cart—impressed that the Reverend had found one that would support his weight—fired up the engine, and drove the route that he could travel in his sleep. Despite knowing that the Reverend's message was urgent, Hellboy couldn't resist the temptation to take a couple of side corridors and pull a few wheelies. Then it was back to business.

He parked the cart at the set of steps that led up into the basement of what used to be one of the fancier hotels in Cedar Hill back in the day, until a casket-factory fire took most of three city blocks on a sweltering night in August of 1969. A section of the hotel had remained all but untouched by that fire, and the Reverend had somehow convinced the city leaders to let him set up shop—a.k.a. The Cedar Hill Open Shelter—in what was left of it. So Cedar Hill boasted the only homeless shelter in the nation that had an Italian-marble floor and an honest-to-Pete crystal chandelier.

Entering the basement of the Open Shelter, Hellboy closed the door behind him and then speed-dialed the Reverend's private number on his cell phone.

"You're in the basement, right?" said the Reverend.

"Good to hear your voice, as well," replied Hellboy.

"I'll take that as a yes. Walk over toward the showers."

"I've done my hygiene routine for the day, thanks."

"*Walk toward the showers.*"

Hellboy walked toward the showers.

"Stop when you get to the lockers on the left."

"Your wish, cha-cha-cha."

"Open locker #713."

Hellboy did—and was greeted by a well-lighted, if slightly narrow, staircase.

"My gift," said the Reverend. "Come on up."

Hellboy had to take most of the stairs sideways, but it was an easy-enough walk. The Reverend knew that, while Hellboy never scared away fans and admirers (or even the merely curious), given a choice, he preferred to move about as unnoticed as possible, for as long as possible.

He reached the top of the stairs and knocked on the inside of the other locker door he found waiting there.

A moment later, the Reverend said: "Dave's not here, man."

"Very funny." He opened the door and stepped into the Reverend's office—which also served as the man's bedroom, kitchen, living room, entertainment area, and bathroom. At the moment, a little girl of about eight or nine years of age was sleeping on the little sofa in the corner of the office. She looked pale, weak, and tired, and—judging from the discolored stains that could only have been dried blood that covered her clothes like patchwork—like she'd not had the best of days. Or lives, for that matter.

"Is she the urgent matter?" asked Hellboy.

"Yes and no," said the Reverend. He brushed some hair out of his eyes, finished washing his hands at the sink, and then came over and embraced Hellboy. "Good of you to come."

"Never could turn down a breakneck ride in a golf cart. It's a character flaw." He examined the Reverend for a moment, then nodded. "That whole *Is-He-Jesus-or-Charles-Manson?* look is working for you. You got a new collar, didn't you?"

The Reverend reached up and flicked his thumbnail against the annoying white clerical collar around his neck. "Blue-light special at the Vatican Garage Days Sale, ten for a buck."

The little girl on the sofa rolled over, made a soft, pained noise, and dropped the small stuffed blue pony she was holding. The Reverend picked up the pony and held it toward Hellboy. "These things still give you the willies?"

"Yes," replied Hellboy, taking a step back. "Don't ask me why, I know it's just a damned stuffed animal, but ponies are *creepy.* Evil, even. Evil pony. Get it away from me."

The Reverend grinned, slipping the evil pony back into the little girl's arms. "In case you were about to ask—and I suspect you were—I found her in an alley about a mile from here. She'd been beaten, starved, and left to die, yet through all of that she somehow managed to hang on to her stuffed animal. It never ceases to amaze me how resilient children are."

"What's going on, Reverend?"

The Reverend stared at him for a moment, and then knelt next to the nameless little girl on the sofa and began stroking her hair. "The ancient Greeks believed in two kinds of time, HB: *chronos* and *kairos*. *Kairos* is not measurable. In *kairos*, you simply *are*, from the moment of your birth on. You *are*, wholly and positively. *Kairos* is especially strong in children, because they haven't learned to understand, let alone accept, concepts such as time and age and death. In children, *kairos* can break through *chronos*: when they're playing safely, drawing a picture for Mommy or Daddy, taking the first taste of the first ice-cream cone of summer, when they sing along to songs in a Disney cartoon, there is only *kairos*. As long as a child thinks it's immortal, it is. Think of every living child as being the burning bush that Moses saw; surrounded by the flames of *chronos*, but untouched by the fire. In *chronos*, in the everyday world, the one where you're going to eventually die, you're nothing more than a set of records, fingerprints, your social security number; you're always watching the clock, aware of time passing—but in *kairos*, you were, are, and always will be."

"Okay . . . ?"

"I need to know you understand that. It's important."

"Man, you sound a little freaked."

"Maybe that's because I *am* a little freaked—and you *know* what it takes to do that to me, right?"

"Now *I'm* getting freaked."

"Look at me, HB. Look at—there you go. You understand what I just told you, right?"

"Yeah, *chronos* sucks, *kairos* rules, I got it."

"In a few minutes, as the *chronos* flies, you're going to be meeting someone whose duty—one among many, anyway—is to make certain that *chronos* and *kairos* stay separated, that one never bleeds into the other long enough for it have a permanent effect. Especially for children like little Sara here."

Hellboy stared down at little Sara and her evil pony, and as he watched, some of the physical wounds she'd had just a few moments ago—some tiny scars, several facial bruises, badly scraped knuckles, and a handful of open cuts—began to heal with the Reverend's every touch. "How special is she, little Sara here?"

The Reverend shook his head. "As far as the people in her life are concerned, she's just a sack of human meat, unwanted detritus, a burden to bear. She's not special in the least, not her or a million other children just like her."

Hellboy held up his left hand, palm out. "Don't go all high and mighty on me, Reverend, okay? You're preaching to the choir, so save your breath, I get it, and I agree. So why am I here?"

"Ever read Dickens?"

"Yeah, but I like the movies better, especially the ones with Ronald Colman. Why?"

"The heart of Dickensian philosophy—at least insofar as it was useful to the *Star Trek* films so they could make everyone think they were being deep and thoughtful—was that sometimes the needs of the many outweigh the needs of the few—"

"—or the one, right. *Wrath of Khan*. I dug that one."

"Is that something you personally agree with? That sometimes the needs—"

"Heard you the first time, Reverend. And, yeah, I can see how that might apply in certain situations."

"Could you apply it to a certain situation if you had to?" The intensity in the Reverend's voice and behind his gaze caused Hellboy's right hand to actually begin shaking.

"Could you be a little less hypothetical?"

The Reverend rose and began walking toward Hellboy, his eyes never blinking. "I really don't mean for all of this to make you nervous."

"You'll buy the drinks later. Be specific."

The Reverend stood less than two feet away from Hellboy now; if anything, his gaze was even more electrifying and unsettling. "If it were absolutely necessary, could you—?"

"Not your job, Reverend," came another voice from the far side of the room.

Both Hellboy and the Reverend looked over just in time to see a figure emerge from the wall like a bas-relief painting that had decided it had no use for the boundaries of three dimensions. When it was fully free of the wall, the figure shook itself as if tossing off a deep, wearying chill, and then turned to face them.

"Wow," said Hellboy. "Don't take this personally, but you are one ugly son of a bitch. What happened, you try to French kiss an airplane propeller while it was still running?"

"That's it, exactly," said the figure. "And it never returned my calls, either. The nerve of some things." Looking at the Reverend, the figure raised its hand and gave a small wave. "Reverend, always a thrill."

"As is the never-not-annoying manner of your entrances, Rael."

"Just keeping my hand in the parlor-tricks game while I still can."

The Reverend pointed between Rael and Hellboy. "Do I need to make formal introductions?"

"Nah," said Rael. "He's already heard you call me by name, and we have satellite television and magazine subscriptions. Everybody knows who Hollywood is." He started toward little Sara and her evil pony. "Damn, Reverend—you didn't tell me that the big K was *this* intense in her."

"I thought it might be a nice surprise, given the circumstances."

"You're right. Thanks, man." Rael put a hand on the Reverend's shoulder and continued staring down at Sara. This close to Rael, Hellboy saw how much worse Rael's face actually was than he'd first believed.

There was very little soft tissue on the upper portions of his face, and what flesh there was had become hardened to the point where it more resembled scales on a lizard's back; in places this scalelike flesh was semi-translucent, allowing Hellboy to see the red and blue veins that spiderwebbed the areas where most people had cheeks. Rael had no nose, only two tear-shaped caves through which he breathed, both of which seemed to leak constantly. His left eye was a good quarter inch lower on his face than his right, and he had no ears to speak of, just bits of dangling flesh on either side of his head. Though his jaws were intact, he possessed almost no chin; the flesh under his lower lip had only the smallest of rounded bone fragment beneath it, the rest simply blended into his neck like melted candle wax, creating a thick, disturbing wattle that pulsed with every leak from his nose caves.

The worst part, though, was the overall shape of his face and head; his skull seemed to have been wrenched apart with a crowbar, then pieced back together by someone with no knowledge whatsoever of human anatomy; there were lumps where none should have been, craters where there should have been lumps, and one section, beneath his too-low left eye, where the cracked and yellowed bone was actually exposed to the elements; Hellboy caught a glimpse of something metal and realized there was a rusty pin holding those two small sections of his faceplate together.

"Didn't anyone ever teach you that it's rude to stare?" said Rael.

"Sorry. It's just . . . you're quite a sight."

Rael looked at the Reverend. "Sensitive, tactful sort, isn't he?"

"Yes. Remind you of anyone?"

"What are you?" asked Hellboy.

" 'What,' is it? 'What?' This, coming from the poster boy for why you should never fall asleep in a tanning bed."

"Rael is an angel," said the Reverend.

"Technically," said Rael, "I am a Hallower: a half-human descendant of the Rephaim Grigori, who were among the Fallen Angels. In retaliation for God's not having shared all Knowledge with them, the Fallen Angels stole the *Book of Forbidden Knowledge* and came down to Earth and gave countless Secrets to Man. Most of the Grigori coupled with human women during their time on Earth, and my race was one of many that issued from that coupling—though there aren't many of us left, of any of the races, not now. I am a descendant of, among others, the Fallen Angel Kokabel. He gave mankind the Forbidden Knowledge of Time and Science and assisted the Grigori Penemue in giving children the Knowledge of the lonely, bitter, and painful." Rael lifted his left hand, palm facing outward. "He also tainted the Mark of the Archangel Iofiel, who holds dominion over the planet Saturn." He placed the tip of his right index finger at the base of his left middle finger. "It's because of Kokabel that, in Palmistry, the Mount of Saturn brings such deep sadness with it.

"There aren't many of us left, Hollywood. In fact, it's just me and two others, and one of those isn't quite a full blood but I'm in no position to get nitpicky. You see, I am also a *direct* descendant of the Sorcerer of Night, Unkempt, sometimes also known as the Archon Pronoia. My partner in crime is a descendant of the Archon Pthahil. They were the angels who assisted God in creating Adam. Pthahil sculpted Adam's body from several handfuls of earth. Pronoia supplied the nerve tissue. Then God showed them how to give the body life. So we carry with us the knowledge and ability to make Man, and it was that power, that sentient race memory, if you will, that was awakened within us by some kind of survival instinct and forced to the surface at the moment when we should have died. We can create and heal but we can't unmake anything—including ourselves." He pointed to his tragic vaudeville of a face. "Used the old double barrel and only managed to ruin the wallpaper. Not that this *GQ* cover-model face is that bad a representation of what an angel really looks like.

"You see, not all angels are these ethereal, white-robed, wondrous, golden-winged refugees from a beauty contest that you're always seeing depicted in books and movies—oh, no. Many of them—and I'm talking about the ones who sit by God's side and have His favor and love and respect and are the first to get tickets for the WWF Summer Slam—the *good guys, capiche?*—a lot of them are so hideous in their appearance that they make Lovecraft's Great Old Ones look like *Playboy* centerfolds. We're talkin' class-A uggos here, tentacles and dripping teeth and putrescent flesh all dark and oily with larval eruptions that drip phosphorescent goo. And don't get me started on all the *begatting* that's going on at all hours."

"She's stable," said the Reverend.

Rael looked down at Sara's face. "You sure?"

"I'm going to pretend you didn't ask me that."

"Sorry, Reverend. It's just . . . it wouldn't exactly be the high point of the evening if she were to buy the farm on the way home. I need as much Big K as she can provide."

"She'll make it." A breath, a look, a heartbeat. "So that leaves only . . ." And both the Reverend and Rael looked at Hellboy.

"Oh, are we finally getting to it?" said Hellboy. "Someone's going to tell me why you two need me here? Wait, I want to sit down, this is too much excitement." He looked around, couldn't find anything that would support his weight, and so leaned against the locker. "Okay, my heart's all aflutter but I think I'm ready."

Rael looked at the Reverend once again. "I like him. He's a smart-ass."

"And I've got both of you in the same room at the same time," said the Reverend. "Am I the luckiest guy on the planet, or what?"

Hellboy began to speak, but as if reading his mind, Rael walked over and said: "Do you despair, Hollywood? When you look at little Sara over here, can you see what her life has been, that she's not had a good day on this Earth since the moment of her birth, and do you despair?"

Hellboy didn't even have to think about that one. "Damn right, I do."

"And if there were something you could do to help, would you?"

"You know it."

"I do now." He pointed to Sara. "Will you carry her?"

"Do I have to carry the evil pony, too?"

"Yes."

Steeling himself, Hellboy picked up both little Sara and her evil stuffed pony.

"Well, Reverend," said Rael, offering his hand. "It's been—"

"Tell him."

"What?"

"You heard me," said the Reverend, nodding toward Hellboy. "Tell him. Right here, right now. We agreed that it would be his *choice*."

"It will be."

The Reverend shook his head. "Not once you move through the scrim and take him to the others. That would be emotional blackmail—don't say it, I know, that wouldn't be *the intention,* but it would be the result."

Hellboy adjusted Sara in his arms and, whispering so as not to wake her, said: "Tell me what?"

Not taking his eyes from Rael's face, the Reverend replied: "The reason I asked you here on Rael's behalf."

"Not just *my* behalf, Reverend."

"Fine, on both our behalfs, and *all* our behalfs. Now are you going to tell him or should we stand here and argue a half dozen or so more parenthetical points and *really* give *chronos* a chance to tear you a new one?"

"You're not going to let me leave without doing this your way, are you?"

"We agreed, Rael. And you know damned well I could stop you."

"You're about the *only* one who could." He took a deep breath and turned to face Hellboy. And he told Hellboy why he was needed. And it was an awful thing Hellboy was being asked to do. But all he had to do was look down at Sara, and he knew there was no other answer he could give. So he said yes to the awful thing, and he followed Rael through the scrim into a place that was filled with children and sounds and laughter and starlight and he gave Sara to a teenaged girl who said she'd be taken care of and then Rael said Hellboy looked like a sick walrus trying to climb over a rock and then Hellboy felt a deep and aching sadness and thought about pancakes and how few friends he had and then he passed out into a dark unbound corner of the universe . . .

And woke up to see the smallest, most frail-looking little bird-woman watching over him. Her features were tiny, sharp, and delicate. She smiled again—as much as her cleft palate would allow, anyway—and nodded her head, blushing. The veins in her hairless head, already so close to the surface they looked like red and blue strands of webbing, stood out in a way that Hellboy would once have thought grotesque but now found sweet and endearing.

"Hello, little miss," he said.

The bird-woman blushed three shades deeper and buried her head in her arms. She was giggling.

"That's Andrea," said Rael. "She's been here a very long time, Hollywood. In fact, we've got kids in here who—though they may look only eight or nine years old—are older than most of the goddamn *trees* outside. Andrea has agreed to keep you company, providing you read her favorite book."

"Which would be . . . ?"

"*Horton Hears a Who.*"

Hellboy grinned, even though it hurt. "Hey, that's one of my favorites, too."

Andrea was blushing to beat the band now, and as Hellboy smiled at her, at her fragility, at her warmth, at her grace, his brain started to unfog, and bits and pieces of the conversation he'd had with Rael before entering the scrim began swimming their way toward the surface.

"We've already set up a chamber for you and the infected kids," said Rael. "It's very warm, there's comfortable furniture, food, books, movies, music, things to cook with, all the comforts, so to speak."

"How is that possible, movies and working stoves and electricity and . . . all of it?"

"They watch videotapes on VCRs, actually—though we have managed to lay hands on a few DVD players. We don't get cable here, and a satellite dish might eventually draw someone's attention—I lied about our having it; I just wanted to see the look on the Reverend's face. To answer your question, though—portable generators, most of which we've stolen, I'm ashamed to say, along with a lot of other things, but we're not here to discuss the problems I might be having with my conscience. I might be able to do a little sleight of hand with time, *kairos*-wise, but I can't summon electricity from thin air. Most of the 'rooms' are also equipped with portable air filters. A lot of the kids have breathing problems—asthma, allergies, things like that—and the atmosphere in here lately has been making those conditions worse. But we do what we can to make life as good as it can be."

Hellboy struggled into a sitting position. "I feel like my head's been drilled open and filled with cotton candy."

Andrea giggled at the mention of cotton candy.

Looking around, Hellboy saw that the thousands of children from earlier were all back in their rooms.

"I can't chance that I was wrong about *chronos* having little or no part of your makeup," said Rael. "Andrea here will be fine, *kairos* is her middle name, but the rest of the unaffected children . . . can't chance it, Hollywood."

"I understand."

Rael looked around the chamber and then sighed. "You know how sick I am about this, right?"

"What I think doesn't matter."

"Like hell it doesn't. Look at me, Hollywood—you think you're the only one who's alone of your kind? Even if the other Hallowers are where I think they're going to be, we're descended from different Grigori, no two of us are the same race. Like it or not, that's something you have in common with us—and ain't it a bitch that the song is right, that one *is* the loneliest number?"

"How long will you be?" asked Hellboy.

Rael shrugged. "Hopefully less than three days."

"I'll . . . I'll make sure they're happy and well cared for."

"I know you will, Hellboy. The Reverend said you were the only one for the job." Slapping his knees, Rael rose to his feet. "Sorry that you were hit so hard going through the scrim. Knowing that there are areas in reality where the corners don't quite match up and learning how to move through them without getting sick are way different."

"Tell me about it." Hellboy was on his feet now. "So Sara's going to be all right?"

"Yes. She was brought here in time. That's the trick, you know? Find these children before they've suffered so much abuse or neglect or however many different combinations of pain there are to inflict on them that they lose all touch of *kairos*. Sara's got loads of it, still, even after all she's been through. That's really amazing. It should be enough to keep things in place until I get back. As long as the infected kids don't—"

"—I know what I'm supposed to do," said Hellboy. "And you don't need to worry, I'll make sure none of them wander back here."

Rael looked at Hellboy for a moment, then offered his hand. Hellboy shook it.

"I hope you're still here when I get back with the others," said Rael.

"Me too," replied Hellboy—though in his heart he suspected they both knew he wouldn't be.

He and Andrea watched as Rael gathered up his backpack, and then Andrea took hold of Hellboy's hand and guided him through the chambers to the special area Rael had set up for the one hundred and twenty-seven children within whom *chronos* was now rampant.

I can't hold it back much longer on my own, Hollywood, he'd told Hellboy in the Reverend's presence. *I suppose I'm lucky to have held it back this long, but the longer I wait to venture out for the other of my kind, the more hold* chronos *has over the children. I can't let that happen. I can't let one hundred and twenty-seven infected children make the thousands of others sick, as well, and I'm not about to just turn those one hundred and twenty-seven kids out to die in the same world that so hurt them in the first place, and I'm sure as shit not going to allow their final days of life to be spent alone and frightened. Keep them happy for me, Hollywood. Tell them stories. Sing songs to them. Hold their hands. Listen to their prayers. Watch funny movies. Eat junk food. Feel their breath on your cheek when they ask to kiss you good night. Mark the moment when each one passes away, and when it's over, if I haven't gotten back in time with the others to restore* kairos *to everyone, I want you to seal the chamber where their bodies lay, and say a few words for their embattled spirits. Will you do that for me, Hollywood? Will you make sure they all know that their lives weren't just pieces of junk thrown in cupboards or bookshelves to be forgotten? Will you make sure they all know they were loved, and that their lives mattered?*

Hellboy was determined to do all that and more.

Andrea was splendid company. She even stopped blushing after a while.

But when Rael returned with the other Hallowers, only Andrea was there to greet them.

I heard you were back."

Hellboy looked up from his bowl of popcorn to see Tom Manning standing in the doorway to his room. He hoped the director couldn't see the way his puffy eyes still shone. Weeping was not something they were accustomed to.

"Early this morning."

Manning came into the room, closing the door behind him. "So, how did it go?"

Without thinking, Hellboy replied, "I had to sit with one hundred and twenty-seven dying children. They'd been isolated to keep twenty times as many kids alive. The first one died within an hour. It took less than three days for all but one of them to pass." His voice cracked on the last three words, but he held it together.

After a few moments, Manning cleared his throat. "What are you watching?"

"*A Tale of Two Cities.*"

He came around to look at the screen. "Oh, the Ronald Colman version! This is a good one."

Hellboy looked at Manning, hesitated, and then slid over to make room on the extra-large couch. "It just started. Want some popcorn?"

Manning blinked in surprise. Then he nodded. "Love some. Got any beer?"

"In the fridge. Help yourself."

Once upon a time, his father had promised him that there would always be pancakes. And there were, when he wanted them, but they'd never been the same after he was gone. Popcorn, though . . . popcorn was forever.

FEET OF SCIRON
RHYS HUGHES

Foggy Dicks is what they call me. You don't expect me to use my real name in this business, do you? I went into porn because I needed money fast. I looked for other kinds of work but couldn't find any. Yeah, you heard right. Porn. A comedown for the "ectoplasm guy," don't you think? Not all of us land on our feet. Hell, some of us never get off our knees in the first place.

I was on the set of my latest film when I got the call from Hellboy. Without so much as a goodbye I walked out of the studio and caught the first plane to the headquarters of the Bureau for Paranormal Research and Defense in Fairfield. A plane and then a cab, if you want to be picky. He was there to meet me at the gate.

"Good to see you again," he said. He even sounded sincere, the big red brute, his horn stumps glistening.

"Been a long time," I answered.

"What's your new film about?" he asked innocently.

I couldn't bring myself to tell him. I just mumbled something about yoga, the tantric kind. He led me inside and took me to a basement room for a lecture. Then he said:

"Yoga? So you won't be needing a chair?"

In case you're wondering, I was only employed by the Bureau for a month or two. Originally they wanted us to work as a permanent team, Hellboy, Abe, Liz, a few others, but things in the real world aren't like the comic books. People get killed, impaled on giant spikes, fatally slapped by homunculi, the usual stuff, and teams don't stay together. It's not worth it in the long run. Not even in the short run. To be honest my one talent wasn't that useful either. I can extrude ectoplasm from my naked body. From any part.

What use is an agent who has to take off his goddamn shirt or pants every time he wants to lasso a vampire or werewolf with a spooky gloop noose? Way too slow. I left before I was kicked out. Turned out that my talent was more appreciated by the porn industry. Now I was back at the Bureau but it was clearly going to be a one-off job.

The expert in the tweed suit who wanted to talk to me was called Marvin Carnacki and didn't seem comfortable in his surroundings.

"We have reason to believe it's like a maze."

"I beg your pardon?" I asked.

"On the inside," he spluttered impatiently, "the most complex maze ever designed. Worse than what Theseus had to find his way through. Maybe a million times more convoluted."

Then he removed his round spectacles and wiped them carefully on his sleeve. I was aware of Hellboy grinning next to me but I didn't look at him to check. Instead I protested:

"You'll have to start from the beginning."

Marvin Carnacki frowned. "Hasn't anyone told you anything about this case? Time is short."

"Nope, and *whose* time are you referring to?"

So he told me about Theseus, the ancient hero who killed the Minotaur, and the labyrinth he had to get through, and how before doing that, he slew Sciron. And a bunch of other people and monsters too. Sort of cut from the same mold as Hellboy. Except he wasn't red. And didn't have horns. And spoke in Greek. And didn't carry a pistol. Other differences too. Heck, he wasn't even remotely the same.

But that's life, I guess. And death. And mythology.

By the way, Sciron was a giant who liked to kick men off the top of a cliff. First he got them to kneel down before him and kiss his feet. Then he let them have it with the toe of his sandal. It's a scene familiar to me from a dozen films. I've been the kicker and the kicked. Porn is weird. What else do I need to fill you in on? The planet Nekrotzar. A golden barge. A river as long and twisted as a lifespan.

All in good time. Or bad time. Depending.

I'm dictating this from a hospital bed, incidentally, which is where Hellboy put me. He went nuts and threw me around a bit. Broke my ribs, shattered my legs and arms, but the fact of the matter is that he was only defending himself. We'll get to that later.

When the lecture was finished, Hellboy took me for a coffee. I wondered where Liz and Abe were. On a job up north, he said. Then he frowned.

"Marvin confused you, didn't he?"

"He's a nervous man," I answered.

"Because he's a defector."

"Sure, but I still can't work out from which country."

"No country. A rival Bureau."

"We have official enemies?" I croaked.

He shook his impressive head and I sniffed the air carefully but didn't catch the odor of dry-roasted peanuts, which is the way Hellboy smells on a good day. So this had to be a bad day.

Logic, pure and simple. But what makes a genuine demon anxious? If I had worked longer with the Bureau I would have known that Hellboy gets worried just like everybody else and hardly ever smells like a dry-roasted peanut, but for me at that particular moment the lack of snack stench was a negative sign.

I felt afraid then. I calmed myself by muffling my heart in soft pillows of ectoplasm, because I can also extrude the gunk internally, and I flatter myself that Hellboy didn't notice this trick.

"Ready to hear the worst," I said.

"I'll explain briefly," he answered. "Turns out that for many years we've had a secret competitor, a private organization managed by the descendants of the original Carnacki."

"You've lost me already. Carnacki who?"

Hellboy rapped his fingers on the table. "The few people who *do* know the name think he's fictional, the creation of a writer named William Hope Hodgson. The stories Hodgson wrote are a century old but worth reading. Carnacki was a real man, a ghost finder."

"The same way that Sherlock Holmes really lived but was turned into a fictional character by Conan Doyle?"

Hellboy gave a casual wave, no easy gesture with a right hand made of stone. "Yeah. There are a lot of examples. Jules Verne pretended that Phileas Fogg was fictional, H.G. Wells did the same thing with Dr. Moreau, M.P. Shiel with Prince Zaleski, Maurice Richardson with Engelbrecht, the list is endless.

"When he got old, Carnacki decided to create a society dedicated to ridding the natural world of paranormal threats. The same as what the Bureau does but on a smaller scale. The Carnacki Institute never had the resources we did and they were envious of us for a long time. The only advantage they had was that they were aware of our existence. We knew nothing about them."

"They don't seem much of an enemy, more like an alternative, albeit a poor one. We're doing the same job."

Hellboy shrugged. "You'd be surprised at how vicious people can get when they're working for identical goals. Professional jealousy, that kind of thing. The problem is that we *do* have the same objectives."

"I guess I understand that," I responded.

"And Carnacki's descendants aren't as noble as he was. His family had a bad reputation. He was the exception that proved the rule. The others have always been greedy scheming rogues, manipulators, and fraudsters."

"Nice bunch of people!"

"Yeah," nodded Hellboy. "Since it was founded the Carnacki Institute never got the chance to mount a real challenge against us. Not until *now*. Marvin Carnacki, the present director of the Institute, discovered a way to divert Nekrotzar onto a collision course with Earth. There was an old book in a locked attic. He had the good luck to find it. The book outlined the myth of Nekrotzar, gave instructions for a ritual that would change its direction through space."

"And the ritual was performed?" I asked.

Hellboy nodded. "Looks that way."

I finished my coffee. I like regular caffeine hits as much as the next guy but this one suddenly tasted disgusting.

"What the hell is Nekrotzar?"

Myths and legends are generally based on truth, that's common knowledge. Somewhere at the back of every folktale is an event involving real people. Theseus killed the Minotaur and probably there was a real beast for a real man to slay. Before he tackled the Minotaur he killed Sciron and once again that giant was surely an authentic creature. Descriptions are few and far between but Sciron was an ugly mother, that much is certain. And an even more hideous father. Lame joke.

I'll continue more seriously. Bald shiny head, flat round face with bushy eyebrows, thin lips, sagging jowls, lopsided ears, wide nose covered in tough black hairs, bulging belly, muscular frame, relatively short legs, eyes the color of a lake polluted by phosphates and uranium, in one hand a twisted club made of half a tree.

But what was his connection to Nekrotzar?

Nekrotzar was a planet in a distant galaxy, a galaxy not yet identified. The book found by Marvin Carnacki didn't seem too interested in speculating on such details as original locations, so I'll be just as blithe. It was an old planet circling a very old sun, a sun so ancient that it had burnt out. For a million years the planet kept going around anyway but the dead husk of the star was gradually eroded by streams of particles from nearby supernovae and its gravitational attraction became too weak to keep a family of planets in orbit.

Like the other worlds in that system Nekrotzar drifted away on its own, a rogue globe, but people still lived on the surface. The race of beings who always had dwelled there was excessively cruel. Their monarchs were among the most insane in the universe. And another mystery that needs to be solved: they were humanoid, similar in many ways to us.

I've listened to Bureau boffins discuss this enigma. One idea is that in the remote past, long before the Stone Age, humans were more advanced than now. They constructed spaceships and flew off around the universe, colonizing worlds and moving on. Then something happened here, a huge disaster, and the folk who stayed behind on Earth forgot what they knew about technology. So the cosmos is populated with humans and the variations that natural evolution has had time to create.

Plausible. But Nekrotzar is much older than our own planet. Indeed the sun of that world had gone out long before our precious Earth even condensed from stardust. At least that's what Marvin Carnacki's book claimed. And who wrote that book? I don't have a clue. The Bureau is still examining it. Unlike every other book owned by the Carnacki Institute, that volume survived the terrific explosion that followed the ritual.

Whatever the biology of the matter, one thing remains clear: the rulers of Nekrotzar were complete loons. I'll skip over the more lurid accounts of what Kings Humper, Sepsis, and Nobbel got up to. Each was madder than his predecessor. The line ended with the maddest of all, King Sciron, who wanted a palace bigger than those his ancestors had ruled from. In fact he wanted the biggest palace in the history of creation.

Nekrotzar was a very old world and its core had cooled long ago, there was no liquid mantle under the crust, nothing but solid rock. King Sciron gave orders to start mining minerals, shaping blocks and piling those blocks higher and higher into walls.

Eventually he had the biggest palace of all time, the biggest *possible* palace. It didn't make him happy.

The Sciron killed by Theseus was clearly the same guy or else a mythical figure based on the real Sciron. But the question remains how the people on Earth who made up the myth, presumably the ancient Greeks, knew about Nekrotzar in the first place. I found this aspect of the case rather troubling. I thought about ordering a beer, maybe several, but I wasn't even in the mood to get drunk. Hellboy was ready to leave too.

"Time to get moving."

He held open the door of the coffee shop and I passed through and stood blinking in the sunlight. Then he lifted his stone hand to provide shade for both of us. Maybe he thought I needed a cooler head before I was ready to know the rest. If so, he was right.

King Sciron of Nekrotzar never gave the order to stop building. Blocks of stone were cut from the ground and added to other blocks continuously. The walls kept rising and rising. Towers were completed, turrets, domes, and chambers, only to serve as the foundations for more towers, turrets, domes, and chambers. The planet had no magma under its surface. The builders could dig it all up and shape it into blocks if necessary. That's what they did. Eventually the total mass of the planet was converted into the palace. One of the wonders of the universe!

A giant palace adrift in space. King Sciron had his personal chambers at the center. But he often liked to ascend the spiral staircase to the tallest turret. There was a balcony there without a rail that looked over the stars, comets, pulsars, other lost planets. Whenever he wanted to punish someone for an offense, he invited them onto the balcony of that turret and ordered them to kneel before him. Then he kicked them over the edge. The bodies are probably still falling, if they haven't already been burned up in younger suns.

Life is weird. I walk down the street with a big red demon and who's the one that attracts all the attention?

Yeah right. Car horns blared. A grinning fellow came up, tried to shake my hand and didn't look abashed when I refused. "Excuse me, but are you Foggy Dicks? Man, I love your flicks. Never seen anything like them before!"

Yeah, life is weird.

My mind's a little disordered now. It's mostly the drugs, the painkillers they pumped into my veins after Hellboy knocked the crap out of me. I'm still flooded with that liquid junk. But I was strange before my beating. That's what the specialist doctors at the Bureau told me back in the days when they thought I might be team material.

Which reminded me: I still wanted to know where Liz and Abe were. *Up north* was too vague an answer to satisfy me. I can't say I ached to see them—I don't ache much emotionally—but they had been friends, to a small degree at least.

"Mount Snæfell," said Hellboy.

"Iceland? What are they doing there? It's weird: you mentioned Jules Verne in the coffee shop and I remember that he wrote a book about two explorers . . ."

Hellboy just smiled.

"So what part do I play?" I wondered. "What does the Bureau want me to do? You know my talents. Fill me in properly, will you?"

"The book found by Marvin Carnacki outlined many rituals connected with Nekrotzar. Where did this book come from originally? We're still working on that. Marvin himself doesn't know. The rituals are all tantric."

"I'm not the only expert in that," I protested.

"This stuff is extremely advanced. Believe me, you're the only one who can do what's required. The Bureau never lost interest in you."

I was dubious. "Really?"

He rubbed his chin. "What do you think of Marvin Carnacki?"

"Nothing special. An old fuddy-duddy. A typical amateur investigator of the paranormal. Fusty, musty."

"Could you ever consider doing with him the sort of things you do in your films? To save the world . . ."

"Is this a hypothetical question?"

He said nothing, twitched not a facial muscle, and I suddenly knew why the Bureau wanted me. To perform some esoteric tantric-sex ritual with that horrible old man. I was too shocked to utter any word of protest. I stopped in my tracks and closed my eyes and laughed sourly. Hellboy rested his stone hand on my shoulder in a sympathetic manner. Maybe he thought I needed some obvious sign of support before giving my considered reply.

And maybe I did. I said, "We all have to make sacrifices. I'll do what I can."

"Thanks. You're one of the heroes."

Smiling, I acknowledged the compliment, but I was furious with myself. Why had I agreed? Was I going soft?

But I've always been soft.

I'm the ectoplasm guy. Remember?

A special room in one of the least-visited parts of one of the Bureau's old auxiliary buildings had been prepared for the ritual. I wore a gray dressing gown. When Marvin Carnacki entered I wanted to laugh. He was dressed like a pasha from an obsolete Eastern empire. Green curly slippers, loose scarlet pantaloons, a billowing orange blouse, an elaborate turban of blue silk. His fingers glittered with silver rings.

"Let's get it over with," I snorted.

Marvin took offense. "No need to be so blunt. I'm swallowing my pride as well."

"Now you've raised the issue," I remarked, "I still don't understand why you came to the Bureau in the first place. Descendant of the famous ghost finder! The first Carnacki would disown you if he knew. Why can't you handle the crisis back at your own institute?"

"Can't you guess?" he sneered.

"You discovered the existence of Nekrotzar and diverted it onto a collision course with Earth. You knew that astronomers would detect it soon enough and warn the governments of the world. You gambled that the Bureau would get involved but be powerless to prevent the catastrophe. Then the Carnacki Institute would step in and put everything right, because only your group had the necessary rituals at their disposal. It was supposed to be a way of showing the Bureau you were a force to be reckoned with."

"The boy has some brains," sniffed Marvin.

"That's right, buddy," I said.

"Nothing turned out the way we planned. We performed the tantric ritual to divert the course of Nekrotzar but there were errors in the procedure."

I shook my head. "Sloppy work, my friend."

"How right you are! A few small mistakes with big side effects. There was a blast that destroyed the antique furniture and killed the membership of the institute, all except me . . ."

"An explosion. Any other side effects?" I asked casually. I've always found that indulging in light conversation helps to reduce the embarrassment. Not by much, true, but we take what little we can get in this world. And in the next.

"Nothing major. One random dead person from Earth has possibly been resurrected on Nekrotzar."

I smiled mirthlessly at the irony of the situation. Diverting Nekrotzar onto a collision course with Earth had been the easy part, achievable from a distance, but diverting it a second time, *away* from our own world, was a far harder task. Somebody had to actually go there and physically steer it.

The book had mentioned a rudder in the throne room of King Sciron, unbelievable as that sounds. Hellboy was the only one capable of doing this. Marvin and I were just there to open up a doorway.

"There were twenty others involved in the first tantric ritual," pointed out Marvin. "You'll have to mimic the roles of them all. Can you do that?"

"Just watch this," I bellowed.

I prefer to leave out most of the details of what happened next. You'll have to use your imagination. I'll just say that Marvin held up a book during the ritual and began reciting in an unintelligible language. Then a mist thickened in the air and I knew it was time to extrude my ectoplasm. He ignored me and kept chanting.

I began to realize he was more perverse than anyone I had encountered before. Now I knew what Hellboy meant when he referred to the Carnacki family as decadent. The mist began congealing into blobs and falling to the floor. On the floor those blobs ran about like drops of mercury before flattening into discs. Then the discs slid together.

"The doorway to Nekrotzar!" somebody shouted.

"Get ready!" was the response.

"Another few minutes!" cried the first voice, and I was aware of the big face of Hellboy looming through the remaining mist. He had stepped from behind the screens. Time seemed to slow. Then a sudden thought made me shudder. If Hellboy managed to cross to Nekrotzar, how the hell would he get back?

He had to pass me on his way to the shimmering doorway and I thought about blocking his path and begging him not to go, even though it wasn't strictly my business what happened to him on the other side. Then Marvin distracted me.

"Listen carefully," he said. "I've got a proposal. How much are these Bureau creeps paying you? Well I can offer more. The Carnacki Institute has many bank accounts and now the other members are dead. So I'm extremely rich. You want half this money? It's yours if you perform one simple service."

"You think I'm so cheap?" I spluttered.

"Yes I do. The Carnacki family was big and influential. All I want is to rebuild some of my destroyed pride. That's not much to ask. My institute diverted Nekrotzar onto a new trajectory but couldn't put it back on its original course. I don't mind admitting I've lost face."

"State your terms," I growled, believing myself beyond temptation, but none of us are ever that.

"All you have to do is enroll as a member of my institute. I can formally welcome you aboard right now. There's nobody left to veto my decision. I *am* the Carnacki Institute."

"What good will that do either of us?"

"Cross over to Nekrotzar with Hellboy. He'll have to make the perilous trip through the palace to the throne room. The instant he arrives near the throne, you can jump forward and take hold of the rudder. The credit for saving the world will belong to the institute again! You agree? By the power invested in me I accept you as a full member!"

I arched my eyebrows. "How can I persuade Hellboy to let me accompany him on the mission? I'm not a field agent. I'm just here for this."

"Don't give him a choice. Hitch a ride all the way!"

And he whispered into my ear. His idea was so treacherous I still don't understand why I didn't break his evil jaw with my fist. Maybe it was the hypnotic quality of his eyes. Whatever the reason, I was infected with his madness. I howled. The mystic doorway was ready and Hellboy was striding toward it. I transformed myself entirely into ectoplasm, flapped across the surface of the floor, flung myself over Hellboy's shoulders like a cloak.

Not really like a cloak. Closer than that. Like a second skin. In fact the astral molecules of my ectoplasm meshed with the molecules of his real skin, bonding with the moisture in his cells. I'm no expert on the biology of demons and maybe that moisture wasn't water, but it served its purpose. He paused for a moment.

"What the hell are you doing? This isn't part of the ritual!"

"I've changed my allegiance," I hissed.

"You're making a mistake. I don't want to hurt you."

"Buddy, there's no way you can remove me now. Not without surgery. I've sold you out for money, same way I sold myself out, years ago."

In a few minutes the doorway would close. Hellboy had no time to reason with me. He had to cross over *now*, with me draped on his back. I planned to stay exactly where I was for as long as possible. I was drunk with a feeling of power, far more drunk than I had ever been on beer.

Half a minute later I was totally punch drunk . . .

We had underestimated the big red lunatic. No mortal man could reach around behind himself and pull off his own skin without even blinking! It should go without saying that Hellboy wasn't a man. First he shook me out like a sheet, then he rolled me up and snapped me like a whip against the floor, forcing me to change back into a man. I had betrayed the Bureau and had this coming to me . . .

That should have been the end of it, but I was still infected with the madness Marvin Carnacki had induced in my soul. I flung myself at Hellboy again and again. He tried to brush me off lightly but I just wouldn't back off. So he was forced to get rough.

"Sorry, Foggy," he said, and the regret in his voice was genuine.

Witnesses to the incident later told me that the whole thing lasted thirty seconds. I believe it. But in that short period a mangling occurred that I surely will never forget. Having said that, I don't recall the actual beating. The bruises are my mementos. And the scars. Very rapidly I faded in and out of consciousness like a flickering lightbulb, then I distinctly remember hearing a shouted warning that the doorway was starting to vanish. Maybe my life was saved by that yell. Hellboy turned his attention to his mission.

As he passed through the door, he began to shimmer. Just before he was entirely gone, he glanced over his shoulder at Marvin Carnacki and jerked a thumb. "I'll be back for you."

Despite my condition I managed to laugh.

But Marvin only sneered. "How will you do that? Nekrotzar is located in outer space. If you succeed in diverting it from its present course you'll never see planet Earth again!"

It was a fair point, well made. Yes.

And that's how I ended up in the hospital. The surgeons worked hard to repair the damage. When I came to my senses I felt different, lighter, but in a way I couldn't identify. I realized I was in one of the Bureau's secret sickbays. The nurses were friendly but didn't engage too intimately in conversation. I asked for a newspaper. Many weeks had passed since the assault. A single paragraph on one of the back pages of one of the crankier tabloids reported that the actor Foggy Dicks had been injured by falling scenery on the set of his latest film. I smiled thinly at this. The Bureau can pull any strings it wants to.

I found myself growing obsessed about the progress of Hellboy's weird mission on an alien world. Nobody could give me any information. As for Marvin Carnacki, I didn't even ask about him, partly because I didn't care, partly because the merest thought gave me painful cramps inside. I know that sounds very mixed up, but I *was* very mixed up right then. As I recovered I tried simple exercises with my ectoplasm gland, attempting to shoot forth tendrils of gloop to lasso the jug of water on my bedside table. But nothing worked. My injuries were still serious. Frustrating.

So I have to relate the story of Hellboy's exploits on Nekrotzar secondhand, the same way I received it from the big red brute in question. Might as well get down to that task now. My pillow is comfortable enough. After he stepped through the doorway, our stump-browed hero emerged through an almost identical portal on the other side that vanished behind him like a broken cobweb. He was in a vast hall, the lobby of the palace, and the sight of his surroundings was impressive even to him, and he's seen a lot of odd sights in his career, believe me.

You don't have to take my word for that, or for anything else, of course, but your doubts aren't important to me. Anyway, Hellboy gazed at the horizons, then craned his head to look up at the distant ceiling. Stormclouds were gathering in one corner of the room, bumping back and forth between the place where the ceiling met a wall and a row of columns rising from the floor. When King Sciron had given his order to start work on the palace, he forgot the inconveniences of geography. The landscapes of his home planet became enclosed in the edifice.

Mountain ranges, river valleys, deserts, steppes, icecaps, glaciers, even entire oceans—these don't just disappear simply because you roof them over and enclose them between gigantic walls in absurdly immense rooms. The forests die, this is true, because of the lack of sunlight, but Nekrotzar's sun had gone out millennia before anyway. The only vegetation Hellboy found on his visit was various kinds of fungus, some toadstools as big as redwood trees and puffballs like the severed heads of bloated corpses. And all illumination was provided by the perpetual electric storms . . .

Why didn't he arrive directly in the throne room? Why did he now have to travel all the way from the lobby to the center of the palace? Who knows for sure? The rulers of Nekrotzar had been devoted to games of mischief; it was in their nature to be capricious. Hellboy began walking over a moldy carpet as big as a savanna. He was aware of many pairs of eyes watching him from the shadows, some from above, but sensations like that were part of a day's work for him. Something flapped high above. A lump of pterodactyl crap hit his shoulder.

"So that's how it's going to be?" he muttered.

He crested a rise, a warp in the carpet, and stood gazing down at a small inland sea. Mists obscured most of its expanse, but at the wide mouth of a lazy river was a wooden jetty with a golden boat moored to it. A man stood on the jetty and something made him look in Hellboy's direction. Fingering the pistol in its holster but not drawing it, Hellboy ambled down the incline to meet the man. They stood a few yards apart, squinting at each other, then both slowly nodded, as if reassured.

"I know you," said Hellboy.

"Yeah?" came the reply. "Well I ain't Anubis."

Hellboy moved closer. "You're Philip José Farmer, the writer. What are you doing on an alien world?"

The boatman shrugged. "For some reason I've been resurrected here. No explanation was ever offered by anyone. I thought at first that maybe every other human who had ever died would join me somewhere along the length of this mighty river, but it didn't turn out like that. I'm alone."

"You're a new Charon, an infernal ferryman?"

"Nah, I just rent out the boats. Been waiting for my first customer since my rebirth. You're the one."

"Honored," said Hellboy, "but I don't have time to work out this new mystery. I reckon it might not even be connected to my main quest. It could be just a fluke.

I don't care because you have what I need, namely a boat. I have to ask the price first, I guess."

"Look buddy, I like you, don't know why. You can have the barge for free. Money's no use to me. Maybe I shouldn't tell you this, but there's an endearing quality about you and I want to help properly."

"Thanks for the observation."

"This river is exactly one million miles long and terminates in the throne room. If you use the boat to paddle there it'll take at least a century. But there's a shortcut. The river loops like a knotted piece of string. If you're strong enough, drag the boat overland to the next room and rejoin the river there. That way you'll bypass a long stretch, because first it flows into the lower levels and then around and up through most of the turrets before returning to this level."

"Thanks. You're one of the good guys."

"Smile when you call me that, stranger," said Philip José Farmer.

"How much of the river will I bypass?"

The answer came with a grin. "Ninety-nine percent."

There wasn't a need for further decision making. Hellboy grabbed hold of the mooring rope and dragged the boat up the river bank. Then off he set across the carpet in the indicated direction. Seeing him preoccupied with his burden, the pterodactyls took their opportunity to swoop and sink their talons into his shoulders. They tried to carry him off to their clifftop nests. Bad mistake. Soon the ground was littered with broken long heads and the flapping remnants of torn wings.

Hellboy entered the adjacent room by passing through a wet curtain, the spume of a waterfall that cascaded from a high shelf directly over the door. A curiously formed rainbow undulated away into pale brown light. Desert sands whipped abrasive particles against his bare legs and arms. He ignored them and the biting insects that regarded him as a potential supper. Hellboy is the sort of guy who lights an *ordinary*-length cigarette from the crater lip of an active volcano. Talking about those, there were none, for Nekrotzar was a geologically dead world.

Small mercies. Hellboy spied the river in the distance. He plunged into a petrified forest, snapping stone trunks left and right. Then he was set on by a group of telepathic winking tyrannosaurs. Swinging the boat on the end of its rope he knocked those down like Cretaceous skittles. Their winking days were over. Damage to the hull was thankfully minimal. He pushed the golden barge out into midstream and jumped aboard, determined to enjoy the ride. But others in the equation had different ideas about that. And here was one of the most bizarre aspects of the entire adventure. What the hell were *Nazis* doing on Nekrotzar?

They ambushed him in the next room, which was a sort of lounge filled with giant sofas and occasional tables. They sniped at him from behind the cover of weirdly shaped rocks, from both banks of the narrowing river. He cursed, fired back and made every bullet count. As for the Nazis, they were old men, clearly marooned here for many decades, but how and why? I don't think Hellboy killed every one, at least he doesn't reckon he did, just most of them. Good enough.

Plenty of things happened to him after this, mostly bad things, but each time he won through. One percent of a million miles is still a hell of a long way. The rooms he passed into all contained their own dangers. Snakes the size of oil pipelines, golems fabricated from riverbank mud, armies of evil spiders with tiny human faces, muttering warlocks sitting inside caves who cast bolts of spluttering green fire. And Hellboy lost all sense of direction. He just took what came to him and responded appropriately. After a while he even stopped wondering why.

Marvin Carnacki hadn't lied. The palace *was* a maze, a labyrinth worse than the famous one Theseus found his way through. But Theseus used an unwinding cord to retrace his steps and Hellboy only had the river to follow. Inside Hellboy was a growing conviction that he wouldn't be stuck on Nekrotzar forever but he didn't want to appear too confident. Tempting fate and all that. He just kept working the oars and only broke his rhythm to deal with hostile assaults. He thinks it was the T'ao T'ieh that really made him cynical about the threats.

The T'ao T'ieh, he later explained, is an inverse variation of Cerberus, the guardian hound of Hell. Whereas Cerberus has one body and three heads, the T'ao T'ieh has only one head but two bodies. Anyway, at a bend in the river, just before it plunged into a chasm between two looming easy chairs, the dog in question jumped into the water from the shore and started swimming toward the boat. Hellboy lifted one oar and used it as a club to pulverize the hound's skull. A single stroke was enough. No contest. The corpse spiraled to the bottom.

Then he entered a space longer and narrower than any encountered so far, more of a corridor than a room, and he guessed it was the approach passage to the throne room. He squinted in the dim light and made out the flight of steps that led up to the plush chair of a king. It was unoccupied at the moment but on the bottom step stood something that could only be one of the authentic inhabitants of Nekrotzar. Then Hellboy knew that the other things he'd fought weren't original to this world. The realization gave him some relief. It confirmed a guess.

The source of the river was a broken fountain halfway along the corridor but Hellboy didn't wait to reach it. He jumped out of the boat and sauntered toward the shape that blocked his progress up the steps. Bald shiny head, flat round face with bushy eyebrows, thin lips, sagging jowls, lopsided ears, wide nose covered in tough black hairs, bulging belly . . . It was the last king of Nekrotzar himself. Or was it?

"King Sciron, I presume?" asked Hellboy.

"Yes and no. The original Sciron perished centuries ago, but not before he had cloned himself many times. Each of those clones experimented with further clones, improving the basic model until the optimum example was achieved. That's me, in case you're wondering!"

Hellboy rubbed his jaw. "Are you going to let me pass? I have a job to do."

"Nope. I intend to kick you into oblivion."

"I knew something like this would happen. Let's finish it . . ."

Sciron rushed at Hellboy, jumped and kicked him in the face. The force of this impact should have knocked Hellboy halfway down the corridor but it only unbalanced him for a moment. Then Sciron began circling Hellboy, lashing out with his foot as often as possible, but Hellboy just stood there and he even had the audacity to casually insert a cigarette between his lips and flick open his lighter.

"Lie down, will ya?" Sciron screeched hysterically.

Hellboy reached out and snatched Sciron around the waist, throwing him to the floor with a quick twist. Then Hellboy stood on Sciron's hand until a cry of surrender was forthcoming. Perception clouded by pain, the last king of Nekrotzar was scarcely aware of being loaded on the barge and sent drifting off downstream.

"A million miles," called Hellboy, "and if you make it all the way in one piece you deserve this mercy."

He waved farewell but didn't pause to hear what the reply was.

Hellboy bounded up the steps into the throne room. Next to the ornate chair was the rudder that controlled the direction of the palace through space. He gripped it in his left hand, then gazed at a pair of screens below that indicated velocity and direction. Hellboy smiled, then released his hold on the rudder. A lesser hero might have sat on the throne at this point but he stood where he was and waited.

An hour later the voices came to him from the rear of the throne room. Abe and Liz stepped from the shadows.

"Trevor Bruttenholm was right all along," Hellboy said.

"He knew his stuff, for sure."

Hellboy grinned. "When I was younger he told me all about Nekrotzar and he stressed that it really was a *very* old planet. He also mentioned that it was a lot smaller than Earth. The collision between the two worlds has already happened, billions of years ago, but the Earth was just a cloud of stardust then and congealed around Nekrotzar, trapping the palace in what eventually became the Earth's crust, forty miles under what is now Iceland."

"Shame the Carnacki freaks didn't know that when they tried to divert its course," said Abe.

"Yeah, could have saved themselves a lot of trouble. Their ritual made Nekrotzar shift not even one foot. It was already where they wanted it to be. That's what I call irony."

"Jules Verne was right all along as well," said Liz.

Hellboy laughed. "Giant mushroom forests always interest me. Let's collect samples on the way back."

Hellboy came to see me in the hospital not long after. Liz and Abe had mapped the tunnels from the surface down to the palace and they emerged from the crater of Mount Snæfell with sooty faces two days later. They showered in Reykjavík and then boarded a special Bureau jet for the supersonic flight to Fairfield. I was delighted to see Hellboy and grateful for the time he spent with me in the following weeks.

He answered all my questions with candor.

"It's a well-known fact the Nazis kept exploring deep caves in the Earth's crust," he told me. "Maybe they were looking for secure hiding places for stolen gold. On three occasions Himmler gave orders for battalions to penetrate the interiors of extinct volcanoes. No news was ever sent back and it was assumed the soldiers had died. From what happened to me it's clear one battalion reached Nekrotzar."

"And when you saw them, it gave you reassurance?"

He nodded. "That's when I knew I wasn't in outer space but only a few dozen miles below the Earth's surface. I had to go all the way to the throne room just to be absolutely certain. It's amazing how small an area a million-mile river can occupy if it's tightly looped. Also I wanted to get back to the surface and I'd arranged to meet Liz and Abe by the throne. So I kept going."

"They took a big risk going down to meet you."

"Yeah. It wasn't easy for them. We thought a double approach to the problem was the best course of action. Liz and Abe went down the volcano on the assumption that Nekrotzar was lodged in the Earth's crust, but I went by the supernatural gateway, just in case we were wrong."

"How did you defeat Sciron so easily?" I asked.

"Because he was actually very feeble. The legend of Theseus and Sciron gave me an initial clue. Theseus was just a man, Sciron was a giant, but the battle was won too easily. Theseus had no trouble whatever kicking Sciron off his own cliff. So then I knew."

"Yeah, but knew *what?*" I protested.

"That the inhabitants of Nekrotzar were weaklings. Millions of years of decadent living had made them soft. Sciron was a giant like the other members of his race, but he wasn't physically powerful on Earth. His enormous size was just for show. His strength was relative to the conditions of Nekrotzar . . ."

"And this also applied to his clones?" I asked.

"Exactly," agreed Hellboy. "The Sciron faced by Theseus was one of the copies that somehow found an escape out of the palace and up to the Earth's surface."

"I have an idea," I said, "to help navigate the labyrinth of the palace if you decide to return there."

"Go ahead and tell me," he responded.

"Take my ectoplasm gland. I don't want it. You can use it to generate a cord long enough to stretch through all the caverns on the way down and through all the rooms when you arrive."

He rubbed his big red chin. "The surgeons already took it out. It wasn't my idea. But that's the way it is."

"I don't care," I responded.

"You *are* one of the good guys," said Hellboy.

His surprise was genuine but mild. It's hard to rattle that big red demon. Yes indeed. He helped me up and let me use him as a crutch as I lurched down the corridor. It was nice just to walk again. I didn't think we had a definite destination, but then I realized we were heading toward the canteen. My nose twitched. The odor of frying mushrooms permeated the corridors. I wasn't sure if the smell was utterly tempting or totally foul. A minor paradox.

"We have a new cook," explained Hellboy.

"You're training him to prepare really strange meals?"

"He has a vested interest in the paranormal. He'll also have a hell of a lot of washing up to do."

I didn't need to visit the kitchens to know that Marvin Carnacki was in there, sleeves rolled up, chopping fungi the size of trees into pieces small enough for an enormous pot.

"Risotto today. For every staff member," said Hellboy. "Tomorrow it's pizza. Someday people will relate legends about the man who cooked more meals than humanly possible."

"Talking about legends, Theseus was always getting into trouble. Just like you. Is there some connection?"

"Nah," protested Hellboy with a chuckle. "He got into trouble because every Theseus creates an Anti-Theseus. I get into trouble because it's my style. Different situations."

I couldn't argue with that. We shared a table in the canteen. I'd describe the meal as chthonic if anyone ever asked me.

I hope they never do.

MONSTER BOY
STEPHEN VOLK

For the first six months of his life Ethan Salt didn't have a name. This was typical of his father, Vic, who didn't set out for anywhere unless he was already late, and his mother, Diane, who was so indecisive and unpredictable that her relatives called the two of them The Secret Society—you never knew what they were going to do next, and neither did they, most of the time.

Like all parents, though, their only concern was that baby came out with all his bits and bobs in the requisite place and in the requisite number. They took their bundle of joy home from Llantrisant Royal to their smallish house on a perpetually almost-finished housing estate called Coed Coch (which meant something red; Welsh was never Vic's strongest subject) on the outskirts of the market town of Pontypridd, halfway between Cardiff and Merthyr in the coalfields of South Wales. Not that there was any coal there now. Or rather, there *was*, but nobody was digging it. The few miners still employed in the area worked as tour guides at the Big Pit Museum near Abergavenny, or up at the Heritage Centre, where you could try on the helmets, and learn about canaries and Davy lamps, and have a not-bad Sunday dinner.

Ethan's early years were uneventful, except for a scare when they suspected he had viral meningitis and he was rushed to hospital in the back of Vic's VW. As a boy growing up Ethan would never know that his father sat outside the room in which the doctors did their tests, elbows on the knees of his tracksuit bottoms, weeping into his hands until they were as wet as if he'd plunged them into a bucket of water.

As an infant the lad was anything but talkative (though in later years he'd certainly make up for it). When he was three, Mrs. Idris, a woman with beetroot-colored glasses, came and moved her index finger horizontally in front of his face and shook a rattle next to his ears. It was concluded as she shut her briefcase that he might be a late developer. "I notice his eye contact isn't very good," she said matter-of-factly to his mother. "Well, it's all right when he's talking to *me*," said Diane. Defensively.

If he was a late talker, he wasn't a late listener. He'd be drawing or writing, and hear his family avidly discussing his latest school reports, saying they were good, look how clever he is, look how brainy, there's nothing wrong with this one, how can they say anything's *wrong* with this kid? And, out of the corner of his eye he'd see his grampa drawing a line across his lips with his index finger. And he'd pretend he hadn't heard, or seen. Sometimes Ethan thought that was the main thing to learn about growing up: pretending that you hadn't heard, or seen.

Things he *had* heard were his nan saying: "They talk about *syndrome* this, *syndrome* that—they never talked about syndrome when our boys were in school. Not a good mixer, they'd say."

And: "Spectrum? What do they mean by *spectrum?* His reports are good, what more do they want? Flipping troublemakers these days, they are. Lot of nonsense they talk. Honest to God."

And his grampa would shake his copy of the *Echo* to get the spine straight, and wink at him from behind it.

"All right, butty?"

And Ethan would smile.

It was an incontrovertible formula, that. *Wink. Smile.* So sure and comforting and inarguable that it should have been taught in Chemistry. The peculiar, poetic chemistry between two human beings bridged by seventy years of life on this planet.

Secretly, deep down, Ethan knew he was a worry to his family. His parents in particular. He didn't know why. It was a mystery like a hundred million elastic bands knotted up in a big ball in his head. That was why he worked as hard as he could. He saw how happy and relieved they were when he did well in school, and for a short while, looking at their grinning faces and feeling them ruffle his hair (his father saying, "Well done, mate"), it made him think, fleetingly, that they were happy about him. But that feeling quickly faded away, and the feeling came back inside that they weren't, and couldn't be, and never would be. The feeling of a hole somewhere that needs some chocolate biscuits in it, or needed to see a grandfather's wink, or hear the snap of the *Echo* being opened.

He was a "good scholar," as his nan would say. He paid attention in class and the information went in. He didn't understand why the other children were so slow and so stupid. Why they spent time nattering and talking about how they felt about each other. He just wanted to be there to learn stuff. So he did.

Often when he arrived home his mum would ask, "Make any friends today, soldier?" And he'd say, "No." Just like that. And her heart would sink a little bit, but she tried not to show it, not to let it upset her, though Vic saw sometimes it did. She tried to content herself in the knowledge he was happy with his own company, and that was a good thing, wasn't it? He wasn't like other kids, but that wasn't necessarily a bad thing, was it? He was eccentric. He was *special.* And he was clever. She could see him being a doctor, lawyer, prime minister if he wanted to. So what if he didn't have friends?

It didn't seem to bother Ethan. He had his books. He had his DVDs, his computer games, his card collections. And he had his monsters.

"D ad, if all the different enemies of Godzilla had a fight, which one do you think would win?"

Vic sighed. He'd barely reversed out of the driveway. In fact, he was barely awake and it was the first thing his son had said to him that morning. "Jesus Christ, Ethan."

"All right, all right," said the little boy with *The Movie Treasury of Horror Movies* open across his lap. "But do you think it's Mothra, the giant moth, which is a bit crappy looking, or the Smog Monster, or do you think it's King Kong in *Godzilla vs. King Kong* because King Kong is a monster in his own right and really, really powerful."

Ethan. For God's *sake,* his father wanted to shout. But instead he said:

"Seat belt."

"I think it's King Kong, I do."

"Do you? Well that's really interesting," Vic murmured under his breath, knowing his son was impervious to sarcasm. "Seat belt."

Begrudgingly, Ethan tugged the strap across him and clicked it into its buckle. He frowned, balancing the open covers of the hardback on his knees. Didn't his father realize he had more important things to be thinking about?

"T he first things that terrified him, before he'd even looked inside, were the covers. A green-lit grotesque with one eyeball hanging out and saliva dangling from a wide-open chasm of a mouth. The gimlet eyes and duck's-feet ears of Gorgo. Claude

Rains's Phantom of the Opera, even in the *mask*. Karloff's Frankenstein, the iconic, sculpted head as formidable as a concrete wall. Slithery Lugosi. Chaney's leering and twisted Hunchback. He didn't know their names, at first. He just saw their pictures. Page after page of them, image after image, nightmare after nightmare in glorious black and white. He was terrified, yes, and mesmerized, just as much.

He'd take out a selected issue of Grampa's old *Famous Monsters of Filmland* whenever he went round there, which was every weekday after he was dropped off by the school bus, because neither his mum nor his dad finished work till six. Soon he looked forward specifically to that activity and planning which magazine he would delve into next—King Kong with his inhumanly flaring nostrils, or Karloff's Im-Ho-Tep in his eerie red fez?—methodically asking his grandfather to identify each character in each picture throughout, and elaborate on the stories behind each film within.

It was an illicit activity he and his grampa shared, and part of the excitement of it was that it was forbidden fruit. Both knew equally instinctively that his mother and father would not approve; that they would see his interest as unwholesome and unhealthy, but for some reason the universe (the Universal universe, often) of these mutant and reprehensible creatures *meant* something to Ethan. In a way he could not express, he thrilled to them and felt for them in a manner he didn't feel for people around him most of the time. He was absorbed by these wonders now, and could no more shake them off than he could shake off his own skin.

The monsters had him. He was caught in the Wolf Man's hairy grip. He was hypnotized by Bela's unconvincingly hypnotic (but nevertheless disturbing) stare, which affected him on a far deeper level than mere fear. Within those film stills of grainy graveyards, blasted heaths, and shadow-laden laboratories, way before he'd seen any of the actual films, he knew he *belonged*—like he belonged nowhere else.

He learned about Bram Stoker, about James Whale, about Frederic March, about Edgar Allan Poe and Lon Chaney (Sr. and Jr.). He knew every actor who played every Frankenstein's monster pre- and post-Karloff, from Thomas Edison's short through Hammer horror and beyond. He knew who played spidery Dr. Pretorius in *Bride of Frankenstein* and the Dracula film in which Michael Ripper played a police inspector.

Sometimes he would ask questions, and his grampa would answer as best he could, but the old man realized that these were characters that Ethan had grown to love, and love was never about logical explanations. The essential "unknowableness" was what the boy adored, as he had adored it himself at that age. To enjoy it was enough. To enjoy, and be terrified.

When the kids in the playground talked about best friends and football and boyfriends, to Ethan it was like they were speaking a different language, but the world of monsters was familiar, homely, comforting, compared to the nasty and unpredictable world he faced every day when he opened the front door. It was scary, but it was understandable. It was understandable that to make a man come back to life you'd put electricity through bolts in his neck. It was understandable that you put a stake through a vampire's heart and he wouldn't come after you anymore.

"Jekyll and Hyde," Grampa would say by way of education. "Who you are and who you want to be, and the price you have to pay."

He'd tell the boy that Ray Bradbury wrote *The Beast from 20,000 Fathoms,* and the special-effects dinosaur in that film was created by Ray Harryhausen.

"Shaky monsters!" Ethan would cry, using their shared pet expression for stop-frame animation. *"Jason and the Argonauts!"*

"That's right. And the two of them were friends since they were little boys. The two Rays. Two little boys in America whose heads were full of monsters. And they both went on to create them—one by writing them, one by making them."

He hung on his grampa's every word.

He'd sit, wonderfully anxious, anxiously full of wonder, watching *Bride of Frankenstein* on the floor between his grandfather's bony knees, occasionally given the bounty of one of the chocolates the old man lined meticulously along the armrest. And if his heart *did* skip a beat, or if he *did* have to look away at the scary part—like when, on another occasion, the camera panned to the Wolf Man for the very first time, in that mist-shrouded wood, in Wales, and his eyes were sparkling and his fur looked *so real*—his grampa was there protecting him. And sometimes when there was a night scene and the TV screen was dark, Ethan could see a grandfatherly smile reflected in it, hovering somewhere in Transylvania, while his nan was in the kitchen making him beans on toast.

He remembered the day his grampa had said, "Watch this, it will make you cry," and first put on his video of *King Kong*—the Willis O'Brien original. As soon as it started, with its creaky old titles and music, Ethan had mumbled, "Crap, that is." "Don't be a critic. Hush," reprimanded the old man sternly. And by the time *The End* came up, the boy sat gazing at the screen in awed silence, as if he had been witnessed a kind of miracle. Which, in a way, he had.

"Still think it was crap, then?"

"No." Ethan down-tilted his head slightly, reluctant to concede his change of heart. "It was good, that was," he said.

Grampa nodded, a twinkle in his eye. "Attaboy," he said, sinking back in the armchair, knowing he had a convert at last.

"D ad, if the giant Ymir from *20 Million Miles to Earth* and Gwangi from *The Valley of Gwangi* had a fight, who d'you think would win?"

Vic's back was hunched over the steering wheel, knuckles as white as his pallor. "Ethan, honest to God now, I'm really not interested in the slightest, OK?"

"No, but . . ."

"Never mind 'No, but . . .'"

"Yeah but, say they had an *encounter* and . . ."

"Really, Ethan." He raised his voice. "I know you don't believe me now, but I've got no interest whatsoever, all right?"

His son went silent, dropped his chin to his chest, and said nothing for the rest of the drive to school. Inevitably, Vic wondered what he was thinking. Was he thinking what a bad, horrible, nasty father he had? Was he thinking that all he wanted was a little show of fake interest from his dad, for once? Not much, just a little?

He stopped the car just beyond the school crossing. Ethan got out of the passenger seat, hauled his bag onto his shoulder and shut the door after him. Vic wasn't thinking about work any more.

"Okay, butty?"

Ethan nodded.

Vic watched his son trudge in through the gates. He seemed strangely apart from the flow of chatting, skipping children around him—a sad and lonely little boy. Tears prickled Vic's eyes and he quickly shut out the rest of his thoughts and concentrated on driving to work.

"Oi! Gay!"

Dylan Drew was not the archetype of a bully. If there was an *American Idol* of bullies, he wouldn't even get through the first set of auditions.

"Oi! Gay boy, I'm talking to you. Why aren't you walking over here with us?"

Ethan didn't look up. He kept his eyes strictly focused on his own shadow in front of him on the pavement.

"Not *gay* enough for you, are we?"

Ethan said *Shut up* in his head and for a moment he was scared he'd said it out loud, but they didn't need that kind of incitement. He knew that in seconds he'd be surrounded by Dylan and his brainless musketeers, Huw Gronow and Matthew Pamplin. Shit, shit, shit.

They walled him off. Dylan in front, nonchalantly walking backward, the others keeping pace. Ethan tried not to slow his speed, tried not to look up. But Gronow immediately started picking at the *Creature from the Black Lagoon* sticker on his shoulder bag. Ethan shrugged him off but he was like a seagull going for a crust of bread.

"He do like monsters, gay boy do!"

"Van Helsing."

Ethan thrust his elbow back. "I don't even *like* that film." He gave a quick jab back with the other elbow. Pamplin was pinching the skin at the back of his neck, causing Ethan to duck down in his collar like a tortoise into its shell.

"It's his favorite, favorite film. Bless!"

"Get lost! It's a *kids'* film!" Ethan protested.

"That's what I mean. He loves it."

"I *don't!* It's stupid. It has Dracula wanting to produce babies. Why does Dracula want to produce babies when he reproduces by biting people and . . ."

"Oo-ee, he knows all about ree-*pro*-duction, guys." Drew wobbled his jaw from side to side. "Not bad for a *gay boy.*"

Ethan had had enough. "*Stupid . . .*" he said before he could stop it coming out. He was halfway through barging past the boy in front of him, who stood with his hands on his hips, but already Ethan realized he was too close and he should have kept his trap shut.

"Who are you calling stupid, *freak?*"

Dylan had caught Ethan round the head with the hook of his arm and wasn't letting go in a hurry. In the same blur of motion one of the others had snatched Ethan's bag off his shoulder and was swinging it in the air in big circles. "*Freak!*" That was the word they always used, and he hated it. "Skinny fucking freak-a-zoid *twat!*"

No! Ethan kicked backward with one foot but hit only air.

"Oi! Less of that!"

He felt his own school bag hit his left leg just below the buttock. Dylan had let go and one of them—Ethan thought it was Gronow again—held his head at arm's length.

"What have you got in here?" Dylan was doing an inventory of Ethan's belongings, now being shaken out of his school bag all over the road. "Nutri-Grain Bar. Nice." He held up the offending object. A rectangle of protein, nuts, sultanas: a healthy substitute for sweets in his lunch box, Ethan's mum told him.

"Don't," said Ethan.

Dylan unwrapped one corner. "Shit. Looks like what fucking parrots eat. You a bloody parrot, freak?"

"No. Give it here."

Gronow sniggered. "Jesus. It looks as if it's been shoved up a goat's arse."

"Smells as if it's come *out* of a goat's arse," said Pamplin.

"Give it here!" said Ethan.

"Why?" said Dylan, walking toward him, waving the Nutri-Grain Bar in front of Ethan's face like a flick-knife. "Do you want to shove it up your *own* arse, gay-o?

Is that it, freak-o?" He stabbed it toward Ethan's face but Ethan turned one cheek then the other.

"You know what?" Ethan said. "My mum says you are what you eat, and she must be right because you eat *shit.*"

Gronow laughed—it was an ill-formed rejoinder but amusing, he thought—then quickly bit his lip because Dylan wasn't laughing *at all.*

"You know what your mother eats? Your father's fat prick every night." He threw the Nutri-Grain Bar into the gutter.

"Yeah. Probably," said Ethan cheerfully.

Dylan's nostrils flared. "Are you trying to be a funny fuck?"

"No."

"Well don't."

"I'm not."

"Well shut up when I'm talking to you."

Ethan did.

Dylan came up close, closer even than before. So close he had to tuck his chin in. "Friday. By the park gates. Straight after school," he said, showing Ethan his fist at close range as if he wanted him to examine it. "*I'm going to beat your fucking head in.* All right?"

Though it sounded like a question, Ethan, sensibly, decided it probably didn't require an answer.

After they'd gone Ethan's heart started thumping as he walked to the bus stop. *I'm going to beat your fucking head in.* He didn't like that word. Didn't hear it that much at home, but when he did he knew there was going to be trouble, so he covered his ears till the nastiness was over.

But he knew this time the nastiness wouldn't be over. On Friday Dylan Drew would hurt him. Hurt him really badly like he bashed other boys and made really strong boys cry and scream. Ethan knew the sweet tingly feeling of a nosebleed and he knew it would be worse than that. He knew the way boxers came at each other and hit and hit, and hurt and hurt and he wondered if he could stand that, and what would happen if the hitting didn't stop, didn't stop ever, and then you'd die? What would happen then, he wondered?

Three months before, Ethan's nan and grampa had cheerfully decided one day to drive over to the Abergavenny open-air market to give it the once-over, seemingly oblivious to the fact that it was the hottest day on record for several decades and there were warnings on the radio for old people not to go outdoors at all. Grampa was eighty and his wife was seventy-six. Vic was mad at them afterward, more angry than upset, or so it seemed to Ethan. It seemed like he was being like Diane was with Ethan when he stepped out into traffic without looking, and she slapped him on the back of the legs. If Grampa hadn't been old, Vic would have slapped his legs too, Ethan reckoned.

The heat had got to him in Abergavenny and he'd fallen over, too heavy for Nan to steady him, and she'd cried out for help as he slumped to the ground. As luck would have it, a nurse was passing and they got him to the nearest hospital, where he recovered, weak, wheezing, and embarrassed, and the diagnosis was "heart failure." When Ethan heard that expression from his dad he thought it sounded like failing an exam: as if his grampa's heart had been told "must try harder."

From that point on, the old man became more fragile day by day. The word "complications" started to be used. The boy didn't want to ask what that word meant—"complications." But inevitably he saw the result of his grandfather's steady decline.

He was told increasingly, when he got overexcited or boisterous, that "Gramp gets tired quickly now, love"—which he knew. He could see. He wasn't blind. He could see him get breathless and cough more and use his puffer more often. He wasn't *stupid*.

He still went there from school and gave him the lowdown on what monster films he'd seen, and the two of them would discuss the verdict: "Crap" or "Good." But Grampa didn't look at him so much and sometimes Ethan had to touch his chin and turn his face to him, and when he did he thought his eyes were a little bit glazy looking. But Grampa said he was just tired, that's all.

Sometimes Ethan would put his hand on the old man's cardigan sleeve and shake it gently. He didn't want him to be tired. *He* wanted to *talk. Come on.*

"No more monsters."

"Just one," Ethan would say.

The old man would sigh. "All right, then. Go on then."

And sometimes his nan would look in at them as if she was going to cry too. Everybody had that bleary, reddy, cry-y look about them these days.

Ethan knew something was wrong. He knew Grampa wasn't chatting so much, and ran out of steam, and didn't like his ham sandwiches anymore, and didn't want anything but a nice cup of tea. Where he once took ten tablets a day he now took thirty. "Bloody tablets." Once he said to Ethan, "you know what I think they should do? Stop all the bloody tablets and then see what happens." Ethan thought of Dr.

Jekyll taking his potion, gripping his throat, writhing in agony on the laboratory floor. "Bloody tablets." In his mind's eye he saw a transformation. But transformation into what?

Grampa's arms were always fattish, roundish, but now he had the arms of a skeleton. When Ethan felt them there was nothing there because he wasn't eating—only jelly and ice cream, not "proper food" as his nan called it. Which was when she'd dab her eyes with a tissue.

Gradually the old man became sad, gray, and wizened. Ethan thought he had the gray cardboard color of a zombie from *Plague of the Zombies*. He thought his grampa might be turning from color into black and white. Is *that* what happens when people get old, he wondered? Because all those old films are black and white, aren't they?

His skin was dry like parchment, like a really old manuscript. Like something precious from a museum. Ethan would touch the back of the old man's hand—dry, so dry, so unlike the softness, the *pinkness* of his own—and think of Boris Karloff in *The Mummy*. Wrinkles upon wrinkles upon wrinkles, century upon century. So this is death. This is how we turn into frightening things. Mummies. Zombies. *Night of the Living Dead*. It happens *now*.

The boy was frightened; he didn't know of what.

He was afraid sometimes when the old man was groaning in his chair and he didn't know if he was sleeping or awake.

Then he'd brighten again when his grampa would ask him to fetch something, and go:

"Attaboy."

They had the bed moved downstairs. Ethan's dad put a second banister rail beside the stairs (a better job of DIY than he ever did at home, Diane said), and a seat in the shower. But by then his grandfather had difficulty getting out of his chair, let alone upstairs. Ethan would stand in front of him and take him by the hands, and help him up.

"*Att*-aboy!"

Medically speaking, one thing happened after another in swift succession. Grampa got an infection in his chest. That was the point at which Diane said, "He looks bloody awful, get the doctor up here," and they called 999 and whipped him into hospital that night.

Ethan didn't visit him after that, the last time he went into hospital. His father told him he didn't think it was a good idea.

A few nights later Ethan heard his mum say not to worry but his dad, Vic, was sleeping up at the hospital that night, in Grampa's room. Again Ethan nodded, and when Diane asked if he was OK, nodded again and returned to his Game Boy. It upset him that he didn't know what he was expected to say.

One night he was watching the end of *The Day the Earth Stood Still* in his bedroom and he heard his dad downstairs saying something about "pumping lots of morphine"—except Ethan thought the word was "morphing" and he thought of his grampa "morphing" into some new, strange creature, like the Alien Mother from *Aliens* or the shape-changing being from John Carpenter's *The Thing*.

He crept downstairs. His dad hugged him and went back to hospital that fifth night, after telling his son to be tough and strong for his mother. Ethan sat and watched TV with her, and Diane held his hand on the sofa and sometimes kissed his fingers one by one and got them wet and sticky.

The next morning she threw back his curtains and the light that came in blinded him with its whiteness and before he could even open his eyes he could feel her holding him but not see her as she said, fast, like it was glue she didn't want to stick: "We've all got to be brave now, baby. Grampa's gone. He's not hurting any more and he was peaceful like he was sleeping. He's just gone into a deep, deep sleep and we've all got to be strong, sweetheart."

And Ethan cried. Or rather, he pretended to cry. Oh yes, he *howled*, because he knew that's what you were *supposed* to do when people died, so he'd better, or he might be in trouble. His eyes were still tightly shut and the room was full of sunlight he didn't want to see, and he could feel warm breasts against his cheek. Poor Ethan. Sobbing his little heart out against his mother's chest. He just wasn't sure what he felt, or whether he felt anything at all.

When he got home from his encounter with Dylan, after his dad picked him up from his nan's, his mum had fish fingers and oven chips ready for him on the table. He dumped his school bag, sat and looked down at his food but didn't feel hungry.

"Anything wrong, love?"

He shook out a dollop of ketchup.

"No."

All he wanted to do was go upstairs and watch the skeleton fight from *Jason and the Argonauts,* and the scene with the Harpies. *Shaky monsters. Ray Harryhausen.* Grampa had liked that scene, and Ethan loved the way their color shimmered, like they were half in one world and half in another.

Thursday night came all too quickly. He tried to slow down time in his mind but it didn't work. His bedroom light was switched off, and in the dark, like all anxieties, Ethan's anxiety about the next day's fight grew to Godzilla proportions.

"Oh God, oh God, oh God," he sobbed quietly into his pillow.

He tossed and turned, trying to get himself to sleep—except he didn't want to sleep because sleep would only bring the morning faster. His pajamas started to feel sticky with sweat, tugging and riding up in the wrong places. He tried to rid his mind of bad thoughts, but it was no good. He wrestled with his blanket. Tried to count sheep. Sheep were useless—they just turned into Dylan Drew and his flock, sidling up to him, hands in pockets.

It was pelting outside. Hammering on the roof. Tamping hard on the window panes. Lightning lit the room sporadically. He thought of Boris Karloff's hand flexing. He thought of a jagged trident in the sky above a castle. He thought about monsters.

Kreeeeee-AAAAAA!

His eyes popped open wide, glistening in the dark.

It was the thunder. It had to be. It was in the street but it sounded like it was in his head. He felt his bladder slacken and he needed the bathroom but didn't want to go there. He held himself between the legs.

KKKKKAAAAAaaaaiiieeeee-cccchhhhhh-AAAARRRRR!

It sounded like King Kong and Gwangi in hideous cacophony. It was nothing—of *course* it was. But what were thunder and lightning *for*, he thought, his heart pounding, but to *make things arise?*

He threw back the covers and rolled out of bed. He shuffled over to the window on his knees and threw back the curtains, not knowing what he would see beyond the glass semiopaque with rivulets of rain.

His back straightened and his throat took in a gasp of air so sudden his lips and teeth went cold.

He saw the song the Harpies sang.

As real as the magician scattering the teeth of the Hydra like beans and waiting for skeletons to sprout.

As real as the shriek of Elsa Lanchester when she first beholds the ugliness of her mate.

As real as the demon at the end of *Night of the Demon*, swathed in locomotive smoke, plucking the flesh stuffing out of the dreadful Karswell as a child might do to a teddy bear.

As real—no . . . *more* real.

Kreee! Kreee! SchrAAAAAAAAAAAAKKK!

It wasn't like something out of a dream. It was better than that. It was like something out of a *movie*.

The dragon had squat, muscular humanoid legs and a reptilian tail that swished and spiraled spasmodically as if trying to corkscrew a nonexistent bottle. As it turned he saw the thing had a mouth like a whale, bright pink and clean inside, and its leathery wings flapped like the vast sails of a galleon. The mouth opened as wide as its body, the jaw fell impossibly down to its ankles, exposing triple rows of fangs—sharp, sharper, sharpest—and Ethan could only imagine the acrid dead-meat tang of its breath.

But it was the *second* creature that made Ethan's eyes widen.

This one had the first secured in a head lock. It was male and looked like a shaved version of *Mighty Joe Young* on steroids. He had no idea of its size. Maybe eight feet tall. Maybe more. Its arms were beyond muscular, the insides seeming to want to burst from skin the color of uncooked steak. But its gigantic right hand was what he saw first—a huge stone paw that looked like it had been unearthed in the Valley of the Kings, the dust blown off its cryptic inscriptions by some soon-to-be-deceased archaeologists of knucklebones—smashing like a sledgehammer into its opponent's face. Its leather trench coat was torn in places, revealing patches of lobster-red skin mottled with sprigs of hair. Its nose was tiny, making its chiseled jaw even more like something hewn from Mount Rushmore. The horns on its head had been reduced to stumps, and under its fearsome row of piano-keyboard teeth it wore a neat black goatee.

Ethan watched.

As it pummeled the gravy out of its scaly dance partner, the sound of broken bone covered up by the poundings of the storm, it moved surprisingly nimbly on its cloven hooves. He didn't know if it was the devil from that movie *Legend* where Tom Cruise played Tom Thumb, or Jack the Giant Killer, or somebody; or if it was some Notre Dame gargoyle friend of Quasimodo come to life; or if he was witnessing one of those one-to-one duels that were always the climax of a Harryhausen film, like the centaur-cyclops fighting the gryphon, or Perseus versus Medusa.

Goggle-eyed, he wasn't sure *what* he was watching, but he didn't want to miss a second.

Next morning he dressed and came downstairs, helping himself to an unusually large bowl of Kellogg's Frosties and shoveling them into his mouth with little sign of restraint.

"Everything all right, love?"

Ethan nodded.

"What's wrong?" asked his mother.

"Nothing."

For once, she thought he meant it.

When the car door slammed, Vic took a deep breath, preparing himself for the inevitable barrage of monster questions. He geared himself up. Got ready to roll with the punches.

But this time, nothing came.

He looked over at his boy, who sat obediently looking out through the windscreen with his school bag on his lap and the seat belt across his body like a crossing-out.

"All right, son?"

Ethan nodded, and his father felt a strange pang of regret.

The car sounded a little empty today.

At lunchtime he pulled on his anorak and walked to his grandmother's house, a few streets away, and rang the doorbell. "I left some work. I did it when I was here on Sunday. I need it for this afternoon." He didn't like lying to her and already felt he wasn't being very convincing. "Geography," he added.

"Oh," said his nan. "Shall I get it for you?"

"No, I'll get it," said Ethan. "I know where it is."

"Got time for a cup of tea, love?" she asked as he went into the middle room, where he always did his homework.

"No thanks."

"Biscuit? Nice piece of cake?"

"No thanks."

When he was sure she'd gone, he crept upstairs and shut the door to the back bedroom behind him. It was Grampa's room.

The old man's belongings were still in evidence. Obviously his nan hadn't yet had the heart to pack them away; maybe she never would. The five or six paperbacks with the elephant bookends. The digital camera Vic had bought him last birthday which he'd never used. The single bed he'd slept in alone ever since his coughing and insomnia had started to keep his wife up all night. The nylon avocado bed linens with not a crease in them. On the dressing table under the triptych of the vanity mirror, a Burgundy-striped rugby club tie, still in its cellophane.

Ethan slid open the drawer underneath. It was full of his grandfather's clothes. Pullovers, cardigans. Shirts—some, maybe old Christmas presents even, still in their wrappers. The strong smell of mothballs wafted out. It made him think that the objects were being preserved. He wondered if he was a grave robber of some kind, like in *Curse of the Mummy's Tomb*. Whether he would be punished in some way by forces beyond his understanding. But this wasn't beyond his understanding. This was his grampa.

Underneath the Marks & Spencer shirts Ethan found what he wanted. He slid his hand into one of his grandfather's brown leather gloves. It was much too big, and when he clenched his fist the tops of the fingers were empty and bent against the heel of his hand.

His nan heard the front door slam, and was surprised her grandson hadn't poked his head round the door to say goodbye. But he was a funny little boy, she knew that. Much as she loved him to pieces, mind.

Dylan Drew was waiting like a gunfighter. His amigos lolled in sullen poses nearby. Huw Gronow, hood up and acne ridden, was munching a Lion bar and Matthew Pamplin was idly rearranging his genitals due to ill-considered boxer shorts. They hadn't forgotten their promise and were waiting for him. And so were a half dozen other hangers-on and rubberneckers who'd heard the rumors that had been percolating and turned up in the hope of seeing some blood spilled. To them, it could be the high point of an otherwise dreary week.

"I'm bored now," one girl in pandalike mascara said. "Honest to bloody God now." One of her mates passed her a cigarette, to shut her gob. Their ringside seat was near the fence and Dylan was watching their miniskirts edge up their white thighs when Gronow's voice, behind him, alerted him to the arrival of his foe.

"Showtime!"

The gunslinger turned, a massive smirk commandeering his face.

"Hey, freaky dick!" called Pamplin. "You haven't forgotten have you?"

Ethan had his head down and was walking straight toward them at a steady pace. Dylan stood with his arms crossed and his legs wide apart—which proved not to be the greatest idea. A frown etched into Gronow's brow and Pamplin's chin dropped dumbly as they saw Ethan . . . *accelerate*.

Dylan suddenly and all-consumingly thought of his testicles. The message was traveling from his brain while Gronow, immobilized by disbelief, saw Ethan take his hand from his anorak pocket and at the end of it registered this enormous brown fist like the hammer of Thor. This giant hand, this *slab*—pulling back with a crook of the elbow, then embedding itself hard into Dylan's stomach, bending him double.

The girls went into caterwauls of horror.

In a blur the leather fist drew back and administered a *second* blow, an uppercut to Dylan's chin. With no choice in the matter he followed the trajectory of his jaw, vertically, a dog on a leash yanked skyward.

Then fell on his ass. Before anyone had time to blink.

Ethan just kept on coming. Or rather the stone fist did. It smashed in right and left, crunching Dylan's face into the grass, first one cheek, then the other. The bewildered bully's flailing arms did nothing to diminish the onslaught. Two to the head, two to the body, two more to the head. Ethan hardly even paused for breath.

"Oi!"

"Little fucker!"

The friends, on their feet now.

Dealing with it.

How?

While they figured that out for themselves, Ethan continued beating the holy hell out of Dylan Drew, the boy's ears turning redder with every stinging blow, but not as red as the mist in front of Ethan's eyes. It was as if the stone fist had a will of its own now, and Ethan back behind the red mist wasn't in control of it anymore. The fist was empowering him, *changing* him, making him someone or something and he didn't know what. Something hot and alien was running through his veins. Mascara girl shrieked, "Stop it! Stop it!" But Gronow and Pamplin were still too stunned, too scared, to move.

The mist in front of Ethan coagulated in the air. It became a stream of blood which was coming from Dylan's nostrils and soon smeared his upper lip. The muscular crunch of the blows grew duller and duller in Ethan's ears and he could hear—distantly—another of the girls yelling, "Do something! Do something!" But nobody did.

Anyway, Dylan was weeping now the hitting had stopped, and Ethan was standing looking down at him, breathing through locked teeth, seeing his own breath as his adversary curled in a ball, wailing and sobbing and dripping blood from his broken nose.

And a shadow, giant, drew back from over him like an unrolled blanket.

And Ethan walked away, with no one standing in his path, and no words of abuse ringing in his ears. Only the sound of his own loud breathing, sounding like he'd run a hundred miles. But feeling he could run another thousand if he wanted to.

He took his hand out of his anorak pocket. Peeled off the oversized leather glove he was still wearing and pressed it flat back on top of its twin in the drawer.

"Everything all right, love?" said his nan, from down in the kitchen.

He saw a small red smear on its brown knuckle and touched it with his fingertip. He realized his heart was beating hard, still, as he slid closed the drawer and saw himself reflected in the dressing-table mirror.

He wondered if he was a monster or a hero.

He guessed he'd have to wait until he was a grownup to find out.

Dedicated to the memory of Dilwyn Mills Volk
(1924–2007)

EVOLUTION AND
HELLHOLE CANYON
DON WINSLOW

D esert species are larger.
  This isn't just my observation; it's an evolutionary fact. Species in the
desert have adapted larger body mass to diffuse the sun's intense heat. It's
true of the mammals, with their bigger frames, larger ears, and thicker tails. It's true
of the reptiles—they're just, well, bigger.

I thought about this and my own long, thick tail as I stared at the rattlesnake.
I'm adapted to the desert, an evolved creature, if you will; just like the snake that
hissed at me, its large rattler making music like some kind of ancient ritual from the
extinct people that inhabited this canyon for thousands of years.

They hadn't evolved.

But my concern now was not with them, but with the snake blocking my path,
a narrow passage between two red-rock boulders twice as high as my head. The whole
canyon was strewn with boulders, a geological anarchy, strewn about as if some god
had had a temper tantrum and thrown his toys all over the place.

Unintelligent design; again, if you will.

It was this maze of sun-baked rock that I was trying to work my way through.
I was already hot, tired, and thirsty; and now this rattlesnake was in my way. In the

desert, time equals survival. The longer you stay, the hotter you get, the more you dehydrate, the less chance your large body has to diffuse the heat. This is even more true in the narrow canyons where the sun reflects off the rocks, which store the heat and then disperse it, creating an oven.

I wanted out of the oven. I wanted to make it up to the oasis of palm trees, do my job, and get out of Hellhole Canyon.

The snake was a big one, all right, and it knew it. It had all the arrogance of the A-male, the dominant individual of its species. This boy was clearly successful, healthy, fat from hunting rats and mice. If a snake could be said to swagger, this one had swagger.

"We have a problem, big boy?" I asked.

"*We* don't," it hissed. "*You* might."

"Yeah?" I asked. "What's that?"

I tried to sound light and tough at the same time, but I was alert and ready to move. So was the snake; it was coiled to strike.

"It's one thing to go up a canyon," it said. "Another thing to come back down."

"Thanks for the wisdom," I said. "Are you going to let me through?"

Or do I have to swing my hammer-fist down and crush you, which I really don't want to do. Or *try* to do. I'm fast, but was I as fast as that rattler? It was a question to which I really didn't want an answer. Take it from a guy who's been in a lot of scrapes—talking is always better than fighting. Guys who say different are usually standing on the sidelines, men in white shirts and two-hundred-dollar ties who sit in offices and encourage other men to go out and fight and die.

I doubted that the snake's bite could pierce my tough hide, but the fangs that it was showing me were big, and this was another question I preferred to leave to the realm of conjecture. Didn't want it on my headstone, *He Guessed Wrong About The Fangs.*

And it wasn't like anyone was going to come rushing in with the antidote. I was a long way from anywhere, in the desert a hundred miles east of San Diego, hard by the Mexican border.

Which was the point.

I looked down at the snake with a *Well?* look in my eye.

"I'll let you through," it said, "if you think you really want to go."

Want to go? Does anyone *want* to go on a gig like this? Since when did *want* have anything to do with it? You do your job, whether you *want* to or not.

Evolution is not a choice.

"Stamp my ticket," I said. "I'm going for the ride."

"Suit yourself," the snake said. "Just don't say I didn't warn you."

Then it was just gone, disappeared into a crack in the boulder I didn't even realize was there. But then again, it had evolved to do just that. If it hadn't, it would long ago have fallen prey to one of the hawks that even now circled above, issuing its single-note, plaintive cry like another warning I wasn't going to heed. Higher in the sky three vultures wafted on a thermal, their keen eyes looking down, searching for the dead and dying.

They were large animals—desert species.

"Not yet, you bastards," I muttered. "You're early for the party. Very bad manners."

I took a gulp of hot air and then bounded up the next section of the canyon, my red skin blending in with the rock, my tail switching from side to side, providing stability and balance, my tough skin impervious to the cholla and barrel cactus that lined the canyon like angry sentinels. It was easy to imagine dinosaurs in this place that sang of the prehistoric.

Is that me? I wondered.

Am I a dinosaur, too?

In some ways, I hoped so.

It took me ten minutes to climb to a flat stretch of rock from which I could see the palm oasis a half mile above me, a patch of dark green cut into a narrow notch between red cliffs. I stopped and let my heartbeat slow down, and when it did, I could hear running water above me in the oasis.

I laid flat down on the sheet of rock, blending in as much as I could.

Laid still as death, and watched.

Twenty minutes later I saw a flicker of movement in the palms. A flash of white fabric. A cool color for desert heat, but a mistake in this country of buff, tan, terracotta, and red. You don't wear white in the desert if you don't want to be seen.

The snake can discern the strange temperature of the color.

The hawk can see you.

So can the vultures.

And me.

I moved carefully now. Slowly, making my own boulderlike body become just another rock in this garden of rock as I made my way up toward the oasis.

And I left the trail.

It's axiomatic in the desert—you leave the trail, you die. Every year out here, two or three hikers do it and don't make it back. They run out of water, the heat gets to their brains and they become disoriented. What look like easy, shallow canyons become narrow death traps. They can find their way in; they can't find their way out. Sometimes it's years before their bodies are found. If they're found, if they're not consumed first by the foxes, coyotes, and lions—big ones—that live out here.

That's what the snake was trying to tell me.

It's one thing to go up a canyon. Another thing to come back down.

Yeah.

But I went off the trail and up, making a wide loop to the right to blend in against the rocks of the cliff face and to get up above the oasis. They'd be looking down the canyon for any threat. They'd never think it would come from above. The terrain above the oasis is impassable.

For a human being.

Now I knew why they sent me. Your garden-variety *Homo sapiens* couldn't have made it. Neither up the canyon or down. He'd have been spotted and shot down before he got halfway up. Simply not built to do that.

It took me three long hours. Three hours of heat, thirst, heart-straining effort and pain to make the long loop away from the trail and then back again, above the oasis. I followed the sound of water, and if you don't think that's ironic in the desert, well, you don't know irony. But that's what I did—I could hear the stream of water as it sluiced through tiny cracks in the rocks and tumbled off cliffs and boulders, and the sound was my guide.

I'll admit it, by the time I got above that damn oasis I was hurting. I was just to the top, out of breath, gasping for even this baked air and stretched out flat on a rock above the stream, when the hawk landed in a creosote bush beside me and laughed.

It was a red-tailed hawk, big and beautiful.

"There are four of them," it said.

"Why are you helping me?"

Suspicion is an evolutionary trait in my business. Develop it or become extinct. Beautiful or not, I had no reason to trust this hawk. Well, I trusted its eye, I didn't trust its heart. I certainly don't trust beauty. Maybe it's envy rather than suspicion.

"A suitcase bomb?" it said. "Radiation kills hawks, too."

"Got it."

"You're going to die," the hawk said.

"Says who?" I asked.

"The vultures," the hawk said, tilting its head upward. "They're impatient. Hungry. It's been a slow day, and you'd make a large feed."

"Tell them I have a tastier meal in mind for them."

"They'll be glad to hear it," the hawk said. Then, "Two AKs, a MAC-10, one Uzi. Two of them are asleep, one's getting water, the other is on lookout."

"Looking down," I said.

"That's right." It looked at me carefully, curiously, and then it asked the question it had on its mind. "What are you? I haven't seen a thing like you before."

No one has, I thought.

What am I?

Good goddamn question.

"I'm a desert species," I said, for lack of a better answer. Time was an issue, and I wasn't in the mood for explanation or introspection. Time for that after the job was done. Yeah, you're kidding yourself, I thought—there's never time for that.

The hawk said, "You're not of the desert."

"No?"

It shook its head and then flew off.

It didn't like being lied to.

Can't say I blamed it; neither do I.

I got busy and started to scuttle down the stream until I came to a flat shelf of rock behind some Indian tobacco brush. I laid out flat—well, as flat as I can get—and peered through the bush, down into the palm oasis.

The hawk had been telling the truth.

Four of them.

They had come across the border in the desert, left the truck down near Ocotillo Wells and hiked in. Were waiting in the canyon for the chopper that would come in that night. They would meet it down in the flats and from there . . .

Radiation kills hawks, too.

I knew they were going to be tough. Good fighters, hardened in the mountains of Afghanistan and the Kashmir. But they hadn't seen or heard me. Their instincts were honed for other kinds of predators—helicopters and drones—death from the sky. The two sleepers were still asleep on a long rock that slanted above a pool, where the one getting water had filled the canteens and was now just bathing in the little pool. The lookout sat in the shade at the lower edge of the oasis—he was looking out down the canyon, away from me.

The suitcase sat by his hip, the small camo net thrown over it inadequately for the purpose of disguise. The bright midday sun exposed it for what it was—shiny, metal, modern, and lethal. An indiscriminate mass murderer that I'd been sent to fetch like some kind of mutant golden retriever after an equally mutant stick.

Stealth or speed—the basic choice of the evolutionary engineer. Every predator is equipped with greater or fewer quantities of those qualities, and I knew that if I was going to get that suitcase, I was going to need both. First, the stealth to get into range, and then the burst of speed to close the deal.

Starting with stealth, I slid off the rock, becoming one with the water—Zen Hellboy. I landed in a pool of water, crawled to the edge and did the same with the next little waterfall, and the next, until I reached the palm trees. Suddenly I was in another world. It seemed almost impossible, to be so quickly out of the harsh sun and baked rock into a realm of deep cool shade, running streams, and little waterfalls.

No wonder the ancient people cherished this place, their paintings even now evident on the gray rock faces above the little pools.

Water is sacred.

Water is life.

I pushed through some palms into a little grotto, slid down one of the waterfalls and stood stock still, like a rock, my hooves planted at the bottom of the pool, my head behind the falling water. Tiny frogs, green and blue, clung to the moss by my face. I looked at them, my eyes begging them to be quiet.

I can't really tell you if they nodded their agreement. I thought they did. Anyway, they were smart enough to keep their mouths shut.

The bather looked almost innocent. Naked as Adam, he sat in the pool and splashed the cool, clean water on his face. The third time he did it I was on him. Grabbed him by the neck and shook him until he blacked out. I left him at the water's edge.

Now came the speed portion of the show. I dashed up the slanting rock and hit the first sleeper before he could wake up. The second sleeper reached for his AK but I got to it first and tossed it, the rifle clattering down the rock, metal scraping on stone. Then I tossed him.

Bullets smacked the rock around my head as the lookout came charging toward me, firing his MAC-10 from the hip. The frogs jumped off into the water. I dove right after them, but the water was shallow and provided little cover. I could feel the rounds zipping into the pool beside me and then I got my hooves under me, pushed, and drove up and out of the water.

He panicked.

Hell, I'd panic too if I'd never seen me before. There are times I catch my image in the mirror, or a store window, and . . .

Never mind.

Anyway, I was a species he'd never seen and he panicked and ran and that was all I needed. I didn't enjoy running him down, even though I knew the immense evil he was here to perpetrate. There was something nasty about it, something atavistic, primordial, if you will; a battle for a nuclear weapon reduced to a chase of one species by another.

He couldn't win.

It wasn't a matter of will, or skill. It was just physical—I had the superior construction for this. He outpaced me at first, but then he came against a boulder and that was that. He tried to climb it, but I was on him even as he had a desperate, futile hand-grip on the top.

I swung my hammer fist.

The hawk cried.

I looked up and saw it land in a palm tree. Then I saw the vultures tightening their circle, dropping in a spiral, descending for that promised meal that meant another day of life.

Bon appétit, I thought.

The water tasted good. I knelt beside a pool and drank myself full. It was clear and cold and clean. After I drank my fill I jumped into the water and washed myself clean.

Well, not *clean.*

The suitcase was lying in the shade under a palm. I picked it up and started down the canyon. Good golden retriever. Good Hellboy.

They came from the sky. I should have known it, foreseen it, sensed it, but I heard their cry and then looked back to the oasis and the men were gone, their crumpled bodies lifted up and changed into the super-sized vultures that were now starting into their dives, sharp beaks and razor talons aimed for my eyes. Of course they morphed, I thought. It was the desert. You change, you evolve, or you go extinct.

I broke into a run down the canyon, balancing myself against a fall that would be fatal. If I went down they'd be on me. Hell, even if I stayed on my feet they'd be on me.

The hawk saved me.

It plunged from the sky in a headlong dive into the first vulture, a clash that exploded in a mushroom cloud of feathers, and then a mutual death spiral as, locked together, they spun and plummeted to the ground. The other three just gave it up—it took the heart right out of them. Soon they were just specks in the sky.

I kept moving, wanted to get out of the canyon before they recovered their morale and decided to take another shot. The sun pounded on my head like a hammer and wedge, as if it was trying to split my skull in half, leave me here with the scattered mineral detritus of the Pleistocene temper tantrum. It hurt like hell, but this was Hellhole Canyon and I was Hellboy, so what the hell could I expect? I wasn't going to let it stop me.

Ditto the snake.

It met me on the way down in the same spot it stopped me on my way up. This time it was spread out, relaxed, absorbing the heat it would need to survive the frigid desert night.

"Surprised to see me?" I asked.

"No," it said. Then, "A little, maybe."

Its strike came out of nowhere. I never had a chance to move. It struck me in the leg, then looked up in surprise and horror when its fangs didn't penetrate.

Part of me wanted to step on it, crush it under my weight. Or pick it up and fling it, send it helicoptering against a rock, make it a blood smudge like a painting. The worse part of me wanted to do that, the better part of me decided that there had been enough—more than enough—death for one day.

I stepped over it and walked down the canyon.

I guess you could say I'd evolved.

Bigger, maybe.

A ROOM OF ONE'S OWN
CHINA MIÉVILLE

"Don't you ever wish it could be different?" Liz Sherman sat with her knees up on her bed, like a teenager waiting for a phone call.

"Nope," Hellboy said. "Sure, if you didn't sometimes think about that stuff you wouldn't be human . . ." He paused as if for an unheard laugh track. "There's stuff all of us would like. *Wish* you could have a few days off. *Wish* you had a few more damn choices than 'Shoot at the giant caterpillar' and/or 'Bash the werewolf biting your ass.' Sure, might be nice, but none of us gets much in the way of choice, you got to make do, got to have your breakfast and smile."

Liz stared at him. She waved her hand at her B.P.R.D. quarters.

"The walls," she said. "Beige. This décor. Don't you ever wish it could be different?"

"I knew you meant that," Hellboy said. "I was kidding."

"Sure." Liz stood and swiped her fingers at the paint. "Who picks these colors? You're never tempted to do stuff to yours, make it more homey?"

"I did."

"When you got rid of the Babar the Elephant wallpaper? It took you forty-some years, and you only did it because me and Abe were calling you Zephir the monkey."

"And now it's how I like it."

"Yeah?" Liz turned, hands on hips. "What color are your walls?" Seconds of silence. "You don't know what color your own room is."

"That's how I like it."

Liz shook her head. "I'm bored of home being an office catalog. I've got plans." She turned in the center of the room, looking slowly at every aspect.

Back outside his own rooms, Hellboy paused and scratched his chin.

"Brown," he said. "Gray? Brown."

"What are you doing?"

"Hey Kate," Hellboy said. "What color's your room?"

"Here?" Kate Corrigan leaned against the wall. "Light brown. In my apartment? Blue."

"What color's my room?"

"Oxblood."

"What the hell's oxblood?"

"The color of your room. Oh, you've been talking to Liz. It's good she's decorating, isn't it?"

"It is?"

"You know what it's been like for her. She was like a lab rat here." She glanced around. "There are people in the Bureau who'd still rather she was kept in a fireproof cell. It's Manning who insisted she got a proper room. So if she's doing her place up, she's decided it's home. So yeah, it's good. I'm helping her out. Said I'd help her pick furniture and paint. She's looking through stuff from the licensed suppliers."

"Licensed?"

"Anyone who does decoration here has to have clearance, because they're going to see stuff. There're three interior-decorating companies licensed by the B.P.R.D. Tell us if you want to do your place up."

"Nah. I'm good. With the . . ." He opened the door and peered. "That's oxblood? Doesn't that clash with my skin?"

That night Hellboy got called on a mission. Ten days later he returned, tired and crotchety, with his coat still smoldering. His bed was reinforced but it made its usual panicked noise when he sat on it and threw his bits and pieces onto the floor.

"You stink," Kate said. "How was France?"

"Don't you knock? France was nice, except for the zombies. How's it been here?"

"Fine. Come see Liz's room."

"You finished it?"

"Pretty much." She led him through the hallways. "This one decorator, turns out they're the ones who did Professor Bruttenholm's apartments in the center, back in the day. The woman who runs it now just took over. Anyway her pop's pop, who started the business, was friends with the professor from way back. Maybe you remember him? They used to sit around and talk literature and interior design."

"Design? Professor Bruttenholm?"

"Said she overheard. Mr. Margolyse? Any bells? She remembers them arguing what color the front door of Wuthering Heights would be. That's one of their schticks, they'll print up stuff from old stories, pictures, whatever. Sirbilex Designs does lots of the *olde worlde* stuff." She said it *oldee worldee.*

"Liz likes that? Would think she'd want something a bit more . . ."

"Funky town? Yeah. Turns out she's got time for a bit of old-style stuff, found some cool old designs there. Furniture's more Ikea though. Be nice, Hellboy. She's mixing it up a bit."

She was.

"Hey Liz," Hellboy said. "Wow."

"I'm not taking any home-furnishing advice from you, Hellboy," Liz said, turning up the little stereo on her desk. Liz sat in an uncomfortable but expensive-looking plastic molded chair. The desk she leaned on was some chrome-legged thing, the sea scenes and landscapes that had come with the room were replaced with old movie posters, and there were new garish greenish-orangish-reddish curtains (all the colors that went into them were *–ish,* like they were loath to commit). Surrounding the whole thing was a jaundice-colored wallpaper printed with flouncy scribbled designs.

"Holy . . . ," Hellboy said.

"Too kind," Liz said. She grinned.

"If it cooks your potatoes, I'm happy for you." Hellboy prodded the wall with his stone forefinger. "That is impressively ugly."

"Isn't it?" said Liz. She touched it herself. "How are you supposed to walk away from that?" she said. "I like all the little paths." She traced one of the pee-colored curlicues with her fingertip, almost dreamily, getting it lost in the design's maze.

"Big seller?" Hellboy said.

"Custom job," Kate said, when Liz didn't respond. Hellboy shook his head as he retreated from the sickly buttery walls.

Even in a slow period the B.P.R.D. had regular briefings—somewhere someone was always hearing a banshee, finding their crops flattened in a mandala, getting their goats sucked.

"Still no word on what that thing in Bodmin in England is," Manning said, flicking through his papers. "We're hearing some weird stuff coming out of the Ivory Coast . . . Where's Agent Sherman?" Everyone looked around. The corner of the table where Liz usually slouched was empty.

"Maybe she overslept. She's been working hard fixing up her quarters," Abe said with a riffle of his gills.

"On it," said Hellboy. "Quick look at that room should shock *me* awake, at least." Manning folded his arms impatiently. "Back in a minute," shouted Hellboy without turning.

The silence dragged out. When Liz walked in she stopped.

"Whoa," she said. "Did I win a prize or something?"

"Good of you to join us," Manning said. "Where's Hellboy?"

"How should I know?"

"Isn't he with you?"

Liz stared. "I'm not in the habit of bringing Hellboy with me to the john."

"He went to find you in your room," Abe said. "I don't know what's taking him so long . . ."

"I'll go get him," Liz said. "*What's the point of me calling meetings if . . . ,*" Manning started. "Amen," muttered Liz as she went.

The door to her quarters was ajar, but there was no sound from inside. Liz thought Hellboy must have gone. But there he was, standing in the middle of her room, lit up by the morning, staring at nothing. She waited several seconds. She whispered: "Hellboy."

"Yeah," he said, immediately. "Hey Liz." He did not stop staring at whatever nothing it was that held his attention. "You are here. I thought so."

"I'm here now," she said. "What are you doing?"

". . . Thought I . . ." Hellboy hesitated. Looked at her at last. That big jaw and brow and those red stubs made his expressions hard to read. "Thought I saw you. Or heard you or something. It doesn't matter. Come on. Where were you anyway?"

"Jeez, since when is everyone so concerned with my bladder?"

Everyone was still waiting and staring in silence when they returned to the room.

"Liz, Hellboy, this isn't for my own pleasure, you understand?" Manning said. "I need to know you're going to do as ordered. So would you *please* sit down and listen to the damn briefing."

Kate watched Hellboy sit, grumpily obedient. In a place like this, even someone like Hellboy chose to do what he was told, most of the time.

Something woke Liz, in the pit of the night. For several seconds she sat still in her new bed. She stared at the curtains, all colorless in the dark, at their lumpy shadowy shapes. Stared at one particularly large shape, a massive presence of black which she realized, scrabbling upright, was *not* on the curtains, was something standing at the foot of her bed.

The surge of adrenaline made her occult fire-muscles twitch, and Liz's clawed hands ignited, ready to burn. In the sudden, guttering light, the looming figure was visible, and it was Hellboy.

"What are you *doing?*" she gasped at him. "Are you out of your mind?"

Hellboy was in his boxers. He was facing the wall. He did not move.

Liz could not extinguish her flaming hands, and would melt the light switch if she tried to flick it now, so she watched him in the light of her unnatural combustion.

"Hellboy," she said. "What's going on?"

"I needed to check," he said abruptly.

"What?"

"Look." He traced one of the coils on the wallpaper. "Eyes," he said. Pointed to one, two, nubs at the end of the shape. They did look a bit like eyes. "Like I thought. You were in there. I was trying to help."

Liz stood, and shook her hands, and clenched her innards until the fires went out.

"Hellboy," she said. "Come on now." She put her arm around him. Glanced at the wall, as if she could see anything. She remembered the outrageous angles and uncertain curves, the ill unclean smoldering faded color. Liz led Hellboy to the door, gently steering his bulk.

"I saw you, Liz," he said. "I think it was you." He shook his head twice. "What the hell? Guess I should lay off the, uh, cheese before bed."

"You going to be okay to get back to your room?"

"Sure."

"Okay. Sleep well." Liz stood, arms crossed, blinking against the corridor light, watching Hellboy stomp slowly back to his room. He moved normally enough. He sounded like himself. When she went back to bed she even convinced herself, more or less, that that was the last of it, that whatever little brain fart had happened to him was done now. But she wasn't really convinced. She knew that because, when she woke up in the morning and he was there, again, at the foot of her bed, staring at nothing, she was not surprised.

"Liz," he said. "I need to swap rooms."

Liz came to the briefing that morning with a suitcase full of clothes. Hellboy did not come at all. When she told them what had happened, there was something spooked enough in her demeanor that, though Manning had started striding quickly enough toward her room, he'd slowed considerably by the time he got close to the door. Abe, Kate, and Liz followed him.

"I told him no," Liz said. "He kept saying yes. He kept saying, 'I have to find you, I'm sure you're there.' His voice was so weird I got spooked and left him to it."

"Spooked?" Abe said. "Frightened? You don't mean to say . . ."

"No," Liz said. "He may be acting weird but it's Hellboy. He wouldn't hurt me. He kept saying, 'I need to help you.' It wasn't me I was scared for. It was him."

"Hellboy." Even Manning's voice was careful. The B.P.R.D. dealt with possessions, doppelgängers, illusions, and shape-shifters, and out-of-character behavior was a red flag. Manning knocked gently. "Hellboy?"

Hellboy stood, his flesh left forefinger tracing a pattern in the wall.

"It's like they commit suicide, the lines in the paper," he said. *Spiral-spiral-stop*, went his finger. *Spiral-spiral-stop*. "They're like bars and someone's behind them. Liz, I can see you. I promise, I'll get you out." *Spiral-spiral-stop*.

"I'm right here, Hellboy," Liz said.

"Yeah," he said, looking at the wall. "Here."

"Hellboy," Manning said. "Come out please. We need to talk."

"Sorry, Tom. I can't come out. How can I? Not with her stuck behind the bars. Aren't we here to help people? There." He prodded. "The woman. Behind the . . . what is that, like a broken neck thing, right?"

There was a long silence.

"I don't see it, Hellboy," Abe said. "Can you come out?"

There was a growing growling sound, something deep, vibrating the knickknacks on Liz's shelves. It grew louder. It was Hellboy. Hellboy was growling. He showed his teeth. Everyone backed away.

"We *help* people," Hellboy shouted. "So let me *help* her. Liz, if you're not going to help me help you, leave me alone. This is where it's at. Who doesn't need a room of their own? Get the hell out."

They got.

"Liz, he thinks he's helping you." Kate said. "Did something happen?"

"No," said Liz. "I don't know what he's saying. I'm fine." Kate, then Manning, then Abe all stared at her. "I know what you're thinking," she snapped. "Test me out."

In the B.P.R.D. labs, the reading was conclusive—Liz was Liz, not some Liz-aping monster of the void, trapping the real Liz behind the wall, for Hellboy to sense. Nothing like that.

"Whatever he's seeing, it's not Liz," the tech said.

"There's something I can't remember," Kate said. "I feel like I know what's going on." A crackle and fuzzy noise interrupted.

"How is he?" Manning asked his radio. There was a long, staticky pause. "Boss," a distorted voice said finally. "You should maybe sort of come see."

It's like you said," the agent said, scurrying to keep up with Manning. "We kept on like you asked, boss, trying to coax him out, but he got madder and madder, and in the end he just slammed the door, and he was screaming, 'Either make this place nice for her, help me help the lady, or get out.'"

They were in the room above Liz's. It was an anonymous office, in which now crouched a little team huddled around a monitor. Attached to it was a wire coiling through a hole in the carpet and the floor.

"Fiber optics," one of them said. "We just acquired the subject."

"You're getting rid of your little spycam from my ceiling when this is done," Liz said. She stopped abruptly when she saw what was on the monitor.

There was Hellboy, in black and white, interrupted by bad reception. He was sitting on the bed. Staring at the walls. Absolutely still.

He was wearing a dress.

"He went through your wardrobe," said an agent. "That's . . ."

"I know exactly what that is," Liz said. "I don't have enough dresses that I don't know them individually."

In tugging it on, Hellboy had split it until it was an obscene drapery of rags over his red skin. He sat, still.

"He's moving his eyes," Kate said. He was. His only motion. "What's he watching?" She closed her eyes, opened them suddenly. "Liz. What did that woman say about her grandfather?"

"What woman . . . ?"

"The designer. What do we know about her family? We have to go to the Sirbilex office. Via a bookshop."

The public end of Sirbilex Designs was a sparse, minimalist, and intensely trendy office, full of catalogs and consultants. The back rooms, where Ellie Margolyse met them, were shabby-chic, cramped, dusty, piled with papers, ledgers, and samples.

"I . . . is there a problem?" Ellie said. She looked from Liz to Kate to Manning to the agents in uniform scanning the room with arcane bits of equipment, running them over the overloaded bookshelves and old furniture. "All our work's under warranty if anything's gone wrong . . ."

"There's no problem with the work," Kate interrupted her. "If anything, it's a bit too damn good. I take it you're not so into your grandfather's look?"

"You mean the way it looks outside compared to this? No . . . Grandpop was a genius, he could do stuff like no one else, ever, but I want to pull this place into the nineties. You can see what it's like. Whenever we have a spare minute we try to pull out a few files and check to see if there's anything useful."

"What happened to your father?"

Ellie stared at Kate.

"What do you know about my dad?"

"Please. Just tell us."

"What is this?" She looked down. "He had a stroke."

"What was he doing? He was going through his father's papers, wasn't he?"

Ellie stared at Kate.

". . . Yes," she said. "How do you know?"

"Please, think carefully—can you remember which papers?"

"What? Are you crazy, I . . ." Ellie stopped suddenly. "You know . . . actually . . . I do know. Because one of them was so weird it stuck in my head." She went to a bookshelf. "Mostly Grandpops was into old gothic novels, nineteenth-century ghost stories, that sort of thing. But one of the things that I found that Dad must have dropped when . . . he had his attack, was some sci-fi thing from like the 1980s, that Grandpop had been scribbling in. I remember because it was *totally* not the kind of thing he normally . . . Here." She turned, a faded magazine in her hand, and froze.

The B.P.R.D. agents all had their pistols out, were aiming them at her. She made a little noise.

"Drop . . . the *Interzone*," Kate whispered, tilting her head and reading the title. Ellie dropped it.

One of the agents crept forward, picked it up with tongs, and placed it into a case that he locked. Kate sagged in relief.

"That issue," Kate said, "has a story in it about a design that short-circuits the human brain. That's what your grandfather was doodling. That's what your dad saw.

"The décor of fiction. That's why he had that issue, because he kept his ear to the ground for any stories like that. Sirbilex. Ex libris. From the books of. He was too talented, Miss Margolyse. He was too good at what he did.

"Where was the file with the designs you found, Liz?" she said.

Liz found it at last, on a low shelf behind an art-deco figure, one box file among many, full of cuttings and Mr. Margolyse's sketches in batches, each folder bearing a one-word title: *Nurseries; Libraries; Attics.*

"Look," said Kate. She held up a hand-drawn picture of a quilt. "That's the bedspread Mrs. Rochester had in her attic. He was so *good* a designer, so sensitive a reader, he could draw the interiors of whatever he read. This *is* the bedspread." Kate waved the picture. "Doesn't matter that Charlotte Brontë never bothered to imagine it. This is it."

"There," said Liz, pointing over Kate's shoulder. "That's the one my design was in. Why does it say 'cave' on the front, there's no pictures of caves . . ."

"Not 'cave,'" Kate said. "What's in here isn't just, you know, the upholstery on the chairs in *Little Women*. This is the folder where the magazine should have been kept. *Cah vay*. Latin. Beware."

She looked at Liz. "You looked at all of these, right? Okay, so there can't be any that smack you down like in the magazine." She went through the papers in the folder. Some were annotated with names. "M.R. James," she read. "Roald Dahl." She held up a picture. "The carpet from Dahl's 'The Wish.' Read it? Don't fall into the black lines if you walk on that. And here it is, Liz. You put it back." She lifted out the strange picture of wallpaper, encoiling lines, a secondary pattern just visible behind them, impossible to make out, its sickly colors, its ugly compulsive designs.

"There's nothing written on this, but I can tell you where it's from," Kate said. "Read it in college. Introduction to Feminist Lit. Ring any bells? Charlotte Perkins Gilman. 'The Yellow Wallpaper.'"

At B.P.R.D. HQ, the feed from the fiber-optic camera had been piped into a briefing room.

Hellboy was on all fours. Hellboy crawled in his ruined dress.

His head moved side to side, still tracing the patterns in the wallpaper around the room. He dragged himself on his limbs, slow like an old animal, along the edge of the room. He had pushed most of the furniture out of the room.

"He's been doing that for hours," Abe said.

"It's in the story," Kate said. She held up the *Collected American Short Stories* which they had all been issued. "Everyone read it now?"

"Yeah, and what the hell was that moaning crap?" Manning said. Kate closed her eyes a moment.

"Charlotte Perkins Gilman. Born 1860. Poet, writer, radical, feminist. 'The Yellow Wallpaper,' 1891. Woman told by doctor husband that she needs a rest cure for depression and quote *hysteria* unquote. Forbidden from working, leaving, or doing anything. Becomes obsessed with the yellow wallpaper. Sees it as bars. With a woman or women creeping behind the patterns. Could be ghosts, could be madness. Becomes obsessed with freeing her, or them. Ends up ripping the wallpaper off the wall to do it. 'I've got out at last,' she says, still crawling. It was her who was trapped." She tapped the slowly circling Hellboy on the screen. "That's the pattern Margolyse drew, and that is what Hellboy's living." They sat silently for several seconds.

"Why don't we just let him finish?" Liz said. "When he rips off the paper, he'll be free, like the woman in the story." Kate stared at her.

"She gets out by going mad."

"Yeah, but she gets out."

"Yeah, by going mad."

They looked at each other.

"We can't risk it," Kate said at last. "If he has to go through the story, we don't know if he can come back from the ending."

"I can't believe I'm hearing this bull," Manning exploded. "This is a *story*. It is not *real*."

"Don't you get it?" Kate shouted. "Margolyse *made* it real. Gilman knew what she was talking about. She was frustrated, like a lot of bored smart women with contrary ideas, so of course she's diagnosed 'depressed and hysterical.' And she got 'prescribed' the so-called rest cure herself by Silas Weir Mitchell, who was a total celebrity doc back in the day. He ordered her into her room and, get this, not to write. Not to *think*. The story's her trying to fight his misogynist crap. Don't roll your eyes, Manning, *listen*." She flicked through papers. "This is from *Fat and Blood*, Mitchell's book about his so-called 'cure' for women like her. He says you need to seclude them not just for their sake but for everyone else's. Says a hysterical girl is, listen, 'a vampire who sucks the blood of the healthy people about her,' that you have to take control and let her know who's boss . . ."

Manning took and scanned the pages. He put them down, pointed at the screen. "Hellboy's not a depressed or hysterical woman. He's Hellboy. Whatever's got into him is some mind game and I'm snapping him out of it. I *know* what's best for him." Manning stormed out, to join the operatives waiting outside Liz's room.

"Wait," said Kate. "You can't . . ." But he was gone. Liz picked up the scattered pages of *Fat and Blood*. "This is not going to go well," Kate said.

On the screen, Hellboy turned his head toward the door. There was no sound on the little monitor. At the edge of the picture, the door burst open and B.P.R.D. operatives streamed in, with Manning behind them.

With a terrible crippled motion, without rising, Hellboy sort of lurch-crawled at them, his tattered dress ripping even more, his hands up, punching and shoving mightily. The agents tried to fan out with stun sticks and prods as if to snag cattle, but even on his knees Hellboy shoved them against walls where they collapsed with broken ribs, hurled them out of the door, slammed them into each other. On the silent black-and-white screen the violence looked like slapstick.

The agents were all incapacitated, crawling away themselves, dragging their comrades with them. Hellboy resumed his slow all-fours shuffle. In his path lay one prone figure. Manning, still unconscious. Hellboy delicately crawled over his body, continued his penitent's circumnavigation of the room.

". . . No good," a voice gasped from Kate's walkie-talkie. "Jesus he's strong! Can't even get near him. 'Got to help her!' he keeps saying. Asked us if we were there to make the room nicer, then he went for us . . ."

"Why does he think Liz is in there?" Abe said. Liz did not look up from the papers.

"It's like the story," Kate said. "She talks about 'the woman' a long time before she talks about herself. I guess it's not easy to admit that you're the one who's being . . . who's . . ."

"How long do we have? Until he starts ripping the walls?" Abe said.

"And why is that a problem again?" Liz said.

"If he goes by the story, not long," Kate said. "Liz, maybe you're right. Maybe he'll rip it all off, stand up, sniff, take off the dress and walk out. But what if he doesn't? What if the wallpaper wins? You want to risk it?"

"If we enter and try to incapacitate him," Abe said, "we might seriously hurt him. If we don't incapacitate him he might seriously hurt us. And if we leave him he might go seriously mad."

They watched. Not wanting to risk another incursion, Manning's agents managed to snare him with a makeshift lasso, and drag him out at last into the corridor.

"What is that?" Abe said. He pointed at the screen. "I thought it was a flaw in the electronics, but . . ."

In the corner of the room, something hovered. A figure, barely, hazily, just. It stuttered in and out of focus, and presence. A shadow. They stared. No one breathed. There was nothing, then nothing, then as Hellboy continued his slow crawl, it appeared again, behind him. Watching him. Moving.

"It's a woman," said Abe.

"You think?" said Kate. "I thought it looked like . . . I thought it looked like Hellboy." They both squinted. The shuddering shadow watched Hellboy's terrible slow progress. It guttered like a candle, a woman-shade, then nothing, then a horn-stubbed thing, gone again, then a thinner remnant, something else again, shadowed with—what was that?—a ghost beard. Gone, and only Hellboy remained, crawling.

"It was a woman. The trapped woman. And the trapped Hellboy too," Liz said. "And that other thing was . . . the other part of the presence haunting that room." She waved the papers. "The one with the cure for uppity women. Doctor Silas Weir Mitchell.

"'You must morally alter as well as physically amend,'" she read from *Fat and Blood*. "You need to control the woman 'with a firm and steady will . . . with no regard to her complaints . . .' He's there to make sure the rest cure goes the distance. He's the bars in the wallpaper."

"Oh my god," breathed Kate. "What are we going to do . . . ? It's trapping him." On the screen that baleful presence was there again, close up to the camera suddenly, leering, behind Hellboy.

"Listen," Liz said. "Hellboy keeps asking if we'll improve the room. That's the wallpaper asserting itself." She read again. "'If circumstances oblige us to treat such a person in her own home, let us at least change her room, and also have it well understood how far we are to control her surroundings.' That kind of improvement's okay because it's all about power. Which is what that damn wallpaper wants."

"So?" Kate said. "Even if Hellboy or the room or the wallpaper lets us in, it'll only be to throw in some cushions or something."

"Even when Hellboy, and the woman, fight him to try to get out, they're stuck in that room," Liz said. "They're secluding themselves, just like the wallpaper wants. There's a whole chapter on seclusion in this." She waved the papers. "That wallpaper wants them in there *alone*. The last thing it wants is another presence."

"Well it's not going to get it." Kate said, "Hellboy won't let us in there . . ."

She stopped. She and Liz stared at each other.

Kate dialed Sirbilex. "Where," she said, "is your grandfather's folder? How fast can you run up a design?"

Fast, it turned out. A quick block printing, some speedy sewing. Under this kind of pressure, Ellie produced a pair of curtains within a few hours.

"He's started picking at the walls," Abe said urgently when Kate returned. They pushed very gently at the unlocked door, looked into the room where Hellboy knelt in his ragged dress, a strip of the strange wallpaper in his hand, an end still anchored like skin to the wall. Behind him, the shadow stained the air. They felt an onrush of malevolent attention as the spirit of the wallpaper regarded them across the oppressive yellow atmosphere.

"Hellboy." Liz said, quickly. Hellboy hesitated in his crawl, and looked up at her.

"You here to help you . . . her . . . out, Liz?" Hellboy said. His voice was heartbreaking.

"No, Hellboy," she said. "You can do that. I trust you. I'm here to make the room nicer. Can I? You were right. Those curtains are terrible." She dangled the cloth she held for him to see.

"What's going on?" Approaching from the end of the corridor was Manning, his head bandaged. Kate clapped her hand over his mouth.

"Hush," she whispered. He stared at her. "Liz has got this."

"Yeah," they heard Hellboy mutter. "Those curtains are kind of ugly. C'mon in."

Liz stepped carefully past him. The something, the whatever, the ugliness in the room parted for her. She stepped past the remaining furniture. Hellboy's constant circling had worn a smear across the wallpaper, in the lower half of the wall.

"She's trying to get out," he whispered. "I'll have her out in a moment."

Liz bit her lip. "Don't rush," she said. She could feel the wallpaper watching her, with its little bud-pattern-ugly-nub yellow eyes. She stood on a chair by the window. "This'll make it nicer in here," she said. "This'll go better."

She fiddled with the runners, threading the curtains onto them, replacing the violently multicolored ones she had so recently put in place. Their replacements were strange and old fashioned. Their pattern was of rippling vertical stripes like tresses, interspersed with coils of ribbon. The bands joined together in clutches at the top of the curtains. Liz stepped back.

"There you go," she said. "Much more appropriate." The odd pattern was not much more attractive, but was at least more subdued in color, more antique in design. "Good luck, Hellboy," Liz said as she left.

"You're giving him new *curtains?*" Manning muttered.

Liz closed the door. They crept to where they had brought the monitor, in sight of the door.

Hellboy tugged at the rip of wallpaper. He tore it slowly from the wall. They watched him on the screen and heard his sigh, a moan, of relief or sadness or something, through the door.

"Come on," Kate whispered. Hellboy reached with his great right hand, and with strange delicacy snagged another piece of the wallpaper, and began to tear it. There was a whispering in the room, of women, men, somethings. Behind the kneeling Hellboy, the shadow appeared again, the woman, Hellboy, the controlling doctor, insinuations in wallpaper spirit, overseeing another mind tearing itself apart to freedom. "We're too late," whispered Kate.

Wordlessly, Liz pointed at a further corner of the screen. At the curtains. They billowed. Though the window was closed, and there was no draft. Something was moving behind them. The viewers froze.

Hellboy tore another strip from the wall. The wallpaper-presence stuttered out of sight for several seconds as Hellboy paused.

Behind him, crawling low out of the shadows below the curtains, something was coming toward him. Something like a cadaverous human figure, reaching out with bony arms, it and all its limbs all covered with reams of unnatural long hair. The thing crept, spidery, toward the frozen Hellboy.

"What the hell . . . ?" Manning whispered.

"You," said Abe, "could perhaps benefit from reading more ghost stories."

"The curtains," Kate said. "From 'The Diary of Mr. Poynter.' Ghost story by M.R. James."

W hat is it?"
   "According to James's story," Kate said, urgently, as the hair-thing advanced, "probably the ghost of Everard Charlett, notoriously dissolute seventeenth-century rake. *Kind* of his ghost. Or at least the ghost of his hair."

"*Fictional* rake, yes?" Manning said. "Wait, his *hair?*"

"Yeah. It's invoked by the pattern on those curtains, which are based on his hair. Whatever, it's hair related."

"And vain," Abe added. "I've read the story."

"And predatory," said Liz. "Damn it, it's coming for him!" The hair-thing stalked, ungainly and vile, toward where Hellboy sat.

Hellboy did not move. He still held a strip of wallpaper. In his hand, and around the room, it was growing agitated. The patterns on it were *flexing*. There were women visible behind its bars, and faint, faint reproductions of Hellboy, crawling. The shade-thing that emanated from it flickered around the room, agitated, stopped, suddenly, darker than before, between the approaching curtain-thing and Hellboy.

"Neither of them wants competition," Liz said. "They both want him."

The two pattern-spirits stared at each other. The newcomer rose, tottering, in baleful inhuman motion. It stood, a humanoid shape in flamboyant locks, facing the rest-cure-and-seclusion-enforcing spirit, a twisting figure-coagulum of wallpaper pattern, a constantly plaiting twist of yellow skeins.

"Look," said Kate. The women were clearer on the walls now, the vague Hellboy-shapes with them, as the intricate curling patterns that trapped them faded, and the wallpaper-spirit grew more tangible, more *yellow*, so yellow the slippery color seemed visible like urine even on the black-and-white screen.

"They're getting out," said Liz. The crawling woman-shapes, the vague, crawling Hellboy-shapes, escaping from the bar-free walls, their hidden coloration and contours moving swiftly and disappearing, as the spirit of the yellow wallpaper, outraged at the intrusion of another predator decoration, took its attention away from its prisoners and turned to the curtain-monster of hair.

The wallpaper-spirit reached up with a limb made of pattern and shoved the curtain-apparition in its hairy chest.

The curtain-thing staggered, regained its footing, and shoved the wallpaper back.

The two aspects of evil interior design circled each other warily, as the last of the shadows in the wall slipped away. Finally, the two presences began to punch each other. Somewhat ineffectually.

Hellboy shook his head, dropped the little trail of wallpaper he held and turned. He saw the shoving match between monstrous invocations of patterns, pushing each other like thirteen-year-olds in a playground. Still sitting down, scootching along backward on his haunches, Hellboy retreated slowly to the door, as the curtain-spirit kicked the wallpaper-spirit in the crotch.

"Oooh!" Everyone gathered around the monitor winced as the curlicue-thing doubled over, and the hair-creature swaggered closer, only for the enraged yellow manifestation to grab it in an incompetent wrestling hold and trip it up. All without a sound.

Hellboy opened the door, slipped out, and closed it again. A few feet from him, Abe, Liz, Kate, and Manning stared at a screen. He cleared his throat. They looked up, and gestured him over.

"Hey, big guy!"

"You got out!"

"Come check this!"

Hellboy steepled his fingers as best he could given the differences between his two hands.

"I have three questions," he said. "One. What was I doing in Liz's room? Two, why was something that looks like evil wallpaper squabbling with something that looks like evil curtains? And three." He looked slowly down at himself. At the extraordinarily filthy, yellow-smeared, ripped-up dress still hanging off his shoulders. "Three . . ." he said, and fingered the material. "Whatever the answer to three," he said, "it *never happened*. Clear? We *never speak of it*."

"They're squabbling over you," Kate said. "Well, they were at first. Hellboy, come and watch. We can explain. Which do you think's stronger: male dominance and social control, or cruel and sadistic vanity? I've got five bucks on misogyny. Abe's backing narcissism. At the moment they're pretty evenly matched—ouch!" One of the décor-things scored some painful hit.

"Winner can buy me a pizza," Hellboy said. "I'm going back to the oxblood palace. Liz, you want your dress back?"

CONTRIBUTORS

AMBER BENSON is the author of *Death's Daughter*, the first novel in an upcoming series from Ace Books. She cocreated, cowrote, and directed the animated supernatural web series *Ghosts of Albion* with Christopher Golden, followed by a series of novels including *Witchery* and *Accursed*, and the novella *Astray*. Benson and Golden also coauthored the novella *The Seven Whistlers*. As an actress, she has appeared in dozens of roles in feature films, TV movies, and television series, including the fan-favorite role of Tara Maclay on three seasons of *Buffy the Vampire Slayer*. Benson wrote, produced, and directed the feature films *Chance* and *Lovers, Liars, and Lunatics*.

✠

GARY A. BRAUNBECK is the creator of the critically praised Cedar Hill series of stories, novellas, and novels set in the fictional town of Cedar Hill, Ohio. His work has been translated into French, German, Russian, Japanese, and Italian. Among his most popular novels are *Prodigal Blues*, *In Silent Graves*, *Mr. Hands*, and the recent *Coffin County* (all set in Cedar Hill). His collections include the Stoker Award–winning *Destinations Unknown*, *Things Left Behind*, two volumes of *The Collected Cedar Hill Stories*, and the forthcoming *Rose of Sharon* and *Other Dark Detours*. He has received numerous awards for his fiction, including the International Horror Guild Award and three Bram Stoker Awards. He lives in Columbus, Ohio, with his wife, author Lucy A. Snyder, and five cats who will not hesitate to draw blood if he forgets to feed them on time. To learn more about Gary and his work, please visit him online at www.garybraunbeck.com.

✠

KEN BRUEN is the author of twenty-three novels, two-time winner of the Shamus award, and winner of the Macavity Award and the Barry. He holds a PhD in Metaphysics and lives in Galway, Ireland.

✠

A two-time winner of the British Fantasy Award, **MARK CHADBOURN** is the author of eleven novels and one nonfiction book. His current fantasy sequence, *Kingdom of the Serpent*, continued with *The Burning Man* in April 2008. A former journalist, he is now a screenwriter for BBC television drama. His other jobs have included running an independent record company, managing rock bands, working on a production line, and as an engineer's "mate." He lives in a forest in the English Midlands.

✠

CHRISTOPHER GOLDEN is the author of dozens of novels for adults, teens, and young readers, most recently *The Lost Ones*, *Poison Ink*, and (with Tim Lebbon) *Mind the Gap*. With Mike Mignola, he cowrote the lavishly illustrated novel *Baltimore, or, The Steadfast Tin Soldier and the Vampire*, which they are currently scripting as a feature film. In the world of Hellboy, he has written three novels (*The Lost Army*, *The Bones of Giants*, *The Dragon Pool*), cowritten the first B.P.R.D. miniseries (*The Hollow Earth*), and edited all three short story collections. He lives in Massachusetts with his wife and three children. His original novels have been published in fourteen languages in countries around the world. Please visit him at www.christophergolden.com.

✠

CODY GOODFELLOW is the author of untold human suffering and three novels, *Perfect Union*, *Radiant Dawn*, and *Ravenous Dusk*. His short fiction has appeared in *Cemetery Dance*, *Hot Blood*,

Horrors Beyond, and *Daikaiju*. He lives in a benign polyp in best-selling author John Skipp's sigmoid colon. (The view sucks, but it has an awesome hot tub.)

☩

B orn in 1951, **BARBARA HAMBLY** is a native Californian, though she spent a year of college at the University of Bordeaux, France. She attended the University of California–Riverside, obtaining both a Master's Degree in Medieval History and a black belt in karate, both of which have been equally useful in the writing of fantasy novels. She has taught high school, assisted aerospace engineers with their grammar, modeled, and clerked at an all-night liquor store; she has written horror, fantasy, science fiction, graphic novels, media tie-ins, historical whodunits, and scripts for Saturday morning cartoon shows. She currently teaches one night a week at a community college. She is a widow who lives in Los Angeles.

☩

R HYS HUGHES is a prolific writer of fantasy fiction. Born in Wales in 1966, he now lives in Spain. His intention is to write exactly 1,000 "items" of fiction and link them into one gigantic story cycle. His books include *Worming the Harpy*, *The Smell of Telescopes*, *The Percolated Stars*, *The Less Lonely Planet*, and *The Postmodern Mariner*. His most recent novel is *Engelbrecht Again*, a sequel to *The Exploits of Engelbrecht*, Maurice Richardson's classic series of stories about a "dwarf surrealist boxer" who fights clocks, zombies, witches, robots, and Martians.

☩

B RIAN KEENE is the best-selling author of *Ghost Walk*, *Dark Hollow*, *The Rising*, *Ghoul*, *Kill Whitey*, *City of the Dead*, *Terminal*, and many more. Several of his short stories have been adapted into graphic novels and several of his novels are slated for film and video-game adaptations. The winner of two Bram Stoker awards, Keene's work has been praised in such diverse places as the *New York Times*, The History Channel, CNN.com, *Publishers Weekly*, *Fangoria* magazine, and *Rue Morgue* magazine. You can communicate with him online at www.briankeene.com or on MySpace at www.myspace.com/brian_keene.

☩

J OE R. LANSDALE is the multi-award-winning author of over thirty novels and two hundred short stories, articles, essays, columns, and reviews. Many of his works have been optioned for film and television. His novella *Bubba Ho-tep* became a cult film by the same name, directed by Don Coscarelli, starring Ossie Davis and Bruce Campbell. Among his awards are two *New York Times* Notable Books, the Edgar, six Bram Stokers, the British Fantasy Award, and the Grinzani Prize for Literature.

☩

C HINA MIÉVILLE's novels include *Perdido Street Station*, *The Scar*, *Iron Council*, and *Un Lun Dun* (for younger readers). He has won the Arthur C. Clarke and British Fantasy Awards twice each. He lives in London and Providence.

☩

M IKE MIGNOLA is best known as the award-winning creator/writer/artist of *Hellboy*, although he began working as a professional cartoonist in the early 1980s, drawing "a little bit of everything for just about everybody." He was also a production designer on the Disney film *Atlantis: The Lost Empire* and visual consultant to Guillermo del Toro on both *Blade II* and the film version of *Hellboy*. He and del Toro cowrote the story for the sequel *Hellboy II: The Golden Army*. Mignola lives in southern California with his wife, daughter, and cat.

GARTH NIX was born in 1963 in Melbourne, Australia. A full-time writer since 2001, he has previously worked as a literary agent, marketing consultant, book editor, book publicist, book sales representative, bookseller, and as a part-time soldier in the Australian Army Reserve. Garth's books include the award-winning fantasy novels *Sabriel*, *Lirael*, and *Abhorsen*; and the cult favorite young-adult science fiction novel *Shade's Children*. His fantasy novels for children include *The Ragwitch*, the six books of the *Seventh Tower* sequence, and the *Keys to the Kingdom* series. More than five million copies of his books have been sold around the world; his books have appeared on the bestseller lists of the *New York Times*, *Publishers Weekly*, *The Guardian*, and *The Australian*; and his work has been translated into thirty-seven languages. He lives in a Sydney beach suburb with his wife and two children.

✠

JOHN SKIPP remains one of America's most cheerfully perplexing Renaissance mutants: *New York Times* best-selling author turned filmmaker, satirist, cultural crusader, musical pornographer, splatterpunk poster child, purveyor of cuddly metaphysics, interpretive dancer, and all-around bon vivant. Although praised in recent years for his solo work (*Conscience*, *The Long Last Call*, and *Mondo Zombie*), Skipp is perhaps best known for his collaborative efforts with Craig Spector (*The Light at the End*, *The Cleanup*, *The Scream*, *Dead Lines*, *The Bridge*, *Animals*) and Marc Levinthal (*The Emerald Burrito of Oz*). "Second Honeymoon" kicks off a new phase of full-tilt collaboration with Cody Goodfellow. Upcoming work includes *Jake's Wake*, *The Day Before*, a diabolical secret graphic novel, and the long-awaited epic horror *Freek*.

✠

STEPHEN VOLK was born in Pontypridd, South Wales. His first produced screenplay was *Gothic*, directed by Ken Russell, after which he went on to write scripts for US studios such as Universal, Columbia/Sony, TriStar, and MGM, including *The Guardian* for William Friedkin. He shocked the British nation in 1992 with the notorious "live" BBC TV Halloween-night drama *Ghostwatch*, and won a BAFTA for the magical short film *The Deadness of Dad*. His most recent feature credit is the psycho-horror road movie *Octane* starring Madeleine Stowe and Mischa Barton, while for television he created and was lead writer on two seasons of ITV1's multi-award-winning hit series *Afterlife*, about a troubled medium and an even more troubled psychologist. In 2006, his first short-story collection *Dark Corners* was published, from which "31/10" was nominated for both a British Fantasy and a Bram Stoker Award. He lives in Bradford-on-Avon, England, with his wife Patricia, a sculptor.

✠

TAD WILLIAMS is a best-selling novelist whose work is published in more than two dozen languages and occasionally on cocktail napkins and matchbook covers. He has also written film, television, and comic books, all in much less exciting ways than you'd suppose. He believes strongly that Might Should *not* Make Right and that A Person's A Person, No Matter How Small. He also fervently supports changing America's monetary standard to one based on cheese. He lives in the San Francisco Bay Area with his wife Deborah Beale, their two adorable, attack-trained children, three dogs who are all college graduates but live at home because they're having trouble finding work, and two cats that can't solve Sudoku puzzles worth a damn but keep on trying, which is probably admirable.

✠

DON WINSLOW is the author of ten published novels, including *A Cool Breeze on the Underground*, *The Power of the Dog*, and *The Winter of Frankie Machine*. He lives on an old ranch in southern California with his wife and son.

by MIKE MIGNOLA

SEED OF DESTRUCTION
with John Byrne
ISBN: 978-1-59307-094-6 | $17.95

WAKE THE DEVIL
ISBN: 978-1-59307-095-3 | $17.95

THE CHAINED COFFIN AND OTHERS
ISBN: 978-1-59307-091-5 | $17.95

THE RIGHT HAND OF DOOM
ISBN: 978-1-59307-093-9 | $17.95

CONQUEROR WORM
ISBN: 978-1-59307-092-2 | $17.95

STRANGE PLACES
ISBN: 978-1-59307-475-3 | $17.95

THE TROLL WITCH AND OTHERS
with Richard Corben and P. Craig Russell
ISBN: 978-1-59307-860-7 | $17.95

DARKNESS CALLS
with Duncan Fegredo
ISBN: 978-1-59307-896-6 | $19.95

B.P.R.D.: HOLLOW EARTH & OTHER STORIES
by Mignola, Chris Golden, Ryan Sook, and others
ISBN: 978-1-56971-862-9 | $17.95

B.P.R.D.: THE SOUL OF VENICE & OTHER STORIES
by Mignola, Mike Oeming, Guy Davis, Scott Kolins, Geoff Johns, and others
ISBN: 978-1-59307-132-5 | $17.95

B.P.R.D.: PLAGUE OF FROGS
by Mignola and Guy Davis
ISBN: 978-1-59307-288-9 | $17.95

B.P.R.D.: THE DEAD
by Mignola, John Arcudi, and Guy Davis
ISBN: 978-1-59307-380-0 | $17.95

B.P.R.D.: THE BLACK FLAME
by Mignola, Arcudi, and Davis
ISBN: 978-1-59307-550-7 | $17.95

B.P.R.D.: THE UNIVERSAL MACHINE
by Mignola, Arcudi, and Davis
ISBN: 978-1-59307-710-5 | $17.95

B.P.R.D.: GARDEN OF SOULS
by Mignola, Arcudi, and Davis
ISBN: 978-1-59307-882-9 | $17.95

B.P.R.D.: KILLING GROUND
by Mignola, Arcudi, and Davis
ISBN: 978-1-59307-956-7 | $17.95

To find a comics shop in your area, call 1-888-266-4226. For more information or to order direct: •On the web: darkhorse.com •Email: mailorder@darkhorse.com •Phone: 1-800-862-0052 Mon.–Fri. 9 AM to 5 PM Pacific Time.